Henry Wadsworth Longfellow, William Michael Rossetti, Maria
Francesca Rossetti

A shadow of Dante

Being an essay towards studying himself, his world and his pilgrimage

Henry Wadsworth Longfellow, William Michael Rossetti, Maria Francesca Rossetti

A shadow of Dante
Being an essay towards studying himself, his world and his pilgrimage

ISBN/EAN: 9783744722902

Printed in Europe, USA, Canada, Australia, Japan

Cover: Foto ©Andreas Hilbeck / pixelio.de

More available books at **www.hansebooks.com**

SHADOW OF DANTE

𝔅eing an 𝔈ssay

TOWARDS STUDYING HIMSELF, HIS WORLD AND HIS PILGRIMAGE

BY

MARIA FRANCESCA ROSSETTI

Se Dio ti asci, lettor, prender frutto
Di tua lezion

LONDON
LONGMANS, GREEN, AND CO.
AND NEW YORK: 15 EAST 16TH STREET
1894

[*New and Cheaper Edition*]

DEDICATED

TO THE BELOVED MEMORY

OF MY FATHER

Contents.

ILLUSTRATIONS.

TRANSLATION OF THE LEGEND OF THE FRONTISPIECE

The body within which I cast a shadow.
                                    PUR. III. 26.

TRANSLATION OF THE MOTTO OF THE TITLE-PAGE

So may God let thee, Reader, gather fruit
From this thy reading.
                                    INF. XX. 19, 20.

CHAPTER I.

PREFATORY AND INTRODUCTORY.

Dunque che è? perchè, perchè ristai?
What is 't then? wherefore, wherefore hold'st thou back?

Inf. II. 121.

DANTE is a name unlimited in place and period. Not Italy, but the Universe, is his birthplace; not the fourteenth century, but all Time, is his epoch. He rises before us and above us like the Pyramids—awful, massive, solitary; the embodiment of the character, the realization of the science, of his clime and day; yet the outcome of a far wider past, the standard of a far wider future. Like the Pyramids, again, he is known to all by name and by pictorial representation; must we not add, like them unknown to most by actual sight and presence? Who among us has indeed experienced the soul-subduing hush of his solemnity? who beheld all average heights dwarfed by his sublimity?

Even of his fellow-linguists how many have read his great poem through? One of themselves has said it—few have gone beyond the Inferno; nay, most have stopped short at two passages of the Inferno—*Francesca da Rimini* and *il Conte Ugolino.* And of his fellow-cosmopolitans how many have read even so much? If in cultivated society we start him as a topic of conversation, how far is our interlocutor likely to sympathize with our vivid interest? How many young people could we name as having read Dante as a part of their education?

Yet the Divina Commedia has been translated, especially of late years, again and again: copiously treated of by authors of European reputation. The few pore over such works; but what of the many? They have probably glanced through Gustave Doré's illustrations; but as to the poem itself, even those who have learned Italian look upon Dante in his native tongue as too far above their attainments; those who have not never think of making such acquaintance with him as is possible in their own language; while the glosses of commentators are usually bound up with the text, and are at any rate too closely connected with it to be available as independent outlines, even did they not often take for granted in the reader a certain amount of preliminary knowledge and interest. And so it comes to pass that in England comparatively few among cultivated and intellectual people have a thorough and enjoying knowledge of one of the greatest works of man.

As to those who are sufficiently Italian scholars to read Tasso with ease and pleasure, they are simply under a misapprehension in supposing themselves incompetent to pass on to Dante. They would understand him very well with notes; and even highly-educated Italians would not always understand him without. The case is much like that of Shakspeare—Englishmen are disputing to this day as to the meaning of many of his utterances, and so are Italians as to the meaning of Dante. For his difficulties, confessedly

great, are of a kind to meet the reader scarcely less in a
good translation than in the original. At their very head we
must place one of his chief perfections :—conciseness such
that a word often requires expansion into a clause, a clause
into a sentence, which may yet fail of being understood till
amplified into an expository paragraph. Nay, his style is
more than concise : it is elliptical—it is recondite. A first
thought often lies coiled up and hidden under a second ;
the words which state the conclusion involve the premises
and develop the subject. The abstract disquisitions with
which the poem abounds afford the principal, though by
no means the sole, field for the exercise of this marvellous
gift of recondite expression. A reader—could such be
found—equal in knowledge to the poet himself, might still
fail to recognise at a glance each inhabitant of his populous
universe, and to solve at a thought each allusive quasi-
enigma embodying the fictions of mythology, and the truths
of science according to the highest attainments of the
period. Astronomy becomes especially perplexing in his
hands ; the dates of the poem, both as to hour and season,
being hinted in descriptions of the position of the heavenly
bodies, pretty sure to darken the reader's perceptions but
for the friendly aid of the commentator, whose elaborate
notes usually culminate in the one necessary and often
only intelligible fact : ' It was the vernal equinox ;' ' It
was noon, sunset,' etc.

Another of Dante's characteristics is ambiguity—an ambiguity, however, not hazy, but prismatic, and therefore
not really perplexing. Why refuse to discern a double
truth under a single word-presentment in such a passage as
the following ?

'I will be thy guide,
And bring thee hence by an eternal place;
Where thou shalt hearken the despairing shrieks,
Shalt see the ancient Spirits dolorous,
That each one outcries for the second death.'

Inf. I. 113-117

The last line may signify either 'Each cries out on account of the second death which he is suffering,' or 'Each cries out for death to come a second time and ease him of his sufferings.' Both significations being true, why should we narrow our inheritance by rejecting one?

Such, then, is frequently the style in which Dante deals with a range of subject wellnigh encyclopædic. He seems to have familiarly known everything that could be learned, and to have watched with closest attention the men and the politics of his day. Are we of those who, deeply and intelligently interested in the past, love in every period to dive below the surface, and welcome as peculiarly precious every ray of contemporary light thrown on persons and events? Dante is a focus of such rays: bask we in them, and we shall know what at the end of the thirteenth and the beginning of the fourteenth century—among the most intellectual people of the West—were the highest attainments of the highest minds in physical science; what natural and moral problems received an astrological solution; what judgment was passed at the time, or soon afterwards, on such personages as Frederick II. of Germany, Philippe le Bel, Charles of Anjou; what was the character of the petty Italian States and princes of the period; what manners and customs prevailed; what corruptions revolted dignified and pious souls; how nearly on the same level of reality mediæval habits of thought and study placed historic fact and classic fable ; what were the speculations of philo-sophers, what the contemplations of theologians, what the general tone of moral and religious thought in those who by reason of use had their senses exercised to discern both good and evil.

But great as is the profit derived by the mind from the study of the Commedia, greater, far greater, is the profit accruing to the soul which, through the medium of that chain of visions wherein Dante's colossal intellect has embodied its conceptions, contemplates truths the most momentous, spiritual, and ennobling that can engage the thoughts of man.

Any acquaintance with a work so sublime must needs be better than none. A shadow may win the gaze of some who never looked upon the substance, never tasted the entrancement of this Poet's music, never entered into the depths of this Philosopher's cogitations. My plan is very simple. After in some degree setting forth what Dante's Universe is as a whole, and what autobiography and history show his life-experience to have been, I proceed to expound in greater detail—here and there unavoidably with slight repetition—the physical and moral theories on which his Three Worlds are constructed ; and to narrate, now in his own words, now in a prose summary, the course of his stupendous pilgrimage. As in this narration my objects are mainly to carry on his autobiography, to study his character, to be spiritualized by his spirit and upborne on his wings—also, though subordinately, to exemplify his treatment of the subjects above enumerated,—the extracts are such as seem to me best suited to promote these ends ;

the episodes being usually passed over. I use two line-for-line blank verse translations, of the degrees of whose force and beauty the reader will be able to judge : my brother W. M. Rossetti's for the Inferno, Mr. Longfellow's for the Purgatorio and Paradiso, retaining in each case any typographical peculiarity. Difficulties are explained in the text or in footnotes : these last, when taken *verbatim* from the Translators, are distinguished by inverted commas ; and where a passage of any length is paraphrased, the reference at the beginning is repeated at the end. Not without regret, I sacrifice to faithful literality the pleasure of making readers ignorant of Italian acquainted with the exquisite ternary rhyme of the Commedia, so ably preserved in the translations by Mr. Cayley, the Rev. John Dayman, and the Rev. Prebendary Ford. The like faithful literality will be found to characterize my own rendering of passages from Dante's prose works ; the blemish, as it would now by many be considered, of frequent tautology being by no means avoided. The principle of translation should, I think, be one thing, when an author and a style unique and immortal are to be set in living truth before living eyes ; quite another thing when minds merely need to be enabled profitably and pleasurably to assimilate thoughts generated and originally expressed, it may even be with no distinctive force or grace, in a tongue not their own. Whether the tautology of classic Greece and mediæval Italy be in truth a blemish at all, is a question foreign to my present purpose.

Where commentators differ, especially on minor points, I frequently adopt without discussion that view which most commends itself to my own mind. And in any slight hints, whether original or not, on the interpretation of the poem, the one charge I would earnestly deprecate is that of exclusiveness. It is scarcely less difficult to determine what is not, than what is, in Dante. The prismatic character before noticed in particular passages belongs still more to his marvellous work as a whole, and according to each one's tone of mind and groove of thought will be, to a great extent, the contemplations based upon it. A second Dante alone could confidently exclude any sense not intrinsically unworthy of the first.

It only remains to acknowledge my obligations, among Italian commentators, to my late dear Father, to Professor Ferrazzi, and to Signor Fraticelli, whose excellent diagrams have supplied the designs, though not the whole of the letterpress, for three of my own :—among English commentators to Mr. Cayley, and to Professor Longfellow both for the information gathered from his notes, and for his most kind welcome to the use of his eminently faithful and beautiful translation.

THE UNIVERSE.

THE ANGELIC CIRCLES.

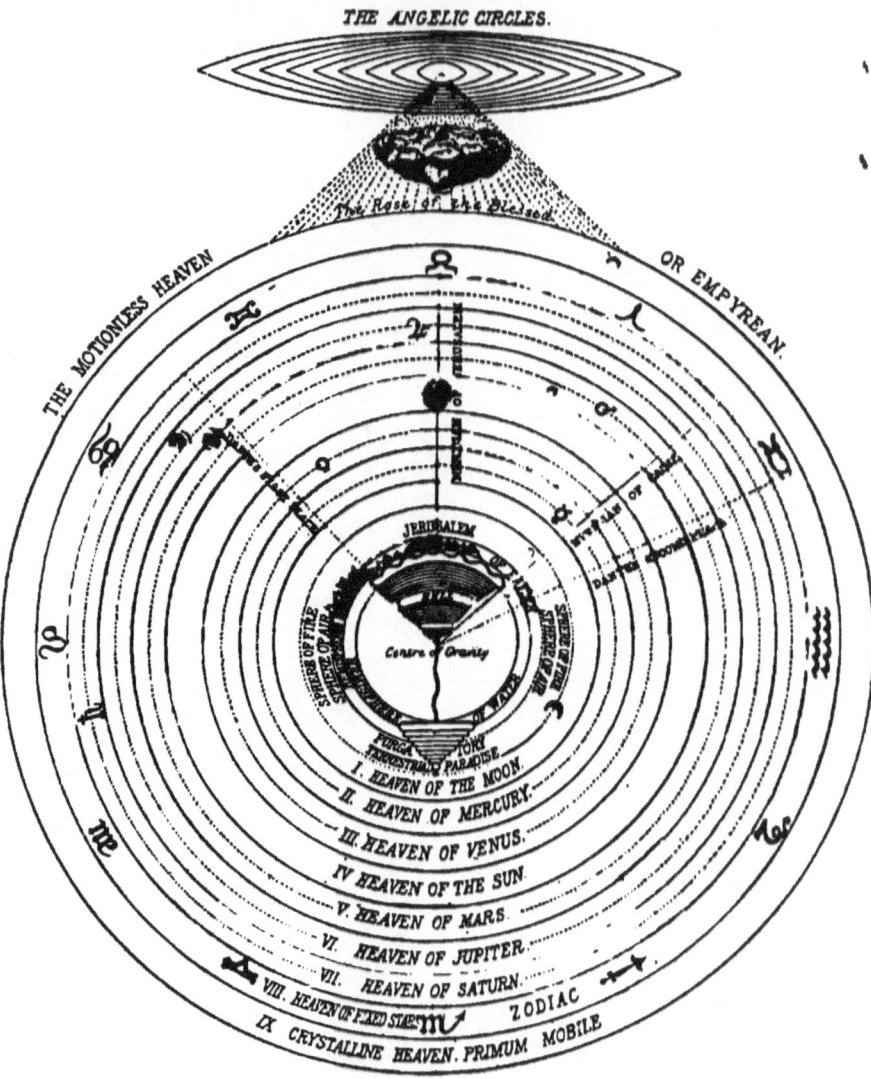

The Rose of the Blessed

THE MOTIONLESS HEAVEN

OR EMPYREAN.

JERUSALEM

Centre of Gravity

SPHERE OF FIRE
SPHERE OF AIR

PURGATORY
TERRESTRIAL PARADISE

I. HEAVEN OF THE MOON.

II. HEAVEN OF MERCURY.

III. HEAVEN OF VENUS.

IV. HEAVEN OF THE SUN.

V. HEAVEN OF MARS.

VI. HEAVEN OF JUPITER.

VII. HEAVEN OF SATURN.

VIII. HEAVEN OF FIXED STARS.

ZODIAC

IX. CRYSTALLINE HEAVEN. PRIMUM MOBILE

(To face Chap. II.)

CHAPTER II.

DANTE'S UNIVERSE.

Mi mise dentro alle segrete cose.
He ushered me within the secret things.
Inf. III. 21.

TO one unacquainted with the Ptolemaic system, and unprovided with suitable maps, the Dantesque cosmology presents difficulties almost as insuperable as those geography would offer to a child destitute of an atlas. The scheme of the Universe has to be picked out here and there throughout the poem; and I propose in this chapter to present my reader with a preliminary bird's-eye view of that world through which we are about to become fellow-pilgrims with the Poet.

The central point of Dante's Universe is that central point of the Earth which constitutes the centre of gravity. Hither with Dante we descend through the Pit of Hell; hence painfully threading our way through the bowels of Earth's opposite hemisphere, emerge on the shore of the single island dotting the vast Ocean; climb with toil the Mountain of Purgatory, situate within the Spheres of Air and Fire, and from the Terrestrial Paradise on its summit ascend through the Nine Heavens: traversing thus all the realms of Time and Space till we attain our final rest in the all-containing, uncontained, timeless, spaceless Empyrean. So marvellous in conception, so perfect in order, so dazzling in glory, is the Universe unfolded to our view. We proceed to consider it in detail.

Dante divides our globe into two elemental hemispheres : the Eastern, chiefly of land; the Western, almost wholly of water. In the midst of the inhabited Land-hemisphere he places Jerusalem; within the same hemisphere, so that its central and Hell's lowest point is exactly under Jerusalem, he places Hell; in the midst of the uninhabited Sea-hemisphere he places Purgatory, as the antipodes to Jerusalem, distant from it by the whole diameter of the globe. Thus on and within the Earth are situated the temporal and the eternal prison-house of sin. Neither, in Dante's view, formed part of God's original creation, wherein sin was not ; but the fall of Lucifer at once produced the one and prepared the other, convulsing and inverting the world which God had made. The rebel Seraph fell headlong from Heaven directly above the Western hemisphere, till then a continent, in whose midst was Eden; and Earth, in the twofold horror of his sight and presence, underwent a twofold change. First, to veil her face, she brought in upon herself the vast floods of the Eastern Sea-hemisphere, transferring to their place all her dry land, save Eden, which thus was left insulated in mid-Ocean. And secondly, to escape his contact, as he sank and sank through her surface, through her bowels, till the middle of his colossal frame, having reached the centre of gravity, remained there fixed from the sheer physical impossibility of sinking any lower, she caused a vast mass of her internal substance to flee before his face ; and leaving eternally void the space it once had occupied to form the inverted pit-cone of Hell.

she heaved it up directly under Eden, amid the new waste of waters, to form the towering mountain-cone on whose peak the Terrestrial Paradise should thenceforth to the end of Time sit far above all elemental strife, and whose sides should, after the Redemption of Man, furnish the Purgatorial stair whereby his foot might aspire once more to tread, his eye to contemplate, his regained inheritance.

Thus two Elements, Earth and Water, hemispherically divided, constitute the Sphere which forms the innermost and immoveable kernel of the Dantesque Universe. It is enveloped by the Sphere of Air, subject to the variations of heat and cold, rain and drought, wind and tempest, and reaching up to that particular point of the Western Mountain where Ante-Purgatory ends, and the Gate of S. Peter admits holy but still imperfect souls to Purgatory proper, which being situated within the Sphere of Fire or Æther, is secure from atmospheric change.

Beyond this highest elemental region lie the Nine Heavens, each alike a hollow revolving sphere, enclosing and enclosed. The First Heaven is of the Moon, the Second of Mercury, the Third of Venus, the Fourth of the Sun (in Dante's time regarded as a planet), the Fifth of Mars, the Sixth of Jupiter, the Seventh of Saturn, the Eighth of the Fixed Stars ; the Ninth is the Starless Crystalline Heaven or Primum Mobile, which, itself the most rapid of all in its revolutions, is the root of Time and Change throughout Creation, and the source and measure of the gradually slackening movement of all the Heavens within it. Without it is the Tenth Heaven, the motionless boundless Empyrean, the special dwelling-place of the Most High God, and the eternal home of His Saints. These, arranged in the form of a Rose, surround a vast effulgent Lake, formed by a reflection of the Uncreated Light on the convex summit of the Primum Mobile, and so placed that a right line drawn downwards from its centre to our globe would touch that earthly Jerusalem, whose bud has so wondrously blossomed into this Jerusalem which is above.

Such is the construction of the Dantesque Universe. But the scheme of natural and moral philosophy set forth in the Divina Commedia includes so complete and complicated a theory of Astrology as bound up with Cosmology and with the action of the Angelic Orders, that I must, even at the risk of tediousness, endeavour to give my reader some insight into the subject.

Around the Divine Essence, manifested in the Primum Mobile as a luminous Atomic Point, circle evermore the Nine Orders of Angels, divided into Three Hierarchies. The first and innermost hierarchy consists of the Seraphim, the Cherubim, the Thrones; the second of the Dominations, the Virtues, the Powers; the third of the Principalities, the Archangels, the Angels. The celestial hosts thus disposed are at once passive and active. All alike, gazing on the Divine Centre, are passively drawn by It,—the Seraphim immediately, the Cherubim through the medium of the Seraphim, the Thrones through that of the Cherubim, and so on, each Order through that next above it. And all alike, as is self-evident, actively draw towards that same Centre, each the Order next below it, till finally the Angels, having none lower of their own nature to draw, draw mankind.

This chain of attraction is, as I conceive, wholly moral. A second chain of influence is partly moral and partly material.

Each Angelic Order moves the Heaven inversely corresponding to it ; the Seraphim as the First Order move the Ninth Heaven, the Cherubim as the Second Order move the Eighth Heaven, and so on in succession through all the Nine. But in the mutual relations between the Circles moving and the Circles moved, while velocity corresponds to velocity, not extension but intensity corresponds to extension. For two are the centres : God Uncreated, Infinite, Highest ; Earth created, finite, lowest. Earth is the centre of the Heavens ;—proximity to the Earth-centre implies contraction of circuit and slackness of motion ; recession from the Earth-centre is proportionate approximation to the manifested Deity, and therefore implies expansion of circuit and acceleration of motion. But the centre of the Angels is God Most High, proximity to Whom implies the utmost perfection whereof the creature is capable. And as, from the very nature of concentric circles, such perfection cannot in this case be expressed by greater extension of circuit, it is expressed by intensity of radiance, and by a velocity of motion which decreases here for precisely the same reason that in the case of the Heavens it increases with expansion of circuit, *i.e.*, that such expansion here implies recession from the Divine Centre and approximation to Earth.

The Universe, thus constructed and governed, presents a marvellous threefold gradation and order :—in highest place pure Form or Mind wholly active, the Nine Angelic Choirs moving the Heavens and not moved ; in middle place Form conjoined with Matter both active and passive, the Nine Heavens moved by the Angels and moving the Elements ; in lowest place pure Matter wholly passive, the Four Elements moved by the Heavens and not moving.

All creatures are immediately or mediately emanations of

the Mind and Will of God, and impressed with His Light. Such as immediately proceed from Him are perfectly enlightened, immortal, incorruptible, and free, as not subject to powers which had no share in their formation. To this perfect class belong not only the Angels as pure Mind, but Man as Mind combined with Matter formed as well as created by the hand of God Himself, so that nought save his own abuse of his free-will could have disfranchised him of his original nobility, and even in his fallen estate the Heavens, however they may influence his inclinations, cannot force his choice. But the Elements and the things thereof compounded, as brute beasts and vegetables, though their matter was of course created immediately by the Almighty, according to this hypothesis derive their light, together with their form or animating principle, through the interposition and influence of the Heavens, and are in consequence imperfectly enlightened, mortal, corruptible, and bond; albeit Divine Providence, infusing the celestial virtues of informing and of ruling, infuses also those of preserving and sustaining the dependent and subject elemental creatures.

Manifold are the philosophic questions in whose answer these theories will be found more or less involved.

A few notes respecting time are needed in conclusion. Dante, in accordance with S. Thomas Aquinas, but not with S. Jerome, makes the creation of the Angels simultaneous with that of the Universe: appealing for confirmation to many passages of Holy Scripture—probably, among others, to that adduced on this subject by the Fathers, ' He that liveth eternally created all things together'[1]—and also

[1] Ecclus. xviii. 1.

to Reason, which cannot allow the Movers to have long remained without their perfection, *i.e.*, without aught to move. The Fall of the rebel Angels he considers to have taken place within twenty seconds of their creation, and to have originated in the pride which made Lucifer unwilling to await the time prefixed by his Maker for enlightening him with perfect knowledge.

The creation of Man would seem, in this system, to have been subsequent to the upheaval of Paradise ; his expulsion thence was effected seven hours after his location there.

At what time, and by what means, the dwelling of our first parents or of their posterity was transferred to the Eastern continent, Dante, so far as I know, leaves untold.[1] One only instance previous to his own pilgrimage does he imagine in which, after this transference, the eye of living man rested on the Western Island-Mountain. With this singularly beautiful narrative I close the present chapter : the speaker is Ulysses, suffering in Hell as an evil counsellor.

> ' When
> From Circe I departed, who beyond
> A year withdrew me near Gaeta there,
> Before Æneas so had named the place,[2]
> Neither son's sweetness, nor the suffering

---

[1] The following curious theory has been conversationally suggested. The Pit of Hell being vast enough to harbour so large a number out of all generations of mankind, the Western Mountain, consisting of the earth thrown up from that pit, is necessarily of the same proportions, and may have sufficed for the dwelling of the entire race until the Deluge, after which event the Ark was providentially guided to deposit its freight on Mount Ararat in the Eastern hemisphere.

[2] 'Gaeta, the ancient Cajeta, is said to have been so named by Æneas after his nurse, who died there.'

Of mine old father, nor the love so due
Which ought to have made glad Penelope,
Could quell in me the ardour which I had
For growing to be expert of the world,
And of the worthiness and vice of men.
But I set off on the high open sea
With one ship only, and that little band
By which I had not been deserted yet.
I saw one shore and other far as Spain,
Far as Morocco, and the isle o' the Sards,
And others which that sea bathes roundabout.
I and my fellows we were old and slow
When we had come unto the narrow pass
Where Hercules has stamped his cautionings
That man should so proceed no further on :
On my right left I Seville ; I had left
Already Ceuta on my other hand.
" O brothers," said I, " ye that are arrived
Through hundred-thousand dangers to the West,—
Unto this now so little waking-time
Which is remaining of your senses still
Endure not to deny the experience
Of the unpeopled world behind the sun.
Consider what is your original :
Ye were not made that ye should live like beasts,
But follow after virtue and the truth."
I with this brief oration so did make
My comrades eager for the journeying
I scarce could have retained them afterwards.
And, having turned our poop into the morn,
We made the oars wings to the maddened flight,
Toward the left hand gaining evermore.
I saw by night already all the stars
Within the other pole, and ours so low

It rose not forth from the marine expanse.
Five times re-kindled and as many razed
Had been the light from underneath the moon
Since we had entered in the lofty pass,
When a brown mountain there appeared to us
Upon the distance, and to me it seemed
So lofty as I had not witnessed one.
We were rejoiced,—and soon it turned to dole ;
For there was born a whirlwind from the new
Country, and struck the fore-side of the ship.
With all its waters thrice it made her wheel ;
The poop rise at the fourth time uppermore,
The prow go down, as pleased Another One,
Till over us again the sea was closed.'

Inf. XXVI. 90-142.

CHAPTER III.

DANTE'S LIFE-EXPERIENCE.

Nel mezzo del cammin di nostra vita.
In midway of the journey of our life.

Inf. I. I.

LET us now inquire what he was, who, born, as he believed, into an universe in the main so ·constructed
and so governed, lived in it fifty-six years, and departed not
till he had tracked a path to aid future generations safely
to work their way from its lowest to its highest sphere :—
what she was, at whose prompting he began, by whose
guidance he completed the pilgrimage wherein he gained
his own experience of that path. Not that this latter inquiry
can be answered as confidently as the former. The
Beatrice of Dante remains to this day the perplexity of
scholars and of commentators, some regarding her as a
personage from first to last purely allegorical. I adopt the
view of Boccaccio and the majority.

Dante Allighieri was born at Florence in May 1265, of
a noble family adhering to the Guelph party. When nearly
nine years old he was taken by his father to a festival held
at the house of Folco Portinari. He there beheld his host's
daughter ; and this first great event of his conscious life,
colouring all its after course, he himself thus narrates :

'Nine times already since my birth had the Heaven of

Light[1] returned almost to the same point in respect of its own gyration, when there first appeared to my eyes the glorious Lady of my mind: who was called Beatrice by many who knew not what she was called. She had already been so long in this life as that, within her time, the Starry Heaven had moved towards the eastern part one of the twelve parts of a degree: so that almost at the beginning of her ninth year she appeared to me, and I saw her almost at the end of my ninth year. And she appeared to me clothed in a most noble colour, a subdued and decorous crimson; girdled and adorned in such wise as was suitable to her most youthful age. . . . I say that thenceforward Love swayed my soul, which was even then espoused to him; and began to assume over me so great and so assured a lordship, empowered thereto in virtue of my imagination, that I must needs perform to the full all his pleasures. He oftentimes commanded me to seek to behold this youngest Angel; wherefore I in my boyhood many times sought her out, and saw her so noble and laudable in bearing, that certes of her might be spoken that word of the poet Homer: She appeared not to be made by any mortal man, but by God. And albeit her image, which abode with me continually, were the triumphant strength of Love to sway me; yet was it of so exceeding noble virtue, that it did at no time suffer Love to rule me without the faithful counsel of Reason in those things wherein such counsel was useful to be heard.'[2]

At ten years old he lost his father; but this did not interrupt the course of his most careful and liberal education. Before he was quite eighteen he wrote his first sonnet, inspired by an incident which he thus records:

[1] *i.e.* the Heaven of the Sun, or Fourth Heaven.
[2] *Vita Nuova* ii.

C

'When so many days had passed as exactly completed nine years from the above-written appearance of this most gracious creature, on the last of the days it happened that this marvellous lady appeared to me, clothed in purest white, between two gentle ladies, who were more advanced in age ; and passing through a street she turned her eyes towards the place where I stood greatly abashed, and. of her ineffable courtesy whose merit is now recompensed in the other world, she saluted me so virtuously that I seemed then to behold the utmost limits of beatitude.   The hour wherein her sweetest salutation reached me was assuredly the ninth of that day ; and whereas that was the first time that her words went forth to come to my ears, I sucked in such sweetness that as one inebriated I departed from the people.' [1]

There is no reason to believe that Dante ever sought Beatrice in marriage, nor any distinct indication that she so much as knew of the pure, lofty, ideal love she had inspired. The very early age at which Florentine fathers affianced their daughters makes it not impossible that even before her ninth year she was engaged to that Simon de' Bardi whose wife, at the age of twenty, she became.   Dante never alludes to her marriage, though he thus touchingly records her father's death in 1288, and his own sympathy in her grief—a sympathy doubtless all the deeper from his personal experience of the like irreparable loss, and further quickened by the virtues of the dead, whose last years had been hallowed by the building and opening of a hospital somewhat strangely characterized at the time as 'the column of the state.' [2]

[1] *Vita Nuova* iii.   [2] Ferrazzi, *Manuale Dantesco*, vol. ii. pp. 21, 22.

'. . . As it pleased that Glorious Lord, Who denied not death to Himself, he who had been the father of so great a marvel as was manifestly this most noble Beatrice, going forth of this life departed in very truth to eternal glory. Wherefore, inasmuch as such parting is painful to those that remain, and have been friends of him that departeth ; and no friendship is there so intimate as that of a good father for a good child, or of a good child for a good father ; and this lady was good in the highest degree, and her father (as is by many believed, and as is true) was good in a high degree, it is manifest that this lady was most bitterly full of grief.'[1]

But ere very long he who had mourned with her was called to mourn yet more sorely for her : first in prophetic vision of her death-chamber, then in agonizing reality. In 1290, at the age of twenty-four, Beatrice died.

'The Lord of this most gracious creature, that is the Lord of Justice, called this noble being to the life of glory under the standard of that blessed queen Mary, whose name was in greatest reverence in the words of this beati-fied Beatrice.'[2]

He proceeds to relate various incidents, taking place as it would seem within the two years and a half following her death : the most prominent of these is his strong temporary attraction towards an unnamed lady descried gazing at him through a window, and touching his feelings first by her evident sympathy in his grief, afterwards by her personal qualities. And here meets us one of the most intricate of Dantesque perplexities. In the Vita Nuova[3] he charac-terizes this attraction or propensity as the 'adversary of Reason,' describes it as beset even while it lasted with mis-

[1] *Vita Nuova* xxii.　　　[2] *Ib.* xxix.　　　[3] *Ib.* xl.

givings and struggles, and relates how it was finally subdued by a 'strong imagination' of Beatrice, in guise like to that wherein he had first beheld her, a child in her ninth year habited in crimson.   Yet in the Convito, in language whose directness it seems impossible to evade, he declares the lady of whom he became enamoured after his first love, and who by a previous passage [1] is identified with the 'lady of the window,' to have been 'the most beautiful and most noble daughter of the Emperor of the Universe, to whom Pythagoras gave the name of Philosophy.' [2]   In most touching words he relates how Philosophy became his consolation : 'I say that as by me was lost the first delight of my soul, of whom mention is made above, I remained pierced with such sadness that no 'comfort availed me. Nevertheless, after a while my mind, which sought out how to be healed, bethought itself (since neither my own nor others' consoling availed) to recur to the mode whereby some mourner had aforetime found consolation.   And I set myself to read that book, not known to many, of Boëthius, wherein he, captive and downfallen, had consoled himself.   And hearing also that Tullius had written another book, wherein, treating of friendship, he had spoken by the way of the consolation of Lælius, a man most excellent, concerning the death of Scipio his friend, I set myself to read that.   And though it were hard to me at first to enter into their purport, at length I entered as far within it as the art of grammar which I possessed and a little of my intellect could do ; by which intellect many things, as in a dream, I saw already ; as in the Vita Nuova may be seen.   And as it often falls out that a man goes in search of silver, and

------

[1] *Conv.* ii. 2.   [2] *Ib.* ii. 16.

beyond his intent finds gold which some hidden cause points out, not perhaps without divine overruling; I, who sought to console me, found not only a remedy for my tears, but words of authors and of science and of books; which considering, I assuredly judged that Philosophy, who was the lady of these authors, of these sciences, and of these books, was a thing exceeding high. And I imagined her in form like unto a noble lady; nor could I imagine her in any attitude save one of commiseration; wherefore so fain was the sense in truth to gaze upon her, that scarcely could I turn it aside from her. And passing beyond this imagining I began to go where she showed herself in very truth, that is, into the schools of the Religious, and to the disputations of philosophers; so that in brief space, perhaps of thirty months, I began to feel so much of her sweetness, that her love expelled and destroyed every other thought.'[1]

How is so astounding a discrepancy to be accounted for? How could such a propensity as this be the adversary of Reason? or the 'strong imagination' of Beatrice, for whom her lover's affection, even in childhood and earliest youth, had never been without the counsel of Reason, have the effect of subduing such a propensity? I would observe first, that we have not the whole of the Convito; fourteen Canzoni with their comment were planned by Dante,[2] three only, alas! were written; and of course it is possible that the mystery was to be cleared up as the work proceeded. Secondly, with very great diffidence I venture to hint at a solution which seems to me not inconsistent with either of the conflicting statements, nor yet with this additional start-ling fact—that in the Commedia Beatrice is herself invested

[1] *Conv.* ii. 13. [2] *Ib.* i. 1.

with the attributes of that wisdom which is asserted in the
Convito to be the body of Philosophy.[1]   It appears, then,
that the effect of this philosophic propensity was so to en-
gross Dante's mind as actually and increasingly to supersede
the thought of his lost treasure,[2] and the at first prominent
consolation of dwelling on her celestial bliss.[3]   It appears
also, from certain passages of the Purgatorio hereafter to be
read in their proper place,[4] that this period of his life was
one of more or less sensual gratification and earthly aim.
Hence it seems natural to infer that his Philosophy was at
this stage of a theoretical rather than of a practical character ; and if so, in a most true though limited sense might
it be termed the adversary of Reason, as all will testify who
have experienced the lulling spell of an intellectual and
sensitive delight in good running parallel with a voluntary
and actual indulgence in evil.   May it not be that after
many alternations of struggling and succumbing despite his
better self and his sage maxims, a most vivid sense of pollu-
tion and of peril, aided by a sudden strong imagination of
Beatrice, came upon him ; and that as entranced he gazed
on her glorified loveliness he instinctively identified with
her his Philosophy already transfigured, potent not only
now to charm and soothe, potent to rule ; to the Intellect
a light, to the Affections a compass and a balance, a sceptre
over the Will ? From the moment of this inward impression
we notice that no more is heard of the lady of the window,
who seems thus to occupy in the Vita Nuova a position
somewhat analogous to that of Virgil in the Commedia : she
representing the speculative pleasures and consolations, he

---

[1] *Conv.* iii. 15.   [2] *Vita Nuova* xxxviii, xxxix.   [3] *Conv.* ii. 10.
[4] *Pur.* xxiii. 115-118, xxx. 55-144, xxxi. 1-90.

the moral laws and suasions of Philosophy. He too will in
turn vanish from before the face of Beatrice, not as counter-
acted, but as included and transcended; her presence
waited on no less by his human than by her own superhuman Virtues. Thus in her one person are finally con-
centrated all nobleness, all beauty, and all rectitude of
Nature and of Grace.

Whether or not this theory can be sustained, it is certain
that in renewed and perpetual allegiance to his First-Beloved
he signs and seals his Vita Nuova :

'. . . There appeared to me a marvellous vision wherein
I saw things, which made me resolve to say no more of
this blessed one until I could more worthily treat of her.
And to come to this I study as much as I can, as she
knows in truth. So that, if it shall be the pleasure of Him
by Whom all things live that my life shall last somewhat
longer, I hope to say of her that which has never been said
of any. And may it then please Him, Who is the Lord of
courtesy, that my soul may go to behold the glory of its
lady, that is, that blessed Beatrice who gloriously gazes on
the face of Him who is blessed throughout all ages.
PRAISE TO GOD.'[1]

In 1291 Dante was persuaded by his friends to espouse
Gemma Donati. She bore him seven children before his
exile ; after it he never saw her again.

So far his private life ; during which, by profound and
extensive studies both in Divine and human science, by the
exercise of all graceful arts and accomplishments, and by
the teaching of inward experience, he was forming and
deepening the character afterwards to be manifested in
public life.

---

[1] *Vita Nuova* xliii.

Public life at that period throughout Italy, and especially in Florence, to all who took a prominent and energetic part, was thorny indeed. The main distinction was that between Ghibellines and Guelphs—two names in their origin far removed from Italy. They were first heard in Germany in 1140, when at Winsberg in Suabia a battle was fought between two contending claimants of the Empire; the one, Conrad of Hohenstauffen, Duke of Franconia, chose for his battle-cry *Waiblingen,* the name of his patrimonial castle in Würtemburg; the other, Henry the Lion, Duke of Saxony, chose his own family name of *Welf,* or *Wölf.* Conrad proved victorious, and his kindred to the fourth ensuing generation occupied the imperial throne; yet both war-cries survived the contest which gave them birth, lingering on in Germany as equivalents of *Imperialist* and *anti-Imperialist.* By a process perfectly clear to philologists, they were modified in Italy into the forms *Ghibellino* and *Guelfo;* and the Popes being there the great opponents of the Emperors, an Italian Guelph was a Papalist. The cities were mainly Guelph; the nobles most frequently Ghibelline.

A private feud had been the means of involving Florence in the contest. In 1215—just three quarters of a century after the victory of Conrad—Buondelmonte de' Buondelmonti, a young nobleman affianced to a maiden of the Amidei, broke his troth and married one of the Donati. The Amidei revenged themselves by his assassination. The Emperor Frederick II., fourth of the House of Suabia, took their part, and the feud once kindled burned on and spread.

But—the Ghibelline party having been expelled from

Florence—this was not the discord with which Dante, on his accession to office, would have to deal.   The Guelph party was split into two factions—the Black and the White, also taking their rise in a private quarrel, originating towards the end of the thirteenth century, not in Florence, but in Pistoja.   A rich merchant of that place, named Cancellieri, had married in succession two wives, whose respective children went by the names of *Whites* and *Blacks ;* names which afforded a too convenient distinction when, in consequence of a gambling dispute, their descendants became involved in deadly feud.   The Florentine family of the Cerchi sided with the Whites, the Donati with the Blacks ; hence multiplied dissensions, involving wellnigh the whole city.

As early as in 1289 Dante had, at the battle of Campaldino and the siege of Caprona, borne arms as a Guelph in civil war.   In 1295 he became a member of the Special Council of the Republic, consisting of eighty of the best and most influential citizens, and in 1300, at the age of thirty-five,

> In midway of the journey of *his* life,

was elected one of the six Priori (chief magistrates of his city) for the months of June and July.   We shall see in the next chapter what view he took of the moral state of Italy, and especially of Florence, at the time of his election.   Suffice it here to say that during his brief tenure of office he concurred with his colleagues in banishing to Sarzana the heads of the White, to Perugia those of the Black faction. But the following year the Whites were recalled by the State ; the Blacks, breaking their ban, returned of themselves, and by intrigue secured, for the so-called pacification of Florence, the intervention of Charles de Valois (brother of Philippe le Bel), then travelling towards Rome in his way to the hoped-for conquest of Sicily.   The wiser members of the Government, seeing through the specious scheme of the Blacks, sent Dante with three others on an embassy to Pope Boniface VIII., whose veto would have nullified the transaction ;—but the prolonged delay in obtaining that veto gave the supporters of the Pacificator ample leisure so to treat Florence that, as historians agree, less evil befalls a city taken by assault.

On the news of these oppressions reaching Rome, Dante hurried homewards, but only to find his house pillaged and burned, and himself accused of undue partiality to the Whites both during and after his tenure of office.   Summoned to answer a charge of peculation, he was not even allowed time to appear, but was in January 1302 condemned, as contumacious, to a heavy fine ; and finally, in March, to perpetual banishment, under pain of being burned alive should he again be found in his native city.

From this time forth, forsaking the Guelph party altogether, Dante was a Ghibelline.   One by one possibilities of return seemed to arise ; one by one they failed.   In March 1304, while he was at Arezzo, the recently-elected Pope Benedict XI. sent Cardinal da Prato on a pacific mission to Florence, but the attempt was unsuccessful, and four months later the ambassador quitted the city, laying it under an interdict.   In July of the same year a military effort of the Poet's fellow-exiles proved most disastrous, and he transferred his residence to Bologna.   In 1312 took place the celebrated Italian enterprise of the Emperor Henry of Luxemburg, and Dante's hopes were excited to the utmost : but yet again they were doomed to bitter disappointment by the sudden death of that illustrious Prince.

In 1316 the State of Florence did indeed publish an amnesty from which Dante was not excepted, but his return was made conditional on payment of a fine, and submission to a public acknowledgment of criminality : and here is a portion of his answer, conveyed in a Latin epistle to a Religious, who seems to have been his kinsman : —

'Is this then the glorious fashion of Dante Allighieri's recall to his country, after suffering exile for wellnigh three lustres? Is this the due recompense of his innocence manifest to all? This the fruit of his abundant sweat and toil endured in study? Far from the man of Philosophy's household this baseness proper to a heart of mire, that he, in the manner of any sciolist and other infamous person, should endure as a prisoner to be put to ransom! Far from the Proclaimer of Justice that he, offended and insulted, to his offenders, as to those who have deserved well of him, should pay tribute! This, Father, is not the way to return to my country : but if by you or by another there can be found another way that shall not derogate from Dante's fame and honour, readily will I thereto betake myself. But if by no honourable way can entrance be found into Florence, there will I never enter. What? Can I not from any corner of the earth behold the sun and the stars? Can I not under every climate of heaven meditate the all-sweet truths, except I first make myself a man of no glory, but rather of ignominy in the face of the people and city of Florence?'

Thus nobly and immoveably resolved, he never again beheld his native land, but at one petty Ghibelline court after another alternated between his own Sphere of Air and Sphere of Fire. Bitter indeed was his experience of what he so touchingly, by the mouth of his ancestor Cacciaguida, describes as his coming fate :

> Thou shalt abandon everything beloved
>   Most tenderly, and this the arrow is
>   Which first the bow of banishment shoots forth.
> Thou shalt have proof how savoureth of salt
>   The bread of others, and how hard a road
>   The going down and up another's stairs.
> And that which most shall weigh upon thy shoulders
>   Will be the bad and foolish company
>   With which into this valley thou shalt fall.
>
> *Par.* XVII. 55-63.

And yet, when enraptured and enrapturing he uttered his unearthly Commedia, he was as one already swallowed up in Infinity and Eternity. Can these words, written as in the Starry Heaven, mean less ?

> The threshing-floor that maketh us so proud,
>   To me revolving with the eternal Twins,
>   Was all apparent made from hill to harbour !
>
> *Par.* XXII. 151-153.

So Dante Allighieri lived, so suffered, and so wrought; till in 1321, at Ravenna, under the protection of Count Guido Novello da Polenta, in his fifty-seventh year, by means of a fever, he passed, we fervently hope, into the full, final, and blessed realization of those things whereof, for our endless good, he had so long and so earnestly testified.

Dante dates his supernatural pilgrimage as taking place A.D. 1300 ; his great poem must therefore be read as historic in all events antecedent to that date, prophetic in all subsequent. Yet, in fact, historic in all. The Vita Nuova, the work as well as the record of early life, has the soft delicacy of Dante's youthful face portrayed by Giotto ; but the Divina Commedia, whether professedly narrating the past or the future, is throughout impressed with the deeper, sterner, sadder lines to be traced in his solemn death-mask.[1]

[1] The authenticity of this death-mask was lately confirmed in a singular manner. In the sepulchral chapel of Braccioforte, contiguous to the tomb of Dante at Ravenna, was discovered, on the 27th May 1865, a box containing human bones, with an inscription declaring them to be the bones of Dante, placed there on the 18th October 1677 by Antonio Santi, a Franciscan friar. To his Order the honour of the great poet's sepulture originally belonged ; and his motive for removing the bones to a receptacle known only to himself, and perhaps a few others, appears to have been dread lest the Municipality of Ravenna should make good a repeatedly-urged claim against the Friars to jurisdiction over the tomb. In that secret shelter the precious relics lay hidden till discovered as above related. The most careful and scientific investigation by the Government verified them so far as possible as the bones of Dante Allighieri. The mask was found to correspond in many important parts to the head of the skeleton. The cavity of the cranium being filled with rice, the weight of this was ascertained to be 1420 grammes. [Professor Huxley states that the heaviest brain weighed by Professor Wagner—that of a woman—amounted to 1872 grammes ; next to it comes the brain of Cuvier (1861 grammes), then Byron (1807 grammes), and then an insane person (1783 grammes) : the lightest adult brain recorded (720 grammes) was that of an idiotic female.] Without committing themselves to the science of phrenology, the learned examiners record the following observations on the skull :—Very noticeable are the osseous regions connected with the organs of poetry, music, satire, religion, benevolence, and those which indicate love of authority and independence, self-esteem, pride, loftiness of spirit, self-love ; those also which are connected with the mechanical talents of drawing, sculpture, and architecture. There is a notable development of the parts corresponding to the organs of circumspection and caution. The characteristics of a philosophic mind show themselves ; such a mind as possesses in an eminent degree the inductive faculty, the habit of pondering great matters, the aptitude of discovering the most abstract and remote relations between things—in sum, the organization is that of those universal geniuses who have been the true teachers of the human race. (Relazione della Commissione Governativa eletta a verificare il fatto del ritrovamento delle Ossa di Dante in Ravenna. Firenze, 1865.)

CHAPTER IV.

THE WOOD, AND THE APPARITION OF VIRGIL.

Questa selva selvaggia ed aspra e forte.

What this wood was, savage, and rough, and strong.

Inf. 1. 5.

IN A.D. 1300, the year of the Jubilee; at dawn on the 25th of March, the Feast of the Annunciation, then reckoned as New Year's Day, and happening that year to be also Maundy Thursday; Dante, then nearly thirty-five, and approaching the time of his election to the Priorato, perceived himself to have wandered while half asleep from the right path, and to be actually entangled in the mazes of a dark wood. Before him rose a hill whose sides were clothed with sunshine; but no man walked thereon. Dante took courage to begin the ascent, and had made some little progress in climbing, the lower foot being ever the firmer, when he found himself successively withstood and repelled by three wild beasts, a swift Leopard, a raging Lion, and a craving greedy Wolf. These, but chiefly the last, were gradually and irresistibly forcing him back upon the sunless plain, when suddenly he became aware that he was no longer alone.

> While I was crushing down to the low place,
> To me was offered one before mine eyes
> Who seemed by reason of long silence hoarse.

In the great desert him when I beheld
'Have pity upon me !' I cried to him,
'Who that thou be, or Shade, or certain man.'

He answered me : 'Not man : man once I was ;
Also my parents were Lombardïans,
Mantuans as to country both the two.
Sub Julio was I born, although 'twere latc,
And under good Augustus lived in Rome,
In the time of the false and lying gods.
I was a poet, and I sang that just
Son of Anchises who did come from Troy,
After that haughty Ilion had been burned.
But why to such annoy returnest thou ?
Wherefore not scale the dèlectable mount
Which of all joy is cause and principle ?'

'Art thou that Virgil, then, that fountain-head
Which spreads abroad so wide a stream of speech ?'
Replied I to him with a brow ashamed.
'O of the other poets honour and light,
Avail me the long study and great love
Which have impelled me search thy volumc througl !
My master thou, and thou mine author art :
Thou only art the one from whom I took
The noble style which won me honouring.
Behold the beast because of which I turned :
Do thou against her help me, famous sage,
Because she makes me tremble, veins and pulsc.

'Thee it behoves to hold another course,'
He answered, after that he saw me weep,
'If thou would'st get from out this savage place.

.   .   .   .

Whence I, for thy more good, think and discern
Thou follow me : and I will be thy guide,
And bring thee hence by an eternal place ;
Where thou shalt hearken the despairing shrieks,
Shalt see the ancient Spirits dolorous,
That each one outcries for the second death.
And thou shalt then see those who are content
Within the fire, because they hope to come,
When that it be, unto the blessed race.
To whom thereafter if thou wouldst ascend,
A Soul there'll be more worthy this than I :
Thee will I leave with her, when I depart :
Seeing that Emperor Who above there rules,
Because I was rebellious to His law,
Wills to His city no access by me.
In every part He sways, and there He reigns :
There is His city, and the exalted seat.
Oh happy he whom thither He elects ! '

And I to him : ' Poet, I crave of thee,
And by that God of Whom thou knewest not,
That I may flee this evil so, and worse,
That thou do take me whither now thou saidst,
So that I may behold Saint Peter's gate,
And those whom thou dost make so sorrowful.'

Then on he moved, and I kept after him.

Inf. I. 61-93, 112-136.

But the rayless atmosphere seemed yet again to exert its
baleful influence. Scarcely had they set forward when
Dante, appalled alike at the prospect before him and at
his own unworthiness, expressed his doubts and shrinkings,
and was afresh and more effectually encouraged.

'If I have rightly understood thy speech,'
Replied that Shade of the magnanimous,
'With abjectness thy spirit is oppressed ;
Which oftentimes encumbereth a man,
Diverting him from honoured enterprise,
As seeing false, a beast, when it is dusk.
In order that thou free thee of this fear,
I 'll tell thee why I came, and what I heard
At the first point when I was grieved for thee.
I was among the Spirits in suspense :
A lady called me, blest and beautiful,
Such that I did beseech her to command.
Her eyes were shining more than does the star,
And she began to address me, soft and low,
With voice angelic in her utterance.
"O courteous Spirit thou of Mantua,
Of whom the fame yet in the world endures,
And shall endure as far as motion does,—
One that is mine and is not Fortune's friend
Is so impeded on the desert slope,
Upon his path, that he is turned for dread ;
And he 's so far already strayed, I fear,
That to his help I may be risen late,
By that which I in Heaven have heard of him.
Now do thou move, and with thine ornate speech,
And what behoves to his deliverance,
So succour him that I may be consoled.
I that do make thee go am Beatrice :
I come from where I would return unto :
Love moved me, as it maketh me to speak.
When I shall be in presence of my Lord,
Thee will I praise unto Him oftentimes."
Here she was silent ; and then I began ;—
" Lady of Virtue, oh by whom alone

The human race exceeds the whole contents
Within that heaven which hath its circles least,[1]
So much doth thy commanding pleasure me
As that obeying, though now 'twere, were late :
Needs thee no further open me thy wish.
But tell me wherefore thou dost not beware
Of coming to this centre here-adown,
From the ample place thou burnest to regain."
" Since thou so far within desir'st to know,
I briefly shall apprise thee," she replied,
" Why I am not afraid to come herein.
Only those things are to be had in fear
Which have the potency to do one harm ;
The others not, for they're not terrible.
I, of His grace, am fashioned such by God
That misery of yours touches not me,
Nor, of this burning, flame assails me not.
In heaven a gentle lady is, who grieves
For this impediment I send thee to,
So that she breaks the stern decree above.
Lucia she prayed in her soliciting,
And said : ' Now stands thy faithful one in need
Of thee ; and him to thee I recommend.'
Enemy to all cruel, Lucïa
Moved her, and to the place came where was I,
Who side by side with ancient Rachel sat.
' Beatrice,' said she, ' very praise of God,
Why succourest not him who loved thee so
He issued from the vulgar herd for thee ?
Hearest thou not the anguish of his plaint ?
Seest thou not the death which combats him

---

[1] ' The Lunar Heaven ; in other words, " Through whom the human
race excels every other sublunary thing." '

Upon the flood whereof no sea can boast ? ' [1]
Never were persons in the world so swift
To do their vantage, and to flee their harm,
As I, upon the proffering such words,
Came downward hither from my blessed throne,
Confiding me in thy decorous speech,
Which honours thee and those who 've hearkened it."
After whenas she had discoursed me this,
Weeping, she turned away her shining eyes,
Whereby the swifter made she me to come.
And unto thee I came, as she did will :
Away I took thee from before the beast
Which stopped thee from the fair mount's short ascent.
What is't then ? Wherefore, wherefore, hold'st thou back ?
Wherefore dost harbour in thy heart such fear ?
Daring and valour wherefore hast thou not ?
Seeing such ladies three beatified
Have in the court of heaven a care of thee,
And mine assertion warrants thee such good.'

Like as the flowerets, by the nightly frost
Bent down and closed, when the sun whitens them,
All open on their stalk erect themselves ;
Such I became as to my courage spent :
And to my heart such righteous daring flowed
That, like to one stout-hearted, I began :
' Oh ! she that succoured me compassionate !
And courteous thou who promptly didst obey
The veritable words she proffered thee !
Thou with desiring hast disposed my heart
So to the going forward, by thy words,

---

[1] ' Perhaps an allusion to the hellish river Acheron, which loses itself
in the centre of earth, instead of emptying into any sea.'

That I've reverted to the first intent.
Now go, for there's one only will in both,—
Thou leader, and thou lord, and master thou.'

So said I to him : and, when he had moved,
I entered in the lofty wooded way.

II. 43-142.

These first two cantos of the Inferno must be regarded
as belonging not to it only, but to the whole Divina Commedia, between which and the Vita Nuova they form
the connecting link. Ere we can even inadequately enter
into their meaning, we must have some general notion of
Dante's matured political views as set forth in his treatise
De Monarchiâ. His Ghibellinism was neither a narrow
partisanship, nor a hesitating adherence founded on a nice
balancing of the more of good and less of evil in the two
opposing factions. Rather he had formed a vast sublime
conception, which shall be set forth in his own words :—
'Only Man among beings holds mid¡place between things
corruptible and things incorruptible ; . . . so, alone among
all beings is he ordained to two ultimate ends : whereof the
one is the end of Man according as he is corruptible, the
other his end according as he is incorruptible. Therefore
that unspeakable Providence proposed to Man two ends ;
the one the beatitude of this life, which consists in the
operations of his own virtue, and is figured in the Terrestrial Paradise ; the other the beatitude of eternal life, which
consists in the fruition of the Divine Countenance, whereto
his own virtue cannot mount except it be aided by the
Divine Light—and this is understood by the Celestial
Paradise. To these two beatitudes, as to divers conclu-

sions, by divers means must we come. For to the first we attain by philosophic teachings, provided we follow these, acting according to the moral and intellectual virtues :[1] to the second by those spiritual teachings which transcend human reason, provided we follow these, acting according to the theological virtues, Faith, Hope, and Charity. Therefore these conclusions and means—albeit they be shown us, the one by human reason, which all was made known to us by Philosophers; the other by the Holy Spirit, Who, through Prophets and hagiographers, through Jesus Christ, Son of God Co-eternal to Himself, and through His disciples, revealed truth supernatural and to us necessary—human cupidity would repudiate, unless men like horses, in their bestial nature wandering, by bit and bridle were restrained on the road. Wherefore by man was needed a double directive according to the double end: that is, of the Supreme Pontiff, who, according to Revelation, should lead mankind to eternal life ; and of the Emperor, who, according to philosophic teachings, should direct mankind to temporal felicity. And whereas to this port none or few, and those with overmuch difficulty, could attain, unless mankind, the waves of enticing cupidity being quieted, should repose free in the tranquillity of peace ; this is the aim to be mainly kept in view by the Guardian of the Globe, who is named Roman Prince, to wit, that in the garden-plot of mortals freely with peace may men live.'[2] The expression 'Guardian of the Globe,' is equivalent to 'Emperor of the whole Earth,' for Dante's conception was of nothing less than a temporal supremacy of the Emperor correspondent to the spiritual supremacy of the Pope in

[1] Note here Dante's esteem of Philosophy, and cf. pp. 21-25.
[2] *De Monarchiâ* iii. 15.

universality, in direct derivation from Almighty God, and in indissoluble connexion with the city and people of Rome.

Under the shadow of this world-filling vision we sit down to expound.

The Wood appears, beyond a doubt, to be symbolical of the moral and political condition of Italy just before Dante's election to the Priorato—a state of anarchy rapidly lapsing, in his apprehension, into savagery. *Selva*＝*wood* is the root of *selvaggio*＝*savage; il viver selvaggio*＝*savage life,* is opposed to *il viver civile*＝*civil life ;* the worst of all evils for man on earth is *non esser cive* [1] ＝*not to be a citizen*＝to live in the isolation of a savage. Dante then, before reason had matured within him, found himself a Guelphic member of a Guelphic family, living in a factiously Guelphic community ; and became thus involved in a maze of moral and political disorder. Before his mental eye rose fair the hill of Virtue, illuminated by the sun of Reason, and waiting for the ideal City. He proposed to inaugurate, during his tenure of office, the course which should build and people it :—how colossal was the task, how all but non-existent were the materials, we gather from Boccaccio's record of his silence and his words on a memorable occasion. ‘He being gloriously supreme in the government of the Republic, discourse was held among the chief citizens of sending, for a certain great need (to check the intrigue of the Blacks with Charles of Valois), an embassy to Pope Boniface VIII., and of appointing Dante head of this embassy. And he receiving the proposal in the presence of all who so counselled, and somewhat delaying his reply, one happened to say:

[1] *Par.* viii. 115-117.

" Whereon thinkest thou ?" To which words he answered:
" I am thinking, if I go, who remains ; and if I remain, who
goes ; "—as if he alone among all were strong, and the rest
strong only in him.' The event, as we have seen, justified
this view ; so that it is no wonder to find him in symbolic
imagery proceed to show that scarcely had he begun to act,
securing each onward step before venturing the next, when
behold the three Guelph powers with their characteristic
vices, arraying themselves against him, beset his path ;
Florence in her factiousness, France in her pride, the Court
of Rome in her avarice. He had almost sunk back into
hopeless corruption, when Virgil, the symbol and impersonation of Human Science, especially of Moral and Political
Philosophy, appeared for his deliverance ; and as its only
effectual means, proposed to bring him to a right understanding of the Divine Will both for states and individuals,
by showing him in the Pit of Hell the hideous external and
internal condition of those who contemn it, on the Mount
of Purgatory the painful and toilsome process by which it is
wrought deep into the very texture and essence of the soul.
So far may Human Science teach, and no farther ; for let
Dante but once by perfected moral virtue attain to stand in
the Terrestrial Paradise of the beatitude of this life, and lo,
supernatural light shall dawn, supernatural grace descend
upon him ; his human liberty shall develop into the Divine
liberty of faith, hope, and love ; his human peace into the
Divine peace which passeth all understanding. At that
meeting-point between Heaven and Earth, a higher Guide
shall be vouchsafed him ; he shall be drawn up from the
Terrestrial into the Celestial Paradise, and there grace shall
culminate in that glory of the Beatific Vision whereof

Beatrice, now transfigured into the embodiment of Divine
Science, is at once partaker and interpreter. She indeed
had been the suggester of the whole threefold pilgrimage,
though not its originating cause. For a gracious heavenly
Lady (the Divine Mercy or Prevenient Grace), moved with
pity, had first recommended Dante in his sore need to Lucia
(Illuminating Grace); and Lucia had claimed for him the
aid of his glorified Beatrice, as she sat in the third rank of
celestial thrones beside Rachel (Contemplation). Beatrice,
instantly perceiving that the only hope for her Beloved lay
in the realization of what comes after death, as instantly
descending to Limbo had with tears besought of Virgil the
succour he had hastened to proffer :—and Dante finally, free
of fears and doubts, hailing him as guide, as lord and
master, followed him within the Eternal World.

SECTION OF THE HELL.

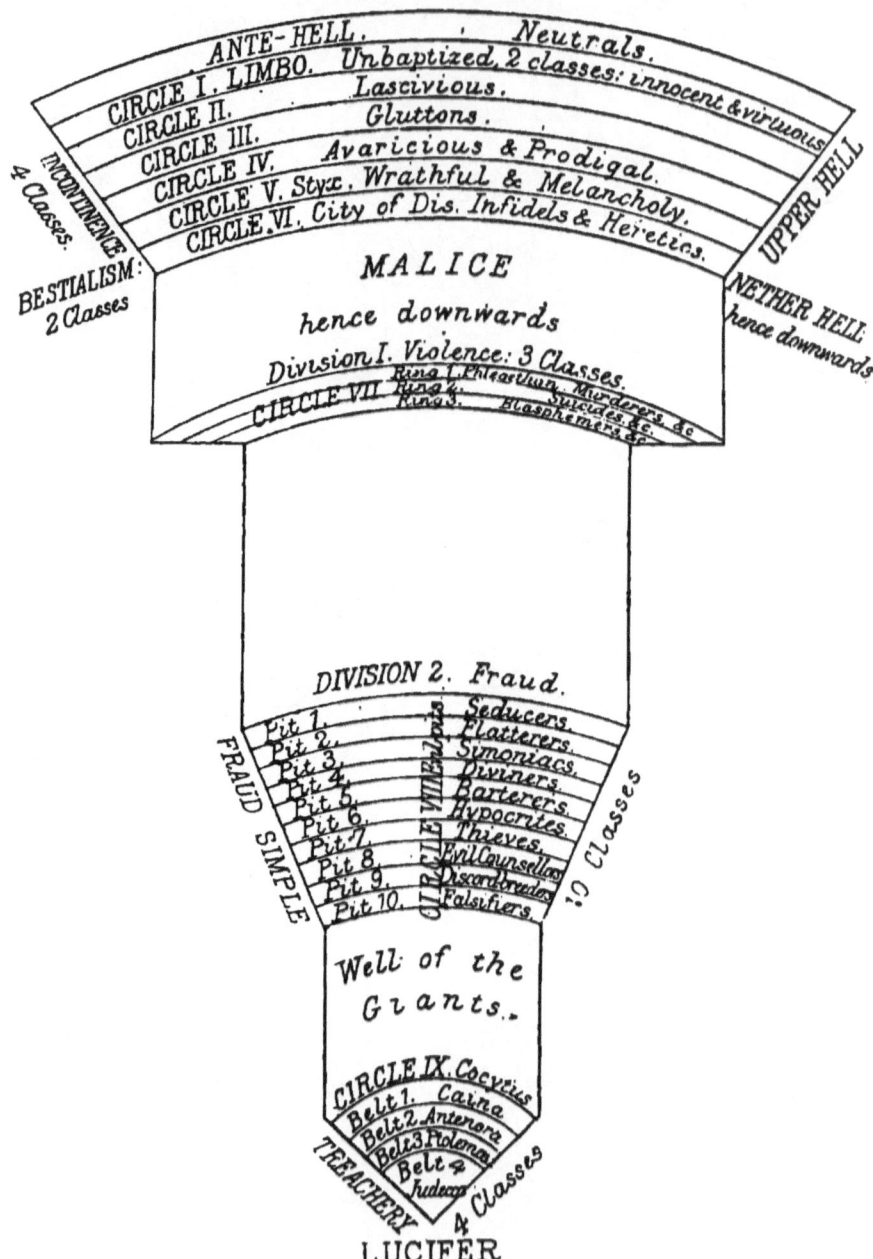

ANTE-HELL. Neutrals.
CIRCLE I. LIMBO. Unbaptized. 2 classes: innocent & virtuous.
CIRCLE II. Lascivious.
CIRCLE III. Gluttons.
CIRCLE IV. Avaricious & Prodigal.
CIRCLE V. Styx. Wrathful & Melancholy.
CIRCLE VI. City of Dis. Infidels & Heretics.

INCONTINENCE. 4 Classes.

BESTIALISM: 2 Classes.

UPPER HELL

NETHER HELL hence downwards

MALICE

hence downwards

Division I. Violence: 3 Classes.

CIRCLE VII. Ring I. Phlegethon. Murderers, &c.
Ring 2.
Ring 3. Suicides, &c. Blasphemers, &c.

DIVISION 2. Fraud.

Pit 1. Seducers.
Pit 2. Flatterers.
Pit 3. Simoniacs.
Pit 4. Diviners.
Pit 5. Barterers.
Pit 6. Hypocrites.
Pit 7. Thieves.
Pit 8. Evil Counsellors.
Pit 9. Discord breeders.
Pit 10. Falsifiers.

FRAUD SIMPLE

CIRCLE VIII. Malebolge.

10 Classes.

Well of the Giants.

CIRCLE IX. Cocytus.
Belt 1. Caina.
Belt 2. Antenora.
Belt 3. Ptolomea.
Belt 4. Judecca.

TREACHERY. 4 Classes.

LUCIFER.

(To face Chab. V.)

CHAPTER V.

THE HELL.

Questo baratro e'l popol che 'l possiede.
This gulf, and eke the folk which it possess.

Inf. XI. 69.

HELL—in Holy Scripture so vividly represented as *the Pit*, that not only is our Blessed Lord said to have descended into the lower parts of the earth, but the dead Samuel complains of being brought *up*, and the living David and Hezekiah deprecate going *down*—is by Dante placed, as we have before seen, within the Earth ; its uppermost central spot directly under that portion of her crust which sustains Jerusalem, its innermost central point her centre of gravity. The annexed plan of a section of the Pit shows its form to be that of a funnel, or hollow inverted cone ; within whose circuit we shall find that, as space contracts, torment intensifies.

Hell is entered through an awful Gate, closed to none ; reft of all fastenings since the day when the Conqueror of Death, fresh from the Cross, forced through it His resistless passage ; and bearing above it, in a dark colour, this inscription :—

' Through me you pass into the grieving realm ;
Through me you pass into the eternal grief ;

Through me you pass among the kin that's lost.
Justice impelled my Maker the All-High ;
The Puïssance Divine created me,
The Supreme Wisdom, and the Primal Love.
Before myself, created things were not,
Unless eternal :—I eternal last.
Leave off all hope, all ye that enter in.'

Inf. III. 1-9.

Immediately beyond this Gate lies a dreary Ante-Hell, the prison of certain Angels who when there was war in Heaven took neither side, and of an inconceivable multitude of human Souls who during their probation lived without infamy and without praise, displeasing alike to God and to His foes, selfishly neutral in the great unceasing conflict between good and evil ;—never alive as noble minds count life ; now most really and most awfully dead. For as they passed their Time trimming and shuffling in the train of public opinion, the sensitive slaves of every gossiping tongue of their acquaintance—even so, disdained alike by Justice and by Mercy, are they left to pass their Eternity hurriedly chasing a hurrying standard, while flies and wasps sting their naked bodies, and disgusting worms absorb their blood and tears.

Ante-Hell is bounded by the Acheron, the first of the four infernal rivers : of whose source a word may fitly here be said.—In Crete, once fertile, now waste, is situate Mount Ida, where Jove was nursed ; and within the cavernous hollow of the mountain there yet stands erect the colossal form of Jove's father Saturn, King of Crete during the Golden Age. As the symbol of Time, he turns his back on Damietta, for the East is of the past ; his face toward

Rome, for the West is of the present and the future. In form he is, with slight variations, the Great Image of Nebuchadnezzar's dream ; his head is of fine gold, his breast and arms of pure silver, his middle of brass, his thighs, legs, and left foot of choice iron, his right foot, on which he chiefly rests, of clay. Thus representing the successive ages of the world in their faultless commencement and gradual degeneracy, in all his substance save the gold he is cleft by a deep fissure, whence trickle the tears of human shame and. sorrow, till they form streams of force to break through the earth's crust, and of volume to constitute the four subterranean rivers—Acheron, Styx, Phlegethon, and Cocytus. With the last three we shall meet in due time ; our present business is with Acheron=Joyless, which flows down from the silver breast ; and on whose brink gather from all lands all human souls that depart under the wrath of God. Charon, the first of a long train of dæmonic personages superhuman, human, and subhuman, is the ferryman : and the miserable Shades are driven into his boat by the sharp inward spurring of the Divine Justice, further enforced upon laggards by blows from the oar.

Hell proper, which begins on the opposite bank, is divided into nine concentric Circles ; each being a landing-place in the descent, having on the one hand the wall of the solid earth, on the other the fearful void of the Abyss.

Circle I. is Limbo, the habitation of two classes of the Unbaptized : Infants who have died too young for actual sin, and such Non-believers of every age and clime as, being in invincible ignorance, have ruled their lives by the law of conscience, or have signally benefited mankind. A third class was once there too—the holy Souls of the chosen nation, who had passed from life in faith in Christ to come, and whom He liberated at His triumphal Descent.

The denizens of Limbo, free from outward inflictions, express by plaints which are only sighs a pain which is only longing : but that hopeless longing is for the Face of God, and that aching pain is the ' pain of loss,' and those ceaseless sighs make the still air tremble into the eternal breeze that constitutes the atmosphere of this thick spirit-wood. Not far down in the descent, amid the gloom, shines a luminous spot, where stands a noble castle guarded by sevenfold high walls, entered by sevenfold gates, entrenched by a fair stream, and enclosing a meadow of fresh verdure :— for even on unchristened man shines the light of brighter Intellect irradiating the deeper shades ; and Virtue with Wisdom builds up a strong and noble habitation for the heroic and philosophic soul ; and the Seven Virtues are high, guarding the Reason and the Will ; and the Seven Sciences give entrance into the inner places of Knowledge ; and Education affords the stream of passage from without, while within the formed mind and character repose in freedom and refreshment. This castle is the utmost point of attainment for non-believers ;—here abide their heroes and heroines, the great ones of their active life ; here too, and in somewhat more exalted place, their poets and sages, the great ones of their contemplative life. Consciously as locally suspended between reward and punishment, baulked and baffled in their whole nature for lack of that which is above nature, keenly sensitive to every wounding token of their separation from the Blessed ; thirsting still for the perfect knowledge they thirsted for on earth, and knowing they must for ever thirst in vain ; desiring without hope that Supreme Good of which they can form higher conceptions than can their fellow-prisoners, yet too self-controlled, as it would seem, to sigh their atmosphere out of its perfect stillness; in countenance neither sad nor glad, but of great authority; slow and grave in gaze, uttering rare speech with modulated voice; retaining the tender affections of their earthly state, and some at least compassionating in all the void with which each and all are aching, these God-sick dwellers on the edge of the 'great gulf fixed' pine on and on eternally, conscious of every natural endowment of kings and priests in the Heavenly City, but wanting alike the anointing oil of grace and the crown of glory.

At the entrance of the Second Circle sits another dæmonic personage—the infernal Judge Minos. All those who, having passed Acheron, stop not short in Limbo, stand in turn before him to confess their sins, and he, discerning to which of the eight penal Circles each Soul belongs,

> Girds himself with his tail as many times
> As he resolves that she be lowered grades.
>
> V. 11-12.

In these eight Circles we first note the three great classes into which Dante, following Aristotle in names, though not altogether in their application, divides sins; viz., Incontinence, Bestialism, and Malice. Incontinence is want of self-control; the sins which proceed from it, and which are punished in the Second, Third, Fourth, and Fifth Circle respectively, are Lasciviousness, Gluttony, Avarice with Prodigality, Anger with Melancholy. Bestialism, punished in the Sixth Circle, and in strict accordance

with the meaning of the Italian word *bestialitade* characterized by Dante as *besotted*, comprises Infidelity and
Heresy in all their forms; the most prominent form being
that Materialism whereof our author says in his Convito,
'Among all bestialisms (*i.e.*, follies) that is most stupid,
most vile, and most hurtful by which any believes, after
this life no other life to be; inasmuch as if we turn over all
the writings as well of philosophers as of other wise writers,
all agree in this, that in us is some part perpetual.' [1]

Malice works others woe either by Violence or by Fraud.
And here—lest my reader should echo Dante's perplexity at
Virgil's statement—I had better premise that some sins of
Malice will appear nearly identical with some of Incontinence; but in each such case the moral difference between
sins of passion and surprise, and sins of wilfulness, delibe-
ration and depravity, must be taken for granted.

Violence is punished in the Seventh Circle according to a
threefold classification of sinners against their neighbour,
themselves, or their God. Further subdivisions distinguish
slayers or injurers of person from robbers, wasters, or destroyers of property; and offenders against the Sacred Person of God by blasphemy, from offenders against the things
of God, *i.e.*, Nature and Art. For as Nature is God's daughter and disciple, so Art, her child and follower, must needs
be His granddaughter and sub-disciple. The offence
against Art is Usury—God's sentence being that man shall
eat bread in the sweat of his brow, *i.e.*, shall by labour of
head and hand utilize natural resources; whereas the usurer,
a mere parasite, derives nourishment from toils he never
shares, and from supplies to which he adds nothing.

[1] *Conv.* ii. 9.

Fraud alone remains to be treated of in its surpassing heinousness as the abuse of man's peculiar and noblest gift of Reason, and in its yet more minute and perplexing classification. Its main distinction is that which assigns to the Eighth Circle ten subdivisions of the simply Fraudulent, who, by deceiving such as had no special reason for trusting them, have broken only the bond of love uniting all men as sharers in a common nature; and to the Ninth Circle four subdivisions of the Treacherous, who, by betraying their kindred, country, friends, or beneficent lords, have broken the closer bond of natural love intertwined with special faith.

Two more points should be premised with regard to all the reprobate. First, that after the Resurrection of the Body their sufferings will increase, inasmuch as sensitiveness to good and evil is in proportion to the perfection of him who experiences either; and though sin be essential imperfection, yet the risen sinner will be so far perfect as to possess both the parts which constitute man. And secondly, that Dante supposes them to have some knowledge of future events in this world, but not of present unless informed from without; whence it follows that all their knowledge will become extinct from that hour in which the door of the future shall be shut.

Having taken this general survey we proceed to particulars.

Incontinence, as we have seen, is want of self-restraint and is the principle of the sins for which four, or perhaps more correctly six, classes of transgressors suffer in four successive Circles.

In Circle II., the prison of the Lascivious, begins the

E

outer darkness of Hell and the 'pain of sense.'   Here they
whose passions have sown the wind reap the roaring whirlwind, and utter most piercing shrieks of terror as ever and
anon they are blown · to the very edge of the yawning
Abyss.

Circle III. is a climate of cold, heavy, dirty-looking,
stench-exhaling, changeless rain and hail and snow, pour-
ing down in ceaseless torrents on the prostrate Gluttons,
whose god was their belly, and who, now and to all Eternity the prey of a sort of personified belly, the demon
Cerberus, are devoured by his teeth, rent by his claws, and
deafened by his barking.

Dante's view of Usury will have prepared us to find that
he regards all misusers of money, whether hoarders or
wasters, as special ignorers of social obligation and breakers
of social order.   Consequently, in the various Circles
wherein they are located, one punishment is of continual
recurrence—made in some way invisible or unrecognisable,
they are cut off from society.   In Circle IV., the realm of the
demon Plutus, are seen but not known a vast multitude of
the two least guilty classes of money-sinners : Misers who
placed their happiness in gold, and who will rise from the
dead with clenched fists ; Spendthrifts who placed theirs in
what gold will buy, and who will rise with close-cropped
hair. (An Italian proverb says of such, 'darebbe tutto fino ai
capelli'='He would lavish all, to his very hair.')[1]   The two
bands for ever crawl in opposite directions half-way round
their dungeon, howling as they impel before them weighty
masses which at each recurring meeting clash in infernal
harmony with their mutual revilings.

[1] G. Rossetti, *Com. An.* vol. i. c. vii. t. 19.

Circle V., the domain of the demon Phlegyas, is the muddy and putrid River Styx=Hatred, Sadness, which, flowing from the brazen middle of Saturn, and here forcing its way through the wall of Hell, harbours the Wrathful= *Iracondi*, and the Melancholy=*Accidiosi:* two classes who seem at first sight to have little in common. S. John the Damascene however speaks of *Ira* as 'a kindling of the blood surrounding the heart, through the *vaporation* of the gall ;'—while S. Thomas Aquinas attributes *Accidia* to 'sad and melancholy *vaporations;*' hence probably their combination by Dante under like punishment by putrid *fumes.* The question is farther complicated by *Accidia*= Melancholy, being in Italian identified with the deadly sin of Sloth, and defined by theologians as 'a certain sadness which weighs down the spirit of man in such wise that there is nothing he likes to do; wherefore *accidia* implies a certain tedium :'[1]—'a sadness of the mind which weighs upon the spirit, so that the person conceives no will towards well-doing, but rather feels it irksome.'[2] Dante in the Purgatorio, as we shall hereafter find, dwells on the sluggish, as here in the Inferno on the gloomy, aspect of the sin. And as he punishes lower down, in the Circle of the Violent, not only suicides as corresponding to murderers, but as corresponding to robbers those spendthrifts and gamblers who have wantonly and obstinately reduced themselves to weep where they were meant to be joyous, so he here punishes with the wrathful enemies of others' peace and happiness the melancholy enemies of their own. These, imbedded in the very dregs of the pool, bewail eternally the absence of those cheering influences of Nature by which they sometime re-

[1] Maestruzzo. [2] Tratt. Pecc. Mort.

fused to be cheered :—while those, partly emerging above its surface, rend and defile each other and themselves after death, as once in life.   It is farther noteworthy that both in the Inferno and in the Purgatorio the Meekness contrary to the sin of Anger is in practice set forth far less as the un-resisting Gentleness which endures evil than as the righteous Indignation which repels it.   For in the Convito, Dante, defining Virtue in general as ‘an elective habit consisting in the mean,’ lays down that Meekness ‘moderates our anger and our too great patience against our exterior ills :’[1] herein following his master Ser Brunetto, who thus speaks : ‘He that is truly meek[2] is angry whereat he ought, and with whom, and as much as, and as, and when, and where. He is wrathful[3] that passes the mean in these things, and forthwith rushes into Anger. The wrathless[4] is he that is not angry where it behoves, and when, and as much as, and with whom, and as; and he is not to be praised.’[5] It is extremely probable that the *Accidiosi* at the bottom of Styx while on earth partook largely of such Wrathlessness, supinely wretched for want of that measured Resentment which, stopping short of revenge, would yet have remedied mischief.[6]

So far Incontinence, which gradually but surely besotting the Understanding and perverting the Will, at length brings to pass that men do not like to retain God in their know-ledge, nor to look forward to the Judgment after death; and so depraves them into that *Bestialism* which seems to

---

[1] *Convito* iv. 17.   [2] *Mansueto.*   [3] *Iracondo.*
[4] *Inrascibile.*   [5] *Tesoro* vi. 21.
[6] G. Rossetti, *Comento Analitico*, Riflessioni sul c. vii.

correspond to the *Folly* of Holy Writ. By it the fool
saith in his heart, 'There is no God,' denying Him in
Whose Image he was made ; by it he mentally remakes
himself in the image of the beasts that perish. Therefore
after the lesser inflictions of Upper Hell, the region of
simple darkness, through the four Circles of the Inconti-
nent, come the torments of Nether Hell, the region of
darkness and of fire ; that fire being, in every instance but
one, the peculiar punishment of such as have dared come
into direct collision with Him Who is a Consuming Fire,
even the Jealous God. It first burns in the one appalling
Circle of the Bestialized—Circle VI., the City of Dis, a
fortified cemetery whose turrets and walls, garrisoned by
demons and guarded by Furies, defend no houses, but keep
under closest watch and ward tombs red-heated by creeping
flames—tombs of souls buried everlastingly, like with like,
for the Infidelity which disbelieved their God's existence
and their own, or for the Heresy which declared their God
other than He has revealed Himself to be. Open as yet,
these tombs will all be closed over the re-embodied souls
after the Judgment Day.

As Incontinence degrades the soul towards Bestialism, so
Bestialism hems it round in Malice. He indeed is the fool
of fools who saith, 'There is no God ;' but he too is a fool
who, saying, 'Tush, the Lord shall not see,' goes on to
annul his Reason by brutish Violence, or to abuse it by
worse than brutish Fraud. Consequently the three remaining Circles, though sunk to a far lower level, are accounted
within the Red City of Dis, and are under the guard of its
fortified enclosure. Its central Void, exhaling the intoler-

able stench of deadliest sin, is the brute-demon Minotaur's prowling-field ; in depth ever a fearful chasm, in character a broken and precipitous landslip from the hour when the earthquake at the Crucifixion, felt throughout the Abyss, left its special and tremendous mark on the prison-houses of the Violence and Fraud which had culminated in Deicide.

At the foot of this chasm spreads Circle VII., the Hell of Violence, divided into three concentric rings. Ring 1, the outermost, is the boiling Blood-river Phlegethon=Burning, issuing from Saturn's iron limbs. Herein stand, at a greater or less depth according to the degree of their guilt, the Violent against their Neighbour's person or property : *i.e.*, Tyrants, Murderers, and Marauders. Their demon-gaolers are the Centaurs, whose arrows keep them down to the pre-scribed depth. Within the circuit of the Blood-river lies Ring 2, the Dolorous Wood, prison and population all in one. For its poison-trees are Suicides, degraded from animal to vegetable bodies, tortured by Harpies, who pluck and eat their leaves, and alone of all the lost doomed after the Judgment Day not to resume their self-despoiled garment of flesh, but hang it on a branch. All about the Wood wanton Spendthrifts and destroyers of their own goods, in utter nakedness, are hunted and rent piecemeal by demon hounds. Phlegethon, here flowing unseen be-neath the soil, reappears at the edge of this grim garland to traverse its enclosure, Ring 3, a scorched and scorching Sand-Waste lying under a rain of fire-flakes.—And here a very curious question presents itself. In the second Can-zone of the Convito, Dante thus speaks of Philosophy, whom he calls his Lady :—

Her beauty raineth down flamelets of fire,
Animate with a noble gracious spirit,
Which is creator of each virtuous thought ;
These break like thunderbolts
The innate vices which make any vile.

And he thus comments on his own words : ' It is to be known that morality is the beauty of Philosophy : for as the beauty of the body results from the limbs, in so far as they are duly ordered; so the beauty of wisdom, which is the body of. Philosophy, as is said, results from the order of the moral virtues, which cause that [wisdom] to please sensibly. And therefore I say that her beauty, that is morality, rains flamelets of fire, that is right appetite, which is generated in the pleasure of moral doctrine ; which appetite separates us even from our natural vices, much more from others. And hence springs that happiness, which Aristotle defines in the first of the Ethics, saying that it is action according to virtue in a perfect life.' [1]   One cannot help asking, Is there a subtle connexion between these two fire-rains? Philosophy, defined as ' a loving use of wisdom,' is said to be ' chiefly in God ; ' [2] and this Third Ring hems in the special violators of the Divine Majesty in His Sacred Person, in His child Nature, and in His grandchild Art. Has that disregarded rain, which welcomed into these Souls on earth would have separated them from their sin, at length penetrated within the earth to punish them and their now eternally inseparable sin together?—However this may be, we certainly see here, as elsewhere, sinners against God under burning torment, endured by Blasphemers supine, as experiencing in the utmost possible degree that the God

[1] *Conv.* iii. 15.   [2] *Ib.* iii. 12.

Who answereth by fire is God indeed ; by breakers of His
laws in Nature walking compulsorily, under a severe penalty
if they stop ; by breakers of His laws in Art seated. These
last, the Usurers, as money-sinners, are not recognised by
personal semblance, and as quasi-fraudulent are located
next to the central Void, here again of appalling depth, with
Phlegethon for its rock-cascade till the stream disappears
once more under the next landing-place. The demon of
this passage is Geryon, a winged monster of human face
and serpent trunk—apt type and embodiment of Fraud.

Circle VIII., Evilpits, is the Hell of Fraud Simple, *i.e.*,
Fraud against those who have no special ground of trust in
their deceiver. Its form, implied in its name, is that of a
series of circular concentric fosses separated by walls, the
outermost wall being of course the solid earth ; and connected by a chain of rock-bridges running all across from
wall-top to wall-top, till cut short by the central Void.
The whole is of a livid stone-colour, and lies on the slope :
the punishment of Fraud in dungeons thus constructed
corresponding to the hidden and lurking character of the
offence.

In Pit 1, Deceivers of women are scourged by demons.—
Pit 2 is a cesspool in which Flatterers are sunk and choked ;
for 'that which cometh out of the mouth, this defileth a
man.' [1]—Pit 3, the tomb of Simoniacs, is perforated throughout bottom and sides with round holes, 'purses' in which
these money-sinners are imbursed from sight, head downward and within the earth, while their feet writhe without,
licked by the fire which torments offenders directly against
God. It is singular that this fire is not in each case

[1] S. Matt. xv. 11.

eternal; as one simoniacal Pope drops upon another in
their special purse, the predecessor sinks wholly within the
rock, and the flame is transferred to the successor.[1]—Pit 4
is ceaselessly perambulated by Diviners, Sorcerers, and
Witches, with heads twisted round upon their necks, so as
to look eternally backward for having sought to look too
forward. Dante seems, however, to condemn them even
more as impostors than as presumptuous searchers into the
secret things of God.—Pit 5 is a lake of boiling pitch,
wherein are submerged Barterers of justice, office, etc., who
on earth found money stick to their hands. They are
under the guard of a troop of peculiarly lying and spiteful
demons with personal and significant names, but classed
together as Evilclaws, who tear them piecemeal with prongs
if they appear above the surface.—Pit 6 lodges the college
of Hypocrites, toiling along under the overwhelming weight
of leaden cloaks and hoods, dazzlingly gilt without. But
the Arch-hypocrites of all time—Caiaphas, Annas, and the
rest of the Council that condemned our Blessed Lord—lie
athwart the way, impaled naked in the form of a cross;
trampled on by each walker in succession, and so crushed,
not by one leaden mantle, but by as many as the Pit contains. Most just and terrible retribution, that the rejecters
at once and instruments of the One Sacrifice for the sins of
the whole world should thus sensibly and visibly bear the
eternal burden of others' sin and pain as well as of their
own. Over this Pit the bridge is broken, and lies a heap
of fragments at the bottom; this being the second special
point at which the earthquake at the Crucifixion took
permanent effect.—Pit 7, the dungeon of Thieves, swarms

[1] G. Rossetti, *Com. An.* vol. 2, c. xix. t. 22.

with a loathsome agglomerate of naked men and serpents; the serpents stinging, the men stung, and each thus alternately transforming and transformed into the other; by a hideous community, not of property only, but of person, 'annihilating the distinction between *meum* and *tuum*.' [1]— Pit 8 presents the sole instance of a sin not directly against God avenged by burning. It is the furnace of Evil Counsellors, whose tongue, a little member set on fire of Hell while yet on earth, has covertly kindled a great matter, yea has set on fire the course of Nature; and who here find how fearful a covering they have all the while been weaving for themselves, even a tongue-shaped winding-sheet of fire unquenchable. Yet they retain a ghastly power of movement and of speech, the tongue within actuating the flame-tongue without.—Pit 9 is the shambles where Schismatics and Discord-breeders are cleft by a sword-bearing Devil: he stationary at a fixed point, they constrained to pace ever round and round; each time reaching the point whole, each time starting from it hacked and mutilated afresh.— Pit 10 is the lazar-house of Falsifiers, sick of various diseases, and so falsified in appearance and condition. [2] They are divided into three classes, according as they have sinned in respect of Substance, of Semblance, or of Fact. The Falsifiers of Substance are Alchemists blotched with leprosy, and Coiners bloated with dropsy. The Falsifiers of Semblance are counterfeiters of the person of another for some evil end: these are out of their mind (Ital. *fuor di se=out of self*). [3] The Falsifiers of Fact are malicious Liars, fever-stricken and prostrate. And some are instruments of further

---

[1] W. M. Rossetti, Trans. Hell, *Gen. Exp.* p. xxx.
[2] Cayley, Notes, p. 109.   [3] W. M. R. p. xxxii.

suffering to others—the sick by brawling and blows, the mad by rabid biting.

We have reached the last portion of the central Void, the Well of the Primæval Giants.   Its denizens are the Nimrod of Holy Scripture, and the Titans and other Giants of classic fable.   Their height may be computed at about seventy feet ; their intellect, speech, power, and freedom are curtailed in inverse proportion.   Their position as in some sort demon-sentinels over the entire region of the Fraudulent—for their heads tower high over the brink of Evilpits, while their feet rest on the frozen bottom of the Abyss—forcibly suggests the retribution slowly but surely dogging the steps of Fraud as the destroyer of the mutual trust on which society is based ;—namely, relapse into that savagery wherein brute force reigns supreme.

And finally we touch Circle IX., the pool Cocytus=Wailing, formed by the coalition of the three rivers at the point where stagnancy must needs ensue from the non-existence of any lower level.   But no mere stagnancy : Cocytus is as fast bound in frost as are the affections of the Traitors therein locked up.   Lying like Evilpits on the slope, it is rather a bason than a plain of ice ; and subdivides into four Belts, distinguishable only by the position of its captives.— Belt 1 is Caina ; here Betrayers of their Kindred are immersed up to the neck.—Belt 2 is Antenora, named from the Trojan Antenor, who according to one author betrayed Troy ; here Betrayers of their Country are immersed up to the throat.—Belt 3 is Ptolemæa, named from Ptolemy the Younger who betrayed Pompey ; here Betrayers of their Friends and Guests are fixed, not as the others, who can hide their faces by bending them downwards, but supine,

face upwards ; and the utter baseness of the sin further subjects the soul committing it to instant reprobation in this
lowest pit, the body informed by a devil still lingering on
earth till the appointed term of life is expired.—Lastly, Belt
4 is Judecca ; here Betrayers of their Beneficent Lords,
wholly imbedded in varying postures, show through the ice
like straws in glass.   Three of these Traitors however are
excepted, as we shall see ere long.

For lo, the bottom of the Bottomless Pit :—What, who
is there ?

Lucifer once, Dis now ; physically as morally self-centred :
half above the ice and half below it, so that his middle corresponds to the precise centre of gravity.   How colossal his
frame we may faintly image when we learn that an ordinary
stature more nearly approaches the seventy feet of the
Giants in the Well than those seventy feet the length of his
arms.   But his ingratitude is past estimation, past imagination, all but infinite : nay, in a true sense, infinite—for
though he be but a creature, and so finite, and though he
were originally endowed, as Dante thinks, with the highest
of all creatures' gifts, and so his endowments were finite too,
yet He Who created him for Himself is Infinite, and the
rejection of the Infinite must needs have a character of
infinity.   Wherefore as by the benefit is estimated the ingratitude, so by the effect of that ingratitude in present
hideousness the pristine beauty ; and if such were indeed
the pristine beauty, and he who was graced therewith yet
rebelled against his Creator and Adorner, duly is he for ever
the summit and the source of mourning.   His head is
triple-faced—the front face ruddy, the right-shoulder face

yellowish, the left black ; in symbol of his dominion over all reprobates from the three parts of the world, the complexions being respectively those of Europe, Asia, and Africa. Beneath each face protrude two monstrous bat-wings, whose flapping creates the wind to freeze Cocytus. In the three mouths are the three excepted Traitors—Judas Iscariot, Marcus Brutus, Cassius ; the first in the front mouth, less tormented by the teeth than by the horrible claws which tear him alone, and so punished far more than the other two, here classed with him as being traitors against what Dante regarded as the most sacred Will and Law of the Almighty, the establishment of the Roman Empire.

What yet remains ? Not Hell, but Earth ; the bowels of the Western hemisphere. Beyond the centre of gravity there is no more going down, but up, head skywards. Half Lucifer's body indeed, reversed in posture, pollutes this hemisphere, but, colossal as it is, it is quickly left behind ; —there is a down-flowing stream, but it can scarcely be formed of matter more virulent than the tears of contrition shed by the already half-beatified tenants of Purgatory ; for all sorrow, pure and purifying though it be, is yet in a sense of the earth, earthy, and so tends to the centre of gravity.[1] Earth's bowels are dark, but afford a way to the light ; the

---

[1] G. Rossetti, *Com. An.* c. xxxiv. t. 44. My theory, wholly suggested by my father's, is yet not absolutely identical with his. He thinks that ' whatever sinfulness is expiated in Purgatory flows down and settles in the kingdom of sin.' I am inclined rather to suppose the stream to consist of the tears of expiation ; the matter flowing from Saturn to form the four great infernal rivers being unquestionably tears, but tears of shame and mere human sorrow.

upward path is rough, but issues in the boundless Ocean, the reedy shore, the free air, the stars that gladden, and the Mount that cleanses.

Some there are who, gazing upon Dante's Hell mainly with their own eyes, are startled by the grotesque element traceable throughout the Cantica as a whole, and shocked at the even ludicrous tone of not a few of its parts.   Others seek rather to gaze on Dante's Hell with Dante's eyes; these discern in that grotesqueness a realized horror, in that ludicrousness a sovereign contempt of evil.   They keep in mind that the mediæval tone of thought bore fruit in the grotesque heads of the lost outside cathedrals, and in a spiritual humorousness which was by no means excluded even from sermons; yea, much more do they remember that the Divine Eternal Wisdom Himself, the Very and Infallible Truth, has, not once nor twice, characterized impiety and sin as Folly; and they feel in the depths of the nature wherewith He has created them that whatever else Folly may be and is, it is none the less essentially monstrous and ridiculous.   In this world of shadows they see it so, in that world of substances they imagine no cause why it should cease to be so; nay why, amid the disenchantments of that atmosphere of Truth, it should not rather be discerned as more so.   A sense of the utter degradation, loathsomeness, despicableness of the soul which by deadly sin besots Reason and enslaves Free Will passes from the Poet's mind into theirs; while the ghastly definiteness and adaptation of the punishments enables them to touch with their finger the awful possibility and actuality of the Second Death, and thus for themselves as for others to dread it more really, to deprecate it more intensely. Dante's Lucifer does appear 'less than Archangel ruined,' immeasurably less; for he appears Seraph wilfully fallen. No illusive splendour is here to dazzle eye and mind into sympathy with rebellious pride; no vagueness to shroud in mist things fearful or things abominable. Dante's Devils are hateful and hated, Dante's reprobates loathsome and loathed, despicable and despised, or at best miserable and commiserated. In the one solitary instance of Francesca da Rimini an unheedful reader might possibly suppose the Poet to sympathize with lawless love; but a careful student will discern abhorrence of moral corruption combined with compassion for sore temptation and grievous suffering. If, in a few other exceptional cases, nobleness of character yet hangs about any of the lost, it is in points wholly distinct from the sin which has been their destruction. Dante is guiltless of seducing any soul of man towards making or calling Evil his Good.

CHAPTER VI.

DANTE'S PILGRIMAGE THROUGH HELL.

O tu che se' per quest' Inferno tratto.

O thou that art conducted through this Hell.

Inf. VI. 40.

WE left Dante at the moment when Virgil's cheering speech had given him courage to enter on the eternal world. The awful inscription over the Gate of Hell, seeming to deny him hope, did indeed well-nigh drive him back again; but a further word and touch nerved him for the first sounds that struck upon his ear— the wailings of the Neutrals in the Ante-Hell :—

Here lamentations, sighs, and strident howls.
Resounded through the air without a star—
Whence I, at the beginning, wept thereat.
Differing tongues and horrid utterances,
And words of anguish and the tones of rage,
High and hoarse voices, and with them a sound
Of hands, a tumult made which circulates
Aye in that air without a season dyed,
Like to the sand whenas the whirlwind blows.

Inf. III. 22-30.

Instructed by Virgil, Dante, refraining from the full gratification of his curiosity respecting these miserable caitiffs, lest he should mitigate their sentence of hopeless obscurity, transferred his attention to the crowd gathering on the brink of Acheron. Charon at first, seeing a living man, and knowing him to be predestined to glory, commanded him to withdraw from among the dead; but Virgil had instant recourse to a formula often needed and often in substance repeated during this grisly descent :

> So is it willed there where's the power to do
> That which is willed ; and thou demand no more.
>
> III. 95, 96.

The boat then crossed with its mournful freight, Dante remaining behind to be first enlightened and comforted by his Master's explanation of the scene he had witnessed, and of the true ground of Charon's refusal to ferry him over ;—then to feel the dark tear-soaked champaign quake under his feet, and in a state of insensibility to be transferred, how he knew not, to the farther shore. His first consciousness was of impenetrable mist, his second of Virgil's sympathetic pallor, his third of the ceaseless sighs which, proceeding from the vast multitudes of both sexes and all ages that people Limbo, stir brooding stillness into tremulous breeze.

> Said the good lord to me : ' Thou askest not
> What Spirits may be these whom thou dost see ?
> I will now, ere thou goest on, thou know
> They did not sin :—and, if they had good works,
> 'Tis not enough, for baptism they had not,
> The door unto the faith which thou believ'st :
> And, if they were before Christianity,
> They did not adequately worship God :—
> And even of these same am I myself.
> For such defaults, and not for other guilt,

F

We're lost, and only are by thus much pained—
That in desire we live, but not in hope.'

Great grief, when I had heard him, took my heart,
Because I knew that people of much worth
Must be suspended in the limbo there.

' Do thou, my master, tell me—tell me, lord—'
Began I, for that I might so be sure
About that faith which conquers error quite,
' Went any ever hence, or by his own
Or other's merit, who was after blessed ? '

And he, who understood my covert speech,
Replied : ' In this condition I was new
When hither I saw come One Powerful
Incoronate with sign of victory.
He took from us the Primal Parent's Shade,
Abel his son's, and that of Noah too,
Of Moses, legist and obedïent,
Abraham patriarch, and David king,
Israel, with his father and his sons,
And Rachel, her for whom he did so much ;
And others many :—and He made them blessed.
And I would have thee know that, before them,
There had not been a human spirit saved.'

IV. 31-63.

In prolonged converse Virgil and Dante passed through
the wood of ghosts till they drew near the home of the more
exalted Spirits ; and while Virgil was yet replying to his
follower's eager question—

In the mean time a voice was heard by me :
' The most high poet honour ye : his Shade,
Which had departed, is returning now.'

Whenas the voice was quiet and at rest,
I four great Shadows saw come unto us ;
Semblance had they nor sorrowful nor glad.

The noble master then began to say :
' Him with that sword behold thou in his hand,
Who comes, as it were sire, before the three :
That one is Homer, poet sovereign.
The other is Horace satirist who comes ;
Ovid the third ; and Lucan is the last.
Because that each one shares along with me
In the same name the single voice did sound,
They do me honour, and thereby do well.'

Assembled thus the goodly school I saw
Of him, the master [1] of the most high song,
Who o'er the others like an eagle flies.
When somewhat they together had discoursed,
They turned to me with gesture of salute ;
My master also smiling at the same.
And more they did me honour yet by much ;
For so they made me of their company
That I became, 'mid so much mind, the sixth.
Thus went we on as far as to the light,
Conversing matters which to hush is good,
As, where I was, the speaking them was so.

IV. 79-105.

After passing in review the dignified inhabitants of the
Castle, and being permanently ennobled in his own eyes by

[1] ' It is questioned whether this " master " is Homer or Virgil. Chronology and modern appreciation would conclude for the first.   If we
consider the three companions of Homer to constitute the " school " to
the exclusion of Virgil, we may do the same : scarcely otherwise from
Dante's point of view.'

the sight, he was led by another way back into the trembling atmosphere.   Thence passing the demon Judge Minos, not unwarned by him, Dante found himself encompassed with the stormy howling darkness of Circle II.   Deep was his compassion as Virgil pointed out among the victims of Lasciviousness many who had peopled his memory and imagination from childhood upwards—Semiramis, Dido and Cleopatra, Helen and Achilles, Paris and Tristram.   But worse was to come.   For here suffered a friend's kinswoman, Francesca da Rimini, coupled with Paolo Malatesta in the soul's death no less than in the body's.   It is said that, deceived by her father, she had given hand and heart to this handsome accomplished youth, and all too late had found that he was but proxy for her real husband, his deformed and repulsive brother Gianciotto.   As now, in a lull of the tempest, she told how the sin of an unguarded moment had been avenged by Gianciotto's hand, her words and her lover's tears affected Dante to fainting; as one dead he fell to the earth, and on recovering consciousness found himself already in Circle III.   To Cerberus's currish menaces Virgil deigned no reply save that of two handfuls of earth cast into his cavernous jaws; and the Poets walked on, placing their feet on the limp shades of the rain-drenched Gluttons.   One of these, the Florentine Ciacco, sitting up as he recognised a fellow-citizen, held detailed converse with him respecting public and private matters both past and future; and excited his pity, though not beyond an inclination to tears.   The colloquy was suddenly broken off by Ciacco losing the power of speech, and dropping back flat into the slush, to emerge thence no more till roused by the Last Trumpet.

Having led his disciple, as always in Hell, towards the left along an arc equal to the ninth part of the Circle, on reaching the steps of descent Virgil had to repel the resistance of Plutus before entering on Circle IV. Dante, feeling some slight pricks of compassion, inquired respecting its tenants, and expressed surprise at not recognising any of the Misers and Spendthrifts he had known on earth. This phenomenon and the nature of their punishment being explained, Fortune and her dealings were thus discoursed of for his comfort under impending spoliation and banishment :—

'Thou now mayst see, my son, the transient puff
Of goods which unto Fortune are consigned,
For which the human race perturbs itself ;
For all the gold that is beneath the moon,
Or that once was, of these outweary souls
Could not make any one of them to pause.'

'Master,' I said to him, 'now tell me still :
This fortune, whereon thou dost touch to me,
What is 't, that has the world's goods so in clutch ? '

And he to me : 'How great that ignorance is,
O foolish creatures, which encumbers ye !
I 'll have thee now digest my text thereof.
The One Whose wisdom transcends everything
He made the heavens, and gave them who conducts,
So that to every part shines every part,[1]
Distributing the light coequally.
Unto the mundane splendours He alike
Ordained a general ministrant and chief,

---

[1] Every part of Heaven to every part of Earth.

Who should in time the vain possessions change
From race to race, from one to other blood,
Beyond preclusion of the human wits;
Wherefore one people rules, one languishes,
All in accordance to the doom of her,
Which is occult, as in the grass the snake.
To her your wisdom has no hindering:
She doth provide, and judge, and prosecute
Her reign, as even theirs the other gods.
Her permutations have not any truce;
Necessity constrains her to be swift,
So oft comes he who proves vicissitude.
And this is she who's put on cross so much
Even by them who ought to give her praise,
Giving her wrongly ill repute and blame.
But she is blessed, and she hears not this:
She, with the other primal creatures, glad
Revolves her sphere, and blessed joys herself.

VII. 61-96.

It was now past midnight; and time pressed.—The next
descent described is not by steps, but by the slope down
which Styx is flowing till it settles into the stagnant pool
that constitutes Circle V., and serves for a moat to the
fortified City of Dis. Here Dante saw the Wrathful tearing
each other piecemeal, and heard of the Melancholy buried
in the black mud at the bottom; the only visible token of
their presence being the bubbling caused on the surface by
their sighs from beneath. The Poets, having walked along
a considerable arc of the space left dry between the solid
wall and the water, found themselves at last at the foot of
a tower, a kind of outwork of Dis, which could only be
reached by crossing the pool. Their gaze had already

been attracted to the summit of this tower by the sudden
appearance of two flames, the demon-sentinels within
having taken them for condemned Souls who must be ferried
over to their allotted prison, and having therefore signalled
to certain comrades in Dis—who counter-signalled by a third
flame, on account of distance barely discernible—to send
the boat. It was soon seen almost flying towards them,
steered by the demon pilot Phlegyas, who having in life
vengefully burned the temple of Apollo, belongs to the
Impious no less than to the Wrathful. Furiously he exulted
in his supposed prey—sorely was galled at learning his mis-
take. He could not however avoid receiving into his
boat these unexampled passengers, the one of whom actually loaded it and depressed its prow.

> While we were running over the dead sluice,
> One did there get before me full of mud,
> And said : 'Who 'rt thou who com'st before the hour ?'
>
> And I to him : 'I stay not, if I come :
> But who art thou, become so hideous ?'
>
> 'Thou seest,' he answered, 'that I'm one which weep.'
>
> And I to him : 'With weeping and with grief,
> Accursed spirit, so continue thou ;
> For thee I know, all filthy as thou art.'
>
> He then upon the boat stretched both his hands :
> Wherefore the master pushed him dextrously,
> Saying : 'Away hence, with the other dogs !'
> He then embraced with both his arms my neck ;
> He kissed my face, and said : 'Indignant soul,
> Blessed the woman who with thee was big !

This was a haughty person in the world ;[1]
No good there is which decks his memory :
Thus is his spirit herein furious.
How many hold them now aloft great kings
Who here will have to be like pigs in slush,
Of themselves leaving horrible misfame.'

And I : ' My master, greatly fain I were
To see him in a smother in this broth,
Before that we shall issue from the lake.'

And he unto me : ' Ere the landing-place
Shall let thee see it, thou 'lt be satisfied :
Such wish it will behove that thou enjoy.'

Soon after this, I saw that massacre
Made, by the muddy people, of this man,
That God I still do therefore praise and thank.
' Upon Filippo Argenti !' all cried out :
The uncouth spirit of the Florentine
Turned with his teeth against himself himself.

VIII. 31-63.

We really cannot help asking here, Is it possible to sympathize with this delight of the disciple, or this rewarding embrace of the Master? Can that be purely righteous indignation which issues in conduct so much too like that of the offender himself?

By this time the Poets were near enough to Dis to perceive the sound of wailing and discern the mosque-shaped fire-reddened turrets ; the pilot however had still to steer some way round before reaching the point of disembarka-

---

[1] 'Filippo Argenti, stated by Boccaccio to have been noted for bodily vigour and furious temper.'

tion. At the gates stood more than a thousand of those rebel Angels aforetime rained down from Heaven, now despitefully saying among themselves, 'Who is this that without death is going through the kingdom of the dead?' In reply, the guiding Sage indicated his wish for a private colloquy; this was granted, but with a threat of retaining him in the city while his pupil should retrace the way alone. Dante, utterly disheartened, adjured his only helper rather to relinquish the enterprise and instantly lead him back to the land of the living; but the answer forbade fear, and enjoined assured confidence in the success of the God-granted pilgrimage. In most anxious suspense he now began to watch the parley he could not hear;—but anon the adverse demons hurried back into the fortress, shutting the door in his leader's face. Yet Virgil, grieved and humbled as he was, ceased not to infuse hope, grounded on the certainty that One without guide or escort was already traversing the Circles behind them to their aid; though under the circumstances no entrance could be effected without wrath.

> And more he said : but I 've it not in mind;
> Because I wholly had mine eye updrawn
> Toward the high turret with the red-hot top ;
> Where in an instant upright fast I saw
> Infernal Furies three, bedyed with blood,
> Who had their limbs and action feminine,
> And who with greenest hydras were engirt :
> They had small serpents for their hair, and asps,
> Wherewith the savage temples were imbound.
>
> And he, who well knew them the abject ones
> Unto the queen of the eternal plaint,

'Look,' said to me, 'the fierce Erinnyes.
Megæra this one is upon the left ;
That is Alecto on the right, who weeps ;
I' the midst Tisiphone :' and here he stopped.

Each one was harrowing with her nails her breast :
They clashed their palms, and cried so loudly out,
That to the poet I strained me, for dismay.
'Let come Medusa ! So we 'll make him smalt,'—
They, looking downwards, uttered all of them :
'On Theseus we revenged the assault not ill.'[1]

'Turn thyself back, and keep thy vision hid ;
For, if the Gorgon show, and thou behold,
'Twould all be o'er with e'er returning up.'
So did the master say ; and he himself
Turned me, and to my own hands trusted not,
But that with his too he should cover me.
O you that have a sane intelligence,
Look ye unto the doctrine which herein
Conceals itself 'neath the strange verses' veil.

And now was coming o'er the turbid waves
A rumour of a sound replete with dread,
Because of which the banks were trembling both ;
Not made in other wise than of a wind
Impetuous by dint o' the adverse heats,
Which smites the forest without any stay,
Rends boughs, and beats them down, and bears along ;
Dusty to vanward, on it goes superb,
And makes the animals and shepherds flee.

He loosed mine eyes, and said : 'Now turn the nerve

---

[1] 'When Theseus and Pirithous attempted to carry Proserpine off
from Hell.'

Of vision up along that ancient foam,
By yonder where that smoke is acridest.'

Like as the frogs before the hostile snake
Scud off along the water one and all,
Until upon the soil each of them squats,—
I saw more than a thousand Souls destroyed
Fly thus in front of one who at the ford
Was passing over Styx with unwet soles.
He from his face was moving that gross air,
Plying the left hand oftentimes in front,
And only with that anguish seemed he tired.
I well perceived he was one sent from heaven,
And to the master turned : and he made sign
I should stay quiet, and to him should bow.
Ah ! of disdain how full he to me seemed !
He reached the gate, and with a little wand
Oped it, that there was no impediment.

' O ye cast out of heaven, a refuse race,'
Upon the horrible threshold he began,
' Whence nurtureth in you this insolence ?
Wherefore 'gainst that Volition do ye kick
To which its end can never be curtailed,
And which hath oft augmented pain to you ?
What booteth it to butt against the fates ?
Your Cerberus, if ye recollect it well,
Keeps yet therefrom his chin and throttle peeled.'

Then he turned back along the noisome path,
And word to us spoke none ; but semblance made
Of a man whom other care constrains and bites
Than that of him who is before his face.
And we toward the fortress moved our feet,
Secure in sequel of the holy words.

IX. 34-105.   :

Quite unopposed the Poets now entered Circle VI., the City of Dis ; and Dante beheld it one vast burial-ground of Infidel and Heretical Souls, bristling with tombs like the cemeteries of Arles and Pola, but after a more bitter fashion, these tombs being all red-hot from the action of fires scattered up and down among them. Speaking the Tuscan dialect as he passed along, he heard himself called by a voice issuing from a sepulchre where lay more than a thousand Epicureans, among them the Emperor Frederick II. The voice was that of the noble Florentine Farinata degli Uberti, who nearly five years before Dante's birth had as the Ghibelline leader defeated the Guelphs at Montaperti, had returned in triumph from banishment, and had then alone and successfully withstood his own party in their parricidal desire to destroy their native city. Long and deep was this patriot's converse with his fellow-citizen, soon like himself, as he plainly predicted, to be an exile, soon like his descendants, now in banishment, to experience the difficulty of returning. Once indeed the discourse was interrupted by Cavalcante de' Cavalcanti, buried in the same sepulchre, starting up to ask news of his son, Dante's friend Guido. His ignorance of the present, whereas Ciacco had known the future,[1] so perplexed his interlocutor as to delay the answer ; and the miserable father, attributing this delay to unwillingness to tell him of his son's death, sank down again in sorest grief. Farinata then took up his own thread just where it had been broken off, and having subsequently explained the mystery of the knowledge of the lost, was intrusted with a message of information and comfort to his fellow-prisoner ; for Guido yet lived, though fated soon to die.

[1] See page 49.

The Poets, having traversed the breadth of Dis, now stood on the edge of a kind of parapet guarding the central Void. The stench rising from the lower Circles was here so putrid as to compel them to seek temporary shelter behind a high tomb; and the consequent delay in their descent furnished opportunity for Virgil to instruct his pupil in that classification of sins under the heads of Incontinence, Bestialism, and Malice, with which the reader is already familiar.

Twenty-two hours had by this time elapsed since the opening of the poem—twelve in the Wood, ten in Hell; Good Friday was dawning on Earth, and further lingering might not be; wherefore the Pilgrims commenced their frightful precipitous descent. The furious Minotaur beset their path, but only to be utterly contemned by Virgil, and by blind raging to afford Dante an opportunity of getting down unmolested till he stood close under the outer wall of Circle VII., and beheld the ghastly Blood-river Phlegethon, which forms its outmost Ring. His progress was opposed by the Centaur Nessus; but Virgil's appeal to Chiron, exempt by his birth and career on earth from the brute violence of his race, obtained the opponent for a guide. Many were the tyrants and blood-shedders of days recent or long, long gone by, pointed out in the deeps of the stream; many indeed the petty oppressors and marauders recognised in its shallows. Where the feet only were covered was the ford, over which Nessus carried Dante on his back, while Virgil cleft the air. They found themselves in the Dolorous Wood, pathless, thicker set than the Tuscan Maremma, its leaves dusky, its boughs knotty and twisted, its sole product poison-distilling thorns: harpies its nest-

building birds, its music their moanings blended with those of
the trees they prey upon. Virgil, desirous to undeceive his
pupil of the imagination that these moans proceeded from
persons hidden in the Wood—and also unable to resist the
temptation to establish as fact his own fiction of the bleeding of the myrtle into which Polydorus had been metamor-
phosed,—suggested the plucking of a twig; but instantly
repented when blood sprang and sorest plaints issued from
the wounded tree—the prison-body of Pier delle Vigne,
Chancellor to the Emperor Frederick II. Envy, 'the
common death and vice of Courts,' had fastened her eyes
on this beloved and trusted counsellor till at length
she succeeded in maligning him to the cruel Prince his
master, by whom he was condemned to a course of torture
and ignominy, begun with blindness and destined to end in
death. That end however came far sooner than was intended, for the victim himself dashed his head against his
prison-wall. He now found some comfort in detailing his
mournful history to such sympathizing listeners, while he
far more briefly answered their inquiries respecting the
state of the tree-bound Souls. The colloquy was at length
suddenly broken off by the precipitous flight of two hound-
hunted Shades of wanton, obstinate Spendthrifts, naked and
thorn-scratched, through the Wood. The one, Lano, had
rapidly wasted a rich patrimony, till at length, having fallen
into an ambush, he desperately rushed among enemies
from whom he might have escaped:—the other, Jacopo di
Sant' Andrea, is recorded to have thrown his money, coin
by coin, into the river, by way of something to do; to
have set alight his tenants' cottages as a bonfire to welcome
his guests, and to have burned down his own magnificent

house in Padua as a spectacle to his fellow-citizens. This hunted madman squatted under a bush, but was none the less torn piecemeal by the hounds, the bush also coming in for its share of suffering. It incorporated an unnamed Florentine suicide, suspected by the commentators of having killed himself to escape the poverty surely coming upon a prodigal; and Dante, constrained by the love of their common birthplace, complied with his request to have his leaves gathered up and restored to him.—Soon the Pilgrims found themselves on the confines of the Sand-Waste, though still compelled to keep just within the Wood, to avoid the scathing of the fire-flakes and the scorching of the sand. Here among the supine Blasphemers they noted the untameable Capaneus; then passing beyond him reached a spot where Dante descried, with a shudder renewed as in after years he wrote of it, Phlegethon reappearing as a boiling Blood-brook to traverse the desert plain. The stream having petrified its bed and banks, he perceived that there must lie the passage across ; yet lingered awhile to hear of the origin of the Infernal Rivers. He then followed his Guide along the stone embankment, the humid exhalation spreading wide enough to extinguish instantly whatever flames might fall upon it, and so preventing its becoming heated like the sand. Already had the Poets left the Wood too far behind to be discernible, when they fell in with a troop of Shades walking. One of these, for all the fire's scathing, was recognisable as Dante's old tutor, Brunetto Latini, eminent as politician, as philosopher, and as author of the encyclopædic Tesoro and the allegorical Tesoretto. As no other contemporary record accuses him of any crime, it has been thought that political motives

may have led to his location here; especially as he is
spoken of throughout the passage with tenderest reverence
and love.   Side by side for a time tutor and scholar walked
and conversed, then once more parted company; and after
some further encounters the Pilgrims reached the point
where Phlegethon becomes an almost deafening torrent,
rushing down the central Void.   Standing by its brink,
Dante was commanded to loose his cord-girdle; and Virgil,
receiving it coiled, threw it down the precipice.   Before
long the loathsome appalling monster Geryon came up and
landed his trunk on the stone dam, while his tail darted
about, sting upwards, in the hollow.—During the Master's
parley with him, the disciple went alone to gaze upon the
Usurers, who, seated along the edge of the sand, were fight-
ing off the burning heat with their hands as best they might.
Not one was recognised by his face, but heraldic bearings
on purses hanging from their necks afforded a clue for their
identification.   These, bordering on Fraud both in offence
and in place, are in tastes and manners the meanest sinners
yet encountered: but plenty of their compeers will be met
with below.   Dante, content, as Virgil had counselled, with
a passing glance at them, on retracing his few solitary steps
found his Leader already seated on the foul monster's back,
and with sinking heart and failing voice obeyed the order
to mount in front, so as to be shielded from too probable
tail-treachery.   As soon as mounted he felt himself firmly
embraced, and heard a charge given to Geryon to descend
gradually, out of consideration for so unwonted a burden.
The downward course accordingly proceeded so gently that
the motion was rendered sensible only by the wind in the
rider's face and beneath him: but it was a sore trial to see

nought save Geryon's form, hear nought save Phlegethon's gurgling and plunging, and when at last eye and ear sought to dive into the depth, perceive nought save fires and wailings. Both riders were finally set down close under the earth-wall; the hateful beast shot away like an arrow from a bow; and Evilpits lay before them.

In Pit 1 they beheld Jason scourged for his successive abandonment of Hypsipyle and Medea:—in Pit 2 Thaïs paying the penalty of her base flattery of Thraso.—Into Pit 3 Dante, whose curiosity was excited by the exceptional sufferings of one of the imbursed Simoniacs, wished to descend. The descent, as in every subsequent instance save one, was effected by the Poets first crossing in its whole length the bridge spanning the pit, and by Virgil then carrying his pupil down—as afterwards again up—the inner wall, which in each pit offers a more gradual slope than the outer one. The tormented Soul proved to be that of Pope Nicholas III., of the Orsini family. In giving account of himself he severely reflected on the character of the actual Pope Boniface VIII.;[1] and foretold the far fouler deeds of Clement V., later to be raised to the Apostolic See through the intrigues of Philippe le Bel. Dante retorted with a strong condemnation of the worldliness which had crept into the Church through the Donation of Constantine:—and was then carried up again by his approving Master.—From the bridge-top was seen, in Pit 4, a long, slow, silent, weeping procession of Soothsayers and Witches, with necks wrung so completely round that the tears streamed down their backs. Such utter degradation

---

[1] Dante's judgment on both Nicholas and Boniface is said to be more severe than that of other historians. (Venturi and Fraticelli, *Inf.* xix.)

of the human image, borne by himself in common with
these reprobates, struck to Dante's inmost soul :

> Certes I wept, leaning on one o' the crags
> Of the hard rock, so that mine escort said
> To me, 'Art thou too of the other fools ?
> Here, when 'tis wholly dead, doth pity[1] live:
> For who can be more wicked than the man
> Who has a passion for God's judgeship ?'
>
> XX. 25-30.

After this gravest remonstrance the Master went on to
point out certain diviners of antiquity, till from naming
Manto he branched off into details concerning the origin of
his own native city Mantua.   These ended, the continuance
of the procession brought under notice various mediæval
sorcerers, among whom occurs the familiar name of Michael
Scott.

Good Friday was over by this time, and the sun of Holy
Saturday was rising on the Earth.   Passing from bridge to
bridge, the Poets discerned through the marvellous obscurity
of Pit 5 the bubbling, swelling, and subsiding of the boiling
Pitch-lake.   Soon a black Devil was seen to run along the
rocky chain, clenching the ankles of a Barterer slung across
his shoulder.   Hurled down into the pitch this sinner soon
came up again, but was forthwith once more submerged by
the prongs of the Evilclaws.   Virgil, whose mind apparently
misgave him that obstacles similar to those of Dis would
here arise, enjoined his charge to squat down for concealment behind a projecting edge of rock, while he himself
should seek a parley.   His first step on the partition-wall

---

[1] *Pietà* meaning both *pity* and *piety*, the sense of this line is: Here
piety lives when pity is wholly dead.

was the signal for a rush of prong-armed Evilclaws, who however at his request deputed their chief, Eviltail, to hear him.

'Bad-tail, dost thou suppose thou seest me
Having come hither,' so my master spoke,
'Already safe from all defence of yours,
Without divine command and favouring fate?
Let me proceed; for it is willed in heaven
I show another on this salvage road.'

His pride was then so fallen that he let
His hook down-tumble to his feet, and said
Unto the rest : 'Now let him not be struck.'

And unto me my lord : 'O thou who sitt'st
Amid the bridge's boulders all asquat,
Return thou to me now securely back.'

Wherefore I moved, and quickly came to him ;
And forward, all of them, the devils came,
So that I feared they would not keep their pledge.
And so erewhile I saw the soldiers fear
Who covenanted from Caprona went,
Seeing themselves amid so many foes.[1]

XXI. 79-96.

So in fact it was; the seeming prohibition was a mere trick, covertly conveying permission to wound him somewhat later; and the disciple proved now far more alive than the Master to the impending danger. Eviltail lied on :

[1] 'Caprona, a Pisan fortress, having capitulated to the Guelph confederates of Tuscany in 1290, the garrison filed out, when the hostile soldiers clamoured (but only to frighten them) to have them hung. Dante is believed to have served among the victors.'

> ''Twill not be possible to go
> Further along this rock, because that all
> The sixth arc's lying at its bottom smashed ;
> And, onward if you still would please to wend,
> Go up then by this cavern : there is nigh
> Another rock, which makes a path along.
> Five hours more on than this is, yesterday,
> A thousand and two hundred sixty-six
> Years finished since the path was broken here.
> I 'm sending thither some of these of mine,
> To see if any airs himself therefrom :
> Go you with them, for they will not be froward.
>
> XXI. 106-117.

Then he thus charged the ten selected for this mission :

> Search ye the boiling bird-lime roundabout.
> Let these as far as the next ledge be safe,
> Which goes on all entire above the dens.
>
> XXI. 124-126.

There was, in fact, no such line of bridges in existence, all those which once spanned Pit 6 lying broken at its bottom : —and the fiends, well knowing this, indulged in an undercurrent of threatening gestures, not one of which was lost on Dante. He begged hard to be spared any save the wonted and trusty escort, but Virgil insisted that there was no danger, and they all started.

> With the ten demons we were going on—
> Ah ! fell companionship ! But, in the church
> With saints, and with the gluttons at the inn.
>
> XXII. 13-15.

On their way they saw seated on the brink the Shade of a former courtier of Theobald II., King of Navarre—Ciampolo, whose words and acts presently disclosed how great an amount of trickery could be carried on by a Barterer even in Hell. Two of the Evilclaws, baffled in their expectation of tormenting him, at length fell foul of each other; and while the whole troop were intent on the scuffle, the Pilgrims made good their escape down the partition-wall into the next Pit. None too soon:—for the pursuing fiends stood directly over them just as their feet touched the bottom; but all peril was past, the appointed officials of Pit 5 being powerless to quit their field of action.

Already in Pit 6, the Poets found themselves in company no longer with demons, but with Hypocrites. At first the nature of their punishment was not apparent, but it was soon explained by one of them, the Bolognese Catalano de' Catalani, of the military and religious Order of Knights of S. Mary, popularly nicknamed Frati Godenti, or Jolly Friars. He, with his colleague Loderingo degli Andalò, had been elected on account of seeming virtues to the office of Podestà in a peculiarly troublous year at Florence, and had acted with the grossest avarice, injustice, and violence. In this Pit not only is courtesy observed—this we might perhaps have expected; but, surprising as it may appear, truth is spoken.—After marvelling over the degraded condition of Caiaphas and his fellow-councillors, Virgil inquired whether there was any opening that might afford him and his companion exit into the next Pit; and learned that he was very near the point where, by clambering up the heaped ruins of the bridge, he would find himself once more on a chain thence to the end unbroken. Half-abashed and half-indignant he resumed his functions, till quite restored to serenity on approaching the pile he seized fast hold of his pupil from behind, and then impelled him upwards from crag to crag. All panting, Dante sat down just as he touched the top : but he was forthwith stirred up again, and soon was vainly peering from the bridge into the thick darkness of Pit 7. From the somewhat lower level of the wall-top however he managed to discern a worse than Libyan desert of Thieves and Serpents, binding and bound, biting and bitten, consuming and consolidating, bewildering and bewildered, men contracting into snakes, snakes expanding into men : none might say whose was whose, or who was who, or what was what :—fit emblem of the social state when habitual contempt of the rights of property makes change the sole unchanging condition. Among these wretches no less than five Florentines were discovered. Two other sinners were specially noticed as belonging by the main course of their lives to the violent Robbers in Circle VII., but weighed down to this lower depth each by a single act of fraud :—Cacus the Centaur (probably now demonized) by his driving Hercules' stolen cattle backwards to falsify their track, and Vanni Fucci of Pistoja by his sacrilegious theft from the sacristy of the Duomo of that city—a crime for which an innocent man had very nearly, if not actually, suffered.

Into Pit 8 it proved but too easy to see, for its flames swarmed thick as fire-flies in the Tuscan valleys—those 'thieving flames' that swathe and conceal Evil Counsellors. Awfully intense was the impression made on the chief Intellect of his day by the doom of souls which, endowed with gifts in some instances even comparable to his own, had sinned as none could sin without those noblest faculties.

> Then grieved I, and I now do grieve again
> When I direct my mind to what I saw,
> And more rein in my thought than I am wont,
> Lest whither virtue guides it not it run ;
> So that, if bounteous star or better thing
> Gave me the good, myself pervert it not.
>
> XXVI. 19-24.

Here two who had led the active life, Ulysses and Diomed, burning together within a double-tongued winding-sheet, were paying the penalty of the bereaved Deidamia, the stolen Palladium, and the fatal Horse :—these two especially excited Dante's attention and interest, and at Virgil's request Ulysses told the tale of his last voyage.[1]—Here also one who after the active life of a warrior had as a Franciscan turned to the contemplative life, Count Guido of Montefeltro in the Apennines, is represented as bearing the irreparable consequences of trusting to Absolution beforehand for sin. His narrative is so painful that it is quite a relief to know how little reason there is for believing it true.[2] No authority save this passage so much as hints at the evil counsel having been given ; Angeli, the historian of the Assisi convent, evidently disbelieves, while Muratori the critic indignantly rejects the story; and Dante himself in his Convito unites with numerous contemporaries in witnessing to the virtues of this 'most noble Latin.'[3] Muratori indeed suggests political motives as not improbably furnishing the key to the accusation. Under this protest let the awful history, as related by the sufferer himself, be read.

---

[1] See page 15.
[2] G. Rossetti, *Com. An.* Riflessioni sul c. xxvii.—Fraticelli *in loc.*
[3] *Conv.* iv. 28.

'I was a man of arms, then cordelier,
Thinking, so girded, to have made amends ;
And certes my belief had come fulfilled,
Were't not for the Arch-priest,[1] whom evil seize,
Who put me back into my former wrongs :
And how and wherefore I will have thee hark.
The whiles I was the form of bones and pulp
My mother gave to me, my doings were
Not lion-like, but rather of the fox.
I knew precautions and clandestine ways,
Each one, and managed so the art of them
That forth the sound went to the end of earth.
When I beheld myself arrived at that
Part of mine age when every one would well
Lower the sails, and gather in the ropes,
That which before had pleased me pained me then,
And penitent I yielded, and confessed,
Alas me wretched ! and it would have served.
The sovereign of the modern pharisees,
Having a war near Lateran to wage,[2]
(And not with Saracens, nor yet with Jews,
Seeing his enemies were Christians all,
And none at Acre had been conquering,[3]
Nor merchandizing in the Soldan's land),[4]
Regarded in himself nor charge supreme,
Nor holy orders, nor in me the cord
Which used to make more lean its girded ones ;
But, as within Soracte Constantine
Prayed Sylvester for cure from leprosy,[5]

---

[1] 'Pope Boniface VIII.'   [2] 'Against the Colonna family.'
[3] 'As the Saracens had done in 1291.'
[4] 'Like the renegade Christians.'
[5] 'The legend ran that, in gratitude for a miraculous cure thus effected on him by Pope Sylvester, Constantine endowed the pontiffs with the government of Rome.'

So unto me prayed this man, as his leach,
Thus from his haughty fever to be cured.
He asked me counsel; and I held my peace,
Because his words appeared intoxicate.
And then said he: "Let not thy heart suspect:
I even now absolve thee; teach me thou
How Penestrino[1] I may throw to earth.
I am able to lock up and unlock heaven,
And this thou knowest; for the keys are two
The which my predecessor[2] held not dear."
The weighty arguments impelled me then,
Where my resolve was silence, to the worse;
And, "Since thou lav'st me, father," I replied,
"From that misdeed which I must fall in now,
Long promising, with short fulfilment, will
Make thee to triumph in the lofty chair."
Then, after I was dead, did Francis come
For me; but one of the black Cherubim
Said to him: "Take him not, nor do me wrong.
He must come down among my sorry folk,
Because he gave the fraudulent advice,
Whereafter at his hair I've been till now:
For who repents not cannot be absolved;
Neither at once can one repent and will,
Because the contradiction bears it not."
Ah woful me! how did I shake myself
Whenas he took me, saying, "Thou perhaps
Didst not imagine I was logic-learned."
He carried me to Minos; and *he* writhed
Eight times his tail about his callous back,
And, after for great rage he'd bitten it,

---

[1] 'Where the Colonnas were still seated.'
[2] Celestin v., who voluntarily abdicated the Papal throne.

Said, " That 's a criminal of the thieving fire."
Wherefore where thou beholdest I am lost,
And rankle, going in this manner clothed.'

When he had thus made ending of his speech,
The flame in anguish took departure hence,
Writing and brandishing its sharpened horn.

XXVII. 67-132.

Standing over Pit 9, Dante was reminded of the bloodiest
battlefields recorded in history.   As he intently gazed on
a Shade split from the chin downwards, it spontaneously
made itself known as Mahomet, and after pointing out Ali
cleft from the chin upwards, set forth the sin and punishment of the whole mutilated troop, and inquired of Dante
who he was, and why there.   The answer came from Virgil,
awakening an amazement which for the moment suspended
the procession, and afforded opportunity for naming some
other Souls.   Among these was Mosca degli Uberti, maimed
of both hands :—the suggester of the bloody revenge taken
by the Amidei for the slight put upon their kinswoman by
Buondelmonte, and so the introducer into Florence of the
Guelph-Ghibelline discord.[1]   The last comer was Bertrand
de Born, Viscount de Hautefort, whom historians accuse as
the inciter of the rebellion of Prince Henry (called 'the
young King,' as having been already crowned) against his
father Henry II. of England.   Here Dante himself shall
speak.

I remained to look upon the troop,
And saw a thing which I should be in fear,
Without more proof, of telling, I alone,
But that my conscience reassureth me,—

[1] See page 26.

The good companion which emboldens man
Under the hauberk of its feeling pure.
I certes saw, and seems I see it still,
A trunk without a head proceeding, so
As went the others of the sorry flock.
And by the hair he held his truncate head,
In guise of lantern, pendulous in hand :
And that gazed on us, and it said, 'Oh me !'
He of himself made light unto himself,
And they were two in one, and one in two :
How it can be He knows Who governs thus.

When he was right against the bridge's foot,
He raised, with all the head, his arm on high,
So to approach to us the words thereof,—
Which were : 'See now the troublous penalty,
Thou who go'st breathing, looking at the dead :
See whether any is so great as this.
And, for that thou mayst carry of me news,
I, know thou, am Bertrand de Born, the man
Who gave the young king ill encouragements.
I mutually made rebels son and sire :
Ahithophel made Absalom no more,
And David, with his wicked goadings-on.
Because I parted persons thus conjoined,
My brain, alas ! I carry parted from
Its principle which is in this my trunk.
So retribution is in me observed.'

The many people and the diverse wounds
Had made mine eyes intoxicated so
That they were fain to stay a-weeping.   But
Virgil said to me : 'What then starest thou on ?

And wherefore prythee does thy vision bend
Down there among the mournful mangled shades ?
Thou hast not done so at the other pits.
Consider, if thou think'st to number them,
The valley turneth twenty miles and two :
Already too the moon's beneath our feet ;
The time is little now that 's granted us,
And there is more to see than thou believ'st.'

' An if thou hadst,' I thereon answered him,
' Attended to the cause for which I looked,
Perhaps thou'dst yet have suffered me to stay.'
My guide was partly going now, and on
I went behind him, making the reply,
And saying furthermore : ' Within that fosse
Whereon so steadfastly mine eyes I set
I think a spirit of my blood doth weep
The guilt which costeth there-adown so much.'

Then said the master : ' Do not let thy thought
Be stumbling from henceforward upon him.
Elsewhere attend, and there let him remáin :
For I beheld him at the bridge's foot
Point thee, and with his finger threaten hard,
And heard him named Geri del Bello.   Thou
Wast so entirely at the time engrossed
With him who held aforetime Hautefort
Thou thither lookedst not, so he was gone.'

' Alas ! my lord, the death by violence
Which is not yet avenged to him,' said I,
' By any that is consort in the shame,
Made him disdainful ; therefore went he off,
As I conceive, without addressing me,
And so he 's made me piteous towards him more.'

XXVIII. 112-142.   XXIX. 1-36.

This Geri del Bello, related to Dante on the father's side, had been killed in a quarrel with one of the Sacchetti ; and, according to the barbarous theory of the day, had a right to expect his kindred to carry on the blood-feud. Dante's non-compliance with this usage, and excuse notwithstanding of his kinsman, are perhaps the sole instances recorded in the Poem of his exercising the virtue of Meekness as opposed to Vindictiveness. Fearful enough was his experience of the woes entailed by blood-feuds upon his city. In the Purgatorio we probably have a further hint of his sentiments on this subject.[1]

But already the Pilgrims stood directly above the Tenth and last Pit, which might have been taken for a hospital wherein all the malaria patients of the worst districts and worst season of Italy were massed together. Dante's ears were quickly stopped with his hands, so piteous were the groans that pierced them ; and his eyes and nose might well have been also stopped from sights and smells no less offensive. Among 'the leprous Alchemists were distinguished two seated back to back, Griffolin d' Arezzo and Capocchio ; among the mad False-Personators Gianni Schicchi, who counterfeiting in semblance a man already dead, but not yet known to be so, had made in his name a fraudulent will ; among the fever-stricken Liars Potiphar's wife, and Sinon the Greek of Trojan infamy ; among the dropsical Coiners Mastro Adamo of Brescia, who for alloying the golden florin had been burned to death by the Florentine Government. Between this last and Sinon a sudden skirmish took place, keen and brisk in word and blow ; and proved, in the Sage's judgment, far too amusing to his pupil.

[1] See page 134.

To listen to them I was wholly fixed,
When 'Look now,' unto me the master said,
'That I am all but quarrelling with thee.'

Whenas I heard him speak to me in wrath,
I turned towards him with so much of shame
That in my memory it whirleth still.
And, as is he who dreams of his mischance,
Who, dreaming, wishes that it *were* a dream,
And longs so, as 'twere not, for that which is ;
Such I became, incapable to speak,
Who wished to make excuse, and all the while
Excused myself, and thought not that I did.

'Less shame will wash a greater foible out,'
The master said, 'than that which thine has been :
Therefore unlade thyself of all distress.
And reckon that I 'm always at thy side
If yet it happen fortune catches thee
Where there are people in a broil like this ;
For wishing to hear that 's a base desire.'

XXX. 130-148.

And now in silence they were crossing the parapet of the
last portion of the awful Void, here probably about 35
feet deep : when lo ! a horn sounded with a blast of force
to hoarsen loudest thunder.   Peering through the twilight,
along the edge of the wide embankment Dante beheld
what he took for many high towers ; Virgil however
quickly informed him that these were no towers, but Giants
disposed at intervals all round the well, so that about half
their person was visible above its brink, and half concealed
within.[1]   Fear came on Dante as error fled ; but soon he

[1] Ampère (*Voyage Dantesque,* 277, quoted by Longfellow, note on
Inf. XXXI. 59) computes the height of Nimrod at 70 feet.

learned how little there was to fear from creatures either powerless or not inclined to harm. Nimrod howled a Babel or pre-Babel jargon which sounded threatening, but made no objection when Virgil reminded him of the horn through which he might vent his rage; Ephialtes, apparently worse disposed, was chained, as was also Briareus; while Tityus and Typhoeus would presumably, if applied to, have been moved by desire of fame to assist the Pilgrims, and Antæus from this motive actually was induced to take them up in a bundle where they stood, and then bending forwards set them down at the foot of the ninth and last earth-wall, on the brink of the frost-bound pool Cocytus. It seemed a bason of glass, not water; its ice so hard that the fall of a mountain would have failed to make even the edge creak.—In its outmost Belt Caina, among other Betrayers of kindred, two wretched brothers, Alessandro and Napoleone degli Alberti, mutual fratricides on account of their patrimony, were seen frozen head to head by the hair.—Next came Antenora:

> Then did I see a thousand faces made
> Doglike by cold; whence shuddering to me comes,
> And always will come, for the frozen fords.
> And, while we were proceeding toward the midst
> Whereunto every weight doth concentrate,
> And I was trembling in the eternal dark,
> Whether 'twas will, or destiny, or hap,
> I know not; but, in walking through the heads,
> I struck my foot hard in the face of one.
>
> On me he weeping cried: 'Why poundest me?
> Unless thou com'st the vengeance to increase
> For Mont' Aperti, why dost me molest?'
>
> XXXII. 70-81.

This reprobate was Bocca degli Abati, a Florentine
Guelph who at the battle of Montaperti had actually
for Ghibelline gold cut off the arm of his own party's
standard-bearer, and so brought on its defeat.

And I : ' My master, now await me here,
That I may get out of a doubt by him :
Then thou shalt hurry me howe'er thou wilt.'

The leader stopped : and unto him I said,
Who in the mean while kept blaspheming hard,
' Who art thou who revil'st another thus ? '

' Now, who art *thou* who go'st through Antenore,
Striking,' he answered, ' on another's cheeks,
So that, were I alive, 'twere overmuch ? '

' Alive am *I;* and, if thou askest fame,
It may be dear to thee,' was my response,
' That I should put thy name 'mong other notes.'

And he to me : ' I wish the contrary :
Arise herefrom, and give me irk no more,
For ill know'st thou to flatter in this plain.'

Then took I hold upon him by the scalp,
And said : ' 'Twill have to be thou name thyself,
Or that no hair remain to thee hereon.'

Whence he to me : ' For thine unhairing me,
I 'll neither tell nor show thee who I am,
If on my head thou fall a thousand times.'

I had in hand his hair already twined,
And I had plucked more than one lock of it,
He barking with his eye concentred down,
When cried another : ' Bocca, what dost want ?
Is 't not enough for thee to sound thy jaws
Unless thou bark'st ?   What devil touches thee ?'

'Now,' said I, 'I 've no wish for thee to speak,
Flagitious traitor ; for, unto thy shame,
I 'll carry of thee veritable news.'

XXXII. 82-111.

But the horror of horrors was yet to come. Just where
Antenora confines with Ptolemæa protruded a head frozen
in one hole with another head, but above it, gnawing and
gnawing it. The gnawer was the Pisan Count Ugolino
della Gherardesca, whose attributed but not attested crime
was the having sold to Florence and Lucca certain castles of
Pisa ; the gnawed was his traitorous friend, Archbishop Ruggieri degli Ubaldini, through whose abhorred machinations
he, with two sons and two grandsons, had been starved to
death in a tower called subsequently the Tower of Famine.
At Dante's entreaty

That sinner from the savage meal his mouth
Uplifted, wiping it upon the hair
Of the head which he 'd wasted from behind.

Then he began : 'Thou 'dst have me to renew
Desperate grief, which presses on my heart
Now only thinking, ere I speak of it.
But, if my words may be a seed to yield
Infamy to the traitor whom I gnaw,
Thou shalt behold me speak and weep at once.
I know not who thou art, nor by what mode
Thou 'rt come down hither : but a Florentine
Thou, when I hear thee, seem'st to me in truth.
I was Count Ugolino, thou must know,
And he Archbishop Roger : now will I
Tell wherefore I 'm a neighbour like to this.[1]

---

[1] ' Why I am such a bad neighbour to Ruggieri (by devouring his head).'

H

That, by the effecting of his evil thoughts,
Confiding in him, I was capturèd,
And after done to death, I need not tell.
Nevertheless, what thou canst not have heard,—
That is, how much my death was cruel,—thou
Shalt hear, and know whether he's injured me.
A scanty opening within the mew
Which has from me the name of Famine, and
Wherein it needs that others too be shut,
Had shown me through its loophole several moo: 5
Already, when I had the evil sleep
Which rent away for me the future's veil.
Master and lord this man unto me seemed,
Chasing the wolf and wolf-cubs to the mount
Because of which the Pisans see not Lucca.[1]
With bitches lean, and eager, and well-trained,
He had Gualandi, with Sismondi and
Lanfranchi,[2] stationed in the front of him.
In little course, the father and the young
Seemed to me tired, and with the sharpened fangs
I seemed to see the flanks of them ripped up.
When I before the morrow was awake,
Weeping amid their sleep I heard my sons
Which were along with me, and asking bread.
Sure thou art cruel if thou grievest not
Already, thinking what was told my heart ;
And, if thou weep'st not, when art wont to weep ?
We now were wakened, and the hour approached
When food was customed to be brought to us,
And each was doubting, on his dream's account :
And I heard locked the exit underneath

---

[1] 'Mount San Giuliano, which stands between the two cities.'
[2] 'Three of the Ghibelline auxiliaries of the Archbishop.'

The horrible turret; whereupon I looked
In my sons' faces, saying not a word.
I wept not, I so petrified within :
They wept; and said my Anselmuccio, "Thou,
Father, art looking so? How is 't with thee?"
I shed no tear, however, nor replied
The whole of that day, nor the after night,
Till issued in the world the other sun.
Whenas some little ray had got itself
Into the painful dungeon, and I marked
My selfsame aspect upon faces four,
I bit for anguish into both my hands :
And they, supposing I did that for need
Of eating, of a sudden raised themselves,
And said : "'Twill give us, father, much less pain
If us thou eat'st of : thou induedst us
This miserable flesh, and doff it thou."
I, not to make them sadder, stilled me then :
That and the next day we remained all dumb ;
Ah ! hardened earth, why openedst thou not?
When to the fourth day we were come, before
My feet, distended, Gaddo threw himself,
Saying, " My father, why not give me help ? "
Herewith he died ; and, as thou seest me,
I saw the three fall one by one, between
The fifth day and the sixth : whereat I took,
Already blind, to groping over each,
And three days called them after they were dead.
Then fasting more availed than sorrowing.'

When he had spoken this, with eyes askew
He took again the wretched skull with teeth
Which like a dog's upon the bone were strong.

XXXIII. 1-78

And Dante, with bleeding heart and burning lips invoking
vengeance on Pisa, passed from the edge into the Belt of
Ptolemæa.   Here not only the supine posture of the lost
made concealment impossible, but the tears, congealing
even as they sprang, blocked up the cavity of the eye with
ice which, while permitting sight, greatly increased torment
by stopping up the vent of pain.

> And, notwithstanding that, as from a corn,
> Every feeling, by the cold's effect,
> Had ceased its lodgment in my countenance,
> I ne'ertheless appeared to feel some wind ;
> Whence I : 'My master, who is moving this?
> Below here is not every vapour quenched?'
>
> And he to me : 'Thou shalt anon be where
> The eye shall give thee answer as to that,
> Seeing the cause which raineth out the blast.'
>
> And one o' the mournful of the freezing rind
> Cried unto us : 'O Spirits cruel so
> As that the final post is given ye,
> Take from my face the hardened veils, that I
> May vent the sorrow which impregns my heart
> A little, ere again the weeping freeze.'
>
> Whence I to him : 'If thou wouldst have mine aid,
> Say who thou wast ; and if I free thee not,
> To the ice's bottom let me have to go.'
>
> XXXIII. 100-117.

Alas for Dante! twice we have mourned him wrathful,
this time far more deeply mourn him false ; for this promise
made to the ear was to be broken to the hope, inasmuch as
he actually wished and prayed *now* to go to the bottom of

the ice.—The Shade went on to name himself Frate Alberigo (of the same order of 'Frati Godenti' as the two Hypocrites met with in Circle VIII., Pit 6[1]), and to refer obscurely to the horrible treachery by which he had murdered his guests at a banquet. Dante, all unknowing of his death, questioned him in surprise, and was informed that Ptolemæa has the 'advantage' of receiving instantly on the consummation of the traitorous deed the traitor's soul, which thenceforward remains utterly ignorant how long, demon-informed, the body walks the earth, and at what moment, demon-deserted, it is buried. Alberigo went on to cite, as perhaps a case in point, that of Branca d' Oria close behind him; and after answering his listener's amazed doubts with a further asseveration of the fact, claimed at length the looked-for relief.

'But hither now betimes stretch out thine hand,—
Open mine eyes.'—And them I opened not,
And to be rude to him was courtesy.

XXXIII. 148-150.

The Pilgrims set foot on the Belt Judecca: and now—

'*Vexilla Regis prodeunt*[2] *Inferni*
Toward us: therefore look in front of thee,
My master said, 'if thou discernest him.

As, at the time when breathes a heavy fog,
Or when our hemisphere is under night,
Appears from far a mill which wind doth turn,

---

[1] See p. 85.
[2] Thus begins the Vespers Hymn for Passion-tide; Virgil adds 'Inferni,' so that the meaning here is, 'The banners of the King of Hell advance.'

Meseemed to see then such an edifice :
Then, for the wind, I strained me up behind
My leader, for no other cave [1] was there.
Already was I (and with fear I put
It into metre) where the Shades were all
Covered, and like a mote in glass showed through.
Down some are lying ; others stand erect,—
That with the head, and with the foot-soles that ;
Another, as a bow, inverts toward
The feet the visage.

　　　　　When so far we'd got
As that my master pleased to show to me
The Creature which had had the noble form,
He from before me moved, and made me stay,
Saying : ' Behold here Dîs, and here the place
Where it befits thou arm with fortitude.'

Thereat how frozen I became, and hoarse,
Ask it not, reader, for I write it not,
For little would be every utterance.
I died not, and I did not keep alive ;
Think for thyself now, if thou 'st flower of wit,
What I became, deprived of one and both.

　　　　　　　　　　XXXIV. 1-27.

Within the deep Dante stood gazing upon the deep,
within the deep of the material Hell upon the deep of the
moral Hell, the form of Lucifer : and in that gaze he knew
what Beatrice had sent him there to learn—what Sin is, and
what it works, and what it suffers in soul and body.

The Lamentable Kingdom's Emperor
Issued from out the ice with half his breast ;

---

[1] ' No other shelter.'

And with a giant more do I compare
Than with his arms do giants : therefore see
How great must be that whole which corresponds
Unto a part so fashioned.   If he was
As beautiful as he is ugly now,
And raised his brows against his Maker, sure
All sorrowfulness must proceed from him.
Ah! how great marvel unto me it seemed
When I beheld three faces to his head !
The one before, and that was vermeil-hue :
Two were the others which adjoined to this,
Over the midst of either shoulder, and
They made the joining where the crown is placed.
And between white and yellow seemed the right ;
The left was such an one to be beheld
As come from there wherein the Nile is sunk.
There issued under each two mighty wings,
Such as 'twas fitting for so great a bird :
I never saw the sails of shipping such.
They had not feathers, but the mode thereof
Was like a bat's ; and these he fluttered so
That from him there was moved a threefold wind :
Cocytus all was frozen over hence.
With six eyes wept he, and three chins along
The weeping trickled, and a bloody foam.
At every mouth he shattered with his teeth
A sinner, in the manner of a brake,
So that he thus made woful three of them.
The biting for the foremost one was nought
Unto the scratching, for at times the spine
Remained of all the skin completely stripped.
'That Soul above which has most punishment
Is,' said my lord, ' Judas Iscariot,
Who has his head within, and outside plies

His legs.   O' the other two, whose head is down,
Brutus is he who from the black head hangs ;
See how he writhes, and does not speak a word :
The other's Cassius, who appears so gaunt.'

XXXIV. 28-67.

But now the Master might release the disciple from his
awful contemplation ; the night of Holy Saturday was
setting in, and nought else remained to see.

I, as it pleased him, did embrace his neck,
And he took vantage of the time and place ;
And, when the wings were opened far apart,
He caught upon the shaggy ribs.   From tuft
To tuft he afterwards descended down
Between the thick hair and the frozen crusts.
When we had got thereunto where the thigh
Turns just upon the thickness of the haunch,
The leader, with fatigue and anguishing,
Turned round his head to where he had his shanks,
And grappled to the hair as one who mounts,
So that I thought I back returned to Hell.

' Now hold on well ; for by such stairs as these,'
The master, panting like a tired man, said,
' It needs from so much ill that we depart.'

Then forth through a stone's orifice he came,
And put me down to sit upon the brink :
He set toward me then his wary step.
I raised mine eyes, and thought I should have seen
Lucifer as I'd left him just, and I
Beheld him holding upperward his legs.
And whether I became then travailed let
The grosser folk conceive, which seeth not
What was the point that I had overpassed.

'Rise up,' the master said, 'upon thy feet ;
The way is long, and sorry is the road,
And now the sun returns to half of three.'[1]

'Twas not the pathway of a palace there
Where we were passing, but a natural cell
Which had soil evil, and no ease of light.

'Or ever I do pluck me from the abyss,
My master,' said I, when I was erect,
'A whit, to loose from error, speak to me.
Where is the ice ?   And how is this one stuck
So topsy-turvy ?   And in time so scant
How has the sun from evening passed to morn ?'

XXXIV. 70-105.

These inquiries the Master answered as we, knowing
beforehand the plan of Dante's Universe, can answer for
ourselves.   The Poets had cleared the centre of gravity
when Virgil had struggled so hard in turning ; they were
now sitting on the earth which forms, so to say, the reverse
of the ice-medal Judecca ; in opposite hemispheres morning
corresponds to evening ;

'And this who makes our staircase with his fell
Is still so planted as he was at first.
Downward in this part did he fall from Heaven ;
And here the earth, which did before project,
Made of the sea, for fear of him, a veil,
And came unto our hemisphere ; and that
Which there appears, and upward rushed, perchance
To flee from him, left vacant here the place.'

XXXIV. 119-126.

---

[1] 'To the half of three hours from the Jewish third hour, *i.e.* to an
hour and a half before noon.'

And now they have but to ascend.

> Down there's a place, remote from Belzebub
> As great a distance as the tomb[1] extends,
> Which not by sight is known, but by the sound
> Made by a runnel which descendeth here
> By a stone's hole which it has eaten out
> During the course it turns ; and little this
> Impends.   My guide and I by that hid path
> Entered to turn again to the clear world :
> And, having not a care of any rest,
> We mounted up, he first and second I,
> So far that I, through a round opening, saw
> Some of the beauteous things which heaven contains :
> And hence we came to re-behold the stars.[2]

XXXIV. 127-139.

---

[1] 'The "tomb" appears to be the entire hollow of Hell from its entrance down to Lucifer. If so, the "place remote from Belzebub" (Lucifer) is the entire space between him and the exit from Hell. Or possibly the tomb is the well or space leading down from the giants to Judecca and Lucifer; in which case the "place" is the particular spot from which Dante now proceeds on his way to Purgatory.'

[2] 'The word stars (*stelle*) ends all the three parts of the Commedia'

THE PURGATORY

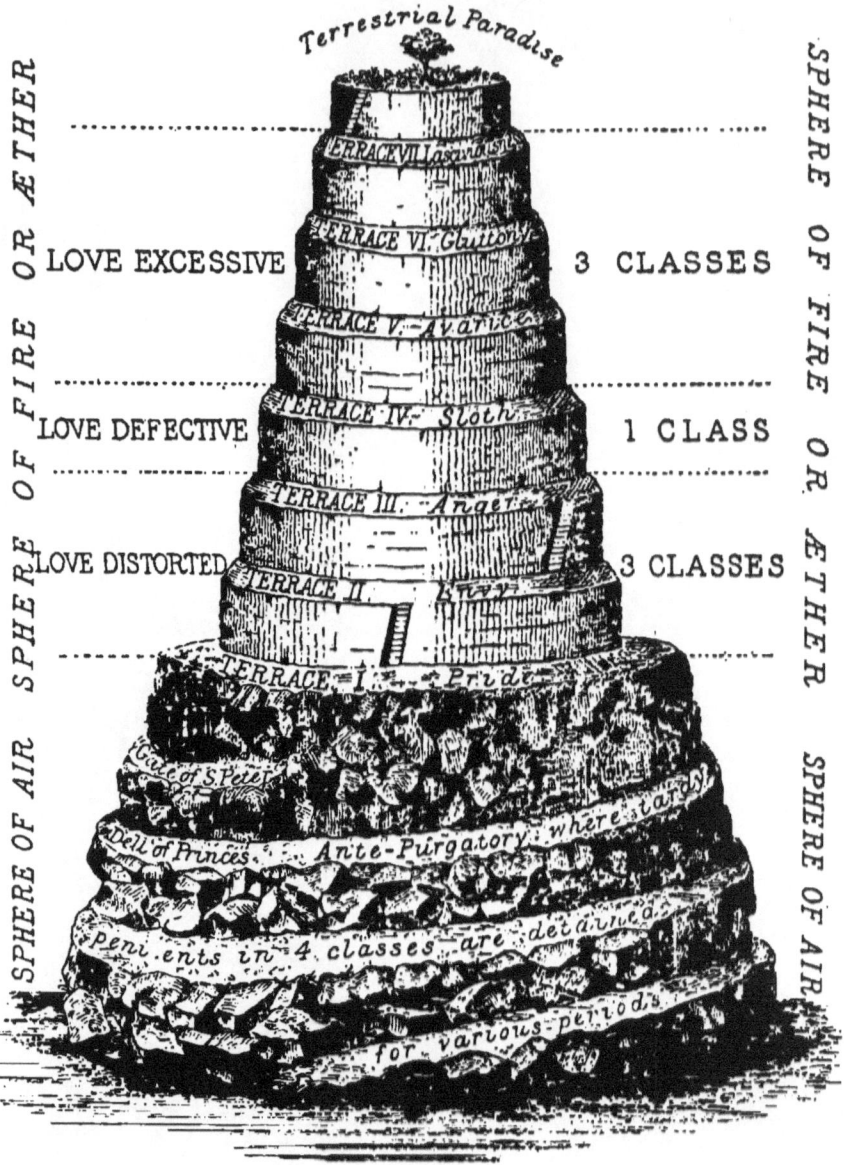

(To face Chap. VII.)

CHAPTER VII.

THE PURGATORY.

Ove l'umano spirito si purga.
Wherein the human spirit doth purge itself.

Pur. 1. 5.

PURGATORY is placed by Dante on the highest mountain in the world, the only land in the Water-hemisphere; an island in the form of an elevated cone blunted at the top, its skirts within the Sphere of Air, its heights within the Sphere of Fire, its transitional confine the Gate of S. Peter, its crown the Terrestrial Paradise. The shores are washed by the vast Western Ocean, across which, from the time of our Blessed Lord's Descent into Hell—till when Dante supposes all the Elect to have gone down to Limbo—comes flying ever and anon the oarless, sailless, Angel-piloted bark that bears the blessed freight of such Souls as, departing in grace, await not on Acheron's but on Tiber's banks the signal for their supreme voyage. For no disembodied Soul but is gathered to one or other of these two streams; and there, all its inferior faculties in abeyance, but Will, Memory, and Understanding far keener than before, attracts and moulds its surrounding air into the shade-body which is thenceforth till the Resurrection to constitute its medium of feeling and expression. In form precisely resembling the fleshly tabernacle so lately put off, and organizing for itself corresponding senses, this aërial unsubstantial body, incapable of fleshly needs, is yet capable of the pains, as hunger and thirst, which accompany them ; of speech and laughter also, of sighs and tears, and of whatever outward signs betoken inward sensation or affection. And Dante imagines that the Angelic boatman ever visiting the mouth of the Tiber himself selects his successive freights of Shades, leaving some and taking others according to his will, which is the reflection of the just Will of God.

As no unbending or leaf-bearing plant could live under the beating of the waves, the low wet shore of the Island grows reeds, and reeds alone ; fit type of the humility which, giving way under the rod, finds it to be for correction and not for destruction. So likewise, the moment a reed is plucked it springs afresh ; for virtues and means of salvation waste not in the using.[1]

And because on the Mount is the healing of moral corruption, its slopes are irradiated by the constellation of the Southern Cross (probably known to Dante through the Catalogue of Ptolemy), whose four stars meetly symbolize the moral virtues of Prudence, Justice, Fortitude, and Temperance. By these even unchristened Man, albeit dubiously and fitfully, may steer his course through this present world ; and so Virgil, the impersonation of Human Science, is still the guide, though oftentimes the hesitating guide, even to the summit of the steep ascent. Sore office for a dweller in Limbo, seeing the sojourners in Purgatory are his fellows in the pain of loss, his worse than fellows in the pain of sense : yet how should he not at every step

[1] Fraticelli, note on *Pur.* I. 135.

fathom the fathomlessness of the great gulf fixed between the Prisoners of Hope and the Prisoner of Hopelessness? Yea, and far more for that the Warden of the Mount is Cato of Utica, brought forth from that same Limbo under the law of leaving behind the affections that bound him there; and—perhaps for his rigid virtue and preference of death to slavery—set over the world where Spirits by energy and suffering pass out of the last remnants of the bondage of corruption into the glorious liberty of the children of God.[1]

The base of the Mountain is the haunt of Souls which, repenting in their last moments, have yet departed under the censures of the Church.   These have to expiate each year of deferred penitence with thirty years of deferred Purgatory; except—and this holds good of every Soul before and during every stage of cleansing—delay be shortened by

[1] Dante most distinctly states (*Par.* XIX. 103-105) that none destitute of faith prospective or of faith retrospective in Christ ever did or ever will enter Heaven.   Yet he places Cato of Utica in Purgatory as a saved soul awaiting a glorified body, and already no prisoner, but a ruler:—and he does so without any such explanation as he gives (*Par.* XX., see pp. 246, 247) in the cases of Trajan and Ripheus.   How is this?   I am tempted to refer to a slight communication made by my brother W. M. Rossetti to *Notes and Queries*.   In the English translation of the mediæval treatise entitled *Cursor Mundi*, Dionysius Cato, a writer of uncertain faith and date, is obviously confounded with one of the two Roman Catos; and is thus (in substance) spoken of: 'Cato, although a pagan, never either spoke or wrote aught contrary to the Christian faith.   He is invariably in accord with Holy Writ: he who follows Cato's precepts follows those of the Bible.   The Holy Ghost, "by reason," seemed to be in Cato.   God grant us grace to follow Cato's precepts, and to be his companions where he dwells.'—This looks as if the author or translator, or both, of this curious old book regarded Cato as having a sort of pre-intuition of Christianity.   If so, may there not have been, in the Middle Ages, some kind of floating tradition to that effect? and might not this possibly account for Dante's exempting him from Hell?   (*Notes and Queries*, 4th S. ii. 229.)

pious prayers on earth. For ampler satisfaction is made to the Divine Justice by love than by time : wherefore one moment of intense supplication may obtain the remission of years of lingering.

Respecting the Mountain itself these two points may be premised :—that the ascent, at first all but too narrow and too steep to be scaled at all, becomes gradually easy and delightful as progress is made ; and that not one upward step can ever be taken after sunset. 'The night cometh, when no man can work.'[1]

Above the base rise the skirts—within the Sphere of Air, therefore subject to atmospheric vicissitudes ; and below the Gate of S. Peter, therefore affording no means of purgation.

On the winding terrace of this Ante-Purgatory are distinguished three successive stages, haunted by three more classes of tardy penitents, who having unlike those at the base died in communion with the Church, are detained only during a period corresponding to that of their delay on earth. The first class comprises those who from negligence put off their conversion to their deathbed :—the second those who, dying by violence, and sinners up to their last hour, repented and forgave after the death-stroke was received : —the third those Princes and Rulers who postponed piety and let slip opportunities of good through absorption in earthly interests and love of earthly greatness ; these last pass the night in a grassy flowery dell in the mountain-side, in colour all one glow, in odour all one fragrance.—The denizens of this whole lower region seem not yet entirely freed from sinful infirmities, neither is their peace untinged

[1] S. John ix. 4.

with care and fear: such as rest sit down under a sense of the hopelessness of making any real progress upward; such as walk chant Miserere as they go; such as converse need and impart consolation; such as humbly dreading the Adversary watch for the nightfall, greet it with the Compline hymn sung with accordant voices and lifted eyes, and are answered by the descent of Guardian Angels, green-winged and robed for hope, golden-haired and radiant-visaged for glory, with fiery swords against the lurking Serpent, with blunted swords towards the reposing Elect, falcons to watch, falcons to fly, moved swifter than seen to move. And as the day is ruled by the Southern Cross of fourfold virtues, so the night by the Alphas[1] of threefold graces, Faith, Hope, and Charity.

Immediately above the termination of the winding terrace, on the frontier of the Sphere of Fire, the Gate of S. Peter firmly set in a cleft of the rock gives or bars access to Purgatory Proper, and so ultimately to the Terrestrial and the Celestial Paradise. The approach to the Gate is by three steps: the first of white marble polished into a mirror; the second of inky-purple stone, rough and calcined, split both lengthwise and athwart; the third of flaming blood-red porphyry. On this rest the feet of him who sits on the adamantine threshold—a dazzling Angel in clothing of ashen hue, having in his hand a drawn flashing sword, under his robe a golden and a silver key, both equally requisite for opening the Gate; the golden the more pre-cious, the silver, as that which unlocks the inmost wards, demanding more skill in its employment. These were committed to him by S. Peter, with a charge rather to err

[1] The *Alphas* of Eridanus, of the Ship, and of the Golden Fish.

I

towards *prostrate* supplicants in opening than in keeping closed. But he who should enter and look back would find himself once more without. 'No man, having put his hand to the plough and looking back, is fit for the Kingdom of God.' [1]

At this point it is indispensable to refer to Dante's own account of his Commedia : 'The subject of all the work, accepted literally only, is the state of souls after death taken simply ; because respecting it and around it the process of all the work revolves. But if the work is accepted allegorically, the subject is Man, in so far as by free-will meriting and demeriting, he is amenable to the justice of reward and punishment.' [2] Therefore, as in the Hell are set forth the moral and penal effects of sin in this world as well as in the world to come, so and yet more in the Purgatory the undoing of those effects, and the formation of habits of virtue in life as well as after death. Contemplated through the medium of this statement, the Mount and the things of the Mount from base to summit are plainly seen. We need hardly be told that the Gate of S. Peter is the Tribunal of Penance, for post-baptismal sinners the transitional confine between the irresolute who in the mutability of passion and sensation linger without the Kingdom of Heaven, and the violent who in the immutability of a steadfast will take it by force. The triple stair stands revealed as candid Confession mirroring the whole man, mournful Contrition breaking the hard heart of the gazer on the Cross, Love all aflame offering up in Satisfaction the life-blood of body, soul, and spirit :—the adamantine threshold-

[1] S. Luke ix. 62.
[2] Epistle to Can Grande della Scala, 7.

seat as the priceless Merits of Christ the Door, Christ
the Rock, Christ the sure Foundation and the precious
Corner-Stone. In the Angel of the Gate, as in the Gospel
Angel of Bethesda, is discerned the Confessor; in the
dazzling radiance of his countenance the exceeding glory of
the ministration of righteousness; in the penitential robe
the sympathetic meekness whereby, restoring one overtaken
in a fault, he considers himself lest he also be tempted; in
the sword the wholesome severity of his discipline; in the
golden key his Divine authority; in the silver the dis-
cernment of spirits whereby he denies Absolution to the
impenitent, the learning and discretion whereby he directs
the penitent.

He who enters by this Gate finds himself at the foot of
a zigzag mountain pass, á veritable needle's eye. This
threaded, he comes out not upon a winding, but upon a
girding terrace. And here we pause for a study of moral
theory and physical construction.

Purgatory proper is the region between the Gate of S.
Peter and the Terrestrial Paradise. It consists of seven
Terraces or landing-places, each presumably equalling in
width the length of a man's body thrice repeated; the successive ascents are by stairs cut out in the rock. Each
Terrace is dedicated to the purgation of one of the seven
Capital Sins; the first three of which spring from Love
distorted, the middle one from Love defective, the last
three from Love excessive. For Love, which is in every
creature the fundamental principle of action, requires two
conditions for its purity and health :—that in its fulness it be
directed towards the Primal Goods, even towards Him, the
only measure of our love of Whom is to love Him without

measure,[1] and towards Virtue which conforms us to His Image :—and that upon all secondary goods it rest in due measure, and no more. For thus is it the seed of every virtue ; but otherwise of every vice whereby man turns the creature against the Creator.—The Distorter of Love loves evil to his neighbour :—if for his own exaltation he desires another's depression, he sins by Pride ; if, esteeming his own power, favour, honour, and fame to be lessened by participation, he desires another's destitution, he sins by Envy ; if because of evil done to himself he desires vengeance on another, he sins by Anger.—The Defaulter in Love loves less than he might the Highest Good, and so striving after It all too slackly sins by Sloth.—The Exceeder in Love loves more than he ought some lower unsufficing good :—if this be money, he sins by Avarice ; if food, by Gluttony ; if sensual pleasure, by Lasciviousness. And the purgation of each sin is double, active and passive. All the penitents alike suffer bodily chastisement vividly representative of the sin wherein they lived, or the penance wherein they failed to live. And all alike, with the whole energy of a body, soul and spirit thrilled with agony, parched and consumed with thirst for God, spurred by examples of virtue (among which comes ever first some act or word of the Blessed Virgin), bridled by instances of vice, exercise themselves night and day, unflinching and unflagging, in the grace contrary to the sin for which they are making satisfaction.

So much applies generally : we pass to what applies specially.

On the first and lowest Terrace is expiated man's worst,

[1] S. François de Sales.

deepest, fundamental corruption—Pride. For how should he be purged of any other taint while this remains ? how of the rebellion of the will while yet exalting himself against the Divine Law ? how of the folly of the understanding while yet despising the Divine Wisdom ? Or how should virtue be acquired by any still counted among the proud whom God resisteth, and not among the humble to whom He giveth grace ? Since then the first Purgatorial experience of each pride-tainted soul must needs be of the irrevocable sentence, 'Every one that exalteth himself shall be abased,'[1]—the penitents of Terrace I. have to creep round and round under weighty masses of stone laid upon their necks to bow them down to the very dust. All along the white marble rock-wall on their left are marvellously sculptured examples of Humility ; on the pavement under their feet instances of Pride. They say the Lord's Prayer as they go, adding to each petition an act of humiliation of heart, mind, or will : and in every word of their converse each studies to abase himself and exalt his fellows. —At the foot of the narrow flight of steps which leads to the next Terrace stands a directing Angel, and the mounting penitent hears voices of sweetness unspeakable chant the now applicable benediction, 'Blessed are the poor in spirit.'

Terrace II. has a general air of monotonous uniformity well suited to the prison-house of a sin which ' is ever where is some equality'[2] between its subject and its object : and which, might it but have its way, would speedily reduce all around it to one dead level of inferiority. Pavement and wall are here not of carved white marble, but of smooth

---

[1] S. Luke xviii. 14.   [2] *Convito* i. 11.

livid stone, symbolizing in colour the Envy to be chastised. The prisoners, mantled in haircloth of like hue, their eyelids sewed up with wire, sit shoulder to shoulder leaning on each other, and all leaning their backs against the bank. Their mean sad-coloured penance-garb in its clinging, teasing, universal prickliness, serves as a corrective parable of their wilful taking—not of pleasure, Envy is no pleasure, but—of pain under the ban of the Royal Law ; pain most wearing in its despicable pettiness, cleaving like a burr to the soul, fastening on all things and all persons within its range.   While in utter helplessness they realize the need of mutual support and assistance, their evil eye, the seat of their sin, learns in blindness and torture to look no more askance on gifts bestowed on each for all.   Vain to those eyes were sculptures; but spirit-voices in the air above them ring or thunder in their ears world-renowned sayings of the Loving and of the Envious.   Their invocations entreat the prayers of all the Saints : their discourse, bitter now only in grave and sad rebuke of their own and others' sin, is sweet in tenderest Brotherly Love, acknowledged interdependence, and heartfelt gratitude.   And their benediction on their release is this : ' Blessed are the merciful,' and ' Rejoice, O Victor.'

Terrace III. is partially beclouded with an all-veiling smoke-fog thicker than the infernal darkness, bitter to the taste, and severely pungent to the eyes.   We have seen in the Hell one probable reason for punishing Wrath with *fumes ;* an additional reason here seems to be the effect of this sin in so obstructing the mental eye as to make it incapable of seeing anything as it really is.   To the sufferers of this Circuit the instances of Meekness and of Anger are

inwardly presented in ecstatic vision ; this mode being probably chosen on purpose to constrain them to keep their
minds in that calm wherein during life they proved so
wofully deficient.   For peace and mercy they address their
unceasing prayer, all one concord in word and tone, to the
Lamb of God That taketh away the sins of the world : thus
they learn to be angry and sin not, mourning over evil only
with the righteous disinterested indignation which would
fain see it wholly converted to good.   And their final dis-
charge is, ' Blessed are the peacemakers, that are without evil anger.'

So far the sins of Love distorted.   The next in order is
Love defective, which as doing little or no good occupies
an exceptional transitional place between the two divisions
of the Love which does evil.

Terrace IV. is a race-course round which the Slothful run
and run at their extremest speed.   Nothing is done for
them, but all by them :—the foremost two lead on, shout-
ing with tears examples of Diligence ; the whole pursuing
troop press on, urge on with words like goads ; the hind-
most two chase on with mordant outcries upon instances of
Sloth.[1]   Nothing is said of any prayers of these athletes ;
they are at last dismissed upwards with the words, ' Blessed
are they that mourn, for their souls shall be queens of consolation.'

From this point extends the region of Love excessive.

Terrace V. is occupied by the Avaricious, and also by
the Prodigal ; indeed every one of the Terraces is stated to
belong to two opposite classes, though here alone is this
circumstance dwelt on.   Prostrate, extended, motionless

---

[1] Sloth=*Accidia.*   See p. 51.

these earth-idolizers lie along the earth ; bound hand and foot because that earth limed their energies away from all the work they should have done for Heaven ; eyes merged within that earth, because while living on it they would raise those eyes no higher.   Their chastisement is expressly said to be as severe as any on the Mount ; what indeed should be sorer to affections set on Heaven than eyes that cannot choose but grovel?   'My soul cleaveth unto the dust' is their sighing plaint ; while now loud, now low, they eulogize by day the Poor and the Liberal, and denounce the Avaricious by night.   And their emancipation blesses those that 'thirst after justice.'

Terrace VI. famishes Gluttons in the midst of plenty. During their ceaseless perambulation two trees, planted probably at opposite spots, keep torturing them with fruitless cravings.   The first tree is the banquet of Tantalus ; in form like a pine, but with head broadening *upwards* that none may climb ; its apples temptingly odorous ; its topmost crown of foliage laved ever by a jet of clearest water streaming upon it from a fount springing high up in the rock-wall.   The smell is of virtue to excite appetite in the utmost possible degree : but still as the hungering thirsting Shades draw nigh a voice issues from the boughs, denying them the feast, and setting before them examples of Temperance.—The second tree is reared from a sprig of the Tree of Knowledge ; but neither here may cries and outstretched hands prevail to obtain one single fruit of the plenteous heavy crop ; the voice amid the leaves again forbids the supplicants, and scares them away with instances of Gluttony.   Unrecognisable in their emaciation these penitents keep their baffled fast, yet chant their tearful vow,

'Thou shalt open my lips, O Lord;' till at length they too are blessed as grace-illumined to hunger no more than in just measure.

Terrace VII.—the last—is a furnace; perhaps through the Fire of this Elemental Sphere manifesting itself at this point in visible sensible flame proceeding from the rock-wall, and only so far blown back by a wind from the edge as to leave clear a passage barely wide enough for one exceeding circumspect to walk along unscorched and un-precipitated.   Two processions of penitents, going contrary ways within the fire, while apart sing low the hymn 'Summæ Deus clementiæ,'[1] wherein Chastity is besought, and pro-claim aloud examples of that virtue; then at each succes-sive encounter embrace and pass on unlingering, crying shame as they separate on instances of Lasciviousness :— till cleansed they are sped upwards with the Angelic valedic-tion, 'Blessed are the pure in heart.'

From this point Purgatory is no more. As impeccable its holy prisoners have entered upon it, so immoveable in the set purpose of making satisfaction to One supremely loved they have endured it unconstrained.   Hence the Wrathful have heedfully kept within their smoke, the Lascivious within their fire; hence the Slothful have raced on even in seeming discourtesy to a guest, the Avaricious cut short pleasant discourse to weep, the Gluttonous sought once and again the trees of emptiness.   But a change comes at last like a flood upon the will; the craving for agony is satiated; the Soul leaps up free for its beatitude. Nature and Grace respond throughout the Sphere of Fire : the Mount trembles sympathetic; Gloria in Excelsis goes

---

[1] The Matins Hymn for Saturday.

up like incense from the whole world of Prisoners of Hope.

One more ladder is scaled—who shall say whether with feet or wings? And lo the indefectible Soul, having with a great sum obtained this freedom, stands on the borders of its redeemed, its reconquered inheritance, the Eden and the Heaven whence it shall go out no more.

CHAPTER VIII.

DANTE'S PILGRIMAGE THROUGH PURGATORY.

> E poi vedrai color che son contenti
> Nel fuoco.
>
> And thou shalt then see those who are content
> Within the fire.
>
> *Inf.* I. 118, 119.

DANTE with Virgil, issuing from within the Earth at earliest dawn, as seems most likely, of Easter Day,[1] stood on the low flat shore of the Western Island.

> Sweet colour of the oriental sapphire,
>   That was upgathered in the cloudless aspect
>   Of the pure air, as far as the first circle,
> Unto mine eyes did recommence delight
>   Soon as I issued forth from the dead air,
>   Which had with sadness filled mine eyes and breast.
> The beauteous planet, that to love incites,
>   Was making all the orient to laugh,
>   Veiling the Fishes that were in her escort.
> To the right hand I turned, and fixed my mind
>   Upon the other pole, and saw four stars
>   Ne'er seen before save by the primal people.
> Rejoicing in their flamelets seemed the heaven.
>   O thou septentrional and widowed site,
>   Because thou art deprived of seeing these !

---

[1] Cayley, note on *Inf.* xxxiv. 105.

When from regarding them I had withdrawn,
　Turning a little to the other pole,
　There where the Wain had disappeared already,
I saw beside me an old man alone,
　Worthy of so much reverence in his look,
　That more owes not to father any son.
A long beard and with white hair intermingled
　He wore, in semblance like unto the tresses,
　Of which a double list fell on his breast.
The rays of the four consecrated stars
　Did so adorn his countenance with light,
　That him I saw as were the sun before him.
' Who are you ? ye who, counter the blind river,
　Have fled away from the eternal prison ? '
　Moving those venerable plumes, he said :
.' Who guided you ? or who has been your lamp
　In issuing forth out of the night profound,
　That ever black makes the infernal valley ?
The laws of the abyss, are they thus broken ?
　Or is there changed in Heaven some counsel new,
　That being damned ye come unto my crags ? '
Then did my Leader lay his grasp upon me,
　And with his words, and with his hands and signs,
　Reverent he made in me my knees and brow ;
Then answered him : ' I came not of myself ;
　A Lady from Heaven descended, at whose prayers
　I aided this one with my company.
But since it is thy will more be unfolded
　Of our condition, how it truly is,
　Mine cannot be that this should be denied thee.
This one has never his last evening seen,
　But by his folly was so near to it
　That very little time was there to turn.
As I have said, I unto him was sent

To rescue him, and other way was none
   Than this to which I have myself betaken.
I 've shown him all the people of perdition,
   And now those Spirits I intend to show
   Who purge themselves beneath thy guardianship.
How I have brought him would be long to tell thee.
   Virtue descendeth from on high that aids me
   To lead him to behold thee and to hear thee.
Now may it please thee to vouchsafe his coming ;
   He seeketh Liberty, which is so dear,
   As knoweth he who life for her refuses.
Thou know'st it ; since, for her, to thee not bitter
   Was death in Utica, where thou didst leave
   The vesture, that will shine so, the great day.
By us the eternal edicts are not broken ;
   Since this one lives, and Minos binds not me ;
   But of that circle I, where are the chaste
Eyes of thy Marcia, who in looks still prays thee,
   O holy breast, to hold her as thine own ;
   For her love, then, incline thyself to us.
Permit us through thy sevenfold realm to go ;
   I will take back this grace from thee to her,
   If to be mentioned there below thou deignest.'
' Marcia so pleasing was unto mine eyes
   While I was on the other side,' then said he,
   ' That every grace she wished of me I granted ;
Now that she dwells beyond the evil river,
   She can no longer move me, by that law
   Which, when I issued forth from there, was made.
But if a Lady of Heaven do move and rule thee,
   As thou dost say, no flattery is needful ;
   Let it suffice thee that for her thou ask me.
Go, then, and see thou gird this one about
   With a smooth rush, and that thou wash his face.

So that thou cleanse away all stain therefrom,
For 'twere not fitting that the eye o'ercast
   By any mist should go before the first
   Angel, who is of those of Paradise.
This little island round about its base
   Below there, yonder, where the billow beats it,
   Doth rushes bear upon its washy ooze ;
No other plant that putteth forth the leaf,
   Or that doth indurate, can there have life,
   Because it yieldeth not unto the shocks.
Thereafter be not this way your return ;
   The sun, which now is rising, will direct you
   To take the mount by easier ascent.'
With this he vanished ; and I raised me up
   Without a word, and wholly drew myself
   Unto my Guide, and turned mine eyes to him.
And he began : 'Son, follow thou my steps ;
   Let us turn back, for on this side declines
   The plain unto its lower boundaries.'
The dawn was vanquishing the matin hour
   Which fled before it, so that from afar
   I recognised the trembling of the sea.
Along the solitary plain we went
   As one who unto the lost road returns,
   And till he finds it seems to go in vain.
As soon as we were come to where the dew
   Fights with the sun, and, being in a part
   Where shadow falls, little evaporates,
Both of his hands upon the grass outspread
   In gentle manner did my Master place ;
   Whence I, who of his action was aware,
Extended unto him my tearful cheeks ;
   There did he make in me uncovered wholly
   That hue which Hell had covered up in me.

Then came we down upon the desert shore
 Which never yet saw navigate its waters
 Any that afterward had known return.
There he begirt me as the other pleased ;
 O marvellous ! for even as he culled
 The humble plant, such it sprang up again
Suddenly there where he uprooted it.

         Pur. I. 13-136.

The sun was rising : when behold another marvel.

We still were on the border of the sea,
 Like people who are thinking of their road,
 Who go in heart, and with the body stay ;
And lo ! as when, upon the approach of morning,
 Through the gross vapours Mars grows fiery red
 Down in the West upon the ocean floor,
Appeared to me—may I again behold it !—
 A light along the sea so swiftly coming,
 Its motion by no flight of wing is equalled ;
From which when I a little had withdrawn
 Mine eyes, that I might question my Conductor,
 Again I saw it brighter grown and larger.
Then on each side of it appeared to me
 I knew not what of white, and underneath it
 Little by little there came forth another.
My master yet had uttered not a word
 While the first whiteness into wings unfolded ;
 But when he clearly recognised the pilot,
He cried : ' Make haste, make haste to bow the knee '
 Behold the Angel of God ! fold thou thy hands !
 Henceforward shalt thou see such officers !
See how he scorneth human arguments,
 So that nor oar he wants, nor other sail
 Than his own wings, between so distant shores.

See how he holds them pointed up to Heaven,
   Fanning the air with the eternal pinions,
   That do not moult themselves like mortal hair !'
Then as still nearer and more near us came
   The Bird Divine, more radiant he appeared,
   So that, near by, the eye could not endure him,
But down I cast it ; and he came to shore
   With a small vessel, very swift and light,
   So that the water swallowed naught thereof.
Upon the stern stood the Celestial Pilot ;
   Beatitude seemed written in his face,
   And more than a hundred·Spirits sat within.
'*In exitu Israel de Ægypto !*'
   They chanted all together in one voice,
   With whatso in that psalm is after written.
Then made he sign of holy rood upon them,
   Whereat all cast themselves upon the shore,
   And he departed swiftly as he came.

II. 10-51.

The newly landed troop first gazed around in perplexity, then seeing two strangers asked the way, but of course in vain. Dante's breathing, as revealing him to be alive, next excited their wondering interest, and anon one pressed forward to embrace him, but could not be embraced in turn ·—thrice the clasping hands met behind the aërial body, thrice returned empty to the embracer's breast. This Shade was his courteous and amiable friend Casella, a consummate Florentine musician in whose singing he had been wont to take delight. At his request now to have that delight renewed, a Canzone of his own was commenced with surpassing sweetness by Casella, and all, even the philosophic Virgil, stood entranced to hear. But not for long : the rigid Warden Cato with one sharp rebuke chased away his charges towards the Mount, and conveyed to Virgil a hint quickly applied.

> He seemed to me within himself remorseful ;
> O noble conscience, and without a stain,
> How sharp a sting is trivial fault to thee !
>
> III. 7-9.

When at length the two Pilgrims felt free somewhat to slacken their hurried steps, Dante, as yet inexperienced in a daylight world of ghosts, and therefore startled to notice no shadow but his own cast on the ground, looked round in sudden anxiety.

> 'Why dost thou still mistrust ?' my Comforter
>   Began to say to me turned wholly round ;
>   'Dost thou not think me with thee, and that I guide thee ?
> 'Tis evening there already where is buried
>   The body within which I cast a shadow ;
>   'Tis from Brundusium ta'en, and Naples has it.
> Now if in front of me no shadow fall,
>   Marvel not at it more than at the heavens,
>   Because one ray impedeth not another.
> To suffer torments, both of cold and heat,
>   Bodies like this that Power provides, Which wills
>   That how It works be not unveiled to us.
> Insane is he who hopeth that our reason
>   Can traverse the illimitable way,
>   Which the One Substance in Three Persons follows !
> Mortals, remain contented at the *Quia;*[1]
>   For if ye had been able to see all,

---

[1] 'Be satisfied with knowing that a thing is, without asking why it is. These were distinguished in scholastic language as the *Demonstratio quia,* and the *Demonstratio propter quid.*'

K

No need there were for Mary to give birth ;
And ye have seen desiring without fruit,
　　Those whose desire would have been quieted,
　　Which evermore is given them for a grief.
I speak of Aristotle and of Plato,
　　And many others ' ;—and here bowed his head,
　　And more he said not, and remained disturbed.

　　　　　　　　　　　　　　　　III. 22-45.

By this time both stood at the foot of the mountain ; the
ascent going up so sheer above them that nothing short of
wings would serve the turn.   As they mused and searched
for a practicable slope, a troop of Souls were seen in slowest
movement more than a mile off ; but the Poets hastening
towards them had soon diminished this distance to a
stone's-throw.   Then the sight of a human shadow excited for
the first time the amazement with which it was to be again
and again greeted :—this amazement removed, the Shades
directed their guests in the way.   As they walked along one
made himself known as Manfred King of Naples and Sicily,
grandson of the Empress Constance ; he did not call himself
son of the Emperor Frederick II., probably because aware
that this last was entombed in the City of Dis, where we
saw him with Farinata and Cavalcante.[1]   Manfred had
been slain at Benevento in battle for his throne against
Charles of Anjou ; and now, after requesting Dante to
obtain for him the prayers of his daughter Constance,
widow of Peter III. of Aragon and mother of the reigning
Kings of Aragon and Sicily, he told of his own death and
burial :—he had at first been interred by order of his victorious rival at the foot of the bridge of Benevento, and a

[1] See page 76.

great pile of stones heaped on his grave; but it is said that
afterwards, by command of Pope Clement v., the Bishop of
Cosenza removed his body to the banks of the River Verde,
on the Neapolitan frontier.   His own words are:

> After I had my body lacerated
>   By these two mortal stabs, I gave myself
>   Weeping to Him, Who willingly doth pardon.
> Horrible my iniquities had been;
>   But Infinite Goodness hath such ample arms,
>   That It receives whatever turns to It.
> Had but Cosenza's pastor, who in chase
>   Of me was sent by Clement at that time,
>   In God read understandingly this page,
> The bones of my dead body still would be
>   At the bridge-head, near unto Benevento,
>   Under the safeguard of the heavy cairn.
> Now the rain bathes and moveth them the wind,
>   Beyond the realm, almost beside the Verde,
>   Where he transported them with tapers quenched.
> By malison of theirs is not so lost
>   Eternal Love, that It cannot return,
>   So long as hope has anything of green.
> True is it, who in contumacy dies
>   Of Holy Church, though penitent at last,
>   Must wait upon the outside of this bank
> Thirty times told the time that he has been
>   In his presumption, unless such decree
>   Shorter by means of righteous prayers become.
> See now if thou hast power to make me happy,
>   By making known unto my good Costanza
>   How thou hast seen me, and this ban beside;
> For those on earth can much advance us here.
>   III. 118-145.

In his absorbed attention to Manfred's words Dante had forgotten all else ; but soon after 9 A.M. the friendly Shades with one voice indicated the sole accessible path, narrower than such a breach in a hedge as might be stopped with one fork-load of brambles, and steeper than probably the very steepest mountain-passes Dante had seen in Italy.

> One climbs Sanleo and descends in Noli,
>   And mounts the summit of Bismantova,
>   With feet alone ; but here one needs must fly ;
> With the swift pinions and the plumes I say
>   Of great desire, conducted after him
>   Who gave me hope, and made a light for me.
> We mounted upward through the rifted rock,
>   And on each side the border pressed upon us,
>   And feet and hands the ground beneath required.
>
> IV. 25-33.

Thus did the Pilgrims manage to struggle to the open mountain-side, and thence to the first stage of the winding terrace ; whereon at length they sat down to rest, looking seawards.   Virgil as usual turned the time to account by explaining some astronomical phenomena of this Antipodal Hemisphere, and was just comforting his disciple with a prospect of easier ascents in the sky-veiled heights and of final rest at the top, when a voice near them saying, ' Perhaps you may want to sit down before that,' made them turn and draw towards a rocky mass till then unnoticed. In its shade were seated a group of very lazy-looking Ghosts, lingering out a time corresponding to that of their negligent delay of conversion.   One with his arms round his knees and his face between them had been the speaker—Belacqua, an acquaintance concerning whose salvation Dante had been

much in doubt, and who now struck into the conversation
in a tone not free from levity.

His sluggish attitude and his curt words
　A little unto laughter moved my lips ;
　Then I began : ' Belacqua, I grieve not
For thee henceforth ; but tell me, wherefore seated
　In this place art thou ?　Waitest thou an escort ?
　Or has thy usual habit seized upon thee ?'
And he : ' O brother, what's the use of climbing ?
　Since to my torment would not let me go
　The Angel of God, who sitteth at the gate.
First Heaven must needs so long revolve me round
　Outside thereof, as in my life it did,
　Since the good sighs I to the end postponed,
Unless, ere that, some prayer may bring me aid
　Which rises from a heart that lives in grace ;
　What profit others that in Heaven are heard not ?'
Meanwhile the Poet was before me mounting,
　And saying : ' Come now ; see the sun has touched
　Meridian, and from the shore the night
Covers already with her foot Morocco.'

I had already from those Shades departed,
　And followed in the footsteps of my Guide,
　When from behind, pointing his finger at me,
One shouted : ' See, it seems as if shone not
　The sunshine on the left of him below,
　And like one living seems he to conduct him !'
Mine eyes I turned at utterance of these words,
　And saw them watching with astonishment
　But me, but me, and the light which was broken !
' Why doth thy mind so occupy itself,'
　The Master said, ' that thou thy pace dost slacken ?
　What matters it to thee what here is whispered ?

Come after me, and let the people talk ;
  Stand like a steadfast tower, that never wags
  Its top for all the blowing of the winds ;
For evermore the man in whom is springing
  Thought upon thought, removes from him the mark,
  Because the force of one the other weakens.'
What could I say in answer but 'I come'?
  I said it somewhat with that colour tinged
  Which makes a man of pardon sometimes worthy.

IV. 121-139. V. 1-21.

The next troop was of some who being while yet uncon-
verted smitten with a violent death-stroke, had in their few
remaining moments been enlightened to repent and to
forgive. Among these was Count Buonconte di Montefeltro, son of that Count Guido whom we already know,[1]
and with whose history his own strikingly contrasts. Buonconte had been slain in the battle of Campaldino, commanding on the Ghibelline side ; and Dante, in that battle his
Guelph opponent, meeting him here eagerly inquired,

          'What violence or what chance
  Led thee astray so far from Campaldino
  That never has thy sepulture been known ?'
'Oh,' he replied, 'at Casentino's foot
  A river crosses named Archiano, born
  Above the Hermitage in Apennine.
There where the name thereof becometh void
  Did I arrive, pierced through and through the throat,
  Fleeing on foot, and bloodying the plain ;
There my sight lost I, and my utterance
  Ceased in the name of Mary, and thereat
  I fell, and tenantless my flesh remained.

---

[1] See page 87.

Truth will I speak, repeat it to the living ;
   God's Angel took me up, and he of Hell
   Shouted : 'O thou from Heaven, why dost thou rob me ?
Thou bearest away the eternal part of him,
   For one poor little tear, that takes him from me ;
   But with the rest I 'll deal in other fashion !'
Well knowest thou how in the air is gathered
   That humid vapour which to water turns,
   Soon as it rises where the cold doth grasp it.
He joined that evil will, which aye seeks evil,
   To intellect, and moved the mist and wind
   By means of power, which his own nature gave ;
Thereafter, when the day was spent, the valley
   From Pratomagno to the great yoke covered
   With fog, and made the heaven above intent,
So that the pregnant air to water changed ;
   Down fell the rain, and to the gullies came
   Whate'er of it earth tolerated not ;
And as it mingled with the mighty torrents,
   Towards the royal river with such speed
   It headlong rushed, that nothing held it back.
My frozen body near unto its outlet
   The robust Archian found, and into Arno
   Thrust it, and loosened from my breast the cross
I made of me, when agony o'ercame me ;
   It rolled me on the banks and on the bottom ;
   Then with its booty covered and begirt me.'

V. 91-129.

To this class of the slain by violence belonged also the
Pisan Farinata degli Scornigiani, whose death is variously
attributed to Beccio da Caprona and to Count Ugolino
della Gherardesca, whom we saw in Hell.[1] It is said that

---

[1] See page 97.

Farinata's father, here expressly called 'the good Marzucco,' a Minorite friar, in company with the other friars attended his funeral, and entreated the whole family to abstain from vengeance.[1]—All this band of Spirits spoke like Belacqua of prayers on earth as their sole possible succour, and unlike him besought Dante to procure them that succour; thus suggesting to his mind a difficulty which his Master professed not confidently to solve.

> As soon as I was free from all those Shades
>   Who only prayed that some one else may pray,
>   So as to hasten their becoming holy,
> Began I : 'It appears that thou deniest,
>   O light of mine, expressly in some text,[2]
>   That orison can bend decree of Heaven ;
> And ne'ertheless these people pray for this.
>   Might then their expectation bootless be ?
>   Or is to me thy saying not quite clear ?'
> And he to me : 'My writing is explicit,
>   And not fallacious is the hope of these,
>   If with sane intellect 'tis well regarded ;
> For top of judgment doth not vail itself,[3]
>   Because the fire of love fulfils at once
>   What he must satisfy who here installs him.
> And there, where I affirmed that proposition,
>   Defect was not amended by a prayer,
>   Because the prayer from God was separate.
> Verily, in so deep a questioning

---

[1] Fraticelli and Longfellow, *Pur.* vi. 17, 18. Various accounts however are given by different authorities.

[2] 'In *Æneid* vi. : "Cease to hope that the decrees of the gods are to be changed by prayers."'

[3] The highest point of God's judgment does not bend.

Do not decide, unless she tell it thee,
Who light 'twixt truth and intellect shall be.
I know not if thou understand ; I speak
Of Beatrice ; her shalt thou see above,
Smiling and happy, on this mountain's top.'

VI. 25-48.

Already the way was felt to be easier, and Dante inspired by the thought of Beatrice was craving more rapid
progress, when suddenly a Shade keeping solitary watch
caught Virgil's eye ; and a request for guidance was answered with an inquiry respecting the Pilgrims' country and
condition. The mere name of Mantua instantly quickened
indifference into interest and love, for this Shade was the
Mantuan Poet-Podestà Sordello ; [1] the name of Virgil awed
love into reverence. The reiterated request to be shown
the shortest way to Purgatory proper now elicited the information that in the rapidly supervening darkness it would
be impossible to get so far, and the welcome offer of introduction into a nocturnal sojourn tenanted by Shades
whose acquaintance would give pleasure.

Little had we withdrawn us from that place,
When I perceived the mount was hollowed out
In fashion as the valleys here are hollowed.
' Thitherward,' said that Shade, ' will we repair,
Where of itself the hill-side makes a lap,

---

[1] It seems to me on the whole most probable that Sordello was both
poet and podestà. Dante (*De Volg. El.* i. 15) speaks of Sordello of
Mantua as a poet ; and all those with whom he is here associated are
Princes and Rulers. Quadrio (*Storia d'ogni Poesia*, ii. 130), though
without giving his authorities, adopts the same conclusion as I have
done respecting this vexed question. (See Longfellow on *Pur.* vi. 74.)

And there for the new day will we await.'
'Twixt hill and plain there was a winding path
 Which led us to the margin of that dell,
 Where dies the border more than half away.
Gold and fine silver, and scarlet and pearl-white,
 The Indian wood resplendent and serene,
 Fresh emerald the moment it is broken,
By herbage and by flowers within that hollow
 Planted, each one in colour would be vanquished,
 As by its greater vanquished is the less.
Nor in that place had nature painted only,
 But of the sweetness of a thousand odours
 Made there a mingled fragrance and unknown.
' *Salve Regina*,' on the green and flowers
 There seated, singing, Spirits I beheld,
 Which were not visible outside the valley.

VII. 64-84.

These Spirits, of whom Sordello himself was one, were
Princes and Rulers who for love of things not in themselves sinful had postponed conversion or been negligent
of good. Long Dante gazed from above as his new friend
pointed out renowned Shade after Shade :—Rodolph of
Hapsburg comforted by his chief opponent Ottocar of
Bohemia ; Philippe le Hardi in consultation with Henry
III. of Navarre, the one father, the other father-in-law, to
the reigning ' Pest of France,' Philippe le Bel ; Peter III.
of Aragon singing in accord with his quondam adversary
Charles I. of Naples. And as the sight of these Princes
suggested the thought of those who now occupied their
thrones, Sordello gave utterance to the reflection—

Not oftentimes upriseth through the branches

The probity of man ; and this He wills
Who gives it, so that we may ask of Him.[1]

VII. 121-123.

Seated alone was Henry III. of England, 'the King of the simple life ;' his posterity is expressly excepted from the censure passed on that of his associates.

We shall find Dante recur in the Paradiso to this subject of the degeneracy of sons from fathers ;[2] it seems to have greatly occupied his mind.   But

'Twas now the hour that turneth back desire
In those who sail the sea, and melts the heart,
The day they've said to their sweet friends farewell,
And the new pilgrim penetrates with love,
If he doth hear from far away a bell
That seemeth to deplore the dying day,
When I began to make of no avail
My hearing, and to watch one of the Souls
Uprisen, that begged attention with its hand.
It joined and lifted upward both its palms,
Fixing its eyes upon the orient,
As if it said to God, ' Naught else I care for.'
' *Te lucis ante* '[3] so devoutly issued
Forth from its mouth, and with such dulcet notes,
It made me issue forth from my own mind.
And then the others, sweetly and devoutly,
Accompanied it through all the hymn entire,
Having their eyes on the supernal wheels.

---

[1] I think the sense of the last line and a half is rather : 'this He wills Who gives it, in order that it may be ascribed to Him.'

[2] See page 229.

[3] The first words of the Compline hymn, which contains a prayer against the Enemy.

Here, Reader, fix thine eyes well on the truth,
 For now indeed so subtile is the veil,
 Surely to penetrate within is easy.
I saw that army of the gentle-born
 Thereafterward in silence upward gaze,
 As if in expectation, pale and humble ;
And from on high come forth and down descend,
 I saw two Angels with two flaming swords,
 Truncated and deprivèd of their points.
Green as the little leaflets just now born
 Their garments were, which, by their verdant pinions
 Beaten and blown abroad, they trailed behind.
One just above us came to take his station,
 And one descended to the opposite bank,
 So that the people were contained between them.
Clearly in them discerned I the blond head ;
 But in their faces was the eye bewildered,
 As faculty confounded by excess.
'From Mary's bosom both of them have come,'
 Sordello said, 'as guardians of the valley
 Against the serpent, that will come anon.'

          VIII. 1-39.

Descending now into the dell with the courteous guide
Dante recognised a friend, the Sardinian Judge Nino de'
Visconti, who seized the opportunity of sending to ask
the innocent prayers of his little daughter Giovanna. Yet
almost as he spoke,

My greedy eyes still wandered up to Heaven,
 Still to that point where slowest are the stars,
 Even as a wheel the nearest to its axle.
And my Conductor : 'Son, what dost thou gaze at
 Up there ?' And I to him : 'At those three torches
 With which this hither pole is all on fire.'

And he to me : ' The four resplendent stars
   Thou sawest this morning are down yonder low,
   And these have mounted up to where those were.'
As he was speaking, to himself Sordello
   Drew him, and said, ' Lo there our Adversary !'
   And pointed with his finger to look thither.
Upon the side on which the little valley
   No barrier hath, a serpent was ; perchance
   The same which gave to Eve the bitter food.
'Twixt grass and flowers came on the evil streak,
   Turning at times its head about, and licking
   Its back like to a beast that smoothes itself.
I did not see, and therefore cannot say
   How the celestial falcons 'gan to move,
   But well I saw that they were both in motion.
Hearing the air cleft by their verdant wings,
   The serpent fled, and round the Angels wheeled,
   Up to their stations flying back alike.

                                   VIII. 85-108.

After converse prolonged through the night, towards dawn of Easter Monday the only Flesh among all these Spirits dropped asleep ; dreamed of Jove's Eagle swooping down and carrying him up into the scorching Fire-Sphere ; and awoke, but not where his sleep had fallen upon him.

Only my Comforter was at my side,
   And now the sun was more than two hours high,
   And turned towards the sea-shore was my face.
' Be not intimidated,' said my Lord,
   ' Be reassured, for all is well with us ;
   Do not restrain, but put forth all thy strength.
Thou hast at length arrived at Purgatory ;
   See there the cliff that closes it around ;
   See there the entrance, where it seems disjoined.

Whilom at dawn, which doth precede the day,
 When inwardly thy spirit was asleep
 Upon the flowers that deck the land below,
There came a Lady and said : " I am Lucìa ;
 Let me take this one up, who is asleep ;
 So will I make his journey easier for him."
Sordello and the other noble shapes
 Remained ; she took thee, and, as day grew bright,
 Upward she came, and I upon her footsteps.
She laid thee here ; and first her beauteous eyes
 That open entrance pointed out to me ;
 Then she and sleep together went away.'
In guise of one whose doubts are reassured,
 And who to confidence his fear doth change,
 After the truth has been discovered to him.
So did I change ; and when without disquiet
 My Leader saw me, up along the cliff
 He moved, and I behind him, tow'rd the height.
Reader, thou seest well how I exalt
 My theme, and therefore if with greater art
 I fortify it, marvel not thereat.
Nearer approached we, and were in such place,
 That there, where first appeared to me a rift
 Like to a crevice that disparts a wall,
I saw a portal, and three stairs beneath,
 Diverse in colour, to go up to it,
 And a gate-keeper, who yet spake no word.
And as I opened more and more mine eyes,
 I saw him seated on the highest stair,
 Such in the face that I endured it not.
And in his hand he had a naked sword,
 Which so reflected back the sunbeams tow'rds us,
 That oft in vain I lifted up mine eyes.
' Tell it from where you are, what is 't you wish ? '

Began he to exclaim; 'Where is the escort?
Take heed your coming hither harm you not!'
'A Lady of Heaven, with these things conversant,'
    My Master answered him, 'but even now
    Said to us, " Thither go; there is the portal."'
'And may she speed your footsteps in all good,'
    Again began the courteous janitor;
    'Come forward then unto these stairs of ours.'
Thither did we approach; and the first stair
    Was marble white, so polished and so smooth,
    I mirrored myself therein as I appear.
The second, tinct of deeper hue than perse,
    Was of a calcined and uneven stone,
    Cracked all asunder lengthwise and across.
The third, that uppermost rests massively,
    Porphyry seemed to me, as flaming red
    As blood that from a vein is spirting forth.
Both of his feet was holding upon this
    The Angel of God, upon the threshold seated,
    Which seemed to me a stone of diamond.
Along the three stairs upward with good-will
    Did my Conductor draw me, saying: 'Ask
    Humbly that he the fastening may undo.'
Devoutly at the holy feet I cast me,
    For mercy's sake besought that he would open,
    But first upon my breast three times I smote.
Seven P's upon my forehead he described
    With the sword's point, and, 'Take heed that thou wash
    These wounds, when thou shalt be within,' he said.

                                        IX. 43-114.

This sevenfold graving of P (the initial of Peccatum =
Sin) signifies the bringing out by reproof of the distinct
marks, already too surely branded within, of the seven

Capital Sins, to be then effaced from body and soul by the works of satisfaction enjoined as sacramental penance. It is noteworthy that no allusion is made to these P's as traced on the forehead of any Shade, and yet none expresses surprise at seeing them on Dante's.

> Ashes, or earth that dry is excavated,
>   Of the same colour were with his attire,
>   And from beneath it he drew forth two keys.
> One was of gold, and the other was of silver ;
>   First with the white, and after with the yellow,
>   Plied he the door, so that I was content.
>   Whenever faileth either of these keys
>   So that it turn not rightly in the lock,'
>   He said to us, ' this entrance doth not open.
> More precious one is, but the other needs
>   More art and intellect ere it unlock,
>   For it is that which doth the knot unloose.
> From Peter I have them ; and he bade me err
>   Rather in opening than in keeping shut,
>   If people but fall down before my feet.'
> Then pushed the portals of the sacred door,
>   Exclaiming : ' Enter ; but I give you warning
>   That forth returns whoever looks behind.'
>
> IX. 115-132.

The Gate opened, *Te Deum laudamus* resounded from within ; the Gate passed, more than an hour was occupied in the zigzag ascent : till at about 10 A.M. one Pilgrim weary, and both uncertain of the way, stood on the First Terrace of Purgatory, and stood there alone.

> Thereon our feet had not been moved as yet,
>   When I perceived the embankment round about,

Which all right of ascent had interdicted,
To be of marble white, and so adorned
    With sculptures, that not only Polycletus,
    But Nature's self, had there been put to shame.
The Angel, who came down to earth with tidings
    Of peace, that had been wept for many a year,
    And opened Heaven from its long interdict,
In front of us appeared so truthfully
    There sculptured in a gracious attitude,
    He did not seem an image that is silent.
One would have sworn that he was saying '*Ave*';
    For she was there in effigy portrayed
    Who turned the key to ope the exalted love,
And in her mien this language had impressed,
    ' *Ecce ancilla Dei*,' as distinctly
    As any figure stamps itself in wax.

                           x. 28-45.

Many more sculptured examples of Humility followed along the bank; and in all, spoken words were after a marvellous fashion rendered sensible to the eye.

He who on no new thing has ever looked
    Was the Creator of this visible language,
    Novel to us, for here it is not found.
While I delighted me in contemplating
    The images of such humility,
    And dear to look on for their Maker's sake,
' Behold, upon this side, but rare they make
    Their steps,' the Poet murmured, ' many people ;
    These will direct us to the lofty stairs.'
Mine eyes, that in beholding were intent
    To see new things, of which they curious are,
    In turning round towards him were not slow.
But still I wish not, Reader, thou shouldst swerve

                         L

From thy good purposes, because thou hearest
How God ordaineth that the debt be paid ;
Attend not to the fashion of the torment,
Think of what follows ; think that at the worst
It cannot reach beyond the mighty sentence.[1]

X. 94-111.

At first sight it may seem surprising that after so awfully setting before his reader the pains of Hell incurred by not forming or not fulfilling good purposes, Dante should fear turning him aside from any such purpose by setting before him his liability, notwithstanding, to the pains of Purgatory. But as we have seen,[2] the subject of the Cantica is not restricted to the purgation of Souls after death ; it likewise exhibits the cleansing from sin and the substitution of good for evil habits in life. The alternative presented will not therefore be at first that between Hell and Purgatory, but that between the ease and pleasures of Vice on the one hand, and the toils and sufferings of resisting Vice on the other.

' Master,' began I, ' that which I behold
Moving towards us seems to me not persons,
And what I know not, so in sight I waver.'
And he to me : ' The grievous quality
Of this their torment bows them so to earth,
That my own eyes at first contended with it ;
But look there fixedly, and disentangle
By sight what cometh underneath those stones ;
Already canst thou see how each is stricken.'
O ye proud Christians ! wretched, weary ones !
Who, in the vision of the mind infirm,   .

---

[1] The Last Judgment.   [2] See p. 112.

Confidence have in your backsliding steps,[1]
Do ye not comprehend that we are worms,
   Born to bring forth the angelic butterfly
   That flieth unto judgment without screen ?
Why floats aloft your spirit high in air ?
   Like are ye unto insects undeveloped,
   Even as the worm in whom formation fails !
As to sustain a ceiling or a roof,
   In place of corbel, oftentimes a figure
   Is seen to join unto its knees its breast,
Which makes of the unreal real anguish
   Arise in him who sees it ; fashioned thus
   Beheld I those, when I had ta'en good heed.
True is it, they were more or less bent down,
   According as they more or less were laden ;
   And he who had most patience in his looks
Weeping did seem to say, ' I can no more !'

' Our Father, Thou Who dwellest in the heavens,
   Not circumscribed, but from the greater love
   Thou bearest to the first effects on high,[2]
Praised be Thy Name and Thine Omnipotence
   By every creature, as befitting is
   To render thanks to Thy sweet Effluence.
Come unto us the peace of Thy dominion,
   For unto it we cannot of ourselves,
   If it come not, with all our intellect.
Even as Thine own Angels of their will
   Make sacrifice to Thee, Hosanna singing,
   So may all men make sacrifice of theirs.

---

[1] You think to advance by means of pride, whereas in truth you recede.
[2] Not as being confined to place, but as bearing greater love to those first and highest creatures who dwell there.

Give unto us this day our daily manna,
   Withouten which in this rough wilderness
   Backward goes he who toils most to advance.
And even as we the trespass we have suffered
   Pardon in one another, pardon Thou
   Benignly, and regard not our desert.
Our virtue, which is easily o'ercome,
   Put not to proof with the old Adversary,
   But Thou from him who spurs it so, deliver.
This last petition verily, dear Lord,
   Not for ourselves is made, who need it not,
   But for their sake who have remained behind us.'

                  X. 112-139.   XI. 1-24.

The Souls in Purgatory need not to deprecate temptation, because so confirmed in grace as to be incapable of sin.

Thus for themselves and us good furtherance
   Those Shades imploring, went beneath a weight
   Like unto that of which we sometimes dream,
Unequally in anguish round and round
   And weary all, upon that foremost cornice,
   Purging away the smoke-stains of the world.
If there good words are always said for us,
   What may not here be said and done for them,
   By those who have a good root to their will?
Well may we help them wash away the marks
   That hence they carried, so that clean and light
   They may ascend unto the starry wheels!

                       XI. 25-36.

Virgil's customary inquiry for a practicable slope was courteously answered, though the posture of the Shades made it impossible to feel sure from whom the answer

came; but it contained an invitation to accompany the
toiling procession, and the inviter made himself known as
the Tuscan Omberto Aldobrandeschi, so hated as to have
been actually murdered by the Sienese for his family sin,
pride of birth :—now he humbly questioned whether his
living guest had ever heard his father Guglielmo's name.

> Listening I downward bent my countenance ;
>   And one of them, not this one who was speaking,
>   Twisted himself beneath the weight that cramps him,
> And looked at me, and knew me, and called out,
>   Keeping his eyes laboriously fixed
>   On me, who all bowed down was going with them.
> ' O,' asked I him, 'art thou not Oderisi,
>   Agobbio's honour, and honour of that art
>   Which is in Paris called illuminating ?'
> ' Brother,' said he, ' more laughing are the leaves
>   Touched by the brush of Franco Bolognese ;
>   All his the honour now, and mine in part.
> In sooth I had not been so courteous
>   While I was living, for the great desire
>   Of excellence, on which my heart was bent.
> Here of such pride is paid the forfeiture ;
>   And yet I should not be here, were it not
>   That, having power to sin, I turned to God.
> O thou vain glory of the human powers,
>   How little green upon thy summit lingers,
>   If 't be not followed by an age of grossness ! [1]
> In painting Cimabue thought that he
>   Should hold the field, now Giotto has the cry,
>   So that the other's fame is growing dim.

---

[1] How shortlived art thou, except an age of ignorance immediately
succeed ; for otherwise the next generation surpasses and effaces thee.

So has one Guido from the other taken[1]
    The glory of our tongue, and he perchance
    Is born, who from the nest shall chase them both.
Naught is this mundane rumour but a breath
    Of wind, that comes now this way and now that,
    And changes name, because it changes side.
What fame shalt thou have more, if old peel off
    From thee thy flesh, than if thou hadst been dead
    Before thou left the *pappo* and the *dindi*,[2]
Ere pass a thousand years ? which is a shorter
    Space to the eterne, than twinkling of an eye
    Unto the circle that in heaven wheels slowest.

                                        XI. 73-108.

The sin of Oderisi had been pride of intellect; that of
the Shade next before him—Provenzan Salvani—pride of
dominion; he had been Podestà of Siena, and unpopular
as such. His death in the battle of Colle having taken
place no earlier than A.D. 1269, Dante, surprised to find
him already beyond the Gate of S. Peter, inquired how his
due period of detention in Ante-Purgatory had been
shortened; and learned that in his lifetime he had merited
this grace by a most painful act of voluntary humiliation.
A friend of his was a war-prisoner of Charles of Anjou, who
would take no less life-ransom than a sum of ten thousand
golden florins: and Provenzano, then at the height of his
glory, had in the garb of a beggar seated himself on a mat
in a public square of Siena, and had successfully begged of
the passers-by aid for his friend.

---

[1] Probably Guido Cavalcanti (see p. 76) from Guido Guinicelli (see
p. 177).

[2] Baby language.

Abreast, like oxen going in a yoke,
  I with that heavy-laden Soul went on,
  As long as the sweet pedagogue permitted ;
But when he said, ' Leave him, and onward pass,
  For here 'tis good that with the sail and oars,
  As much as may be, each push on his barque ; '
Upright, as walking wills it, I redressed
  My person, notwithstanding that my thoughts
  Remained within me downcast and abashed.
I had moved on, and followed willingly
  The footsteps of my Master, and we both
  Already showed how light of foot we were,
When unto me he said : ' Cast down thine eyes ;
  'Twere well for thee, to alleviate the way,
  To look upon the bed beneath thy feet.'
As, that some memory may exist of them,
  Above the buried dead their tombs in earth
  Bear sculptured on them what they were before ;
Whence often there we weep for them afresh,
  From pricking of remembrance, which alone
  To the compassionate doth set its spur ;
So saw I there, but of a better semblance
  In point of artifice, with figures covered
  Whate'er as pathway from the mount projects.
I saw that one who was created noble
  More than all other creatures, down from heaven
  Flaming with lightnings fall upon one side.
I saw Briareus smitten by the dart
  Celestial, lying on the other side,
  Heavy upon the earth by mortal frost.
I saw Thymbræus,[1] Pallas saw, and Mars,
  Still clad in armour round about their father,

---

[1] Apollo.

Gaze at the scattered members of the giants.
I saw, at foot of his great labour, Nimrod,
  As if bewildered, looking at the people
  Who had been proud with him in Sennaar.
O Niobe ! with what afflicted eyes
  Thee I beheld upon the pathway traced,
  Between thy seven and seven children slain !
O Saul ! how fallen upon thy proper sword
  Didst thou appear there lifeless in Gilboa,
  That felt thereafter neither rain nor dew !
O mad Arachne ! so I thee beheld
  E'en then half spider, sad upon the shreds
  Of fabric wrought in evil hour for thee !
O Rehoboam ! no more seems to threaten
  Thine image there ; but full of consternation
  A chariot bears it off, when none pursues !
Displayed moreo'er the adamantine pavement
  How unto his own mother made Alcmæon [1]
  Costly appear the luckless ornament ;
Displayed how his own sons did throw themselves
  Upon Sennacherib within the temple,
  And how, he being dead, they left him there ;
Displayed the ruin and the cruel carnage
  That Tomyris wrought, when she to Cyrus said,
  'Blood didst thou thirst for, and with blood I glut thee !'
Displayed how routed fled the Assyrians
  After that Holofernes had been slain,
  And likewise the remainder of that slaughter.

---

[1] 'Amphiaraüs the soothsayer, foreseeing his own death if he went
to the Theban war, concealed himself to avoid going. His wife Eriphyle, bribed by a " golden necklace set with diamonds," betrayed to
her brother Adrastus his hiding-place ; and Amphiaraüs, departing,
charged his son Alcmæon to kill Eriphyle as soon as he heard of his
death.'

I saw there Troy in ashes and in caverns ;
  O Ilion ! thee, how abject and debased,
  Displayed the image that is there discerned !
Who e'er of pencil master was or stile,
  That could portray the shades and traits which there
  Would cause each subtile genius to admire ?
Dead seemed the dead, the living seemed alive ;
  Better than I saw not who saw the truth,
  All that I trod upon while bowed I went.
Now wax ye proud, and on with looks uplifted,
  Ye sons of Eve, and bow not down your faces
  So that ye may behold your evil ways !

XII. 1-72.

The way thus beguiled brought Dante all unconscious to the noontide hour, and to the point where the liberating Angel awaited him.

  .Towards us came the being beautiful
    Vested in white, and in his countenance
    Such as appears the tremulous morning star.

XII. 88-90.

At the foot of the steep narrow staircase one stroke of the Angel's wings effaced from Dante's brow a P; and the blessing was chanted from the Terrace he was leaving behind.

  Ah me ! how different are these entrances
    From the Infernal ! for with anthems here
    One enters, and below with wild laments.
  We now were mounting up the sacred stairs,
    And it appeared to me by far more easy
    Than on the plain it had appeared before.
  Whence I : ' My Master, say, what heavy thing
    Has been uplifted from me, so that hardly

Aught of fatigue is felt by me in walking ? '
He answered : ' When the P's which have remained
    Still on thy face almost obliterate
    Shall wholly, as the first is, be erased,
Thy feet will be so vanquished by good will,
    That not alone they shall not feel fatigue,
    But urging up will be to them delight.'

                      XII. 112-126.

The cancelling of this first P so greatly deadened all the rest, because Pride lies at the root of all other sins ; without it they would have little virulence, nay often no existence.   And even were this not so, a sinner free from Pride would place no bar in the way of correction.

The Second Terrace reached, in default of any other guide. Virgil besought direction of the Sun, the type of Reason ; then as always in Purgatory turned to the right. A mile's walk brought the Travellers to the point where aërial voices in rapid succession were proclaiming examples of Brotherly Love, the first being the Blessed Virgin's words, ' They have no wine ; ' and directly afterwards their keen gaze detected the penitents for Envy, whose garment rendered it somewhat difficult to distinguish them from the wall.   Great was Dante's compassion at the sight of their pain and blindness, and delicacy of feeling made him anxious to give testimony of his presence by speech. Leave duly obtained, he conversed awhile with Sapia, a lady of Siena, who being banished thence had lived at Colle, and when past her thirty-fifth year had through envy first prayed for and then in most irreverent words rejoiced over the defeat there inflicted by the Florentines on her fellow-citizens under Provenzan Salvani.   She concluded :

' Peace I desired with God at the extreme
   Of my existence, and as yet would not
   My debt have been by penitence discharged,
Had it not been that in remembrance held me
   Pier Pettignano [1] in his holy prayers,
   Who out of charity was grieved for me.
But who art thou, that into our conditions
   Questioning goest, and hast thine eyes unbound
   As I believe, and breathing dost discourse ? '
' Mine eyes,' I said, ' will yet be here ta'en from me,
   But for short space ; for small is the offence
   Committed by their being turned with envy.
Far greater is the fear, wherein suspended
   My soul is, of the torment underneath,
   For even now the load down there weighs on me.'
And she to me : ' Who led thee, then, among us
   Up here, if to return below thou thinkest ? '
   And I : ' He who is with me, and speaks not ;
And living am I ; therefore ask of me,
   Spirit elect, if thou wouldst have me move
   O'er yonder yet my mortal feet for thee.'
' O, this is such a novel thing to hear,'
   She answered, ' that great sign it is God loves thee ;
   Therefore with prayer of thine sometimes assist me.
And I implore, by what thou most desirest,
   If e'er thou treadest the soil of Tuscany,
   Well with my kindred reinstate my fame.'

                                        XIII. 124-150.

Two other Shades, Guido del Duca and Rinieri da
Calboli, then took up the discourse, like Sapia gladly
acknowledging the special grace bestowed on Dante ; and
farther exercising charity by grief for the vices of their native

---

[1] A hermit of Siena.

Romagna and of the Vale of Arno, till at last Guido, desiring leisure to weep over the pictures he himself had drawn,
dismissed his listener.

> We were aware that those beloved Souls
>> Heard us depart ; therefore, by keeping silent,
>> They made us of our pathway confident.
>>> XIV. 127-129.

The thunder-voices that condemn the Envious soon made
themselves heard, Virgil thus commenting upon them :

> ' That was the hard curb
>> That ought to hold a man within his bounds ;
> But you take in the bait so that the hook
>> Of the old Adversary draws you to him,
>> And hence availeth little curb or call.
> The heavens are calling you, and wheel around you,
>> Displaying to you their eternal beauties,
>> And still your eye is looking on the ground ;
> Whence He, who all discerns, chastises you.'
>>> XIV. 143-151.

Then a dazzling brightness told of the Angel's presence ;
the second P was effaced, the Blessing sung, the staircase
benignly pointed out and pronounced easier than had yet
been the case : and the third ascent began, made profitable
by a dialogue on Envy. Guido in his mournful discourse
had thus apostrophized mankind :

> O human race ! why dost thou set thy heart
> Where interdict of partnership must be ?
>> XIV. 86, 87.

And the disciple, doubting of his meaning, now thus
questioned the Master :

' What did the Spirit of Romagna mean,
  Mentioning interdict and partnership ? '
Whence he to me : ' Of his own greatest failing
  He knows the harm ; and therefore wonder not
  If he reprove us, that we less may rue it.
Because are thither pointed your desires
  Where by companionship each share is lessened,
  Envy doth ply the bellows to your sighs.
But if the love of the supernal sphere
  Should upwardly direct your aspiration,
  There would not be that fear within your breast ;
For there, as much the more as one says *Our*,
  So much the more of good each one possesses,
  And more of charity in that cloister burns.'
' I am more hungering to be satisfied,'
  I said, ' than if I had before been silent,
  And more of doubt within my mind I gather.
How can it be, that boon distributed
  The more possessors can more wealthy make
  Therein, than if by few it be possessed ? '
And he to me : [1] ' Because thou fixest still
  Thy mind entirely upon earthly things,
  Thou pluckest darkness from the very light.
That Goodness Infinite and Ineffable
  Which is above there, runneth unto love,
  As to a lucid body comes the sunbeam.
So much It gives Itself as It finds ardour,
  So that as far as charity extends,
  O'er it increases the eternal Valour.
And the more people thitherward aspire,
  More are there to love well, and more they love there,
  And, as a mirror, one reflects the other.[1]

---

[1] Because thy thought still recurs to earthly goods alone, thou de-
rivest darkness from the light of my instruction. But God, the Infinite

And if my reasoning appease thee not,
   Thou shalt see Beatrice ; and she will fully
   Take from thee this and every other longing.
Endeavour, then, that soon may be extinct,
   As are the two already, the five wounds
   That close themselves again by being painful.'
Even as I wished to say, ' Thou dost appease me,'
   I saw that I had reached another circle,
   So that my eager eyes made me keep silence.
There it appeared to me that in a vision
   Ecstatic on a sudden I was rapt,
   And in a temple many persons saw ;
And at the door a woman, with the sweet
   Behaviour of a mother, saying : ' Son,
   Why in this manner hast Thou dealt with us ?
Lo, sorrowing, Thy father and myself
   Were seeking for Thee ' ;—and as here she ceased,
   That which appeared at first had disappeared.

XV. 44-93.

Other examples of Meekness followed, presented like this in inward vision, such being the mode of Terrace III. ; and Virgil's comment was,

What thou hast seen was that thou mayst not fail
   To ope thy heart unto the waters of peace,
   Which from the eternal fountain are diffused.

XV. 130-132.

and Ineffable Good dwelling on high, is attracted by the love of the Blessed, even as a ray by a light-reflecting body.   He gives Himself the more, the more love He finds ; so that the farther charity extends, the wider the Eternal Beatific Virtue spreads above it.   And the more people are intent on that Supreme Vision, the more is present of that same Beatific Virtue, and the more love is there ; and as light is reflected from mirror to mirror, so love from blessed Soul to Soul

It is noticeable that in this and in the Seventh Terrace,
but not in any other, Dante shared the torment of the penitents; in these alone is it of a nature to affect every one
locally present within its range.—He proceeds:

> We passed along, athwart the twilight peering
>   Forward as far as ever eye could stretch
>   Against the sunbeams serotine and lucent;
> And lo! by slow degrees a smoke approached
>   In our direction, sombre as the night,
>   Nor was there place to hide one's-self therefrom.
> This of our eyes and the pure air bereft us.
>
> Darkness of Hell, and of a night deprived
>   Of every planet under a poor sky,
>   As much as may be tenebrous with cloud,
> Ne'er made unto my sight so thick a veil,
>   As did that smoke which there enveloped us,
>   Nor to the feeling of so rough a texture;
> For not an eye it suffered to stay open;
>   Whereat mine escort, faithful and sagacious,
>   Drew near to me and offered me his shoulder.
> E'en as a blind man goes behind his guide,
>   Lest he should wander, or should strike against
>   Aught that may harm or peradventure kill him,
> So went I through the bitter and foul air,
>   Listening unto my Leader, who said only,
>   'Look that from me thou be not separated.'
>   XV. 139-145. XVI. 1-15.

. This blind leaning on the Guide is a parable of the only
safe rule during a temptation to Anger—to hold fast to
known, acknowledged, established principles, seen to be
right before the temptation began: Anger having the property of annulling for the time all true perception.

Voices I heard, and every one appeared
   To supplicate for peace and misericord
   The Lamb of God Who takes away our sins.
Still '*Agnus Dei*' their exordium was ;
   One word there was in all, and metre one,
   So that all harmony appeared among them.
'Master,' I said, 'are Spirits those I hear ?'
   And he to me : 'Thou apprehendest truly,
   And they the knot of anger go unloosing.'

XVI. 16-24.

A voice here commenced a conversation with Dante, the speaker, who named himself Marco Lombardo, reflecting on the utter corruption of the world : and as his interlocutor, fully assenting to this as a fact, requested to be certified whether its cause lay in the influences of the Heavens or in the wills of men—

A sigh profound, that grief forced into Ai !
   He first sent forth, and then began he : 'Brother,
   The world is blind, and sooth thou comest from it !
Ye who are living every cause refer
   Still upward to the Heavens, as if all things
   They of necessity moved with themselves.
If this were so, in you would be destroyed
   Free will, nor any justice would there be
   In having joy for good, or grief for evil.
The Heavens your movements do initiate,
   I say not all ; but granting that I say it,
   Light has been given you for good and evil,
And free volition ; which, if some fatigue
   In the first battles with the Heavens it suffers,
   Afterwards conquers all, if well 'tis nurtured.
To greater force and to a better nature,
   Though free, ye subject are, and that creates

The mind in you the Heavens have not in charge.[1]
Hence, if the present world doth go astray,
   In you the cause is, be it sought in you ;
   And I therein will now be thy true spy.
Forth from the hand of Him, Who fondles it
   Before it is, like to a little girl
   Weeping and laughing in her childish sport,
Issues the simple soul, that nothing knows,
   Save that, proceeding from a joyous Maker,
   Gladly it turns to that which gives it pleasure.
Of trivial good at first it tastes the savour ;
   Is cheated by it, and runs after it,
   If guide or rein turn not aside its love.
Hence it behoved laws for a rein to place,
   Behoved a king[2] to have, who at the least
   Of the true city should discern the tower.
The laws exist, but who sets hand to them ?
   No one ; because the shepherd who precedes
   Can ruminate, but cleaveth not the hoof ;[3]
Wherefore the people that perceives its guide
   Strike only at the good for which it hankers,
   Feeds upon that, and farther seeketh not.
Clearly canst thou perceive that evil guidance
   The cause is that has made the world depraved,
   And not that nature is corrupt in you.'

                              XVI. 64-105.

---

[1] See p. 14. The preceding triplet may be thus paraphrased : To greater strength than that of the Heavens, even to God's Omnipotence, and to a better nature, even to God's Goodness, ye retaining free-will are subject ; and That it is Which creates in you the mind which the Heavens have not in their power.

[2] The Emperor.

[3] Dante seems partly to apply the prohibition to eat beasts that cleave not the hoof, in condemnation of the worldliness practically tainting the Church of his day.

Soon after this the discourse was broken off by the
speakers reaching the skirts of the smoke-fog, beyond
which Marco might not go ; but Dante passed into the
fading sun-light.   The trance wherein he now beheld instances of Anger was suddenly dispelled by the radiance
of the Angel, the preface to confirmed cleanness, freedom
and blessedness.   Lightened of the third P, under the rising
stars he had just time to complete his fourth ascent ere
darkness suspended his power to move upwards, and afforded Virgil opportunity to lay down that theory of the seven
Capital Sins which was in its essential points set forth in
the preceding chapter;[1] and which follows here in full.

> ' Neither Creator nor a creature ever,
>   Son,' he began, ' was destitute of love
>   Natural or spiritual ; and thou knowest it.
> The natural was ever without error ;[2]
>   But err the other may by evil object,
>   Or by too much, or by too little vigour.
> While in the first it well directed is,
>   And in the second moderates itself,
>   It cannot be the cause of sinful pleasure ;
> But when to ill it turns, and, with more care
>   Or lesser than it ought, runs after good,
>   'Gainst the Creator works His own creation.
> Hence thou mayst comprehend that love must be
>   The seed within yourselves of every virtue,
>   And every act that merits punishment.
> Now inasmuch as never from the welfare
>   Of its own subject [3] can love turn its sight,

---

[1] See pp. 113, 114.

[2] The ' natural love ' is the appetite for things needful for the preservation and well-being of the body.

[3] The ' subject of love ' is the person feeling it.

From their own hatred all things are secure ;
And since we cannot think of any being
  Standing alone, nor from the First divided,
  Of hating Him is all desire cut off.
Hence if, discriminating, I judge well,
  The evil that one loves is of one's neighbour,
  And this is born in three modes in your clay.
There are, who, by abasement of their neighbour,
  Hope to excel, and therefore only long
  That from his greatness he may be cast down ;
There are, who power, grace, honour, and renown
  Fear they may lose because another rises,
  Thence are so sad that the reverse they love ;
And there are those whom injury seems to chafe,
  So that it makes them greedy for revenge,
  And such must needs shape out another's harm.
This threefold love is wept for down below ;
  Now of the other will I have thee hear,
  That runneth after good with measure faulty.
Each one confusedly a good conceives
  Wherein the mind may rest, and longeth for it ;
  Therefore to overtake it each one strives.
If languid love to look on this attract you,
  Or in attaining unto it, this cornice,
  After just penitence, torments you for it.
There 's other good that does not make man happy ;
  'Tis not felicity, 'tis not the good
  Essence, of every good the fruit and root.
The love that yields itself too much to this
  Above us is lamented in three circles ;
  But how tripartite it may be described,
I say not, that thou seek it for thyself.'

XVII. 91-139.

Two more dissertations—on the nature of Love, and on

Free Will—had brought midnight near, when the drowsiness just creeping over Dante was forcibly dispelled by a rush of Shades coursing along as if ridden by good-will and just love. ' Mary ran with haste to the mountain,' was the watch-shout of Diligence in the van :—' Quick, quick, let no time be lost for want of love, let energy in well-doing freshen grace,' was the multitudinous spur-cry of the mass : —' Come on with us, and you will find the aperture—our craving for motion is such that we cannot stop—pardon if our righteousness seem discourtesy,' was the hurried direction to the Pilgrims :—then fewest words announced the speaker Abbot of San Zeno in Verona, assigned his date, reprobated the sins of the actual intruded Abbot and of the intruder—and carried him quite out of hearing :—while already the Sloth of the Israelites who died in the wilderness was being vituperated in the rear.

Dante slept at length ; and in the hour preceding the sunrise of Easter Tuesday dreamed once more—dreamed of a woman stammering, squinting, lame of foot, maimed of hands, and ashy pale. He gazed on her, and lo under his gaze her form straightened, her face flushed, her tongue loosened to the Siren's song. But a holy Lady—probably Lucia or Illuminating Grace—arose swift to confound her, calling on Virgil ; and anon the Siren was laid open, the spell broken, the dreamer awake. Then after the fourth benediction and erasure, the fifth ascent began ; and the disciple, yet brooding over the vision which had embodied to his senses the Worldly and Fleshly sins whereof he was about to witness the expiation, was thus admonished by the Master :

> 'Didst thou behold,' he said, 'that old enchantress,
>   Who sole above us henceforth is lamented?
>   Didst thou behold how man is freed from her?
> Suffice it thee, and smite earth with thy heels,
>   Thine eyes lift upward to the lure, that whirls [1]
>   The Eternal King with revolutions vast.'
>
> XIX. 58-63.

Soon both Travellers stood on the Fifth Terrace, amid the sore weeping and wailing of the prostrate Avaricious. The wonted request for direction was answered courteously, but as if to another Shade; and Dante, with Virgil's permission pausing beside the answerer—Pope Adrian V., who had died A.D. 1276, after forty days' reign—thus addressed him:

> 'O Spirit, in whom weeping ripens
>   That without which to God we cannot turn,
>   Suspend awhile for me thy greater care.
> Who wast thou, and why are your backs turned upwards,
>   Tell me, and if thou wouldst that I procure thee
>   Anything there whence living I departed.'
> And he to me: 'Wherefore our backs the Heaven
>   Turns to itself, know shalt thou; but beforehand
>   *Scias quod ego fui successor Petri.*
> Between Siestri and Chiaveri descends
>   A river beautiful, and of its name [2]
>   The title of my blood its summit makes.
> A month and little more essayed I how
>   Weighs the great cloak on him from mire who keeps it;
>   For all the other burdens seem a feather.

---

[1] Lift up thine eyes to the Heavens, which are God's lure to draw them upwards.

[2] The river Lavagna, which gave the title of Counts of Lavagna to the Fieschi family, whence sprang Pope Adrian V.

Tardy, ah woe is me ! was my conversion ;
　　But when the Roman Shepherd I was made,
　　Then I discovered life to be a lie.
I saw that there the heart was not at rest,
　　Nor farther in that life could one ascend ;
　　Whereby the love of this was kindled in me.
Until that time a wretched soul and parted
　　From God was I, and wholly avaricious ;
　　Now, as thou seest, I here am punished for it.
What avarice does is here made manifest
　　In the purgation of these souls converted,
　　And no more bitter pain the Mountain has.
Even as our eye did not uplift itself
　　Aloft, being fastened upon earthly things,
　　So justice here has merged it in the earth.
As avarice had extinguished our affection
　　For every good, whereby was action lost,
　　So justice here doth hold us in restraint,
Bound and imprisoned by the feet and hands ;
　　And so long as it pleases the just Lord
　　Shall we remain immovable and prostrate.'
I on my knees had fallen, and wished to speak ;
　　But even as I began, and he was 'ware,
　　Only by listening, of my reverence,
'What cause,' he said, 'has downward bent thee thus ?'
　　And I to him : 'For your own dignity,
　　Standing, my conscience stung me with remorse.'
'Straighten thy legs, and upward raise thee, brother,'
　　He answered : 'Err not, fellow-servant am I
　　With thee and with the others to one Power.
If e'er that holy, evangelic sound,
　　Which sayeth *neque nubent*, thou hast heard,[1]

---

[1] He means that 'they neither marry,' etc., indicates the abrogation in the next world of *all* earthly relations.

Well canst thou see why in this wise I speak.
Now go ; no longer will I have thee linger,
    Because thy stay doth incommode my weeping,
    With which I ripen that which thou hast said.
On earth I have a grandchild named Alagia,
    Good in herself, unless indeed our house
    Malevolent may make her by example,
And she alone remains to me on earth.'

Ill strives the will against a better will ;
    Therefore, to pleasure him, against my pleasure
    I drew the sponge not saturate from the water.
Onward I moved, and onward moved my Leader,
    Through vacant places, skirting still the rock,
    As on a wall close to the battlements ;
For they that through their eyes pour drop by drop
    The malady which all the world pervades,
    On the other side too near the verge approach.

                    XIX. 91-145. XX. 1-9.

An invocation of Blessed Mary reduced to the Stable of
Bethlehem, followed by the citation of other examples of
Poverty and Liberality, caught Dante's ear as he slowly
made his way along ; and the proclaimer, having gratified
his curiosity by naming himself Hugh Capet, forefather of
the royal line of France, and confirmed his judgment by
heaviest condemnation of the later princes of that line,
concluded by informing him of one point whereof he would
have no other testimony—that the abhorrent recalling of
instances of Avarice is in this Circuit the occupation of the
night.

    From him already we departed were,
        And made endeavour to o'ercome the road
        As much as was permitted to our power,

When I perceived, like something that is falling,
　　The mountain tremble, whence a chill seized on me,
　　As seizes him who to his death is going.
Certes so violently shook not Delos,
　　Before Latona made her nest therein
　　To give birth to the two eyes of the heaven.
Then upon all sides there began a cry,
　　Such that the Master drew himself towards me,
　　Saying, 'Fear not, while I am guiding thee.'
'*Gloria in excelsis Deo,*' all
　　Were saying, from what near I comprehended,
　　Where it was possible to hear the cry.
We paused immovable and in suspense,
　　Even as the shepherds who first heard that song,
　　Until the trembling ceased, and it was finished.
Then we resumed again our holy path,
　　Watching the Shades that lay upon the ground
　　Already turned to their accustomed plaint.
No ignorance ever with so great a strife
　　Had rendered me importunate to know,
　　If erreth not in this my memory,
As meditating then I seemed to have ;
　　Nor out of haste to question did I dare,
　　Nor of myself I there could ought perceive ;
So I went onward timorous and thoughtful.

The natural thirst, that ne'er is satisfied
　　Excepting with the water for whose grace
　　The woman of Samaria besought,
Put me in travail, and haste goaded me
　　Along the encumbered path behind my Leader,
　　And I was pitying that righteous vengeance ;
And lo ! in the same manner as Luke writeth
　　That Christ appeared to two upon the way

From the sepulchral cave already risen,
A Shade appeared to us, and came behind us,
  Down gazing on the prostrate multitude,
  Nor were we ware of it until it spake,
Saying, ' My brothers, may God give you peace ! '
  We turned us suddenly, and Virgilius rendered
  To him the countersign thereto conforming.
Thereon began he : ' In the blessed council,
  Thee may the court veracious place in peace,
  That me doth banish in eternal exile ! '
' How,' said he, and the while we went with speed,
  ' If ye are Shades whom God deigns not on high,
  Who up His stairs so far has guided you ? '
And said my Teacher : ' If thou note the marks
  Which this one bears, and which the Angel traces,
  Well shalt thou see he with the good must reign.'

XX. 124-151. XXI. 1-24.

These words, seeming to speak of the P's as a token
familiar to the inquirer, constitute, so far as I know, the
only evidence that the penitent Shades may, in common
with Dante, receive these marks.   Virgil went on :

' But because she who spinneth day and night
  For him had not yet drawn the distaff off,
  Which Clotho lays for each one and compacts,
His soul, which is thy sister and my own,
  In coming upwards could not come alone,
  By reason that it sees not in our fashion.
Whence I was drawn from out the ample throat
  Of Hell to be his guide, and I shall guide him
  As far on as my school has power to lead.
But tell us, if thou knowest, why such a shudder
  Erewhile the mountain gave, and why together
  All seemed to cry, as far as its moist feet ? '

In asking he so hit the very eye
  Of my desire, that merely with the hope
  My thirst became the less unsatisfied.
' Naught is there,' he began, ' that without order
  May the religion of the mountain feel,
  Nor aught that may be foreign to its custom.
Free is it here from every permutation ;
  What from itself heaven in itself receiveth
  Can be of this the cause, and naught beside ;
Because that neither rain, nor hail, nor snow,
  Nor dew, nor hoar-frost any higher falls
  Than the short, little stairway of three steps.
Dense clouds do not appear, nor rarefied,
  Nor coruscation, nor the daughter [1] of Thaumas,
  That often upon earth her region shifts ;
No arid vapour any farther rises
  Than to the top of the three steps I spake of,
  Whereon the Vicar of Peter has his feet.
Lower down perchance it trembles less or more,
  But, for the wind that in the earth is hidden
  I know not how, up here it never trembled.
It trembles here, whenever any Soul
  Feels itself pure, so that it soars, or moves
  To mount aloft, and such a cry attends it.
Of purity the will alone gives proof,
  Which, being wholly free to change its convent,
  Takes by surprise the Soul, and helps it fly.
First it wills well ; but the desire permits not,
  Which Divine Justice with the self-same will
  There was to sin, upon the torment sets.
And I, who have been lying in this pain
  Five hundred years and more, but just now felt

---

[1] Iris : the rainbow.

A free volition for a better seat.
Therefore thou heardst the earthquake, and the pious
 Spirits along the mountain rendering praise
 Unto the Lord, that soon He speed them upwards.'
So said he to him ; and since we enjoy
 As much in drinking as the thirst is great,
 I could not say how much it did me good.
And the wise Leader : ' Now I see the net
 That snares you here, and how ye are set free,
 Why the earth quakes, and wherefore ye rejoice.
Now who thou wast be pleased that I may know ;
 And why so many centuries thou hast here
 Been lying, let me gather from thy words.'

         XXI. 25-81.

The released Shade replied that he was the Latin poet
Papinius Statius, author of the Sylvæ, the Thebaid and the
Achilleid, the latter work being, however, cut short by his
premature death about A.D. 96.   He continued :

' The seeds unto my ardour were the sparks
 Of that celestial flame which heated me,
 Whereby more than a thousand have been fired ;
Of the Æneid speak I, which to me
 A mother was, and was my nurse in song ;
 Without this weighed I not a drachma's weight.
And to have lived upon the earth what time
 Virgilius lived, I would accept one sun
 More than I must ere issuing from my ban.'
These words towards me made Virgilius turn
 With looks that in their silence said, ' Be silent ! '
 But yet the power that wills cannot do all things ;
For tears and laughter are such pursuivants
 Unto the passion from which each springs forth,
 In the most truthful least the will they follow.

I only smiled, as one who gives the wink ;
   Whereat the Shade was silent, and it gazed
   Into mine eyes, where most expression dwells ;
And, 'As thou well mayst consummate a labour
   So great,' it said, 'why did thy face just now
   Display to me the lightning of a smile ?'
Now am I caught on this side and on that ;
   One keeps me silent, one to speak conjures me,
   Wherefore I sigh, and I am understood.
'Speak,' said my Master, 'and be not afraid
   Of speaking, but speak out, and say to him
   What he demands with such solicitude.'
Whence I : 'Thou peradventure marvellest,
   O antique Spirit, at the smile I gave ;
   But I will have more wonder seize upon thee.
This one, who guides on high these eyes of mine,
   Is that Virgilius, from whom thou didst learn
   To sing aloud of men and of the Gods.
If other cause thou to my smile imputedst,
   Abandon it as false, and trust it was
   Those words which thou hast spoken concerning him.
Already he was stooping to embrace
   My Teacher's feet ; but he said to him : 'Brother,
   Do not ; for Shade thou art, and Shade beholdest.'
And he uprising : 'Now canst thou the sum
   Of love which warms me to thee comprehend,
   When this our vanity I disremember,
Treating a shadow as substantial thing.'

Already was the Angel left behind us,
   The Angel who to the sixth round had turned us,
   Having erased one mark from off my face ;
And those who have in justice their desire
   Had said to us, '*Beati,*' in their voices,
   With, '*sitio,*' and without more ended it.
               XXI. 94-136.   XXII. 1-6.

Note here how expressly Dante appropriates to himself the cancelling of the P.   If the Shades receive these prints at all, we must I think conclude the erasure to be in their case effected by their purgative sufferings.

Going up the sixth staircase, Statius at Virgil's request further detailed his own history.   He had endured these five ages of penance not for the love of money which constitutes Avarice, but for the love of money's worth which tempts to Prodigality; and which would have consigned him to the Fourth Circle of Hell had not Virgil's words, 'To what dost not thou, O accursed hunger of gold, drive the appetite of mortals?' enlightened and corrected him. And to Virgil he owed yet a third benefit, a second and greater enlightenment.   He read in the Fourth Eclogue the celebrated quotation of the Sibylline prophecy, 'The last era of Cumæan song is now arrived; the great series of ages begins anew; now the Virgin returns, returns the Saturnian reign; now a new Progeny is sent down from the high Heaven.' [1]   And reading he perceived the agreement of the words with the preached Gospel, sought out its preachers, believed and was baptized; compassionated and helped his persecuted brethren, yet lacked courage openly to profess his and their faith, and for this cowardly Sloth had to race round the Fourth Terrace above four hundred years; the remaining three centuries since his death having been passed, as we must conclude, lower down.—His narrative ended, he heard from his countryman news of former friends and other inhabitants of Limbo, interesting to him on account of their works, or as the heroines of his own poems.   At last Terrace VI. was reached; and the con-

[1] Longfellow's translation.

versation of the Latin Bards was teaching their art to their
Italian follower—

> But soon their sweet discourses interrupted
>   A tree which midway in the road we found,
>   With apples sweet and grateful to the smell.
> And even as a fir-tree tapers upward
>   From bough to bough, so downwardly did that ;
>   I think in order that no one might climb it.
> On that side where our pathway was enclosed
>   Fell from the lofty rock a limpid water,
>   And spread itself abroad upon the leaves.
> The Poets twain unto the tree drew near,
>   And from among the foliage a voice
>   Cried : ' Of this food ye shall have scarcity.'
> Then said : ' More thoughtful Mary was of making
>   The marriage feast complete and honourable,
>   Than of her mouth which now for you responds ;
> And for their drink the ancient Roman women
>   With water were content : and Daniel
>   Disparaged food, and understanding won.
> The primal age was beautiful as gold ;
>   Acorns it made with hunger savourous,
>   And nectar every rivulet with thirst.
> Honey and locusts were the aliments
>   That fed the Baptist in the wilderness ;
>   Whence he is glorious, and so magnified
> As by the Evangel is revealed to you.'
>
> The while among the verdant leaves mine eyes
>   I riveted, as he is wont to do
>   Who wastes his life pursuing little birds,
> My more than Father said unto me : ' Son,
>   Come now ; because the time that is ordained us
>   More usefully should be apportioned out.'

I turned my face and no less soon my steps
   Unto the Sages, who were speaking so
   They made the going of no cost to me ;
And lo ! were heard a song and a lament,
   ' *Labia mea, Domine,*' in fashion
   Such that delight and dolence it brought forth.
' O my sweet Father, what is this I hear ? '
   Began I ; and he answered : ' Shades that go
   Perhaps the knot unloosing of their debt.'
In the same way that thoughtful pilgrims do,
   Who, unknown people on the road o'ertaking,
   Turn themselves round to them, and do not stop,
Even thus, behind us with a swifter motion
   Coming and passing onward, gazed upon us
   A crowd of Spirits silent and devout.
Each in his eyes was dark and cavernous,
   Pallid in face, and so emaciate
   That from the bones the skin did shape itself.

               XXII. 130-154. XXIII. 1-24.

These Shades were macerated out of all knowledge ; but one of them, Forese de' Donati, recognising in Dante a friend, a brother-in-law, and—as will presently appear by the Poet's own words to him—a companion in more or less of evil, was in turn recognised by his voice. He could not however obtain information on any one subject till he had satisfied Dante's strong desire to know the cause of his wasted condition.

   ' That face of thine which dead I once bewept,
      Gives me for weeping now no lesser grief,'
      I answered him, ' beholding it so changed !
   But tell me, for God's sake, what thus denudes you ?
      Make me not speak while I am marvelling,

For ill speaks he who's full of other longings.'
And he to me : ' From the eternal counsel
 Falls power into the water and the tree
 Behind us left, whereby I grow so thin.
All of this people who lamenting sing,
 For following beyond measure appetite
 In hunger and thirst are here re-sanctified.
Desire to eat and drink enkindles in us
 The scent that issues from the apple-tree,
 And from the spray that sprinkles o'er the verdure ;
And not a single time alone, this ground
 Encircling, is renewed our pain,—
 I say our pain, and ought to say our solace,—
For the same wish doth lead us to the tree
 Which led the Christ rejoicing to say *Eli*,
 When with His veins He liberated us.'
And I to him : ' Forese, from that day
 When for a better life thou changedst worlds,
 Up to this time five years have not rolled round.
If sooner were the power exhausted in thee
 Of sinning more, than thee the hour surprised
 Of that good sorrow which to God reweds us,
How hast thou come up hitherward already?
 I thought to find thee down there underneath,
 Where time for time doth restitution make.'
And he to me : ' Thus speedily has led me
 To drink of the sweet wormwood of these torments,
 My Nella with her overflowing tears ;
She with her prayers devout and with her sighs
 Has drawn me from the coast where one awaits,
 And from the other circles set me free.
So much more dear and pleasing is to God
 My little widow, whom so much I loved,
 As in good works she is the more alone ;

For the Barbagia of Sardinia[1]
  By far more modest in its women is
  Than the Barbagia I have left her in.
O brother sweet, what wilt thou have me say?
  A future time is in my sight already,
  To which this hour will not be very old,
When from the pulpit shall be interdicted
  To the unblushing womankind of Florence
  To go about displaying breast and paps.
What savages were e'er, what Saracens,
  Who stood in need, to make them covered go,
  Of spiritual or other discipline?
But if the shameless women were assured
  Of what swift Heaven prepares for them, already
  Wide open would they have their mouths to howl;
For if my foresight here deceive me not,
  They shall be sad ere he has bearded cheeks
  Who now is hushed to sleep with lullaby.
O brother, now no longer hide thee from me ;
  See that not only I, but all these people
  Are gazing there, where thou dost veil the sun.'
Whence I to him : ' If thou bring back to mind
  What thou with me hast been and I with thee,
  The present memory will be grievous still.
Out of that life he turned me back who goes
  In front of me, two days agone when round
  The sister of him yonder showed herself,'
And to the sun I pointed. ' Through the deep
  Night of the truly dead has this one led me,
  With this true flesh, that follows after him.
Thence his encouragements have led me up,
  Ascending and still circling round the mount

---

[1] A wild mountainous district, almost barbarous.

N

That you doth straighten, whom the world made crooked.
He says that he will bear me company,
  Till I shall be where Beatrice will be ;
  There it behoves me to remain without him.
This is Virgilius, who thus says to me,'
  And him I pointed at ; 'the other is
  That Shade for whom just now shook every slope
Your realm, that from itself discharges him.'

XXIII. 55-133.

Many Shades were then pointed out by name :—considering that this had been done in every preceding Circuit, one
is somewhat surprised at Forese's statement that it is allowed
here on account of their altered semblance.   At last the
second Tree was seen, and its warnings against Gluttony
heard.   About a mile further on, at two o'clock P.M., the
usual processes set free the Poets for the seventh ascent ;
and as they performed it, Statius explained the nature and
formation of the shade-body.

And now unto the last of all the circles
  Had we arrived and to the right hand turned,
  And were attentive to another care.
There the embankment shoots forth flames of fire,
  And upward doth the cornice breathe a blast
  That drives them back, and from itself sequesters.
Hence we must needs go on the open side,
  And one by one ; and I did fear the fire
  On this side, and on that the falling down.
My Leader said : 'Along this place one ought
  To keep upon the eyes a tightened rein,
  Seeing that one so easily might err.'
' *Summæ Deus clementiæ,*' in the bosom
  Of the great burning chanted then I heard,

Which made me no less eager to turn round ;
And Spirits saw I walking through the flame ;
   Wherefore I looked, to my own steps and their
   Apportioning my sight from time to time.
After the close which to that hymn is made,
   Aloud they shouted, ' *Virum non cognosco* ';[1]
   Then recommenced the hymn with voices low.

XXV. 109-129.

On this Terrace Dante talked with the poet Guido
Guinicelli of Bologna, a man of science, and one of the
earliest writers in pure Italian; and was by him asked to
say an intercessory Paternoster up to the point where it
ceases to be applicable to the impeccable. The Provençal
troubadour Arnault Daniel, being requested to tell his
name, made graceful reply in his native tongue ; and as
he wholly disappeared within the fire, the Pilgrims stood
opposite the eighth staircase.

[2]As when he vibrates forth his earliest rays,
   In regions where his Maker shed His blood,
   (The Ebro falling under lofty Libra,
And waters in the Ganges burnt with noon,)
   So stood the Sun :[2] hence was the day departing,
   When the glad Angel of God appeared to us.
Outside the flame he stood upon the verge,
   And chanted forth, '*Beati mundo corde*,'
   In voice by far more living than our own.
Then : ' No one farther goes, souls sanctified,

---

[1] The B. Virgin's words as an example of Chastity, 'I know not a
man.'

[2] ' When the Sun is rising at Jerusalem, it is setting on the Mountain
of Purgatory ; it is midnight in Spain, with Libra in the meridian, and
noon in India.'

> If first the fire bite not ; within it enter,
> And be not deaf unto the song beyond.'
>
> XXVII. 1-12.

We must conclude that nowhere round this whole Terrace is there any break in the flame-wreath ; wherefore
no penitent Shade but must needs pass through it, whether
tainted or not with the special sin chastised by sojourning
within it.   The reason may perhaps be that S. Paul apparently includes each and every soul that has built upon the
One Foundation 'wood, hay, stubble,' in the class saved
'so as by fire.'[1]   And Dante himself elsewhere uses 'the
fire,' 'the temporal fire,' as terms equivalent to 'Purgatory.'[2]

> When we were close beside him thus he said ;
>   Wherefore e'en such became I, when I heard him,
>   As he is who is put into the grave.
> Upon my claspèd hands I straightened me,
>   Scanning the fire and vividly recalling
>   The human bodies I had once seen burned.
>
> XXVII. 13-18.

Yes, and in that awful conflict he must have called up
with more agonizing intensity a more appalling vision—for
he was himself under sentence of death by fire should he
again be found in Florence.

> Towards me turned themselves my good Conductors,
>   And unto me Virgilius said : ' My son,
>   Here may indeed be torment, but not death.
> Remember thee, remember ! and if I
>   On Geryon have safely guided thee,

---

[1] 1 Cor. iii. 10-15.   [2] *Inf.* i. 119.   *Pur.* xxvii. 127.

What shall I do now I am nearer God?
Believe for certain, shouldst thou stand a full
    Millennium in the bosom of this flame,
    It could not make thee bald a single hair.
And if perchance thou think that I deceive thee,
    Draw near to it, and put it to the proof
    With thine own hands upon thy garment's hem.
Now lay aside, now lay aside all fear,
    Turn hitherward, and onward come securely ;'
    And I still motionless, and 'gainst my conscience !
Seeing me stand still motionless and stubborn,
    Somewhat disturbed he said : ' Now look thou, Son,
    'Twixt Beatrice and thee there is this wall.'
As at the name of Thisbe oped his lids
    The dying Pyramus, and gazed upon her,
    What time the mulberry became vermilion,
Even thus, my obduracy being softened,
    I turned to my wise Guide, hearing the name
    That in my memory evermore is welling.
Whereat he wagged his head, and said : ' How now ?
    Shall we stay on this side ?' then smiled as one
    Does at a child who's vanquished by an apple.
Then into the fire in front of me he entered,
    Beseeching Statius to come after me,
    Who a long way before divided us.
When I was in it, into molten glass
    I would have cast me to refresh myself,
    So without measure was the burning there !
And my sweet Father, to encourage me,
    Discoursing still of Beatrice went on,
    Saying : ' Her eyes I seem to see already !'
A voice, that on the other side was singing,
    Directed us, and we, attent alone
    On that, came forth where the ascent began.

'*Venite, benedicti Patris mei,*'
  Sounded within a splendour, which was there
  Such it o'ercame me, and I could not look.
'The sun departs,' it added, 'and night cometh ;
  Tarry ye not, but onward urge your steps,
  So long as yet the west becomes not dark.'
                       XXVII. 19-63.

But no haste availed: Dante's shadow went out before
him with the Sun's last ray behind him ; not another upward step was possible ; and he with his two companions
lay down for the night, each on a several stair between the
high walls of the strait ascent.

  Little could there be seen of things without ;
    But through that little I beheld the stars
    More luminous and larger than their wont.
  Thus ruminating, and beholding these,
    Sleep seized upon me,—sleep, that oftentimes
    Before a deed is done has tidings of it.
  It was the hour, I think, when from the East
    First on the mountain Cytherea beamed,
    Who with the fire of love seems always burning ;
  Youthful and beautiful in dreams methought
    I saw a lady walking in a meadow,
    Gathering flowers ; and singing she was saying :
  'Know whosoever may my name demand
    That I am Leah, and go moving round
    My beauteous hands to make myself a garland.
  To please me at the mirror, here I deck me,
    But never does my sister Rachel leave
    Her looking-glass, and sitteth all day long.
  To see her beauteous eyes as eager is she,
    As I am to adorn me with my hands ;
    Her, seeing, and me, doing satisfies.'
                       XXVII. 88-108.

Leah is the symbol of the Active Life; Rachel of the Contemplative, which is the more perfect. But neither wife could Jacob obtain without previous long and toilsome service. Even so has the Mount of Purgation now led up to the lower or Terrestrial Paradise of Action; which again will serve as the stepping-stone to the higher or Celestial Paradise of Contemplation.

And now Easter Wednesday is dawning.

> And now before the antelucan splendours
>   That unto pilgrims the more grateful rise,
>   As, home-returning, less remote they lodge,
> The darkness fled away on every side,
>   And slumber with it; whereupon I rose,
>   Seeing already the great Masters risen.
> 'That apple sweet,[1] which through so many branches
>   The care of mortals goeth in pursuit of,
>   To-day shall put in peace thy hungerings.'
> Speaking to me, Virgilius of such words
>   As these made use; and never were there guerdons
>   That could in pleasantness compare with these.
> Such longing upon longing came upon me
>   To be above, that at each step thereafter
>   For flight I felt in me the pinions growing.
> When underneath us was the stairway all
>   Run o'er, and we were on the highest step,
>   Virgilius fastened upon me his eyes,
> And said: 'The temporal fire and the eternal,
>   Son, thou hast seen, and to a place art come
>   Where of myself no farther I discern.
> By intellect and art I here have brought thee;
>   Take thine own pleasure for thy guide henceforth;

---

[1] True Happiness.

Beyond the steep ways and the narrow art thou.
Behold the sun, that shines upon thy forehead ;
   Behold the grass, the flowerets, and the shrubs
   Which of itself alone this land produces.
Until rejoicing come the beauteous eyes
   Which weeping caused me to come unto thee,
   Thou canst sit down, and thou canst walk among them.
Expect no more or word or sign from me ;
   Free and upright and sound is thy free-will,
   And error were it not to do its bidding ;
Thee o'er thyself I therefore crown and mitre !'

                                  XXVII. 109-112.

CHAPTER IX.

THE GARDEN OF EDEN, AND THE DESCENT OF BEATRICE.

> Questo luogo, eletto
> All' umana natura per suo nido.
>
> This place
> Elect to human nature for its nest.
>
> *Pur.* XXVIII. 77, 78.

A ND so the crowned King and mitred Priest entered
upon his kingdom and temple of Paradise.

Eager already to search in and round
   The heavenly forest, dense and living-green,
   Which tempered to the eyes the new-born day,
Withouten more delay I left the bank,
   Taking the level country slowly, slowly
   Over the soil that everywhere breathes fragrance.
A softly-breathing air, that no mutation
   Had in itself, upon the forehead smote me
   No heavier blow than of a gentle wind,
Whereat the branches, lightly tremulous,
   Did all of them bow downward toward that side
   Where its first shadow casts the Holy Mountain ;
Yet not from their upright direction swayed,
   So that the little birds upon their tops
   Should leave the practice of each art of theirs ;
But with full ravishment the hours of prime,
   Singing, received they in the midst of leaves,

> That ever bore a burden to their rhymes,
> Such as from branch to branch goes gathering on
>   Through the pine forest on the shore of Chiassi,
>   When Eolus unlooses the Sirocco.
> Already my slow steps had carried me
>   Into the ancient wood so far, that I
>   Could not perceive where I had entered it.
> And lo! my further course a stream cut off,
>   Which tow'rd the left hand with its little waves
>   Bent down the grass that on its margin sprang.
> All waters that on earth most limpid are
>   Would seem to have within themselves some mixture
>   Compared with that which nothing doth conceal,
> Although it moves on with a brown, brown current
>   Under the shade perpetual, that never
>   Ray of the sun lets in, nor of the moon.
> With feet I stayed, and with mine eyes I passed
>   Beyond the rivulet, to look upon
>   The great variety of the fresh May.
> And there appeared to me (even as appears
>   Suddenly something that doth turn aside
>   Through very wonder every other thought)
> A lady all alone, who went along
>   Singing and culling floweret after floweret,
>   With which her pathway was all painted over.
>
>   *Pur.* XXVIII. 1-42.

This lady is named Matilda, and no further defined. But as any 'Elizabeth' as barely named in an English poem would be unhesitatingly identified with our great Queen Elizabeth, so is it scarcely possible not to identify this lovely poetic vision with Matilda Countess of Tuscany, of unique celebrity in mediæval history. Born somewhat before the middle of the eleventh century, she succeeded

her father Boniface in his vast possessions, comprising
not only Tuscany, but Mantua, Parma, Reggio, Placentia,
Ferrara, Modena, a part of Umbria, the duchy of Spoleto,
Verona, almost all the country afterwards called the Patrimony of S. Peter, and part of the Marches of Ancona. She
adhered with the utmost devotion to Pope Gregory VII.,
and to his successors, in all their contests with the Emperors,
and dying childless bequeathed her territories to the Holy
See. Her unvarying espousal of the Papal as opposed to
the Imperial cause seems the only point that can reason-
ably cast a doubt on the identity of the two Matildas,
Dante holding, as we have seen, a view essentially different.
But in any case the Flower-culler of Eden, the only permanent inhabitant appearing there, would seem to be the
realization and development of the dream-Leah, and so the
Christian type of the Active Life in the Paradise of Earth :
Beatrice standing in the same relation to the dream-Rachel,
and to the Contemplative Life in the Paradise of Heaven.

> ' Ah, beauteous lady, who in rays of love
>   Dost warm thyself, if I may trust to looks,
>   Which the heart's witnesses are wont to be,
> May the desire come unto thee to draw
>   Near to this river's bank,' I said to her,
>   ' So much that I may hear what thou art singing.
> Thou makest me remember where and what
>   Proserpina that moment was when lost
>   Her mother her, and she herself the Spring.'
> As turns herself, with feet together pressed
>   And to the ground, a lady who is dancing,
>   And hardly puts one foot before the other,
> On the vermilion and the yellow flowerets
>   She turned towards me, not in other wise

Than maiden who her modest eyes casts down ;
And my entreaties made to be content,
   So near approaching, that the dulcet sound
   Came unto me together with its meaning.
As soon as she was where the grasses are
   Bathed by the waters of the beauteous river,
   To lift her eyes she granted me the boon.
I do not think there shone so great a light
   Under the lids of Venus, when transfixed
   By her own son, beyond his usual custom ![1]
Erect upon the other bank she smiled,
   Bearing full many colours in her hands,
   Which that high land produces without seed.
Apart three paces did the river make us ;
   But Hellespont where Xerxes passed across,
   (A curb still to all human arrogance,)
More hatred from Leander did not suffer
   For rolling between Sestos and Abydos,
   Than that from me, because it oped not then.
' Ye are new-comers ; and because I smile,'
   Began she, ' peradventure, in this place
   Elect to human nature for its nest,
Some apprehension keeps you marvelling ;
   But the psalm *Delectasti* giveth light
   Which has the power to uncloud your intellect.'

XXVIII. 43-81.

' Delectasti' begins verse 5 of Psalm xci. (Vulgate) [2] which
says, ' Thou, Lord, hast made me glad through Thy works :
and I will rejoice in giving praise for the operations of Thy
hands.' Matilda having thus explained the source of her
smiling joy, declared herself ready to answer any farther

---

[1] When he accidentally shot into her the arrow of love for Adonis.
[2] In the English Prayer-Book version, Psalm xcii. 4.

questions; and Dante was not slow to ask how breeze and stream could exist where, as Statius had told him, there was neither wind nor rain. The reply taught him first of the breeze :—The winds and rains from which Eden by its upheaval is exempt, are those caused below the Gate of S. Peter by the Sun's heat drawing up exhalations from Earth and Water. But the movement of the Heavens from East to West carries with it that of the Spheres of Air and Æther (or Fire) :—in the Sphere of Air the weather-vicissitudes completely break up this movement and render it insensible, while in the free Sphere of Æther it is unbroken and sensible, and constitutes the breeze wherewith the forest is tremulous and musical. The stricken plants in their turn impart to that breeze a virtue which it then in its gyration diffuses all around, fertilizing the generous soil with abundant plant-growth diverse in qualities. The Paradisiacal table-land contains within itself every kind of seed producing fruit; and if perchance any plant in Earth's baser hemisphere seem to spring up without seed, its germination must be attributed to some seed whirled and dropped from Eden ; albeit no such fruit may be hoped for here as it there would have brought forth. And as to the stream—

> ' The water which thou seest springs not from vein
>   Restored by vapour that the cold condenses,
>   Like to a stream that gains or loses breath ;
> But issues from a fountain safe and certain,
>   Which by the Will of God as much regains
>   As it discharges, open on two sides.
> Upon this side with virtue it descends,
>   Which takes away all memory of sin ;

On that, of every good deed done restores it.
Here Lethe, as upon the other side
 Eunoë, it is called ; and worketh not
 If first on either side it be not tasted.
This every other savour doth transcend ;
 And notwithstanding slaked so far may be
 Thy thirst, that I reveal to thee no more,
I 'll give thee a corollary still in grace,
 Nor think my speech will be to thee less dear
 If it spread out beyond my promise to thee.
Those who in ancient times have feigned in song
 The Age of Gold and its felicity,
 Dreamed of this place perhaps upon Parnassus.
Here was the human race in innocence ;
 Here evermore was Spring, and every fruit ;
 This is the nectar of which each one speaks.'
Then backward did I turn me wholly round
 Unto my Poets, and saw that with a smile
 They had been listening to these closing words ;
Then to the beautiful lady turned mine eyes.

Singing like unto an enamoured lady
 She, with the ending of her words, continued :
 ' *Beati quorum tecta sunt peccata.*'[1]
And even as Nymphs, that wandered all alone
 Among the sylvan shadows, sedulous
 One to avoid and one to see the sun,
She then against the stream moved onward, going
 Along the bank, and I abreast of her,
 Her little steps with little steps attending.
Between her steps and mine were not a hundred,
 When equally the margins gave a turn,
 In such a way, that to the East I faced.

---

[1] ' Blessed is he—whose sin is covered.'—Ps. xxxii. 1.

Nor even thus our way continued far
  Before the lady wholly turned herself
  Unto me, saying, 'Brother, look and listen!'
And lo! a sudden lustre ran across
  On every side athwart the spacious forest,
  Such that it made me doubt if it were lightning.
But since the lightning ceases as it comes,
  And that continuing brightened more and more,
  Within my thought I said, 'What thing is this?'.
And a delicious melody there ran
  Along the luminous air, whence holy zeal
  Made me rebuke the hardihood of Eve;
For there where earth and heaven obedient were,
  The woman only, and but just created,
  Could not endure to stay 'neath any veil;
Underneath which had she devoutly stayed,
  I sooner should have tasted those delights
  Ineffable, and for a longer time.

                    XXVIII. 121-148. XXIX. 1-30.

Marvellous indeed was the procession now advancing along Matilda's side of Lethe. The brightness quickly resolved itself into seven golden candlesticks all aflame, the melody into distinct Hosannas; and here a wondering look towards Virgil was answered only in kind, for Pagan Rome and Limbo taught not of the songs of Sion, nor of the Sevenfold Gifts of the Holy Ghost. On and on, majestically slow, and preceding a white-robed train of Patriarchs, Prophets, and others who died in faith not having received the promises, came the seven flames, each trailing behind it a luminous aërial pennon of such hue that the seven pennons completed the rainbow typical of the seven Sacraments. Then followed, two and two, twenty-

four Elders crowned with lilies; the twenty-four Books of
the Old Testament[1] personified and crowned with the grace
of Faith.   Then the four Living Beings of Ezekiel and
S. John, symbolic of the four Gospels : and in the square
whereof they formed the corners the chariot of the Church,
resting on the two wheels of the two Covenants, and
drawn by the Gryphon blended of golden-plumed Eagle
and Lion white and ruddy, meet emblem of our Blessed
Lord in His two Natures Divine and Human ; with Feet
resting on Earth and Wings stretching sheer up into Heaven.
Beside the Christian right wheel danced three damsels,
white, green, and red—the Theological Virtues : beside the
Jewish left wheel four purple-robed—the Cardinal Virtues ;
triple-eyed Prudence leading her sisters.—Then followed
the Writers as quasi-personifications of the remaining Books
of the New Testament, two of them in consequence presented and re-presented under varying aspects.   With S.
Paul bearing the sword of the Spirit walked in physician's
garb his historian S. Luke; behind them SS. James, Peter,
John, and Jude, in humble seeming as authors of the
short Canonical Epistles; last of all S. John once more,
aged and solitary, in keen-faced slumber as the Seer of
the Apocalypse.   These were habited like their elder
Brethren, excepting that their wreaths, as emblematic of
Love rather than of Faith, were of roses and other red
flowers.

[1] The 45 books of the Old Testament according to the Vulgate are
thus counted as 24.   The Pentateuch = 5 ; Joshua, Judges, Ruth = 3 ;
4 of Kings = 1 ; 2 of Chronicles = 1 ; 2 of Ezra = 1 ; Tobit, Judith,
Esther, Job = 4; Psalms = 1 ; the Sapiential Books = 4 ; the Song
of Songs = 1 ; 5 Major Prophets = 1 ; 12 Minor Prophets = 1 ; 2
of Maccabees = 1.

But now thunder gave the signal for a halt; and Solomon from among the Twenty-four sang thrice 'Come, Spouse, from Lebanon;' and a many-voiced echo went up from his companions.

Even as the Blessed at the final summons
    Shall rise up quickened each one from his cavern,
    Uplifting light the reinvested flesh,
So upon that celestial chariot
    A hundred rose *ad vocem tanti senis*,[1]
    Ministers and messengers of life eternal.
They all were saying, '*Benedictus qui venis*,'[2]
    And, scattering flowers above and round about,
    '*Manibus o date lilia plenis.*'[3]
Ere now have I beheld, as day began,
    The eastern hemisphere all tinged with rose,
    And the other heaven with fair·serene adorned;
And the sun's face, uprising, overshadowed
    So that by tempering influence of vapours
    For a long interval the eye sustained it;
Thus in the bosom of a cloud of flowers
    Which from those hands angelical ascended,
    And downward fell again inside and out,
Over her snow-white veil with olive cinct
    Appeared a lady under a green mantle,
    Vested in colour of the living flame.
And my own spirit, that already now
    So long a time had been, that in her presence
    Trembling with awe it had not stood abashed,
Without more knowledge having by mine eyes,

[1] 'At the voice of so venerable an old man.'
[2] 'Blessed art thou that comest.'
[3] *Æneid* vi. 833: Give lilies in handfuls.

O

Through occult virtue that from her proceeded
Of ancient love the mighty influence felt.
As soon as on my vision smote the power
Sublime, that had already pierced me through
Ere from my boyhood I had yet come forth,
To the left hand I turned with that reliance
With which the little child runs to his mother,
When he has fear, or when he is afflicted,
To say unto Virgilius : ' Not a drachm
Of blood remains in me, that does not tremble ;
I know the traces of the ancient flame.'
But us Virgilius of himself deprived
Had left, Virgilius, sweetest of all fathers,
Virgilius, to whom I for safety gave me :
Nor whatsoever lost the ancient mother [1]
Availed my cheeks now purified from dew,
That weeping they should not again be darkened.

XXX. 13-54.

Crownless Human Science had given place to Divine
Science olive-crowned, grace-vested, having an Unction
from the Holy One and knowing all things ; the Leader,
Lord and Master of Intellect to the Treasure of Memory
and of Love. Even at the point where Dante had laid her
down dead would he now have taken her up living ; but
she would take him up, not such as in vision he went forth
of her death-chamber, but such as intervening life had
made and set him before her then and there.

' Dante, because Virgilius has departed
Do not weep yet, do not weep yet awhile ;
For by another sword thou needs must weep.'

---

[1] The terrestrial Paradise forfeited by Eve.

E'en as an admiral, who on poop and prow
　　Comes to behold the people that are working
　　In other ships, and cheers them to well-doing,
Upon the left-hand border of the car,
　　When at the sound I turned of my own name,
　　Which of necessity is here recorded,
I saw the Lady, who erewhile appeared
　　Veiled underneath the angelic festival,
　　Direct her eyes to me across the river.
Although the veil, that from her head descended,
　　Encircled with the foliage of Minerva,
　　Did not permit her to appear distinctly,
In attitude still royally majestic
　　Continued she, like unto one who speaks,
　　And keeps his warmest utterance in reserve :
' Look at me well ; in sooth I 'm Beatrice !
　　How didst thou deign to come unto the Mountain ?
　　Didst thou not know that man is happy here ? '
Mine eyes fell downward into the clear fountain,
　　But, seeing myself therein, I sought the grass,
　　So great a shame did weigh my forehead down.
As to the son the mother seems superb,
　　So she appeared to me ; for somewhat bitter
　　Tasteth the savour of severe compassion.
Silent became she, and the Angels sang
　　Suddenly, '*In Te, Domine, speravi :*'[1]
　　But beyond *pedes meos*[1] did not pass.
Even as the snow among the living rafters
　　Upon the back of Italy[2] congeals,
　　Blown on and drifted by Sclavonian winds,

---

[1] ' In Thee, O Lord, have I hoped '—' my feet.'—Psalm xxx. 2-9,
Vulgate ; xxxi. 1-9, English Prayer-Book version.
[2] The Apennines

And then, dissolving, trickles through itself
  Whene'er the land that loses shadow breathes,[1]
  So that it seems a fire that melts a taper ;
E'en thus was I without a tear or sigh,
  Before the song of those who sing for ever
  After the music of the eternal spheres.
But when I heard in their sweet melodies
  Compassion for me, more than had they said,
  ' O wherefore, lady, dost thou thus upbraid him ? '
The ice, that was about my heart congealed,
  To air and water changed, and in my anguish
  Through mouth and eyes came gushing from my breast.
She, on the right-hand border of the car
  Still firmly standing, to those holy beings
  Thus her discourse directed afterwards :
' Ye keep your watch in the eternal day,
  So that nor night nor sleep can steal from you
  One step the ages make upon their path ;
Therefore my answer is with greater care,
  That he may hear me who is weeping yonder,
  So that the sin and dole be of one measure.
Not only by the work of those great wheels,
  That destine every seed unto some end,
  According as the stars are in conjunction,
But by the largess of celestial graces,
  Which have such lofty vapours for their rain
  That near to them our sight approaches not,
Such had this man become in his new life
  Potentially, that every righteous habit
  Would have made admirable proof in him ;
But so much more malignant and more savage
  Becomes the land untilled and with bad seed,

---

[1] When the wind blows from Africa, shadowless at noon within the Tropics.

The more good earthly vigour it possesses.
Some time did I sustain him with my look ;
　　Revealing unto him my youthful eyes,
　　I led him with me turned in the right way.
As soon as ever of my second age [1]
　　I was upon the threshold and changed life,
　　Himself from me he took and gave to others.
When from the flesh to spirit I ascended
　　And beauty and virtue were in me increased,
　　I was to him less dear and less delightful ;
And into ways untrue he turned his steps,
　　Pursuing the false images of good,
　　That never any promises fulfil ;
Nor prayer for inspiration me availed,
　　By means of which in dreams and otherwise
　　I called him back, so little did he heed them.
So low he fell, that all appliances
　　For his salvation were already short,
　　Save showing him the people of perdition.
For this I visited the gates of death,
　　And unto him, who so far up has led him,
　　My intercessions were with weeping borne.
God's lofty fiat would be violated,
　　If Lethe should be passed, and if such viands
　　Should tasted be, withouten any scot
Of penitence, that gushes forth in tears.'

'O thou who art beyond the sacred river,'
　　Turning to me the point of her discourse,
　　That edgewise even had seemed to me so keen,
She recommenced, continuing without pause,
　　'Say, say if this be true ; to such a charge

---

[1] The second age, or Adolescence, was reckoned to begin at 25, of which Beatrice wanted 9 months at her death.

Thy own confession needs must be conjoined.'
My faculties were in so great confusion,
   That the voice moved, but sooner was extinct
   Than by its organs it was set at large.
Awhile she waited ; then she said : 'What thinkest ?
   Answer me ; for the mournful memories
   In thee not yet are by the waters injured.'
Confusion and dismay together mingled
   Forced such a Yes ! from out my mouth, that sight
   Was needful to the understanding of it.
Even as a cross-bow breaks, when 'tis discharged
   Too tensely drawn the bowstring and the bow,
   And with less force the arrow hits the mark,
So I gave way beneath that heavy burden,
   Outpouring in a torrent tears and sighs,
   And the voice flagged upon its passage forth.
Whence she to me : ' In those desires of mine
   Which led thee to the loving of that good,
   Beyond which there is nothing to aspire to,
What trenches lying traverse or what chains
   Didst thou discover, that of passing onward
   Thou shouldst have thus despoiled thee of the hope ?
And what allurements or what vantages
   Upon the forehead of the others [1] showed,
   That thou shouldst turn thy footsteps unto them ?'
After the heaving of a bitter sigh,
   Hardly had I the voice to make response,
   And with fatigue my lips did fashion it.
Weeping I said : ' The things that present were
   With their false pleasure turned aside my steps,
   Soon as your countenance concealed itself.'
And she : 'Shouldst thou be silent, or deny

---

[1] The other desires, *i.e.* of worldly goods and pleasures.

What thou confessest, not less manifest
  Would be thy fault, by such a Judge 'tis known.
But when from one's own cheeks comes bursting forth
  The accusal of the sin, in our tribunal
  Against the edge the wheel doth turn itself.
But still, that thou mayst feel a greater shame
  For thy transgression, and another time
  Hearing the Sirens thou mayst be more strong,
Cast down the seed of weeping and attend ;
  So shalt thou hear, how in an opposite way
  My buried flesh should have directed thee.
Never to thee presented art or nature
  Pleasure so great as the fair limbs wherein
  I was enclosed, which scattered are in earth.
And if the highest pleasure thus did fail thee
  By reason of my death, what mortal thing
  Should then have drawn thee into its desire ?
Thou oughtest verily at the first shaft
  Of things fallacious to have risen up
  To follow me, who was no longer such.
Thou oughtest not to have stooped thy pinions downward
  To wait for further blows, or little girl,
  Or other vanity of such brief use.
The callow birdlet waits for two or three,
  But to the eyes of those already fledged,
  In vain the net is spread or shaft is shot.'
Even as children silent in their shame
  Stand listening with their eyes upon the ground,
  And conscious of their fault, and penitent ;
So was I standing ; and she said : ' If thou
  In hearing sufferest pain, lift up thy beard
  And thou shalt feel a greater pain in seeing.'
With less resistance is a robust holm
  Uprooted, either by a native wind

Or else by that from regions of Iarbas,[1]
Than I upraised at her command my chin :
   And when she by the beard the face demanded,
   Well I perceived the venom of her meaning.
And as my countenance was lifted up,
   Mine eye perceived those creatures beautiful
   Had rested from the strewing of the flowers ;
And, still but little reassured, mine eyes
   Saw Beatrice turned round towards the monster,[2]
   That is one person only in two natures.
Beneath her veil, beyond the margent green,
   She seemed to me far more her ancient self
   To excel, than others here, when she was here.
So pricked me then the thorn of penitence,
   That of all other things the one which turned me
   Most to its love became the most my foe.
Such self-conviction stung me at the heart
   O'erpowered I fell, and what I then became
   She knoweth who had furnished me the cause.

                     XXX. 55-145. XXXI. 1-90.

This sufficed. The memory of sin had done its work, and might now be for ever left behind in the waters of Lethe. Ere yet Dante had recovered consciousness Ma-

---

[1] 'Iarbas, King of Gœtulia, from whom Dido bought the land for building Carthage.'

[2] Orig. *fiera = wild animal ;* not necessarily, though in modern Italian usually, =*beast of prey.* This perplexing word is rendered by various translators in various ways. Mr. Johnston simply substitutes ' Gryphon ; ' an expedient I on the whole prefer, considering the extreme difficulty of rendering *fiera* literally, and the surpassing sacredness of the only interpretation I, in common with nearly all commentators, have attached to the symbol. It is not, however, the only interpretation suggested by Mr. Longfellow. And I would remind the reader that, whatever may be the popular use of the term *monster*, it is primarily equivalent to *prodigy.*

tilda had immersed him up to the throat; then having drawn him conscious to the opposite bank she plunged his head for the draught of oblivion. Next, graciously owned and led by the Four Virtues, he was strengthened to behold within the fixed and veiled eyes of Beatrice the double-natured changeless Gryphon changefully mirrored in each nature alternately. And finally, at the acceptable inter-cession of the Three Virtues, the unveiled face beamed full upon him, and he beheld that second beauty into which the first had been transfigured.

After this followed visions embodying the history of the Church and of the Empire, with an exhortation from Bea-trice to bear faithful witness of the things heard and seen:— and behold the time was come to drink of Eunoë and revive the memory of good.

> And more coruscant and with slower steps
>   The sun was holding the meridian circle,
>   Which, with the point of view, shifts here and there,
> When halted (as he cometh to a halt,
>   Who goes before a squadron as its escort,
>   If something new he find upon his way)
> The ladies seven at a dark shadow's edge,
>   Such as, beneath green leaves and branches black,
>   The Alp upon its frigid border wears.
> In front of them the Tigris and Euphrates
>   Methought I saw forth issue from one fountain,
>   And slowly part, like friends, from one another.
> 'O light, O glory of the human race!
>   What stream is this which here unfolds itself
>   From out one source, and from itself withdraws?'
> For such a prayer, 'twas said unto me, 'Pray
>   Matilda that she tell thee;' and here answered,

As one does who doth free himself from blame,
  The beautiful lady : ' This and other things
    Were told to him by me ; and sure I am
    The water of Lethe has not hid them from him
And Beatrice : ' Perhaps a greater care,
    Which oftentimes our memory takes away,
    Has made the vision of his mind obscure.
But Eunoë behold, that yonder rises ;
    Lead him to it, and, as thou art accustomed,
    Revive again the half-dead virtue in him.'
Like gentle soul, that maketh no excuse,
    But makes its own will of another's will
    As soon as by a sign it is disclosed,
Even so, when she had taken hold of me,
    The beautiful lady moved, and unto Statius
    Said, in her womanly manner, ' Come with him.'
If, Reader, I possessed a longer space
    For writing it, I yet would sing in part
    Of the sweet draught that ne'er would satiate me :
But inasmuch as full are all the leaves
    Made ready for this second canticle,
    The curb of art no farther lets me go.
From the most holy water I returned
    Regenerate, in the manner of new trees
    That are renewed with a new foliage,
Pure and disposed to mount unto the stars.

                       XXXIII. 103-145.

THE ROSE OF THE BLESSED.

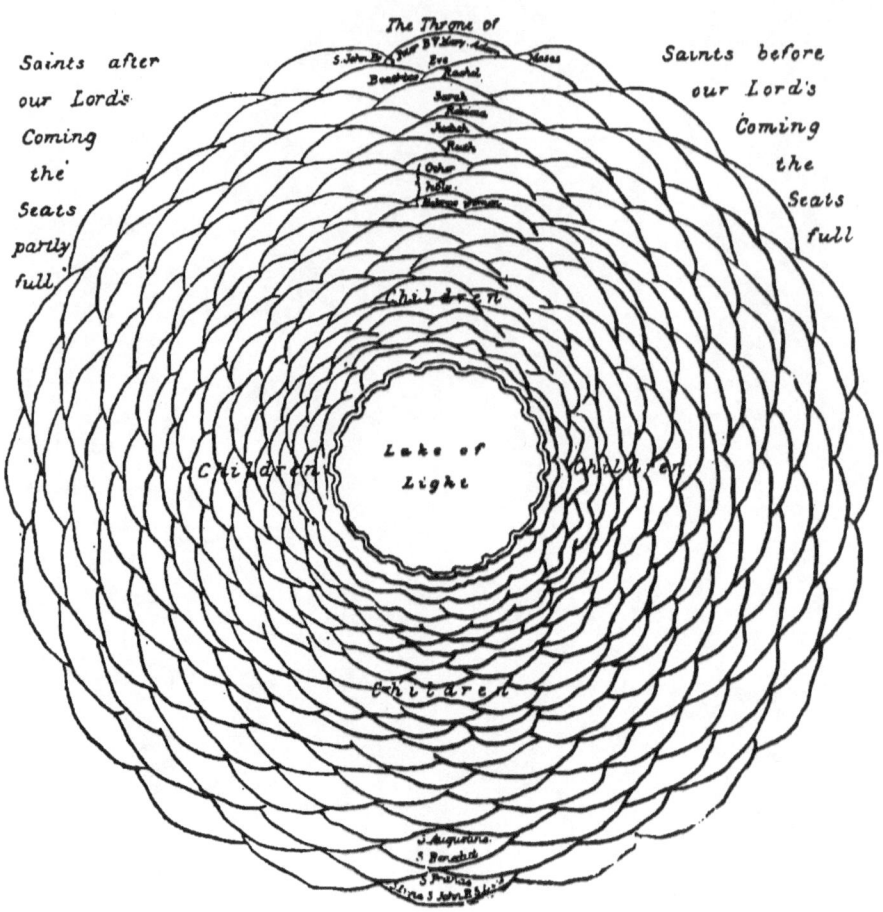

CHAPTER X.

THE PARADISE.

La forma general di Paradiso.
The general form of Paradise.

Par. XXXI. 52.

PARADISE consists, as we have seen, of Nine Heavens, each a revolving hollow sphere enclosing and enclosed, and of the uncontained Empyrean which contains them all.

As star differeth from star in glory, so Saint from Saint. Whereof Dante has constructed a marvellous parable :—for in each successive Heaven, as he ascends, Blessed Souls manifest themselves visibly and audibly as denizens, while yet each in very truth has his immoveable eternal seat in the ineffable Rose of the Empyrean. And so the lower or higher place of manifestation serves for a token whereby human sense may apprehend the lower or higher degree of that vision of God which constitutes beatitude. When therefore Saints are spoken of as dwelling in any Heaven below the highest, the statement must be understood not of real but of apparent or representative abode. In all, however, beatitude is perfect according to the capacity of each ; for entire conformity with the Divine Will produces entire satisfaction in the appointments of that Will, and in the exact order resulting throughout the Universe from exact

justice in the apportionment of rewards.   As Bellarmine
illustrates this subject—if a father clothe all his children in
cloth of gold, the measure fits the growth of each, yet all
are alike complete in covering and adornment.

In their apparent Star-abodes the Saints show themselves
swathed in cocoons of light, flashing brighter with each
accidental increase of joy or charity ; in their real Rose-
seats they are seen without this raiment.

Their gaze is ceaselessly fixed on the Beatific Vision, and
their motion rapid in proportion to the vividness wherewith
they apprehend that Vision.   Their knowledge is unerring,
because they behold mirrored in God all things meet for
them to know ; their speech is the flawless reflection of
that unerring knowledge.

In Hell, as we have seen, the utmost possible perversion
of the Understanding by the Bestialism or spiritual Folly
of Unbelief and Misbelief occupies the exceptional transitional Circle between four upper and three lower Circles of
less and of more perverted Will ; the frailty of Incontinence
being above, the depravity of Malice below.   In Heaven
a somewhat similar arrangement may perhaps be traced.
The utmost possible sanctification of the Understanding by
the spiritual gifts of the Wisdom and Knowledge growing
out of Faith and Orthodoxy, occupies the Heaven of the
Sun, apparently exceptional and transitional between three
lower and four upper Heavens of less and of more sanctified
Will ; the imperfection of Earthliness being below, as far
as Earth's shadow extends to the celestial spheres ; the
perfection of Heavenliness above, in light unshadowed.

We will now consider the special characteristics of each
Planet and its denizens.

The First Heaven, revolved by the Angels as the lowest · of the Nine Orders, is that of the waxing and waning Moon, and therefore of Wills imperfect through Instability. Here dwell Nuns whose vows failed of entire fulfilment; inasmuch as, removed by violence from the cloister, and bearing thereto a changeless persevering love, they yet braved not all evils to return thither so soon as freed from bodily constraint.

The Second Heaven, revolved by the Archangels, is that of Mercury, 'more veiled from the solar rays than is any other star':[1] the abode of Wills imperfect through that Love of Fame which half puts out within the soul the rays of the Love of God even as they dart upward. Here are men of activity and eloquence, who used their powers for good, but not without regard to the praise of their fellow-creatures.

The Third Heaven, revolved by the Principalities, is that of Venus, now before and now behind the Sun, and the last to which Earth's shadow reaches; indwelt by Wills imperfect through excess of mere human love.

The Fourth and middle Planetary Heaven, revolved by the Powers, is that of the Sun, the chief material light, and the dwelling of the great spiritual and intellectual lights, the holy and eminent Doctors in Divinity and Philosophy.

The Fifth Heaven, revolved by the Virtues, is that of blood-red Mars, the abode of Martyrs, Confessors, and Warriors on behalf of the Faith.

The Sixth Heaven, revolved by the Dominations, is that of Jupiter brilliantly white, inhabited by Rulers eminent for Justice.

[1] *Convito* ii. 14.

The Seventh and last Planetary Heaven, revolved by the Thrones, is the cold orbit of Saturn, fit dwelling of those Monks and Hermits who, refined by severest abstinence, rose to that heavenly Contemplation whereto this star was believed to influence men.

The Eighth or Starry Heaven, revolved by the Cherubim, is that of the Fixed Stars, including of course the constellations of the Zodiac. Hither descends the Triumph of Christ, here linger the Apostles with the Saints of the Old and of the New Testament.

The Ninth or Starless Crystalline Heaven is the Primum Mobile, revolved by the Seraphim; here it is that the Nine Orders of the Celestial Hierarchy circle in fiery rings around the Light Which no man can approach unto, manifested as an Atomic Point.

No more of Time, no more of Space: left behind in the Crystalline Primum Mobile, they have no place in the Still Fire-Heaven, the Empyrean, Essential Light, Essential Love, possessing all things, and in very contentment motionless. But the Elect have place there, yea have no place save only there; Time and Space may furnish a parable of their condition, Time and Space can construct no home for their abode. Their home is the mystical White Rose into which they are composed around the Lake of Divine Light whose circumference would outgird the Sun, and which constitutes the central Yellow of this Flower ineffable. Petals upon petals, petals upon petals, petals upon petals; the narrowest circuit encompasses the Sun-outmeasuring Lake, what should suffice to fill the widest? And what should be hidden, what withheld from the enthroned Souls that form those petals, seeing that they gaze into the Very

Light, and that the multitude of the Heavenly Host as bees deposit amid their recesses the Peace and Glow brought down from the Bosom of God? All eyes and all love are here set one way, even towards God Triune.

The order of the Rose includes both a horizontal and a vertical division. The horizontal division takes place at mid-height, all the Blessed thence downwards having died in infancy, all thence upwards at years of discretion. Among the infants no less than among the adults there are varying degrees of glory, corresponding to the varying degrees of grace wherewith Dante—arguing from the difference made before birth between Jacob and Esau— believes them to have been endowed. The vertical division takes place at two opposite points of the circumference, the left half of the thrones being filled by those who looked forward to Christ Coming, the right half as yet only partially occupied by those who looked backward to Christ Come. On the one side the dividing line consists of a chain of holy women, five of those designated by name being ancestresses of our Blessed Lord : at the top of course S. Mary, under her Eve, then Rachel, beside whom, as we learned at the beginning of the poem, is seated Beatrice ; then Sarah, Rebekah, Judith, Ruth ; the rest are unnamed. On the other side, opposite S. Mary, S. John the Baptist forms the head of the second dividing line, which consists of holy Mandriarchs ; S. Francis, S. Benedict, S. Augustine being alone named. To the right of the Blessed Virgin sit S. Peter first, next S. John the Evangelist ; to her left first Adam, next Moses. To the left of S. John the Baptist, opposite S. Peter, is S. Anne, Mother of the Blessed Virgin ; to his right, opposite Adam, S.

P

Lucia, Virgin and Martyr, and the type of Illuminating Grace.

Above and beyond this there is and can be nought save the Alpha and Omega, the First Beginning and the Last End: the Ever-Blessed Trinity in Unity, Whereinto is taken for evermore the Glorified Humanity of God Incarnate.

CHAPTER XI.

DANTE'S PILGRIMAGE THROUGH PARADISE.

Presso di lei e nel mondo felice.

Close at her side and in the Happy World.

Par. XXV. 139.

THE means by which Dante was lifted from the Terrestrial Paradise into the wholly unearthly Fire of the last Elemental Sphere, and thence through each successive Heaven (except one) even into the Empyrean, was a fixed gaze into the eyes of Beatrice; and the increase of bliss in each ascent was typified by the increase in the beauty of her smile. For inasmuch as Beatrice is the figure of Divine Science, ' in her face appear things that tell of the pleasures of Paradise; and . . . the place wherein this appears . . . is in her eyes and her smile. And here it should be known that the eyes of Wisdom are the two demonstrations, by which is seen the truth most certainly; and her smile is her persuasions, in which is shown forth the interior light of Wisdom under some veil : and in these two things is felt that highest pleasure of beatitude, which is the greatest good in Paradise.' [1]

The Sun, which rises on the world through divers pas-

[1] *Convito* iii. 15.

sages, was now in the most favourable of all, that is, the equinoctial :

> Almost that passage had made morning there
>> And evening here, and there was wholly white
>> That hemisphere, and black the other part.
> When Beatrice towards the left-hand side
>> I saw turned round, and gazing at the sun ;
>> Never did eagle fasten so upon it !
> And even as a second ray is wont
>> To issue from the first and reascend,
>> Like to a pilgrim who would fain return,
> Thus of her action, through the eyes infused
>> In my imagination, mine I made,
>> And sunward fixed mine eyes beyond our wont.
> There much is lawful which is here unlawful
>> Unto our powers, by virtue of the place
>> Made for the human species as its own.[1]
> Not long I bore it, nor so little while
>> But I beheld it sparkle round about
>> Like iron that comes molten from the fire ;
> And suddenly it seemed that day to day
>> Was added, as if He Who has the power
>> Had with another sun the heaven adorned.
>
>>>>>>> *Par.* I. 43-63.

In that instant Dante had been drawn up from the Terrestrial Paradise into the upper region of the Elemental Fire, where the music of the Spheres soon burst upon his ear.

> With eyes upon the everlasting wheels
>> Stood Beatrice all intent, and I, on her
>> Fixing my vision from above removed,

---

[1] The Garden of Eden.

Such at her aspect inwardly became
  As Glaucus, tasting of the herb that made him[1]
  Peer of the other gods beneath the sea.
To represent transhumanize in words
  Impossible were ; the example, then, suffice
  Him for whom Grace the experience reserves.
If I was merely what of me Thou newly
  Createdst, Love Who governest the Heaven,
  Thou knowest, Who didst lift me with Thy light!
When now the wheel, which Thou dost make eternal[2]
  Desiring Thee, made me attentive to it
  By harmony Thou dost modulate and measure,[2]
Then seemed to me so much of Heaven enkindled
  By the sun's flame, that neither rain nor river
  E'er made a lake so widely spread abroad.
The newness of the sound and the great light
  Kindled in me a longing for their cause,
  Never before with such acuteness felt ;
Whence she, who saw me as I saw myself,
  To quiet in me my perturbed mind,
  Opened her mouth, ere I did mine to ask,
And she began : ' Thou makest thyself so dull
  With false imagining, that thou seest not
  What thou wouldst see if thou hadst shaken it off.
Thou art not upon earth, as thou believest ;
  But lightning, fleeing its appropriate site,

---

[1] Glaucus was a fisherman, who seeing some fish caught by him revive on touching the salt-meadow-grass growing on the shore, ate of the same herb and so became a sea-god.

[2] ' According to Plato the Heavens ever move seeking the Soul of the World, and desirous to find it ; that Soul is God.' (Fraticelli *in loc.*) The sense of these lines is : When now the heavenly revolution, which Thou, O Love, dost render perpetual through the desire Thou infusest for Thyself, attracted my attention by its harmony—*i.e.* the music of the Spheres.

Ne'er ran as thou, who thitherward returnest.'
If of my former doubt I was divested
   By these brief little words more smiled than spoken,
   I in a new one was the more ensnared ;
And said : 'Already did I rest content
   From great amazement ; but am now amazed
   In what way I transcend these bodies light.'
Whereupon she, after a pitying sigh,
   Her eyes directed tow'rds me with that look
   A mother casts on a delirious child ;
And she began : 'All things whate'er they be
   Have order among themselves, and this is form,
   That makes the universe resemble God.

     .   .   .   .   .   .

The Providence that regulates all this
   Makes with Its light the Heaven for ever quiet,
   Wherein that turns which has the greatest haste.
And thither now, as to a site decreed,
   Bears us away the virtue of that cord
   Which aims its arrows at a joyous mark.
True is it, that as oftentimes the form
   Accords not with the intention of the art,
   Because in answering is matter deaf,
So likewise from this course doth deviate
   Sometimes the creature, who the power possesses,
   Though thus impelled, to swerve some other way,
(In the same wise as one may see the fire
   Fall from a cloud,) if the first impetus
   Earthward is wrested by some false delight.
Thou shouldst not wonder more, if well I judge,
   At thine ascent, than at a rivulet
   From some high mount descending to the lowland.
Marvel it would be in thee, if deprived
   Of hindrance, thou wert seated down below,

As if on earth the living fire were quiet.'
Thereat she heavenward turned again her face.

I. 64-105, 121-142.

For the Elemental Fire is no abode of glorified Spirits ;
and therefore

The con-created and perpetual thirst
    For the realm deiform did bear us on,
    As swift almost as ye the Heavens behold.
Upward gazed Beatrice, and I at her ;
    And in such space perchance as strikes a bolt
    And flies, and from the notch unlocks itself,
Arrived I saw me where a wondrous thing
    Drew to itself my sight ; and therefore she
    From whom no care of mine could be concealed,
Towards me turning, blithe as beautiful,
    Said unto me : ' Fix gratefully thy mind
    On God, Who unto the first star[1] has brought us.'
It seemed to me a cloud encompassed us,
    Luminous, dense, consolidate and bright
    As adamant on which the sun is striking.
Into itself did the eternal pearl[2]
    Receive us, even as water doth receive
    A ray of light, remaining still unbroken.
[3] If I was body, (and we here conceive not
    How one dimension tolerates another,
    Which needs must be if body enter body,)
More the desire should be enkindled in us
    That Essence to behold, Wherein is seen[3]

[1, 2] The Moon.

[3] If I was in the body (a thing wholly incomprehensible to us on earth, inasmuch as we cannot conceive of one physical dimension enduring the insertion of another and yet remaining unchanged, which needs must have been if my body had entered within the Moon's body),

How God and our own nature were united.
There will be seen what we receive by faith,
  Not demonstrated, but self-evident
  In guise of the first truth that man believes.
I made reply : ' Madonna, as devoutly
  As most I can do I give thanks to Him
  Who has removed me from the mortal world.'

II. 19-48.

Dante then inquired respecting the Moon's spots, and
was answered that they are the diverse effect of the Divine
virtue infused through the Angelic Movers of the First
Heaven. He was about to confess himself convinced of
the erroneous nature of his previous theories on this subject—

But there appeared a vision, which withdrew me
  So close to it, in order to be seen,
  That my confession I remembered not.
Such as through polished and transparent glass,
  Or waters crystalline and undisturbed,
  But not so deep as that their bed be lost,
Come back again the outlines of our faces
  So feeble, that a pearl on forehead white
  Comes not less speedily unto our eyes ;
Such saw I many faces prompt to speak,
  So that I ran in error opposite
  To that which kindled love 'twixt man and fountain [1]
As soon as I became aware of them,
  Esteeming them as mirrored semblances,
  To see of whom they were, mine eyes I turned,

---

then so great and blessed a marvel as a human bodily presence in
Heaven ought the more to enkindle in us the desire to behold that
Essence of our Incarnate Lord, Wherein, etc.

[1] Narcissus took a reflected for a real face, Dante took real faces for
reflected.

And nothing saw, and once more turned them forward
   Direct into the light of my sweet Guide,
   Who smiling kindled in her holy eyes.
' Marvel thou not,' she said to me, ' because
   I smile at this thy puerile conceit,
   Since on the truth it trusts not yet its foot,
But turns thee, as 'tis wont, on emptiness.
   True substances are these which thou beholdest,
   Here relegate for breaking of some vow.
Therefore speak with them, listen and believe ;
   For the True Light, which giveth peace to them,
   Permits them not to turn from It their feet.'
And I unto the Shade that seemed most wishful
   To speak directed me, and I began,
   As one whom too great eagerness bewilders :
' O well-created Spirit, who in the rays
   Of life eternal dost the sweetness taste
   Which being untasted ne'er is comprehended,
Grateful 'twill be to me, if thou content me
   Both with thy name and with your destiny.'
   Whereat she promptly and with laughing eyes :
' Our charity doth never shut the doors
   Against a just desire, except as One[1]
   Who wills that all her court be like herself.
I was a virgin sister in the world ;
   And if thy mind doth contemplate me well,
   The being more fair will not conceal me from thee,
But thou shalt recognise I am Piccarda,
   Who, stationed here among these other blessed,
   Myself am blessed in the slowest sphere.'

III. 7-51.

Piccarda was the sister of Dante's wife Gemma de'

---

[1] The Blessed Virgin.

Donati, and of that Forese, whom in Purgatory we saw expiating the sin of Gluttony.[1]   She continued :

' All our affections, that alone inflamed
   Are in the pleasure of the Holy Ghost,
   Rejoice at being of His order formed ;[2]
And this allotment, which appears so low,
   Therefore is given us, because our vows
   Have been neglected and in some part void.'
Whence I to her : ' In your miraculous aspects
   There shines I know not what of the divine,
   Which doth transform you from our first conceptions.
Therefore I was not swift in my remembrance ;
   But what thou tellest me now aids me so,
   That the refiguring is easier to me.
But tell me, ye who in this place are happy,
   Are you desirous of a higher place,
   To see more or to make yourselves more friends ?'[3]
First with those other Shades she smiled a little ;
   Thereafter answered me so full of gladness,
   She seemed to burn in the first fire of love :
' Brother, our will is quieted by virtue
   Of charity, that makes us wish alone
   For what we have, nor gives us thirst for more.
If to be more exalted we aspired,
   Discordant would our aspirations be
   Unto the will of Him Who here secludes us ;
Which thou shalt see finds no place in these circles,
   If being in charity is needful here,
   And if thou lookest well into its nature ;
Nay, 'tis essential to this blest existence
   To keep itself within the Will Divine,

---

[1] See page 173.   [2] Professed nuns of His order.
[3] More the friends of God.

Whereby our very wishes are made one ;
So that, as we are station above station
    Throughout this realm, to all the realm 'tis pleasing,
    As to the King, who makes His Will our will.
And His Will is our peace ; this is the sea
    To which is moving onward whatsoever
    It doth create, and all that nature makes.'
Then it was clear to me how everywhere
    In Heaven is Paradise, although the grace
    Of good supreme there rain not in one measure.
But as it comes to pass, if one food sates,
    And for another still remains the longing,
    We ask for this, and that decline with thanks,
E'en thus did I, with gesture and with word,
    To learn from her what was the web wherein
    She did not ply the shuttle to the end.
' A perfect life and merit high in-heaven
    A lady[1] o'er us,' said she, ' by whose rule
    Down in your world they vest and veil themselves,
That until death they may both watch and sleep
    Beside that Spouse Who every vow accepts
    Which charity conformeth to His pleasure.
To follow her, in girlhood from the world
    I fled, and in her habit shut myself,
    And pledged me to the pathway of her sect.
Then men accustomed unto evil more
    Than unto good, from the sweet cloister tore me ;
    God knows what afterward my life became.'
III. 52-108.

Her brother Corso had forced Piccarda away from her cloister, and married her to Rosselin della Tosa ; she survived the marriage only a few months. She went on :

---

[1] S. Clara, foundress of the Poor Clares.

‘ This other Splendour, which to thee reveals
   Itself on my right side, and is enkindled
   With all the illumination of our sphere,
What of myself I say applies to her ;
   A nun was she, and likewise from her head
   Was ta’en the shadow of the sacred wimple.
But when she too was to the world returned
   Against her wishes and against good usage,
   Of the heart’s veil she never was divested.
Of great Costanza this is the effulgence,
   Who from the second wind of Suabia
   Brought forth the third and latest puissance.’

III. 109-120.

Constance was the daughter of Roger I., King of Naples
and Sicily, who was succeeded immediately by his son
William the Bad, next by his grandson William the Good.
This last reigned but a very short time ; and as his early
childless death was foreseen, Constance, his aunt and sole
heiress, was taken, say various ancient but not uncontra-
dicted historians,[1] from her convent at Palermo, and compelled to marry Henry VI., son of the Emperor Frederick
Barbarossa of Suabia, and father by her of Frederick II., in
his turn father of the Manfred who in Purgatory styled
himself Constance’s grandson.[2]

Thus unto me she spake and then began
   ‘ *Ave Maria* ’ singing, and in singing
   Vanished, as through deep water something heavy.
My sight, that followed her as long a time
   As it was possible, when it had lost her
   Turned round unto the mark of more desire,
And wholly unto Beatrice reverted ;

---

[1] Fraticelli *in loc.*   [2] See page 128.

> But she such lightnings flashed into mine eyes,
>> That at the first my sight endured it not ;
> And this in questioning more backward made me.
>
>> III. 121-130.

Dante had two questions to ask : the one, suggested by
what he had seen, was concerning the abode of the Blessed ;
appearances seeming to justify Plato's hypothesis of the
return of disembodied souls to the stars.   Beatrice, discerning in his mind this unexpressed doubt, thus solved it :

> ' He of the Seraphim most absorbed in God,
>> Moses, and Samuel, and whichever John
>> Thou mayst select, I say, and even Mary,
> Have not in any other Heaven their seats,
>> Than have those Spirits that just appeared to thee,
>> Nor of existence more or fewer years ;
> But all make beautiful the primal circle,
>> And have sweet life in different degrees,
>> By feeling more or less the eternal Breath.
> They showed themselves here, not because allotted
>> This sphere has been to them, but to give sign
>> Of the celestial which is least exalted.
> To speak thus is adapted to your mind,
>> Since only through the sense it apprehendeth
>> What then it worthy makes of intellect.
> On this account the Scripture condescends
>> Unto your faculties, and feet and hands
>> To God attributes, and means something else ;
> And Holy Church under an aspect human
>> Gabriel and Michael represents to you,
>> And him who made Tobias whole again.'
>
>> IV. 28-48.

Dante's second question, suggested by what he had heard,
was—how violence suffered at the hands of another can

lessen the merit of one whose good-will endures unchanged.
Beatrice replied by explaining the distinction between
absolute and relative will:

> [1]‘ That as unjust our justice should appear
>   In eyes of mortals, is an argument ·
>   Of faith, and not of sin heretical.[1]
> But still, that your perception may be able
>   To thoroughly penetrate this verity,
>   As thou desirest, I will satisfy thee.
> [2] If it be violence when he who suffers
>   Co-operates not with him who uses force,
>   These Souls were not on that account excused ;
> For will is never quenched unless it will,
>   But operates as nature doth in fire,
>   If violence a thousand times distort it.
> Hence, if it yieldeth more or less, it seconds
>   The force ;[2] and these have done so, having power
>   Of turning back unto the holy place.
> If their will had been perfect, like to that
>   Which Lawrence fast upon his gridiron held,
>   And Mutius made severe to his own hand,
> It would have urged them back along the road
>   Whence they were dragged as soon as they were free ;
>   But such a solid will is all too rare.

---

[1] That heavenly Justice should appear unjust in the eyes of mortals
is a reason why they should exercise faith, not why they should fall
into heresy.

[2] If that only be properly called an act of violence in which he who
is forced co-operates not in the least degree with him who forces, these
Souls cannot be excused as having suffered violence. For Will never
can be quenched except by its own consent ; even as fire, after enduring a thousand attempts to make it burn downward, invariably burns
upward the moment it is left to itself. If then, bodily force ceasing,
the Will still yields more or less, it does co-operate with that force ;
and these, etc.

And by these words, if thou hast gathered them
  As thou shouldst do, the argument is refuted
  That would have still annoyed thee many times.
But now another passage runs across
  Before thine eyes, and such that by thyself
  Thou couldst not thread it ere thou wouldst be weary.
I have for certain put into thy mind
  That Soul beatified could never lie,
  For it is ever near the primal Truth,
And then thou from Piccarda might'st have heard
  Costanza kept affection for the veil,
  So that she seemeth here to contradict me.
Many times, brother, has it come to pass,
  That, to escape from peril, with reluctance
  That has been done it was not right to do,
E'en as Alcmæon (who, being by his father
  Thereto entreated, his own mother slew)
  Not to lose pity pitiless became.[1]
At this point I desire thee to remember
  That force with will commingles, and they cause
  That the offences cannot be excused.
Will absolute consenteth not to evil ;
  But in so far consenteth as it fears,
  If it refrain, to fall into more harm.
Hence when Piccarda uses this expression,
  She meaneth the will absolute, and I
  The other, so that both of us speak truth.'
Such was the flowing of the holy river
  That issued from the fount whence springs all truth :
  This put to rest my wishes one and all.
' O love of the first Lover, O divine,'
  Said I forthwith, ' whose speech inundates me

---

[1] 'Not to lose *piety*' is the sense ; but then the play on *pietà* = *piety* and *pity*, would be lost.   See also Note 1, p. 150.

And warms me so, it more and more revives me,
My own affection is not so profound
   As to suffice in rendering grace for grace ;
   Let Him, who sees and can, thereto respond.
[1] Well I perceive that never sated is
   Our intellect unless the Truth illume it,
   Beyond which nothing true expands itself.
It rests therein, as wild beast in his lair,
   When it attains It ; and it can attain It ;
   If not, then each desire would frustrate be.
Therefore springs up, in fashion of a shoot,
   Doubt at the foot of truth ; and this is nature,
   Which to the top from height to height impels us.[1]
This doth invite me, this assurance give me
   With reverence, Lady, to inquire of you
   Another truth, which is obscure to me.
I wish to know if man can satisfy you
   For broken vows with other good deeds, so
   That in your balance they will not be light.'

                       IV. 67-138.

The answer was :

'The greatest gift that in His largess God
   Creating made, and unto His own goodness
   Nearest conformed, and that which He doth prize
Most highly, is the freedom of the will,
   Wherewith the creatures of intelligence

---

[1] Well do I see that our intellect can never be fully satisfied, except it be irradiated by that Truth which Itself so includes all truth that aught outside It is not truth, but falsehood. In the aforesaid Truth our intellect rests as a wild beast in his lair, so soon as it has attained thereto ; and thereto it is able to attain, else would its every desire be frustrate. Therefore at the foot of every ascertained truth there ever springs a shoot of doubt concerning some further truth ; such is man's nature, impelling him from peak to peak even to the summit.

Both all and only were and are endowed.[1]
Now wilt thou see, if thence thou reasonest,
  The high worth of a vow, if it be made
  So that when thou consentest God consents ;[2]
For, closing between God and man the compact,
  A sacrifice is of this treasure made,
  Such as I say, and made by its own act.
What can be rendered then as compensation ?
  Think'st thou to make good use of what thou'st offered,
  With gains ill gotten thou wouldst do good deed.'

V. 19-33.

Nevertheless, the essence of a vow being the binding of
the will rather than the particular point wherein it is bound,
Holy Church has a dispensing power to which recourse may
lawfully be had on just occasion :—

'But let none shift the burden on his shoulder
  At his arbitrament, without the turning
  Both of the white and of the yellow key;
And every permutation deem as foolish,
  If in the substitute the thing relinquished,
  As the four is in six, be not contained.
Therefore whatever thing has so great weight
  In value that it drags down every balance,
  Cannot be satisfied with other spending.'[3]

V. 55-63.

But from all this it obviously follows that vows must not be
lightly made.

And then Beatrice with her neophyte passed into Mercury,

---

[1] All rational creatures, and none but rational creatures, are endowed
with free will.

[2] So that it be made according to the known Will of God.

[3] Cannot be made up for by any other offering.

where shine the Spirits of men eloquent and active in good, but not free from the love of fame.   Here Dante conversed at great length with the Emperor Justinian, who traced out the progress and achievements of the Roman Eagle from the days of Æneas to those of Augustus, and added :

> ' But what the standard that has made me speak
>   Achieved before, and after should achieve
>   Throughout the mortal realm that lies beneath it,
> Becometh in appearance mean and dim,
>   If in the hand of the third Cæsar seen
>   With eye unclouded and affection pure,
> Because the living Justice that inspires me
>   Granted it, in the hand of him I speak of,
>   The glory of doing vengeance for its wrath.
> Now here attend to what I answer thee ;
>   Later it ran with Titus to do vengeance
>   Upon the vengeance of the ancient sin.'
>
> VI. 82-93.

' The vengeance of the ancient sin ' is the Death of our Blessed Lord as the atoning Victim for the entire race of man.   That in any view of this most awful subject the human instrumentality whereby that precious Death was effected should be regarded otherwise than as the uttermost stretch of wickedness, seems to us no less blasphemous than inconceivable ; yet it is the loving and reverent Dante who writes of such instrumentality as ' the glory ' of ' the Third Cæsar ' Tiberius.   The whole passage is incomprehensible till read in the light of the elaborate argument whereby, in the treatise *De Monarchiâ*, Rome is professedly demonstrated to be by Divine right the centre of empire over the whole

terrestrial globe. The crowning proofs adduced are two.
First, our Saviour's having implicitly approved Augustus'
claim of world-wide sovereignty, by willing to be so born as
to be registered his subject. Secondly, the Divine accept-
ance of the Crucifixion as a punishment making satisfaction
for the sins of all mankind ; which it could not have been
if inflicted by any one save the ordinary judge, or by any
ordinary judge not having jurisdiction over all mankind.[1]
By us, of course, the conclusion is only less inadmissible
than the argument. But we probably have here the key to
a perplexing problem—why Pontius Pilate is nowhere met
with in Hell.

After glancing at Charlemagne, Justinian went on severely
to reprehend the ill-doing both of Guelphs and Ghibellines,
and then set forth the condition of himself and his companions :

‘ This little planet doth adorn itself
　With the good Spirits that have active been,
　That fame and honour might come after them ;
And whensoever the desires mount thither,
　Thus deviating, must perforce the rays
　Of the true love less vividly mount upward.
But in commensuration of our wages
　With our desert is portion of our joy,
　Because we see them neither less nor greater.
Herein doth living Justice sweeten so
　Affection in us, that for evermore
　It cannot warp to any iniquity.
Voices diverse make up sweet melodies ;
　So in this life of ours the seats diverse
　Render sweet harmony among these spheres ;

---

[1] *De Monarchiâ*, ii. 10, 11.

And in the compass of this present pearl
   Shineth the sheen of Romeo, of whom
   The grand and beauteous work was ill rewarded.
But the Provençals who against him wrought,
   They have not laughed, and therefore ill goes he
   Who makes his hurt of the good deeds of others.
Four daughters, and each one of them a queen,
   Had Raymond Berenger, and this for him
   Did Romeo, a poor man and a pilgrim ;
And then malicious words incited him
   To summon to a reckoning this just man,
   Who rendered to him seven and five for ten.
Then he departed poor and stricken in years,
   And if the world could know the heart he had,
   In begging bit by bit his livelihood,
Though much it laud him, it would laud him more.'

VI. 112-142.

He who is here called Romeo (probably not a proper name, but a term equivalent to ' pilgrim to Rome '[1]), arriving a stranger at the court of Raymond Berenger Count of Provence, became his trusted seneschal, tripled his income while maintaining his grandeur, and contrived the brilliant marriages of his four daughters—Margaret to S. Louis of France, Eleanor to Henry III. of England, Sanctia to Richard Earl of Cornwall elected King of the Romans, Beatrice to Charles Count of Anjou, afterwards by Papal investiture King of Naples. The sequel is but too clear.

The Saints vanished with singing ; and Beatrice discerning in Dante's mind a perplexity arising from Justinian's words respecting that vengeance on Jerusalem whereof Titus was the minister, proceeded thus to instruct him :

[1] *Vita Nuova* xli.

'According to infallible advisement,
    After what manner a just vengeance justly
    Could be avenged has put thee upon thinking,
But I will speedily thy mind unloose;
    And do thou listen, for these words of mine
    Of a great doctrine will a present make thee.
By not enduring on the power that wills
    Curb for his good, that man who ne'er was born,
    Damning himself damned all his progeny;
Whereby the human species down below
    Lay sick for many centuries in great error,
    Till to descend it pleased the Word of God
To where the nature, which from its own Maker
    Estranged itself, He joined to Him in person,
    By the sole act of His eternal love.
Now unto what is said direct thy sight;
    This nature when united to its Maker,
    Such as created, was sincere and good;
But by itself alone was banished forth
    From Paradise, because it turned aside
    Out of the way of truth and of its life.
Therefore the penalty the cross held out,
    If measured by the nature thus assumed,
    None ever yet with so great justice stung,
And none was ever of so great injustice,
    Considering Who the Person was that suffered,
    Within Whom such a nature was contracted.
From one act therefore issued things diverse;
    To God and to the Jews one Death was pleasing;
    Earth trembled at it and the Heaven was opened.
It should no longer now seem difficult
    To thee, when it is said that a just vengeance
    By a just court was afterward avenged.
But now do I behold thy mind entangled

From thought to thought within a knot, from which
  With great desire it waits to free itself.
Thou sayest, "Well discern I what I hear ;
  But it is hidden from me why God willed
  For our redemption only this one mode."
Buried remaineth, brother, this decree
  Unto the eyes of every one whose nature
  Is in the flame of love not yet adult.
Verily, inasmuch as at this mark
  One gazes long and little is discerned,
  Wherefore this mode was worthiest will I say.
[1] Goodness Divine, which from Itself doth spurn
  All envy, burning in Itself so sparkles
  That the eternal beauties It unfolds.[1]
[2] Whate'er from This immediately distils
  Has afterwards no end, for ne'er removed
  Is Its impression when It sets Its seal.
Whate'er from This immediately rains down
  Is wholly free, because it is not subject
  Unto the influences of novel things.
The more conformed thereto, the more it pleases ;
  For the blest Ardour that irradiates all things
  In that most like Itself is most vivacious.
With all of these things has advantaged been
  The human creature ; and if one be wanting,
  From his nobility he needs must fall.
'Tis sin alone which doth disfranchise him,
  And render him unlike the Good Supreme,[2]
  So that he little with Its light is blanched,[3]

---

[1] The Divine Goodness, wholly free from aught that is contrary to charity, in the ardour of Its own Love so sparkles as to take pleasure in manifesting and communicating Its Eternal Beauty.

[2] See pp. 13, 14, ' All creatures,' etc.

[3] Irradiated.

And to his dignity no more returns,
　Unless he fill up where transgression empties
　With righteous pains for criminal delights.
Your nature when it sinned so utterly
　In its own seed, out of these dignities
　Even as out of Paradise was driven,
Nor could itself recover, if thou notest
　With nicest subtilty, by any way,
　Except by passing one of these two fords :
Either that God through clemency alone
　Had pardon granted, or that man himself
　Had satisfaction for his folly made.
Fix now thine eye deep into the abyss
　Of the eternal counsel, to my speech
　As far as may be fastened steadfastly !
Man in his limitations had not power
　To satisfy, not having power to sink
　In his humility obeying then,
Far as he disobeying thought to rise ;
　And for this reason man has been from power
　Of satisfying by himself excluded.
Therefore it God behoved in His own ways[1]
　Man to restore unto his perfect life,
　I say in one, or else in both of them.
But since the action of the doer is
　So much more grateful, as it more presents
　The goodness of the heart from which it issues,
Goodness Divine, that doth imprint the world,
　Has been contented to proceed by each
　And all Its ways to lift you up again ;
Nor 'twixt the first day and the final night
　Such high and such magnificent proceeding

---

[1] Mercy and Justice.

By one or by the other was or shall be ;
  For God more bounteous was Himself to give
  To make man able to uplift himself,
  Than if He only of Himself had pardoned ;
And all the other modes were insufficient
  For justice, were it not the Son of God
  Himself had humbled to become incarnate.'

VII. 19-120.

The ascent to Venus, insensible at the moment, was after taking place revealed by the increased beauty of Beatrice. Here within the star's light were seen circling other lights, their charity such that albeit they revolved with the Heavenly Principalities, yet, as one testified, Dante's desire to converse with them would render a pause no less blissful than unbroken revolution.

After these eyes of mine themselves had offered
  Unto my Lady reverently, and she
  Content and certain of herself had made them,
Back to the light they turned, which so great promise
  Made of itself, and, ' Say, who art thou ?' was
  My voice, imprinted with a great affection.
O how and how much I beheld it grow
  With the new joy that superadded was
  Unto its joys, as soon as I had spoken !
Thus changed, it said to me : ' The world possessed me
  Short time below : and, if it had been more,
  Much evil will be which would not have been.
My gladness keepeth me concealed from thee,
  Which rayeth round about me, and doth hide me
  Like as a creature swathed in its own silk.
Much didst thou love me, and thou hadst good reason ;
  For had I been below, I should have shown thee
  Somewhat beyond the foliage of my love.'

VIII. 40-57 .

This Saint was Charles Martel, the eldest son of Charles II. of Naples by his wife Mary of Hungary, and thus doubly born a King, though the paternal crown he did not live to inherit, dying at the age of twenty-three. This virtuous prince and early friend of Dante now bitterly lamented the fate of Naples under his money-loving brother Robert I., degenerate from their large-natured father.—Yet when a son is not the speaker, Charles II. himself is throughout the poem unfavourably mentioned. In another passage of the Paradiso [1] largeness of nature is indeed probably alluded to as his one virtue ; but in the Purgatorio he is actually included in Hugh Capet's denunciation of the avarice of his house,[2] and is spoken of by Sordello as degenerate from his own father Charles I.[3] Such degeneracy, of which various instances were then under contemplation, was, as we saw, attributed by the speaker to its primary cause, the Will of Almighty God [4] that all the glory of human virtue should be ascribed to Himself. Dante now, desiring farther light on the subject, asked of Charles Martel how of sweet seed can come bitter, and heard the astrological doctrine of the secondary cause and its practical result :—that the star under which nativity takes place counteracts and modifies by its influence the otherwise unvarying rule of the resemblance of child to parent ; and that in all glaring instances of contrast between a man's self and his state of life, the blame should fall, not on Nature for not adapting him to his state, but on himself and his advisers for not adapting his state to him.

[1] *Par.* xix. 127-129.
[2] *Pur.* xx. 79-81.
[3] *Pur.* vii. 124.
[4] See pp. 136, 137.

Other Spirits of this Third Heaven then conversed with
their guest; and Rahab was pointed out to him as its most
exalted inhabitant.

But behold him now free of the region of imperfect
Wills; the transitional Heaven of the Sun lies before him,
the peculiar kingdom of Wisdom and Knowledge.—The
Sun was in Aries,

> And I was with him; but of the ascending
>   I was not conscious, saving as a man
>   Of a first thought is conscious ere it come;
> And Beatrice, she who is seen to pass
>   From good to better, and so suddenly
>   That not by time her action is expressed,
> How lucent in herself must she have been!
>   And what was in the sun, wherein I entered,
>   Apparent not by colour but by light,
> I, though I call on genius, art, and practice,
>   Cannot so tell that it could be imagined;
>   Believe one can, and let him long to see it.
> And if our fantasies too lowly are
>   For altitude so great, it is no marvel,
>   Since o'er the sun was never eye could go.
> Such in this place was the fourth family
>   Of the high Father, Who for ever sates it,
>   Showing how He breathes forth and how begets.
> And Beatrice began : ' Give thanks, give thanks
>   Unto the Sun of Angels, Who to this
>   Sensible one has raised thee by His grace !'
> Never was heart of mortal so disposed
>   To worship, nor to give itself to God
>   With all its gratitude was it so ready,
> As at those words did I myself become;
>   And all my love was so absorbed in Him,

That in oblivion Beatrice was eclipsed.
Nor this displeased her ; but she smiled at it
  So that the splendour of her laughing eyes
  My single mind on many things divided.
Lights many saw I, vivid and triumphant,
  Make us a centre and themselves a circle,
  More sweet in voice than luminous in aspect.
Thus girt about the daughter of Latona
  We sometimes see, when pregnant is the air,
  So that it holds the thread which makes her zone.[1]
Within the court of Heaven, whence I return,
  Are many jewels found, so fair and precious
  They cannot be transported from the realm ;
And of them was the singing of those lights.
  Who takes not wings that he may fly up thither,
  The tidings thence may from the dumb await !

X. 34-75.

S. Thomas Aquinas from out the garland made known himself and his companions, among whom were Albertus Magnus ; Gratian ; Peter Lombard ; Solomon ; S. Dionysius the Areopagite, whose treatise De cœlesti Hierarchiâ is the foundation of Dante's own theory respecting the Angelic Orders ; Severinus Boëthius ; and the Venerable Bede. On Boëthius we may dwell a moment longer ; he had been a Roman Senator whom the Gothic King Theodoric in consequence of some suspicion imprisoned at Pavia, and who there wrote the treatise De consolatione Philosophiæ, Dante's comfort in the bitter mourning of his youth,[2] as doubtless also in the exile of his maturer age. This eighth radiance of the garland was thus specially commended to notice :

[1] The colours which form the halo.
[2] *Convito* ii. 13 (see page 22).

‘ Now if thou trainest thy mind's eye along
   From light to light pursuant of my praise,
   With thirst already of the eighth thou waitest.
By seeing every good therein exults
   The sainted Soul, which the fallacious world
   Makes manifest to him who listeneth well ;
The body whence 'twas hunted forth is lying
   Down in Cieldauro, and from martyrdom
   And banishment it came unto this peace.'.

X. 121-129.

All aglow with charity, the great Dominican Saint proceeded to dilate first on the glories, not of his own Founder,
but of the ‘seraphic’ S. Francis of Assisi ; and then, while
exalting S. Dominic, severely to condemn the corruptions
which had crept into his Order. But anon round the first
saintly garland formed a second, among whose component
roses were Hugh de S. Victor, the Prophet Nathan, S.
Chrysostom, S. Anselm, and S. Bonaventura the Franciscan,
who emulous of S. Thomas' humility and charity first
narrated the acts of the ‘cherubic’ S. Dominic : and alas !
found hardly less reason to conclude by censuring his own
Order than by extolling its Founder S. Francis.

Then S. Thomas spoke again. In naming one by one
the Saints of the first garland he had said of Solomon, the
Singer of the Canticles and the wisest of mankind,

‘ The fifth light, that among us is the fairest,
   Breathes forth from such a love that all the world
   Below is greedy to learn tidings of it.
Within it is the lofty mind, where knowledge
   So deep was put, that, if the true be true,
   To see so much there never rose a second :’

(X. 109-114)

and this concluding assertion had wrought in his hearer's mind a perplexity which the Angelic Doctor removed by explaining that Regal Prudence is the one and only point of this King's unique eminence among the sons of men. And after an admonition against hasty sentence in matters of reasoning, he gave yet more solemn warning against self-intrusion into the Eternal Judgment-Seat :

> ' Nor yet shall people be too confident
>   In judging, even as he is who doth count
>   The corn in field or ever it be ripe.
> For I have seen all winter long the thorn
>   First show itself intractable and fierce,
>   And after bear the rose upon its top ;
> And I have seen a ship direct and swift
>   Run o'er the sea throughout its course entire,
>   To perish at the harbour's mouth at last.
> Let not Dame Bertha nor Ser Martin think,
>   Seeing one steal, another offering make,
>   To see them in the arbitrament divine ;
> For one may rise, and fall the other may.'
>
> XIII. 130-142.

Beatrice next besought on Dante's behalf instruction respecting another truth.

> ' This man has need (and does not tell you so,
>   Nor with the voice, nor even in his thought)
>   Of going to the root of one truth more.
> Declare unto him if the light wherewith
>   Blossoms your substance shall remain with you
>   Eternally the same that it is now ;
> And if it do remain, say in what manner,
>   After ye are again made visible,
>   It can be that it injure not your sight.'

As by a greater gladness urged and drawn
    They who are dancing in a ring sometimes
    Uplift their voices and their motions quicken;
So, at that orison devout and prompt,
    The holy circles a new joy displayed
    In their revolving and their wondrous song.
Whoso lamenteth him that here we die
    That we may live above, has never there
    Seen the refreshment of the eternal rain.
The One and Two and Three who ever liveth,
    And reigneth ever in Three and Two and One,
    Not circumscribed and all things circumscribing,
Three several times was chanted by each one
    Among those Spirits with such melody
    That for all merit it were just reward;
And, in the lustre most divine of all
    The lesser ring, I heard a modest voice,[1]
    Such as perhaps the Angel's was to Mary,
Answer: [2]'As long as the festivity
    Of Paradise shall be, so long our Love
    Shall radiate round about us such a vesture.
Its brightness is proportioned to the ardour,
    The ardour to the vision; and the vision
    Equals what grace it has above its worth.[2]
When, glorious and sanctified, our flesh
    Is reassumed, then shall our persons be
    More pleasing by their being all complete;
For will increase whate'er bestows on us
    Of light gratuitous the Good Supreme,

---

[1] Solomon's.
[2] So long as Paradise shall last, so long shall God our Love radiate this vesture of light around us. Its brightness is in proportion to the ardour of our charity, that ardour to our vision of God; and that vision is in proportion to the grace bestowed upon the soul over and above its natural powers.

Light which enables us to look on Him ;
Therefore the vision must perforce increase,
    Increase the ardour which from that is kindled,
    Increase the radiance which from this proceeds.
But [1]even as a coal that sends forth flame,
    And by its vivid whiteness overpowers it
    So that its own appearance it maintains,
Thus the effulgence that surrounds us now
    Shall be o'erpowered in aspect by the flesh,[1]
    Which still to-day the earth doth cover up ;
Nor can so great a splendour weary us,
    For strong will be the organs of the body
    To everything which hath the power to please us.'
So sudden and alert appeared to me
    Both one and the other choir to say Amen,
    That well they showed desire for their dead bodies ;
Nor sole for them perhaps, but for the mothers,
    The fathers, and the rest who had been dear
    Or ever they became eternal flames.
And lo ! all round about of equal brightness
    Arose a lustre over what was there,
    Like an horizon that is clearing up.
And as at rise of early eve begin
    Along the welkin new appearances,
    So that the sight seems real and unreal,
It seemed to me that new subsistences
    Began there to be seen, and make a circle
    Outside the other two circumferences.
O very sparkling of the Holy Spirit,
    How sudden and incandescent it became
    Unto mine eyes, that vanquished bore it not !

---

[1] Even as a coal sending out a flame does yet by its own vivid brightness so overpower that flame as to be still distinguished as coal, so will the risen body of flesh be distinguishable notwithstanding the effulgence.

But Beatrice so beautiful and smiling
   Appeared to me, that with the other sights
   That followed not my memory I must leave her.
Then to uplift themselves mine eyes resumed
   The power, and I beheld myself translated
   To higher salvation with my Lady only.
Well was I ware that I was more uplifted
   By the enkindled smiling of the star,
   That seemed to me more ruddy than its wont.
With all my heart, and in that dialect
   Which is the same in all, such holocaust
   To God I made as the new grace beseemed ;
And not yet from my bosom was exhausted
   The ardour of sacrifice, before I knew
   This offering was accepted and auspicious :
For with so great a lustre and so red
   Splendours appeared to me in twofold rays,
   I said : ' O Helios who dost so adorn them ! '
Even as distinct with less and greater lights
   Glimmers between the two poles of the world
   The Galaxy that maketh wise men doubt,
Thus constellated in the depths of Mars,
   Those rays described the venerable sign
   That quadrants joining in a circle make.
Here doth my memory overcome my genius :
   For on that cross as levin gleamed forth Christ,
   So that I cannot find ensample worthy ;
But he who takes his cross and follows Christ
   Again will pardon me what I omit,
   Seeing in that aurora lighten Christ.
From horn to horn, and 'twixt the top and base,
   Lights were in motion, brightly scintillating
   As they together met and passed each other.

                                    XIV. 10-111.

An ineffable melody of a hymn to the Conqueror of
Death resounded all over the Cross; then the hush of
charity fell upon it that the stranger might speak and hear.
But lo an individual star from out that constellation saluted
him kinsman, giving fervent thanks for the grace super-
abounding towards him, and uttering afterwards things such
as no mortal mind can comprehend. Then most loving
and courteous words invited question ; and question was
made forthwith.

' Truly do I entreat thee, living topaz !
 Set in this precious jewel as a gem,
 That thou wilt satisfy me with thy name.'
' O leaf of mine, in whom I pleasure took
 E'en while awaiting, I was thine own root !'
 Such a beginning he in answer made me.
Then said to me : ' That one from whom is named
 Thy race, and who a hundred years and more
 Has circled round the mount on the first cornice,
A son of mine and thy great-grandsire was ;
 Well it behoves thee that the long fatigue
 Thou shouldst for him make shorter with thy works.
Florence, within the ancient boundary
 From which she taketh still her tierce and nones,[1]
 Abode in quiet, temperate and chaste.
No golden chain she had, nor coronal,
 Nor ladies shod with sandal shoon, nor girdle
 That caught the eye more than the person did.
Not yet the daughter at her birth struck fear
 Into the father, for the time and dower

---

[1] Some say the Hours were sung in the Abbey, others in the Palazzo
Pubblico ; both within the circuit of the ancient walls. (Fraticelli
in loc.)

Did not o'errun this side or that the measure.
No houses had she void of families,
   Not yet had thither come Sardanapalus
   To show what in a chamber can be done ;
Not yet surpassed had Montemalo been
   By your Uccellatojo, which surpassed [1]
   Shall in its downfall be as in its rise.
Bellincion Berti [2] saw I go begirt
   With leather and with bone, and from the mirror
   His dame depart without a painted face ;
And him of Nerli saw, and him of Vecchio, [3]
   Contented with their simple suits of buff,
   And with the spindle and the flax their dames.
O fortunate women ! and each one was certain
   Of her own burial-place, and none as yet
   For sake of France was in her bed deserted.
One o'er the cradle kept her studious watch,
   And in her lullaby the language used
   That first delights the fathers and the mothers ;
Another, drawing tresses from her distaff,
   Told o'er among her family the tales
   Of Trojans and of Fesole and Rome.
As great a marvel then would have been held
   A Lapo Salterello, a Cianghella, [4]
   As Cincinnatus or Cornelia now.
To such a quiet, such a beautiful
   Life of the citizen, to such a safe
   Community, and to so sweet an inn,
Did Mary give me, with loud cries invoked,

---

[1] The Hill of Montemalo overlooks Rome, that of the Uccellatojo Florence, which latter city had now surpassed Rome in the splendour of its buildings.

[2,3] Florentine nobles.

[4] Persons notorious for vice.

And in your ancient Baptistery at once
   Christian and Cacciaguida I became.
Moronto was my brother, and Eliseo ;
   From Val di Pado came to me my wife,[1]
   And from that place thy surname was derived.
I followed afterward the Emperor Conrad,[2]
   And he begirt me of his chivalry,
   So much I pleased him with my noble deeds.
I followed in his train against that law's
   Iniquity, whose people doth usurp
   Your just possessions, through your Pastor's fault.
There by that execrable race was I
   Released from bonds of the fallacious world,
   The love of which defileth many souls,
And came from martyrdom unto this peace.'

XV. 85-148.

Long, long did ancestor and descendant continue to converse of Florence past and present : then the younger besought clear knowledge of that future darkly hinted to him in Hell and in Purgatory ; and the elder, seeing all things reflected in the Eternal Mind as in a mirror, uttered what he saw.

'As forth from Athens went Hippolytus,
   By reason of his step-dame false and cruel,
   So thou from Florence must perforce depart.
Already this is willed, and this is sought for ;
   And soon it shall be done by him who thinks it,
   Where every day the Christ is bought and sold.

---

[1] From Ferrara in the Valley of the Pado or Po. She was of the Aldighieri or Allighieri family.

[2] Conrad III., the first Emperor of the House of Hohenstauffen, was one of the leaders of the Second Crusade.

[1] The blame shall follow the offended party
  In outcry as is usual ; but the vengeance
  Shall witness to the truth that doth dispense it.[1]
Thou shalt abandon everything beloved
  Most tenderly, and this the arrow is
  Which first the bow of banishment shoots forth.
Thou shalt have proof how savoureth of salt
  The bread of others, and how hard a road
  The going down and up another's stairs.
And that which most shall weigh upon thy shoulders
  Will be the bad and foolish company
  With which into this valley thou shalt fall ;
For all ingrate, all mad and impious
  Will they become against thee ; but soon after
  They, and not thou, shall have the forehead scarlet.
Of their bestiality their own proceedings
  Shall furnish proof ; so 'twill be well for thee
  A party to have made thee by thyself.

.   .   .   .   .   .

            Son, these are the commentaries
  On what was said to thee : behold the snares
  That are concealed behind few revolutions ;
Yet would I not thy neighbours thou shouldst envy,
  Because thy life into the future reaches
  Beyond the punishment of their perfidies.'
When by its silence showed that sainted soul
  That it had finished putting in the woof
  Into that web which I had given it warped,
Began I, even as he who yearneth after,
  Being in doubt, some counsel from a person
  Who seeth, and uprightly wills, and loves :

---

[1] As usual in this world, thou who comest off worst wilt be considered in the wrong ; but the vengeance that shall overtake thy persecutors from Him Who is the Truth shall witness to the truth.

'Well see I, father mine, how spurreth on
   The time towards me such a blow to deal me
   As heaviest is to him who most gives way.
Therefore with foresight it is well I arm me,
   That, if the dearest place be taken from me,
   I may not lose the others by my songs.[1]
Down through the world of infinite bitterness,
   And o'er the mountain, from whose beauteous summit
   The eyes of my own Lady lifted me,
And afterward through Heaven from light to light,
   I have learned that which, if I tell again,
   Will be a savour of strong herbs to many.
And if I am a timid friend to truth,
   I fear lest I may lose my life with those
   Who will hereafter call this time the olden.'
The light in which was smiling my own treasure
   Which there I had discovered, flashed at first
   As in the sunshine doth a golden mirror ;
Then made reply : 'A conscience overcast
   Or with its own or with another's shame,
   Will taste forsooth the tartness of thy word ;
But ne'ertheless, all falsehood laid aside,
   Make manifest thy vision utterly,
   And let them scratch wherever is the itch ;
For if thine utterance shall offensive be
   At the first taste, a vital nutriment
   'T will leave thereafter, when it is digested.
This cry of thine shall do as doth the wind,
   Which smiteth most the most exalted summits,
   And that is no slight argument of honour.
Therefore are shown to thee within these wheels,

---

[1] That if I am exiled from my country, I may not for telling unwelcome truths be expelled from every place of refuge.

Upon the mount and in the dolorous valley,
  Only the Souls that unto fame are known ;
Because the spirit of the hearer rests not,
  Nor doth confirm its faith by an example
  Which has the root of it unknown and hidden,
Or other reason that is not apparent.'

                          XVII. 46-69, 94-142.

Comforted in his prospective sorrows by the love and bliss shining on him through the eyes of his Beloved, the future exile from among his fellow-citizens of Florence applied himself to learn from his progenitor some renowned names of his fellow-citizens of Paradise ; each name as it resounded being claimed by the owner's flashing in his place in one or other arm of the Cross. Joshua flashed, and Judas Maccabæus; Charlemagne and Roland; the Crusaders Godfrey of Bouillon, William of Orange, and his kinsman Rinaldo; finally, Robert Guiscard the Norman conqueror of Sicily from the Saracens. Cacciaguida returned to sing at his post within the Cross ; and there was a pause.

To my right side I turned myself around,
  My duty to behold in Beatrice
  Either by words or gesture signified ;
And so translucent I beheld her eyes,
  So full of pleasure, that her countenance
  Surpassed its other and its latest wont.
And as, by feeling greater delectation,
  A man in doing good from day to day
  Becomes aware his virtue is increasing,
So I became aware that my gyration
  With Heaven together had increased its arc,

That miracle beholding more adorned.
And such as is the change, in little lapse
   Of time, in a pale woman, when her face
   Is from the load of bashfulness unladen,
Such was it in mine eyes, when I had turned,
   Caused by the whiteness of the temperate star,
   The sixth, which to itself had gathered me.

                                 XVIII. 52-69.

Here certain radiant Spirits so arranged themselves as successively to form each of the thirty-five letters of the sentence, ‘ Diligite justitiam, qui judicatis terram.’ Then more Lights descended to enwreathe the final *m*, and at length, when all had developed into the form of the crowned Eagle of the Latin Empire, the Saints constituting the Beak began to sing of their own and their fellows’ exaltation hither on account of their Justice and Mercy.

Whence I thereafter : ‘ O perpetual flowers
   Of the eternal joy, that only one
   Make me perceive your odours manifold,
Exhaling, break within me the great fast
   Which a long season has in hunger held me,
   Not finding for it any food on earth.
Well do I know, that if in Heaven its mirror
   Justice Divine another realm doth make,
   Yours apprehends it not through any veil.
You know how I attentively address me
   To listen ; and you know what is the doubt
   That is in me so very old a fast.’
Even as a falcon, issuing from his hood,
   Doth move his head, and with his wings applaud him,
   Showing desire, and making himself fine,
Saw I become that standard, which of lauds
   Was interwoven of the grace divine,

With such songs as he knows who there rejoices.
Then it began : 'He Who a compass turned
  On the world's outer verge, and Who within it
  Devised so much occult and manifest,
Could not the impress of His power so make
  On all the universe, as that His Word
  Should not remain in infinite excess.[1]
And this makes certain that the first proud being,[2]
  Who was the paragon of every creature,
  By not awaiting light fell immature.
And hence appears it, that each minor nature
  Is scant receptacle unto that Good
  Which has no end, and by Itself is measured.
In consequence our vision, which perforce
  Must be some ray of that Intelligence
  With Which all things whatever are replete,
Cannot in its own nature be so potent.
  That it shall not its Origin discern
  Far beyond that which is apparent to it.[3]
Therefore into the justice sempiternal
  The power of vision that your world receives,
  As eye into the ocean penetrates ;
Which, though it see the bottom near the shore,
  Upon the deep perceives it not, and yet
  'Tis there, but it is hidden by the depth.
[4]There is no light but comes from the serene
  That never is o'ercast, nay, it is darkness
  Or shadow of the flesh, or else its poison.[4]

---

[1] Should not infinitely exceed the intelligence of the highest creature.
[2] See page 15.
[3] Discern God its Origin infinitely to surpass its own perceptions.
[4] Nothing is light but that which comes from God's unclouded Brightness ; whatever else claims to be so is darkness, or a shadow cast by the flesh, or the poison of false judgment bred in the senses.

Amply to thee is opened now the cavern
   Which has concealed from thee the living justice
   Of which thou mad'st such frequent questioning.
For saidst thou : " Born a man is on the shore
   Of Indus, and is none who there can speak
   Of Christ, nor who can read, nor who can write ;
And all his inclinations and his actions
   Are good, so far as human reason sees,
   Without a sin in life or in discourse :
He dieth unbaptized and without faith ;
   Where is this justice that condemneth him ?
   Where is his fault, if he do not believe ? "
Now who art thou, that on the bench wouldst sit
   In judgment at a thousand miles away,
   With the short vision of a single span ?
[1] Truly to him who with me subtilizes,
   If so the Scripture were not over you,
   For doubting there were marvellous occasion.'
O animals terrene, O stolid minds,
   The primal Will, that in Itself is good,
   Ne'er from Itself, the Good Supreme, has moved.
So much is just as is accordant with It ;
   No good created draws It to itself,
   But It, by raying forth, occasions that.'
Even as above her nest goes circling round
   The stork when she has fed her little ones,
   And he who has been fed looks up at her,
So lifted I my brows, and even such
   Became the blessed image, which its wings
   Was moving, by so many counsels urged.

---

[1] Truly to him who so subtilely argues with me there would be great occasion to doubt, were not the Scripture far above all human arguments.

Circling around it sang, and said : 'As are
  My notes to thee, who dost not comprehend them,
  Such is the eternal judgment to you mortals.'
Those lucent splendours of the Holy Spirit
  Grew quiet then, but still within the standard
  That made the Romans reverend to the world.
It recommenced : ' Unto this kingdom never
  Ascended one who had not faith in Christ,
  Before or since He to the tree was nailed.
But look thou, many crying are, " Christ, Christ ! "
  Who at the judgment shall be far less near
  To Him than some shall be who knew not Christ.
Such Christians shall the Ethiop condemn,
  When the two companies shall be divided,
  The one for ever rich, the other poor.
What to your kings may not the Persians say,
  When they that volume opened shall behold
  In which are written down all their dispraises ? '

                                     XIX. 22-114.

And then followed the special dispraises of the reigning
Princes of Europe ; of the Emperor Albert I. for his invasion
and occupation of Bohemia, of Philippe le Bel for his de-
basement of the coin, of Edward I. and his Scottish rival for
their pride and ambition, of Charles the Lame of Naples
for the virtue [1] whereof I and the vices whereof M is the
numeral, and of many others of less familiar names on
various grounds.—Songs of unspeakable sweetness filled up
a pause ; and soon the Beak spoke again, giving account
of the six specially exalted Spirits forming the Eye. The
Pupil was David. The first of the five of the Eyebrow was
Trajan, in the Middle Ages popularly believed to have

---

[1] *Par.* viii. 82 (p. 229).

been delivered from Hell and resuscitated on earth through S. Gregory the Great being moved to intercede for him for love of his eminent justice, and in that second brief earthly life to have embraced Christianity, received Baptism, and merited Paradise. The other four were Hezekiah ; Constantine the Great; William the Good of Naples and Sicily; and Ripheus the Trojan, supposed by Dante to have been first enabled by special grace to set all his affections on justice, and so to have passed on to the further grace of foreseeing the future Redemption, reproving idolatry, and having for Baptism the three Theological Virtues. As here no popular or legendary belief seems adducible, we may, I think, assume this last case to be imagined as the Poet's own reply to his recently-cited question respecting Eternal Justice towards a perfectly virtuous heathen ;[1] a reply amounting to this—that no heathen could be perfectly virtuous save by a miracle of grace ; and that supposing this first miracle performed, a second might much rather be expected to infuse a faith that cometh not by hearing, than faith itself be dispensed with as the condition of salvation. The imagination of such a case is in fact an expansion of the Eagle's words before cited,

> ' No good created draws It to itself,
>   But It, by raying forth, occasions that.'
>
> XIX. 89, 90.[2]

The ascent to Saturn was not merely insensible, but unmarked even by the smile of Beatrice, whose glory would at this point have been unendurable by mortal man. Here Jacob's Ladder, the golden-hued symbol of Divine Con-

---

[1] *Par.* xix. 70-78 (p. 245).   [2] See the same page.

templation, stretched up into heights untraceable; and Saints as countless stars shimmered up and down upon it, but sang not—as one of them explained to Dante—for the same reason that Beatrice did not smile. The explainer was S. Peter Damian, a Benedictine monk made by Pope Stephen IX. Cardinal and Bishop of Ostia. His farther statement that not greater love to the Pilgrim guest than his companions nourished, but Divine Election was the cause of his being the one to present himself to hear and to reply, moved Dante to inquire the ground of such election.

> No sooner had I come to the last word,
>   Than of its middle made the light a centre,
>   Whirling itself about like a swift millstone.
> Then answer made the love that was therein :
>   'On me directed is a light divine,
>   Piercing through this in which I am embosomed,
> Of which the virtue with my sight conjoined
>   Lifts me above myself so far, I see
>   The Supreme Essence from which this is drawn.
> Hence comes the joyfulness with which I flame,
>   For to my sight, as far as it is clear,
>   The clearness of the flame I equal make.
> But that Soul in the Heaven which is most pure,
>   That Seraph which his eye on God most fixes,
>   Could this demand of thine not satisfy ;
> Because so deeply sinks in the abyss
>   Of the eternal statute what thou askest,
>   From all created sight it is cut off.
> And to the mortal world, when thou returnest,
>   This carry back, that it may not presume
>   Longer tow'rd such a goal to move its feet.
> The mind that shineth here, on earth doth smoke ;

From this observe how can it do below
That which it cannot though the Heaven assume it?'

XXI. 79-102.

The Saint refused not however to name himself when requested; after which he severely animadverted on the worldliness of the churchmen of the day, and a thunder-cry to the Divine Justice went up from the radiant multitude. Beatrice having calmed her disciple's consequent fear, directed his attention to that multitude. Its largest and brightest pearl, S. Benedict, then declared himself, and pointed out S. Macarius and S. Romuald.

And I to him : 'The affection which thou showest
　Speaking with me, and the good countenance
　Which I behold and note in all your ardours,
In me have so my confidence dilated
　As the sun doth the rose, when it becomes
　As far unfolded as it hath the power.
Therefore I pray, and thou assure me, father,
　If I may so much grace receive, that I
　May thee behold with countenance unveiled.'
He thereupon : 'Brother, thy high desire
　In the remotest sphere shall be fulfilled,
　Where are fulfilled all others and my own.
There perfect is, and ripened, and complete,
　Every desire ; within that one alone
　Is every part where it has always been ;[1]
For it is not in space, nor turns on poles,
　And unto it our stairway reaches up,
　Whence thus from out thy sight it steals away.
Up to that height the Patriarch Jacob saw it
　Extending its supernal part, what time
　So thronged with angels it appeared to him.

XXII. 52-72.

---

[1] The Empyrean is motionless.

He ended with rebuke—the relaxation of the Monastic
Orders supplying the text—

>   . . . and then withdrew
> To his own band, and the band closed together ;
> Then like a whirlwind all was upward rapt.
> The gentle Lady urged me on behind them
> Up o'er that stairway by a single sign,
> So did her virtue overcome my nature ;
> Nor here below, where one goes up and down
> By natural law, was motion e'er so swift
> That it could be compared unto my wing.
> Reader, as I may unto that devout
> Triumph return, on whose account I often
> For my transgressions weep and beat my breast,—
> Thou hadst not thrust thy finger in the fire
> And drawn it out again, before I saw
> The sign that follows Taurus, and was in it.
>
>   XXII. 97-111.

This is the Sign of Gemini, under which Dante, as he
proceeds to relate, was born ; he was now in the Heaven
of the Fixed Stars, contemplating them one by one, and
looking down on Earth through all the Planetary Heavens.

> O glorious stars, O light impregnated
> With mighty virtue, from which I acknowledge
> All of my genius, whatsoe'er it be,
> With you was born, and hid,himself with you,
> He who is father of all mortal life,
> When first I tasted of the Tuscan air ;
> And then when grace was freely given to me
> To enter the high wheel which turns you round,
> Your region was allotted unto me.
> To you devoutly at this hour my soul
> Is sighing, that it virtue may acquire

For the stern pass that draws it to itself.[1]
'Thou art so near unto the last salvation,'[2]
   Thus Beatrice began, 'thou oughtest now
   To have thine eyes unclouded and acute ;
And therefore, ere thou enter farther in,
   Look down once more, and see how vast a world
   Thou hast already put beneath thy feet ;
So that thy heart, as jocund as it may,
   Present itself to the triumphant throng
   That comes rejoicing through this rounded ether.'
I with my sight returned through one and all
   The sevenfold spheres, and I beheld this globe
   Such that I smiled at its ignoble semblance ;
And that opinion I approve as best
   Which doth account it least ; and he who thinks
   Of something else may truly be called just.
I saw the daughter of Latona shining
   Without that shadow which to me was cause
   That once I had believed her rare and dense.[3]
The aspect of thy son, Hyperion,
   Here I sustained, and saw how move themselves
   Around and near him Maia and Dione.
Thence there appeared the temperateness of Jove
   'Twixt son and father, and to me was clear
   The change that of their whereabout they make ;
And all the seven made manifest to me
   How great they are, and eke how swift they are,
   And how they are in distant habitations.
The threshing-floor that maketh us so proud,
   To me revolving with the eternal Twins,

[1] The extreme difficulty of writing of the Supreme Mysteries beheld in the Empyrean.
[2] The highest beatitude.
[3] The theory abandoned by Dante (see p. 212).

Was all apparent made from hill to harbour !
Then to the beauteous eyes mine eyes I turned.

XXII. 112-154.

But there were yet greater things than these to be seen ·
the Triumph of Christ was about to descend.

Even as a bird, 'mid the beloved leaves,
    Quiet upon the nest of her sweet brood
    Throughout the night, that hideth all things from us,
Who, that she may behold their longed-for looks
    And find the food wherewith to nourish them,
    In which, to her, grave labours grateful are,
Anticipates the time on open spray
    And with an ardent longing waits the sun,
    Gazing intent as soon as breaks the dawn :
Even thus my Lady standing was, erect
    And vigilant, turned round towards the zone [1]
    Underneath which the sun displays less haste ;
So that beholding her distraught and wistful,
    Such I became as he is who desiring
    For something yearns, and hoping is appeased.
But brief the space from one When to the other ;
    Of my awaiting, say I, and the seeing
    The welkin grow resplendent more and more.
And Beatrice exclaimed : ' Behold the hosts
    Of Christ's triumphal march, and all the fruit
    Harvested by the rolling of these spheres ! '
It seemed to me her face was all aflame ;
    And eyes she had so full of ecstasy
    That I must needs pass on without describing.
As when in nights serene of the full moon
    Smiles Trivia among the nymphs eternal
    Who paint the firmament through all its gulfs,

---

[1] The South.

Saw I, above the myriads of lamps,
    A Sun[1] that one and all of them enkindled,
    E'en as our own doth the supernal sights,[2]
And through the living Light transparent shone
    The lucent Substance so intensely clear
    Into my sight, that I sustained it not.
O Beatrice, thou gentle guide and dear !
    To me she said : ' What overmasters thee
    A virtue is from which naught shields itself.
There are the Wisdom and Omnipotence
    That oped the thoroughfares 'twixt Heaven and earth,
    For which there erst had been so long a yearning.'
As fire from out a cloud unlocks itself,
    Dilating so it finds not room therein,
    And down, against its nature, falls to earth,
So did my mind, among those aliments
    Becoming larger, issue from itself,
    And that which it became cannot remember.
' Open thine eyes, and look at what I am :
    Thou hast beheld such things, that strong enough
    Hast thou become to tolerate my smile.'
I was as one who still retains the feeling
    Of a forgotten vision, and endeavours
    In vain to bring it back into his mind,
When I this invitation heard, deserving
    Of so much gratitude, it never fades
    Out of the book that chronicles the past.
If at this moment sounded all the tongues
    That Polyhymnia and her sisters made
    Most lubrical with their delicious milk, ·
To aid me, to a thousandth of the truth
    It would not reach, singing the holy smile

---

[1] Our Blessed Lord.   S   [2] The stars.

And how the holy aspect it illumed.
And therefore, representing Paradise,
  The sacred poem must perforce leap over,
  Even as a man who finds his way cut off;
But whoso thinketh of the ponderous theme,
  And of the mortal shoulder laden with it,
  Should blame it not, if under this it tremble.
It is no passage for a little boat
  This which goes cleaving the audacious prow,
  Nor for a pilot who would spare himself.
'Why doth my face so much enamour thee,
  That to the garden fair thou turnest not,
  Which under the rays of Christ is blossoming?
There is the Rose in which the Word Divine
  Became incarnate; there the lilies are
  By whose perfume the good way was discovered.'

                                    XXIII. 1-75.

Dante beheld the Mystical Rose, the Virgin Mother of God, crowned by the Archangel Gabriel in the form of a wreath of light and melody, follow her Adorable Son into the Empyrean.   But the mystical Lilies, the Apostles, and the rest of the Blessed remaining behind, were entreated of Beatrice to bedew her Charge with the waters of that Living Fountain whereof they drink unceasingly.   Their consent was betokened in their flaming velocity of revolution; then from the most beauteous circle stood forth in intensest glow S. Peter:

  And she: 'O light eterne of the great man
    To whom our Lord delivered up the keys
    He carried down of this miraculous joy,
  This one examine on points light and grave,
    As good beseemeth thee, about the Faith

By means of which thou on the sea didst walk.
If he love well, and hope well, and believe,
   From thee 'tis hid not ; for thou hast thy sight
   There where depicted everything is seen.
But since this kingdom has made citizens
   By means of the true Faith, to glorify it
   'Tis well he have the chance to speak thereof.'
As baccalaureate arms himself, and speaks not
   Until the master doth propose the question,
   To argue it, and not to terminate it,
So did I arm myself with every reason,
   While she was speaking, that I might be ready
   For such a questioner and such profession.
' Say, thou good Christian ; manifest thyself;
   What is the Faith ? '   Whereat I raised my brow
   Unto that light wherefrom was this breathed forth
Then turned I round to Beatrice, and she
   Prompt signals made to me that I should pour
   The water forth from my internal fountain.
' May grace, that suffers me to make confession,'
   Began I, ' to the great centurion,
   Cause my conceptions all to be explicit ! '
And I continued : ' As the truthful pen,
   Father, of thy dear brother wrote of it,
   Who put with thee Rome into the good way,
Faith is the substance of the things we hope for,
   And evidence of those that are not seen ;
   And this appears to me its quiddity.'
Then heard I : ' Very rightly thou perceivest,
   If well thou understandest why he placed it
   With substances and then with evidences.'
And I thereafterward : ' The things profound,
   That here vouchsafe to me their apparition,
   Unto all eyes below are so concealed,

That they exist there only in belief,
   Upon the which is founded the high hope,
   And hence it takes the nature of a substance.
And it behoveth us from this belief
   To reason without having other sight,
   And hence it has the nature of evidence.'
Then heard I : ' If whatever is acquired
   Below by doctrine were thus understood,
   No sophist's subtlety would there find place.'
Thus was breathed forth from that enkindled love ;
   Then added : ' Very well has been gone over
   Already of this coin the alloy and weight ;
But tell me if thou hast it in thy purse ?'
   And I : ' Yes, both so shining and so round,
   That in its stamp there is no peradventure.'
Thereafter issued from the light profound
   That there resplendent was : ' This precious jewel,
   Upon the which is every virtue founded,
Whence hadst thou it ?'   And I : ' The large outpouring
   Of Holy Spirit, which has been diffused
   Upon the ancient parchments and the new,
A syllogism is, which proved it to me
   With such acuteness, that, compared therewith,
   All demonstration seems to me obtuse.'
And then I heard : ' The ancient and the new
   Postulates, that to thee are so conclusive,
   Why dost thou take them for the word divine ?'
And I : ' The proofs, which show the truth to me,
   Are the works subsequent, whereunto Nature
   Ne'er heated iron yet, nor anvil beat.'
Twas answered me : ' Say, who assureth thee
   That those works ever were ? the thing itself
   That must be proved, naught else to thee affirms it.'
' Were the world to Christianity converted.'

I said, 'withouten miracles, this one
  Is such, the rest are not its hundredth part ;
Because that poor and fasting thou didst enter
  Into the field to sow there the good plant,
  Which was a vine and has become a thorn !'
This being finished, the high, holy Court
  Resounded through the spheres, 'One God we praise !
  In melody that there above is chanted.
And then that Baron, who from branch to branch,
  Examining, had thus conducted me,
  Till the extremest leaves we were approaching,
Again began : 'The grace that dallying
  Plays with thine intellect thy mouth has opened
  Up to this point, as it should opened be,
So that I do approve what forth emerged ;
  But now thou must express what thou believest,
  And whence to thy belief it was presented.'
' O holy father, Spirit who beholdest
  What thou believest so that thou o'ercamest,
  Towards the sepulchre, more youthful feet,'
Began I, ' thou dost wish me in this place
  The form to manifest of my prompt belief,
  And likewise thou the cause thereof demandest.
And I respond : In one God I believe,
  Sole and eterne, Who moveth all the Heavens
  With love and with desire, Himself unmoved ;
And of such faith not only have I proofs
  Physical and metaphysical, but gives them
  Likewise the truth that from this place rains down
Through Moses, through the Prophets and the Psalms,
  Through the Evangel, and through you, who wrote
  After the fiery Spirit sanctified you ;
In Persons three eterne believe, and these
  One essence I believe, so one and trine

They bear conjunction both with *sunt* and *est*.[1]
With the profound condition and divine
  Which now I touch upon, doth stamp my mind
  Ofttimes the doctrine evangelical.
This the beginning is, this is the spark
  Which afterwards dilates to vivid flame,
  And, like a star in heaven, is sparkling in me.'
Even as a lord who hears what pleaseth him
  His servant straight embraces, gratulating
  For the good news as soon as he is silent ;
So, giving me its benediction, singing,
  Three times encircled me, when I was silent,
  The apostolic light, at whose command
I spoken had, in speaking I so pleased him.

XXIV. 34-154.

Alas that the craving next expressed was never satis-fied !

If e'er it happen that the Poem Sacred,
  To which both Heaven and Earth have set their hand,
  So that it many a year hath made me lean,
O'ercome the cruelty that bars me out
  From the fair sheepfold, where a lamb I slumbered,
  An enemy to the wolves that war upon it,
With other voice forthwith, with other fleece
  Poet will I return, and at my font
  Baptismal will I take the laurel crown ;
Because into the Faith that maketh known
  All souls to God there entered I, and then
  Peter for her sake thus my brow encircled.

XXV. 1-12.

S. James the Great then issued from the Apostolic Choir.

---

[1] *Are* and *is*.

Dante evidently attributes to him—not, like modern commentators, to S. James the Less—the General Epistle which
specially inspires Hope by its boundless promises to prayer :
' If any of you lack wisdom, let him ask of God, that giveth to all men liberally, and upbraideth not ; and it shall be
given him.'   ' Every good gift and every perfect gift is from
above, and cometh down from the Father of lights, with
Whom is no variableness, neither shadow of turning.'[1]

> Smiling thereafterwards, said Beatrice :
>> ' Illustrious life, by whom the benefactions
>> Of our Basilica have been described,
> Make Hope resound within this altitude ;
>> Thou knowest as oft thou dost personify it
>> As Jesus to the three gave greater clearness.'—
> ' Lift up thy head, and make thyself assured ;
>> For what comes hither from the mortal world
>> Must needs be ripened in our radiance.'
> This comfort came to me from the second fire ;
>> Wherefore mine eyes I lifted to the hills,
>> Which bent them down before with too great weight.
> ' Since through His grace our Emperor wills that thou
>> Shouldst find thee face to face, before thy death,
>> In the most secret chamber, with His Counts,
> So that, the truth beholden of this court,[2]
>> Hope, which below there rightfully enamours,
>> Thereby thou strengthen in thyself and others,
> Say what it is, and how is flowering with it
>> Thy mind, and say from whence it came to thee.'
>> Thus did the second light again continue.
>> XXV. 28-48.

---

[1] S. James i. 5, 17.
[2] Having actually beheld the very truth of this Court of Heaven.

But the second question was one Dante could hardly
answer without vainglory :

> And the Compassionate, who piloted   ·
> > The plumage of my wings in such high flight,
> > Did in reply anticipate me thus :
> ' No child whatever the Church Militant
> > Of greater hope possesses, as is written
> > In that Sun which irradiates all our band ;
> Therefore it is conceded him from Egypt
> > To come into Jerusalem to see,
> > Or ever yet his warfare be completed.
> The two remaining points, that not for knowledge
> > Have been demanded, but that he report
> > How much this virtue unto thee is pleasing,
> To him I leave ; for hard he will not find them,
> > Nor of self-praise ; and let him answer them ;
> > And may the grace of God in this assist him ! '
> As a disciple, who his teacher follows,
> > Ready and willing, where he is expert,
> > That his proficiency may be displayed,
> ' Hope,' said I, ' is the certain expectation
> > Of future glory, which is the effect
> > Of grace divine and merit precedent.[1]
> From many stars this light comes unto me ;
> > But he instilled it first into my heart
> > Who was chief singer unto the chief Captain.
> ' *Sperent in Te*,'[2] in the high Theody
> > He sayeth, ' those who know Thy Name' ; and who
> > Knoweth it not, if he my faith possess ?
> Thou didst instil me, then, with his instilling

---

[1] This definition of Hope is from Peter Lombard the Master of Sen-
tences, whom we saw in the First Garland of holy Doctors (p. 231).

[2] Let them hope in Thee.   Ps. ix. 11, Vulgate ; ix. 10, E.P.V.

In the Epistle, so that I am full,
    And upon others rain again your rain.'
While I was speaking, in the living bosom
    Of that combustion quivered an effulgence,
    Sudden and frequent, in the guise of lightning ;
Then breathed : 'The love wherewith I am inflamed
    Towards the virtue still which followed me
    Unto the palm and issue of the field,
Wills that I breathe to thee that thou delight
    In her ; and grateful to me is thy telling
    Whatever things Hope promises to thee.'
And I : [1] 'The ancient Scriptures and the new
    The mark establish, and this shows it me,
    Of all the souls whom God hath made His friends.[1]
Isaiah saith, that each one garmented
    In his own land shall be with twofold garments.
    And his own land is this delightful life.
Thy brother, too, far more explicitly,
    There where he treateth of the robes of white,
    This revelation manifests to us.'
And first, and near the ending of these words,
    '*Sperent in Te*' from over us was heard,
    To which responsive answered all the carols.

                                    XXV. 49-99.

Isaiah's words referred to above are these : 'Therefore in
their land they shall possess the double; everlasting joy
shall be unto them :'[2]—and 'the double' is interpreted of
the soul's beatitude and the body's glorification.

S. John now came and stood with his two brethren : and
Dante, eager to ascertain by his possessing or not a body of

---

[1] Both Testaments fix the mark to be aimed at by all the friends of
God ; and this Heaven in which I stand actually places that mark
before my eyes.   [2] Isaiah lxi. 7.

flesh the truth or falsehood of the belief ' that that disciple
should not die,' gazed at him so fixedly that soon the blindness of dazzling ensued. S. John assured him that none,
save only the Lord and His Mother, wears as yet in Heaven
the twofold garment ; and while blindness still prolonged
inability to discern even Beatrice, consoled him with the
promise of restoration by her power, and examined him
concerning Love, asking first whereon his soul stayed itself.
The answer came :

> ' The Good, that gives contentment to this Court,
>   The Alpha and Omega is of all
>   The writing that love reads me low or loud.'
> The selfsame voice, that taken had from me
>   The terror of the sudden dazzlement,
>   To speak still farther put it in my thought ;
> And said : ' In verity with finer sieve
>   Behoveth thee to sift ; thee it behoveth
>   To say who aimed thy bow at such a target.'
> And I : ' By philosophic arguments,
>   And by authority that hence descends,
>   Such love must needs imprint itself in me ;
> For Good, so far as good, when comprehended
>   Doth straight enkindle love, and so much greater
>   As more of goodness in itself it holds ;
> Then to that Essence (Whose is such advantage
>   That every good which out of It is found
>   Is nothing but a ray of Its own light)
> More than elsewhither must the mind be moved
>   Of every one, in loving, who discerns
>   The truth in which this evidence is founded.
> Such truth he[1] to my intellect reveals

---

[1] Probably Aristotle.

Who demonstrates to me the Primal Love
Of all the sempiternal substances.
The voice reveals it of the truthful Author,
Who says to Moses, speaking of Himself,
" I will make all My goodness pass before thee."
Thou too revealest it to me, beginning
The loud Evangel, that proclaims the secret
Of Heaven to Earth above all other edict.'
And I heard say : ' By human intellect
And by authority concordant with it,
Of all thy loves reserve for God the highest.
But say again if other cords thou feelest
Draw thee towards Him, that thou mayst proclaim
With how many teeth this love is biting thee.'
The holy purpose of the Eagle of Christ
Not latent was, nay, rather I perceived
Whither he fain would my profession lead.
Therefore I recommenced : ' All of those bites
Which have the power to turn the heart to God
Unto my charity have been concurrent.
The being of the world, and my own being,
The death which He endured that I may live,
And that which all the faithful hope, as I do,
With the forementioned vivid consciousness
Have drawn me from the sea of love perverse,
And of the right have placed me on the shore.
The leaves, wherewith embowered is all the garden
Of the Eternal Gardener, do I love
As much as He has granted them of good.'
As soon as I had ceased, a song most sweet
Throughout the Heaven resounded, and my Lady
Said with the others, ' Holy, holy, holy !'

XXVI. 16-69.

Then Beatrice by her healing gaze restored, nay strength-

ened the sight of her Beloved; and amazed he asked
respecting a fourth resplendent Spirit standing with the
three.

> And said my Lady: ' There within those rays
>   Gazes upon its Maker the first Soul
>   That ever the first Virtue did create.'
> Even as the bough that downward bends its top
>   At transit of the wind, and then is lifted
>   By its own virtue, which inclines it upward,
> Likewise did I, the while that she was speaking,
>   Being amazed, and then I was made bold
>   By a desire to speak wherewith I burned.
> And I began : ' O apple, that mature
>   Alone hast been produced, O ancient father,
>   To whom each wife is daughter and daughter-in-law,
> Devoutly as I can I supplicate thee
>   That thou wouldst speak to me; thou seest my wish,
>   And I, to hear thee quickly, speak it not.'
> Sometimes an animal, when covered, struggles
>   So that his impulse needs must be apparent,
>   By reason of the wrappage following it ;
> And in like manner the primeval soul
>   Made clear to me athwart its covering
>   How jubilant it was to give me pleasure.
> Then breathed : ' Without thy uttering it to me,
>   Thine inclination better I discern
>   Than thou whatever thing is surest to thee ;
> For I behold it in the truthful Mirror,
>   That of Himself all things parhelion makes,[1]
>   And none makes Him parhelion of itself.

---

[1] ' Parhelion is an imperfect image of the sun, formed by reflection in
the clouds. All things are such faint reflections of the Creator; but He
is the reflection of none of them.'

Thou fain wouldst hear how long ago God placed me
    Within the lofty garden, where this Lady
    Unto so long a stairway thee disposed.
And how long to mine eyes it was a pleasure,
    And of the great disdain the proper cause,[1]
    And the language that I used and that I made.
Now, son of mine, the tasting of the tree
    Not in itself was cause of so great exile,
    But solely the o'erstepping of the bounds.
There, whence thy Lady moved Virgilius,
    Four thousand and three hundred and two circuits
    Made by the sun, this Council I desired ;
And him I saw return to all the lights
    Of his highway nine hundred times and thirty,
    Whilst I upon the earth was tarrying.
The language that I spake was quite extinct
    Before that in the work interminable
    The people under Nimrod were employed ;
For nevermore result of reasoning
    (Because of human pleasure that doth change,
    Obedient to the Heavens) was durable.
A natural action is it that man speaks ;
    But whether thus or thus, doth nature leave
    To your own art, as seemeth best to you.
Ere I descended to the infernal anguish,
    El was on earth the name of the Chief Good,
    From Whom comes all the joy that wraps me round ;
Eli He then was called, and that is proper,
    Because the use of men is like a leaf
    On bough, which goeth and another cometh.
Upon the mount that highest o'er the wave
    Rises was I, in life or pure or sinful,

---

[1] The precise cause why the eating of the fruit brought on Man the exceeding Wrath of God.

From the first hour to that which is the second,
As the sun changes quadrant, to the sixth.'[1]

XXVI. 82-142.

But lo a change in the face of Heaven.   S. Peter's white effulgence, and sympathetically that of all the Blessed, flushed indignant red as he descanted on the earthliness, worldliness, and violence, too often tainting his Holy See. And after charging him who was to return among men not to hide what he himself had not hidden, with the whole light-storm of triumphant Saints he swept up into the Empyrean.   When they could be seen no more, Beatrice invited one last look towards Earth ; and Dante having beheld it all reduced to pettiness, returned to gaze on the countenance where all was greatness.   Gazing he was again uplifted, and they stood together in the Primum Mobile :

' And in this Heaven there is no other Where
    Than in the Mind Divine, Wherein is kindled
    The love that turns it, and the power it rains.
Within a circle light and love embrace it,
    Even as this doth the others, and that precinct
    He who encircles it alone controls.'

XXVII. 109-114.

And Beatrice lamented the sore corruptions which leave human innocence and faith the portion of babes alone : and Dante turned even from her eyes to contemplate the peculiar vision of the Ninth Heaven, the circling of the Angelic Hierarchy round the Divine Centre. .

A Point beheld I that was raying out
    Light so acute, the sight which It enkindles
    Must close perforce before such great acuteness.

---

[1] See page 15.

And whatsoever star seems smallest here
  Would seem to be a moon if placed beside It
  As one star with another star is placed.'
Perhaps at such a distance as appears
  A halo cincturing the light that paints it,
  When densest is the vapour that sustains it,
Thus distant round the Point a circle of fire
  So swiftly whirled, that it would have surpassed
  Whatever motion soonest girds the world ;
And this was by another circumcinct,
  That by a third, the third then by a fourth,
  By a fifth the fourth, and then by a sixth the fifth :
The seventh followed thereupon in width
  So ample now, that Juno's messenger
  Entire would be too narrow to contain it.
Even so the eighth and ninth ; and every one
  More slowly moved, according as it was
  In number distant farther from the first.
And that one had its flame most crystalline
  From which less distant was the stainless Spark,
  I think because more with Its truth imbued.
My Lady, who in my anxiety
  Beheld me much perplexed, said : ' From that Point
  Dependent is the Heaven and nature all.
Behold that circle most conjoined to It,
  And know thou, that its motion is so swift
  Through burning love whereby it is spurred on.'

XXVIII. 16-45.

Dante inquired why the order of these Angelic Circles is inverse to that of the Heavens, and was answered by his Lady that such inversion is only in respect of extension ; in respect of virtue and influential action there is direct correspondence.[1]

[1] See also page 13.

And soon as to a stop her words had come,
　　Not otherwise does iron scintillate
　　When molten, than those circles scintillated.
'Their coruscation all the sparks repeated,
　　And they so many were, their number makes
　　More millions than the doubling of the chess.
I heard them sing hosanna choir by choir
　　To the fixed Point which holds them at the *Ubi*,[1]
　　And ever will, where they have ever been.

XXVIII. 88-96.

A farther discourse, after teaching the names of the Nine
Angelic Choirs, and their division into three Triads,[2]
assigned the true knowledge of their hierarchic order rather
to S. Dionysius the Areopagite, the disciple of that Master
who had actually been caught up to the Third Heaven,
than to S. Gregory the Great in the points where the two
are discrepant.—And after a pause Beatrice satisfied Dante's
thirst for the knowledge of the where, the when, and the
how of the creation of the Angels.

' Not to acquire some good unto Himself,
　　Which is impossible, but that His splendour[3]
　　In its resplendency may say, ' *Subsisto*,'
In His eternity outside of time,
　　Outside all other limits, as it pleased Him,
　　Into new Loves the Eternal Love unfolded.
Nor as if torpid did He lie before ;
　　For neither after nor before proceeded
　　The going forth of God upon these waters.'

XXIX. 13-21.

---

1 'Their appointed place or whereabout.'
2 See page 12.
3 The Creation, which is the 'splendour' or reflected light of God.

The points next set forth were the relations between active Form or Mind and passive Matter,[1] and the simultaneous creation of the Angels and the Heavens.[2] Beatrice then—digressing by the way to refute an opinion of the Schools and animadvert on the profitless speculations of Preachers—passed on to treat of the rebel Angels; of their Fall, its effect on the Elemental World, its cause :— and of the obedient Angels; of their occupation, their indefectibility, their number, their love proportioned to their mode of perception of the Beatific Vision.

> ' Nor could one reach, in counting, unto twenty
>> So swiftly, as a portion of these angels
>> · Disturbed the subject of your elements.[3]
> The rest remained, and they began this art
>> Which thou discernest, with so great delight
>> That never from their circling do they cease.
> The occasion of the fall was the accursed
>> Presumption of that One, whom thou hast seen
>> By all the burden of the world constrained.
> Those whom thou here beholdest modest were
>> To recognise themselves as of that Goodness
>> Which made them apt for so much understanding ;
> On which account their vision was exalted
>> By the enlightening grace and their own merit,
>> So that they have a full and steadfast will.
> I would not have thee doubt, but certain be,
>> 'Tis meritorious to receive this grace,[4]
>> According as the affection opens to it.
>
> .   .   .   .   .   .

---

[1] See page 13.   [2] See page 14.

[3] ' The subject of the elements is the earth, so called as being the lowest, or underlying the others, fire, air, and water.'

[4] ' The merit consists in being willing to receive this grace.'

This nature doth so multiply itself
　　In numbers, that there never yet was speech
　　Nor mortal fancy that can go so far.
And if thou notest that which is revealed
　　By Daniel, thou wilt see that in his thousands
　　Number determinate is kept concealed.
[1] The primal Light, that all irradiates it,
　　By modes as many is received therein,
　　As are the splendours wherewith It is mated.
Hence, inasmuch as on the act conceptive
　　The affection followeth, of love the sweetness
　　Therein diversely fervid is or tepid.[1]
The height behold now and the amplitude
　　Of the eternal Power, since It hath made
　　Itself so many mirrors, where 'tis broken,
One in Itself remaining as before.'

XXIX. 49-66, 130-145.

But now, even as star after star pales in the effacing
sunlight, so Choir after Choir was extinguished from Dante's
view; and a crowning gaze on Beatrice's consummated
beauty revealed the accomplished ascent into the Empyrean.

From the first day that I beheld her face
　　In this life, to the moment of this look,
　　The sequence of my song has ne'er been severed ;
But now perforce this sequence must desist
　　From following her beauty with my verse,
　　As every artist at his uttermost.
Such as I leave her to a greater fame

---

[1] The Light of God, Which irradiates all this angelic nature, is received therein in modes corresponding in number to the Angels themselves, the splendours or reflected lights wherewith it is united. Hence,
inasmuch as the affection corresponds to the capacity of receiving the
Divine Light, the sweetness of love in this angelic nature is different in
degrees of warmth.

Than any of my trumpet, which is bringing
Its arduous matter to a final close,
With voice and gesture of a perfect leader
She recommenced : ' We from the greatest body
Have issued to the Heaven that is pure light ;
Light intellectual replete with love,
Love of true good replete with ecstasy,
Ecstasy that transcendeth every sweetness.
Here shalt thou see the one host and the other
Of Paradise, and one in the same aspects
Which at the final judgment thou shalt see.'

XXX. 28-45.

The two hosts are of course the Angels and the Saints :
but commentators are not unanimous in deciding which is
referred to as wearing the same aspects that will be seen at
the Last Judgment. Some think the Angels are meant :—
this view is not only based on indisputable fact, but is also
favoured by the order of the words, and by their seeming
exclusion of 'the other' host from that which they predicate.
Others think the Saints are meant; these can allege that
seeming need not be real exclusion, that it would have been
utterly useless to state what it never could enter into
Dante's head to doubt, and that S. Benedict[1] had actually
promised that in the Empyrean the Blessed should be seen
in their proper forms.

The Pilgrim, already by anticipation standing in the
Better Country of his desire, thus continues his narration :

Even as a sudden lightning that disperses
The visual spirits, so that it deprives
The eye of impress from the strongest objects,

---

[1] *Par.* xxii. 58-63 ; page 249.

> Thus round about me flashed a living Light,
>   And left me swathed around with such a veil
>   Of its effulgence, that I nothing saw.
> ' Ever the Love Which quieteth this Heaven
>   Welcomes into Itself with such salute,
>   To make the candle ready for its flame.'
> No sooner had within me these brief words
>   An entrance found, than I perceived myself
>   To be uplifted over my own power,
> And I with vision new rekindled me,
>   Such that no light whatever is so pure
>   But that mine eyes were fortified against it.
>
> XXX. 46-60.

This 'vision new' is as it were the nucleus of that by which it is to be succeeded, and for which it serves to pre-pare the way. The Divine Light is first seen in the form of a River, signifying Its effusion on the creatures :[1] the living Sparks issuing from It are the Angels; the Flowers they ingem, the Saints. Then in the changing of the River's length to the Lake's roundness is figured the return of all creatures into God as their Centre and End.[2] The Rose and the Bees we know already.

> And Light I saw in fashion of a river
>   Fulvid with Its effulgence, 'twixt two banks
>   Depicted with an admirable Spring.
> Out of this river issued living sparks,
>   And on all sides sank down into the flowers,
>   Like unto rubies that are set in gold ;
> And then, as if inebriate with the odours,
>   They plunged again into the wondrous torrent,

[1,2] Venturi *in loc.*

And as one entered issued forth another.
' The high desire, that now inflames and moves thee
    To have intelligence of what thou seest,
    Pleaseth me all the more, the more it swells.
But of this water it behoves thee drink
    Before so great a thirst in thee be slaked.'
    Thus said to me the sunshine of mine eyes ;
And added : ' The river and the topazes
    Going in and out, and the laughing of the herbage,
    Are of their truth foreshadowing prefaces ;
Not that these things are difficult in themselves,
    But the deficiency is on thy side,
    For yet thou hast not vision so exalted.'
There is no babe that leaps so suddenly
    With face towards the milk, if he awake
    Much later than his usual custom is,
As I did, that I might make better mirrors
    Still of mine eyes, down stooping to the wave
    Which flows that we therein be better made.
And even as the penthouse of mine eyelids
    Drank of it, it forthwith appeared to me
    Out of its length to be transformed to round.
Then as a folk who have been under masks
    Seem other than before, if they divest
    The semblance not their own they disappeared in,
Thus into greater pomp were changed for me
    The flowerets and the sparks, so that I saw
    Both of the Courts of Heaven made manifest.
O splendour of God ! by means of which I saw
    The lofty triumph of the realm veracious,
    Give me the power to say how it I saw !
There is a Light above, which visible
    Makes the Creator unto every creature,
    Who only in beholding Him has peace,

And it expands itself in circular form
　To such extent, that its circumference
　Would be too large a girdle for the sun.
The semblance of it is all made of rays
　Reflected from the top of Primal Motion,[1]
　Which takes therefrom vitality and power.
And as a hill in water at its base
　Mirrors itself, as if to see its beauty
　When affluent most in verdure and in flowers,
So, ranged aloft all round about the Light
　Mirrored I saw in more ranks than a thousand
　All who above there have from us returned.
And if the lowest row collect within it
　So great a light, how vast the amplitude
　Is of this Rose in its extremest leaves !
My vision in the vastness and the height
　Lost not itself, but comprehended all
　The quantity and quality of that gladness.
There near and far nor add nor take away ;
　For there where God immediately doth govern,
　The natural law in naught is relevant.
Into the yellow of the Rose Eternal
　That spreads, and multiplies, and breathes an odour
　Of praise unto the ever-vernal Sun,
As one who silent is and fain would speak,
　Me Beatrice drew on, and said : ' Behold
　Of the white stoles how vast the convent is !
Behold how vast the circuit of our city !
　Behold our seats so filled to overflowing,
　That here henceforward are few people wanting !'

　　　　　　　　　　　　　　　　XXX. 61-132.

---

[1] See page 12.

Then Beatrice indicated the throne specially prepared for the Emperor Henry of Luxemburg, and destined to be occupied all too soon for Dante's patriotic hopes :—reproved the blindness of Italy to her true good, and heavily denounced Pope Clement v. as Henry's covert opponent.

> In fashion then as of a snow-white rose
>> Displayed itself to me the saintly host,
>> Whom Christ in His own blood had made His bride.
> But the other host, that flying sees and sings
>> The glory of Him Who doth enamour it,
>> And the goodness that created it so noble,
> Even as a swarm of bees, that sinks in flowers
>> One moment, and the next returns again
>> To where its labour is to sweetness turned,
> Sank into the great flower, that is adorned
>> With leaves so many, and thence reascended
>> To where its love abideth evermore.
> Their faces had they all of living flame,
>> And wings of gold, and all the rest so white
>> No snow unto that limit doth attain.
> From bench to bench, into the flower descending,
>> They carried something of the peace and ardour
>> Which by the fanning of their flanks they won.
> Nor did the interposing 'twixt the flower
>> And that was o'er it of such plenitude
>> Of flying shapes impede the sight and splendour ;
> Because the Light Divine so penetrates
>> The universe, according to its merit,
>> That naught can be an obstacle against it.
> This realm secure and full of gladsomeness,
>> Crowded with ancient people and with modern,
>> Unto one mark had all its look and love.

O Trinal Light, That in a single star
 Sparkling upon their sight so satisfies them,
 Look down upon our tempest here below !
If the barbarians, coming from some region
 That every day by Helice is covered,[1]
 Revolving with her son whom she delights in.[2]
Beholding Rome and all her noble works,
 Were wonder-struck, what time the Lateran
 Above all mortal things was eminent,—
I who to the divine had from the human,
 From time unto eternity, had come,
 From Florence to a people just and sane,
With what amazement must I have been filled !
 Truly between this and the joy, it was
 My pleasure not to hear, and to be mute.
And as a pilgrim who delighteth him
 In gazing round the temple of his vow,
 And hopes some day to retell how it was,
So through the living Light my way pursuing
 Directed I mine eyes o'er all the ranks,
 Now up, now down, and now all round about.
Faces I saw of charity persuasive.
 Embellished by His light and their own smile,
 And attitudes adorned with every grace.
The general form of Paradise already
 My glance had comprehended as a whole,
 In no part hitherto remaining fixed,
And round I turned me with rekindled wish
 My Lady to interrogate of things
 Concerning which my mind was in suspense.
One thing I meant, another answered me ;

---

[1] The Great Bear.   [2] The Little Bear.

I thought I should see Beatrice, and saw
An Old Man habited like the glorious people.
O'erflowing was he in his eyes and cheeks
With joy benign, in attitude of pity
As to a tender father is becoming.
And ' She, where is she ?' instantly I said ;
Whence he : ' To put an end to thy desire,
Me Beatrice hath sent from mine own place.
And if thou lookest up to the third round
Of the first rank, again shalt thou behold her
Upon the throne her merits have assigned her.'
Without reply I lifted up mine eyes,
And saw her, as she made herself a crown
Reflecting from herself the eternal rays.
Not from that region which the highest thunders
Is any mortal eye so far removed,
In whatsoever sea it deepest sinks,
As there from Beatrice my sight ; but this
Was nothing unto me ; because her image
Descended not to me by medium blurred.[1]
' O Lady, thou in whom my hope is strong,
And who for my salvation didst endure
In Hell to leave the imprint of thy feet,
Of whatsoever things I have beheld,
As coming from thy power and from thy goodness
I recognise the virtue and the grace.
Thou from a slave hast brought me unto freedom,
By all those ways, by all the expedients,
Whereby thou hadst the power of doing it.
Preserve towards me thy magnificence,
So that this soul of mine, which thou hast healed,
Pleasing to thee be loosened from the body.'

Through no such medium as our earthly atmosphere, or any other.

Thus I implored ; and she, so far away,
  Smiled, as it seemed, and looked once more at me ;
  Then unto the Eternal Fountain turned.
And said the Old Man holy : ' That thou mayst
  Accomplish perfectly thy journeying,
  Whereunto prayer and holy love have sent me,
Fly with thine eyes all round about this garden ;
  For seeing it will discipline thy sight
  Farther to mount along the Ray Divine.
And she, the Queen of Heaven, for whom I burn
  Wholly with love, will grant us every grace,
  Because that I her faithful Bernard am.'

XXXI. 1-102.

It need hardly be said that this is the great S. Bernard, Abbot of Clairvaux, the singer of the Most Holy Name of Jesus in that sweetest hymn which has kindled and expressed the love of generation after generation from his own day to ours.

As he who peradventure from Croatia
  Cometh to gaze at our Veronica,[1]
  Who through its ancient fame is never sated,
But says in thought, the while it is displayed,
  ' My Lord, Christ Jesus, God of very God,
  Now was Your semblance made like unto this ?'
Even such was I while gazing at the living
  Charity of the man, who in this world
  By contemplation tasted of that peace.
' Thou son of Grace, this jocund life,' began he,

---

[1] The ' Very Image ' of our Blessed Lord, impressed by Him on the handkerchief piously offered Him as He bore His Cross by a holy woman, to whom the same name of *Veronica* is given, her own being uncertain.

' Will not be known to thee by keeping ever
    Thine eyes below here on the lowest place ;
But mark the circles to the most remote,
    Until thou shalt behold enthroned the Queen
    To whom this realm is subject and devoted.'
I lifted up mine eyes, and as at morn
    The oriental part of the horizon
    Surpasses that wherein the sun goes down,
Thus, as if going with mine eyes from vale
    To mount, I saw a part in the remoteness
    Surpass in splendour all the other front.
And even as there, where we await the pole [1]
    That Phaeton drove badly, blazes more
    The light, and is on either side diminished,
So likewise that pacific Oriflamme [2]
    Gleamed brightest in the centre, and each side
    In equal measure did the flame abate.
And at that centre, with their wings expanded,
    More than a thousand jubilant Angels saw I,
    Each differing in effulgence and in kind.
I saw there at their sports and at their songs
    A beauty smiling, which the gladness was
    Within the eyes of all the other saints ;
And if I had in speaking as much wealth
    As in imagining, I should not dare
    To attempt the smallest part of its delight.
Bernard, as soon as he beheld mine eyes
    Fixed and intent upon its fervid fervour,
    His own with such affection turned to her
That it made mine more ardent to behold.

Absorbed in his delight, that contemplator
    Assumed the willing office of a teacher,

[1] The chariot of the Sun.   [2] The Blessed Virgin.

And gave beginning to these holy words :
' The wound that Mary closed up and anointed,
  She at her feet who is so beautiful,
  She is the one who opened it and pierced it.
Within that order which the third seats make
  Is seated Rachel, lower than the other,
  With Beatrice, in manner as thou seest.
Sarah, Rebecca, Judith, and her who was
  Ancestress of the Singer, who for dole
  Of the misdeed said, " *Miserere mei,*"
Canst thou behold from seat to seat descending
  Down in gradation, as with each one's name
  I through the Rose go down from leaf to leaf.
And downward from the seventh row, even as
  Above the same, succeed the Hebrew women,
  Dividing all the tresses of the flower ;
Because, according to the view which Faith
  In Christ had taken, these are the partition
  By which the sacred stairways are divided.
Upon this side, where perfect is the flower
  With each one of its petals, seated are
  Those who believed in Christ Who was to come.
Upon the other side, where intersected
  With vacant spaces are the semicircles,
  Are those who looked to Christ already come.
And as, upon this side, the glorious seat
  Of the Lady of Heaven, and the other seats
  Below it, such a great division make,
So opposite doth that of the great John,
  Who, ever holy, desert and martyrdom
  Endured, and afterwards two years in Hell.
And under him thus to divide were chosen
  Francis, and Benedict, and Augustine,
  And down to us the rest from round to round.

Behold now the high providence divine ;
   For one and other aspect of the Faith
   In equal measure shall this garden fill.
And know that downward from that rank which cleaves
   Midway the sequence of the two divisions,
   Not by their proper merit are they seated ;
But by Another's under fixed conditions ;
   For these are Spirits one and all assoiled
   Before they any true election had.
Well canst thou recognise it in their faces,
   And also in their voices puerile,
   If thou regard them well and hearken to them.'

XXXI. 103-142. XXXII. 1-48.

S. Bernard then, in answer to a doubt he beheld in
Dante's mind, set forth the theory of the varying degrees of
grace and consequently of glory in Elect Babes :—and
further explained that infant salvation has ever depended
on the conjunction of something else with innocence ; in
the earliest ages the faith of parents, in the next period
Circumcision, since the advent of grace Baptism.   He went
on :

' Look now into the face that unto Christ
   Hath most resemblance ; for its brightness only
   Is able to prepare thee to see Christ.'
On her did I behold so great a gladness
   Rain down, borne onward in the holy minds
   Created through that altitude to fly,
That whatsoever I had seen before
   Did not suspend me in such admiration,
   Nor show me such similitude of God.
And the same Love that first descended there,
   ' *Ave Maria, gratia plena,*' singing,

In front of her his wings expanded wide.
Unto the canticle divine responded
   From every part the court beatified,
   So that each sight became serener for it.
' O holy father, who for me endurest
   To be below here, leaving the sweet place
   In which thou sittest by eternal lot,
Who is the Angel that with so much joy
   Into the eyes is looking of our Queen,
   Enamoured so that he seems made of fire ? '
Thus I again recourse had to the teaching
   Of that one who delighted him in Mary
   As doth the star of morning in the sun.
And he to me : ' Such gallantry and grace
   As there can be in Angel and in soul,
   All is in him ; and thus we fain would have it ;
Because he is the one who bore the palm
   Down unto Mary, when the Son of God
   To take our burden on Himself decreed.
But now come onward with thine eyes, as I
   Speaking shall go, and note the great patricians
   Of this most just and merciful of empires.
Those two that sit above there most enraptured,
   As being very near unto Augusta,
   Are as it were the two roots of this Rose.
He who upon the left is near her placed
   The father is, by whose audacious taste
   The human species so much bitter tastes.
Upon the right thou seest that ancient father
   Of Holy Church, into whose keeping Christ
   The keys committed of this lovely flower.
And he who all the evil days beheld,
   Before his death, of her the beauteous bride
   Who with the spear and with the nails was won,

Beside him sits, and by the other rests
  That leader under whom on manna lived
  The people ingrate, fickle, and stiff-necked.
Opposite Peter seest thou Anna seated,
  So well content to look upon her daughter,
  Her eyes she moves not while she sings Hosanna.
And opposite the eldest household father
  Lucïa sits, she who thy Lady moved
  When to rush downward thou didst bend thy brows.
But since the moments of thy vision fly,
  Here will we make full stop, as a good tailor
  Who makes the gown according to his cloth,
And unto the First Love will turn our eyes,
  That looking upon Him thou penetrate
  As far as possible through His effulgence.
                                    XXXII. 85-144.

The Saint invited his neophyte to join in invoking the aid
of the Blessed Virgin, and that aid was granted :

And I, who to the End of all desires
  Was now approaching, even as I ought
  The ardour of desire within me ended.
Bernard was beckoning unto me, and smiling,
  That I should upward look ; but I already
  Was of my own accord such as he wished ;
Because my sight, becoming purified,
  Was entering more and more into the ray
  Of the High Light which of Itself is true.
From that time forward what I saw was greater
  Than our discourse, that to such vision yields,
  And yields the memory unto such excess.
Even as he is who seeth in a dream,
  And after dreaming the imprinted passion
  Remains, and to his mind the rest returns not,

Even such am I, for almost utterly
  Ceases my vision, and distilleth yet
  Within my heart the sweetness born of it ;
Even thus the snow is in the sun unsealed,
  Even thus upon the wind in the light leaves
  Were the soothsayings of the Sibyl lost.[1]
O Light Supreme, that dost so far uplift Thee
  From the conceits of mortals, to my mind
  Of what Thou didst appear re-lend a little,
And make my tongue of so great puissance,
  That but a single sparkle of Thy glory
  It may bequeath unto the future people ;
For by returning to my memory somewhat,
  And by a little sounding in these verses,
  More of Thy victory shall be conceived !
I think the keenness of the living Ray
  Which I endured would have bewildered me,
  If but mine eyes had been averted from It ;[2]
And I remember that I was more bold
  On this account to bear, so that I joined
  My aspect with the Glory Infinite.

                                        XXXIII. 46-81.

And then, confessing himself all impotent to tell, Dante
yet tells as best he may of his consummated grace in the
crowning Vision of God Triune, God Incarnate :

Not because more than one unmingled semblance
  Was in the living Light on Which I looked,

---

[1] The Cumæan Sibyl wrote her oracles on leaves. When she opened
the door of her cavern, these were blown about by the wind ; and she
never cared to re-arrange them.

[2] Unlike the solar ray, this Divine Ray strengthened the fixed eye to
gaze on it.

For It is always what It was before ;
But through the sight, that fortified itself
   In me by looking, one appearance only
   To me was ever changing as I changed.
Within the deep and luminous subsistence
   Of the High Light appeared to me Three Circles,
   Of threefold colour and of one dimension,
And by the Second seemed the First reflected
   As Iris is by Iris, and the Third
   Seemed Fire that equally from Both is breathed.
O how all speech is feeble and falls short
   Of my conceit, and this to what I saw
   Is such, 'tis not enough to call it little !
O Light Eterne, sole in Thyself that dwellest,
   Sole knowest Thyself, and, known unto Thyself
   And knowing, lovest and smilest on Thyself !
That Circulation,[1] Which being thus conceived
   Appeared in Thee as a reflected Light,
   When somewhat contemplated by mine eyes,
Within Itself, of Its own very colour
   Seemed to me painted with our effigy,[2]
   Wherefore my sight was all absorbed therein.
As the geometrician, who endeavours
   To square the circle, and discovers not,
   By taking thought, the principle he wants,
Even such was I at that new apparition ;
   I wished to see how the Image to the Circle
   Conformed Itself, and how It there finds place ;
But my own wings were not enough for this,
   Had it not been that then my mind there smote
   A flash of lightning, wherein came its wish.

---

[1] The Second Person of the Adorable Trinity.
[2] The Human Nature of our Blessed Lord.

U

Here vigour failed the lofty fantasy :
   But now was turning my desire and will,
   Even as a wheel that equally is moved,
The Love Which moves the sun and the other stars.

XXXIII. 109-145.

FINIS.

INDEX I.

EXTRACTS FROM THE DIVINA COMMEDIA.

INDEX II.

QUOTATIONS FROM DANTE'S MINOR WORKS.

Printed by T. and A. CONSTABLE, Printers to Her Majesty,
at the Edinburgh University Press.

THE SILVER LIBRARY.

CROWN 8VO.   3s. 6d. EACH VOLUME.

Arnold's (Sir Edwin) Seas and Lands. With 71 Illustrations. 3s. 6d.

Baker's (Sir S. W.) Eight Years in Ceylon. With 6 Illustrations. 3s. 6d.

Baker's (Sir S. W.) Rifle and Hound in Ceylon. With 6 Illustrations. 3s. 6d.

Baring-Gould's (Rev. S.) Curious Myths of the Middle Ages. 3s. 6d.

Baring-Gould's (Rev. S.) Origin and Development of Religious Belief. 2 vols. 3s. 6d. each.

Brassey's (Lady) A Voyage in the 'Sunbeam.' With 66 Illustrations. 3s. 6d.

Clodd's (E.) Story of Creation: a Plain Account of Evolution. With 77 Illustrations. 3s. 6d.

Conybeare (Rev. W. J.) and Howson's (Very Rev. J. S.) Life and Epistles of St. Paul. With 46 Illustrations. 3s. 6d.

Dougall's (L.) Beggars All. 3s. 6d.

Doyle's (A. Conan) Micah Clarke. A Tale of Monmouth's Rebellion. 3s. 6d.

Doyle's (A. Conan) The Captain of the Polestar, and other Tales. 3s. 6d.

Froude's (J. A.) Short Studies on Great Subjects. 4 vols 3s. 6d. each.

Froude's (J. A.) Caesar: a Sketch. 3s. 6d.

Froude's (J. A.) Thomas Carlyle: a History of his Life.

    1795-1835. 2 vols. 7s.
    1834-1881. 2 vols. 7s.

LONDON AND NEW YORK : LONGMANS, GREEN & CO.

Froude's (J. A.) The Two Chiefs of Dunboy: an Irish Romance of the Last Century. 3s. 6d.

Froude's (J. A.) The History of England, from the Fall of Wolsey to the Defeat of the Spanish Armada. 12 vols. 3s. 6d. each.

Gleig's (Rev. G. R.) Life of the Duke of Wellington. With Portrait. 3s. 6d.

Haggard's (H. R.) She: A History of Adventure. With 32 Illustrations. 3s. 6d.

Haggard's (H. R.) Allan Quatermain. With 20 Illustrations. 3s. 6d.

Haggard's (H. R.) Colonel Quaritch, V.C.: a Tale of Country Life. 3s. 6d.

Haggard's (H. R.) Cleopatra. With 29 Illustrations. 3s. 6d.

Haggard's (H. R.) Eric Brighteyes. With 51 Illustrations. 3s. 6d.

Haggard's (H. R.) Beatrice. 3s. 6d.

Haggard's (H. R.) Allan's Wife, and other Tales. With 34 Illustrations. 3s. 6d.

Haggard's (H. R.) The Witch's Head. With Illustrations. 3s. 6d.

Haggard's (H. R.) Mr. Meeson's Will. With 18 Illustrations. 3s. 6d.

Haggard's (H. R.) Dawn. With Illustrations. 3s. 6d.

Haggard's (H. R.) The World's Desire. By H. RIDER HAGGARD and ANDREW LANG. With 27 Illustrations. 3s. 6d.

Harte's (Bret) In the Carquinez Woods and other Stories. 3s. 6d.

Helmholtz's (Hermann von) Popular Lectures on Scientific Subjects. With 68 Illustrations. 2 vols. 3s. 6d. each.

LONDON AND NEW YORK: LONGMANS, GREEN & CO.

Howitt's (W.) Visits to Remarkable Places. With 80 Illustrations. 3*s.* 6*d.*

Jefferies' (R.) The Story of My Heart : My Autobiography. With Portrait. 3*s.* 6*d.*

Jefferies' (R.) Field and Hedgerow. Last Essays of. With Portrait. 3*s.* 6*d.*

Jefferies' (R.) Red Deer. With 17 Illustrations. 3*s.* 6*d.*

Jefferies' (R.) Wood Magic : a Fable. With Frontispiece and Vignette by E. V. B. 3*s.* 6*d.*

Jefferies' (R.) The Toilers of the Field. With Portrait from the Bust in Salisbury Cathedral. 3*s.* 6*d.*

Knight's (E. F.) The Cruise of the ' Alerte ': the Narrative of a Search for Treasure on the Desert Island of Trinidad. With 2 Maps and 23 Illustrations. 3*s.* 6*d.*

Lang's (A.) Custom and Myth : Studies of Early Usage and Belief. 3*s.* 6*d.*

Lees (J. A.) and Clutterbuck's (W. J.) B. C. 1887, A Ramble in British Columbia. With Maps and 75 Illustrations. 3*s.* 6*d.*

Macaulay's (Lord), Essays and Lays of Ancient Rome. With Portrait and Illustrations. 3*s.* 6*d.*

Macleod's (H. D.) The Elements of Banking. 3*s.* 6*d.*

Marshman's (J. C.) Memoirs of Sir Henry Havelock. 3*s.* 6*d.*

Max Müller's (F.) India, what can it teach us? 3*s.* 6*d.*

Max Müller's (F.) Introduction to the Science of Religion. 3*s.* 6*d.*

Merivale's (Dean) History of the Romans under the Empire. 8 vols. 3*s.* 6*d.* each.

Mill's (J. S.) Principles of Political Economy. 3*s.* 6*d.*

Mill's (J. S.) System of Logic. 3*s.* 6*d.*

Milner's (Geo.) Country Pleasures: the Chronicle of a Year chiefly in a Garden. 3*s.* 6*d.*

Phillipps-Wolley's (C.) Snap: a Legend of the Lone Mountain. With 13 Illustrations. 3*s.* 6*d.*

Proctor's (R. A.) The Orbs Around us: Essays on the Moon and Planets, Meteors and Comets, the Sun and Coloured Pairs of Suns. 3*s.* 6*d.*

Proctor's (R. A.) The Expanse of Heaven: Essays on the Wonders of the Firmament. 3*s.* 6*d.*

Proctor's (R. A.) Other Worlds than Ours. 3*s.* 6*d.*

Proctor's (R. A.) Rough Ways made Smooth. 3*s.* 6*d.*

Proctor's (R. A.) Pleasant Ways in Science. 3*s.* 6*d.*

Proctor's (R. A.) Myths and Marvels of Astronomy. 3*s.* 6*d.*

Proctor's (R. A.) Nature Studies. 3*s.* 6*d.*

Rossetti's (Maria F.) A Shadow of Dante: being an Essay towards studying Himself, his World and his Pilgrimage. With Illustrations by DANTE GABRIEL ROSSETTI. 3*s.* 6*d.*

Smith (R. Bosworth) Carthage and the Carthaginians. With Maps, Plans, etc. 3*s.* 6*d.*

Stanley's (Bishop) Familiar History of Birds. With 160 Illustrations. 3*s.* 6*d.*

Stevenson (R. L.) and Osbourne's (Ll.) The Wrong Box. 3*s.* 6*d.*

Weyman's (Stanley) The House of the Wolf: a Romance. 3*s.* 6*d.*

Wood's (Rev. J. G.) Petland Revisited. With 33 Illustrations. 3*s.* 6*d.*

Wood's (Rev. J. G.) Strange Dwellings. With 60 Illustrations. 3*s.* 6*d.*

Wood's (Rev. J. G.) Out of Doors. 11 Illustrations. 3*s.* 6*d.*

LONDON AND NEW YORK: LONGMANS, GREEN & CO.

Messrs. Longmans, Green, & Co.'s

CLASSIFIED CATALOGUE

OF

WORKS IN GENERAL LITERATURE.

History, Politics, Polity, and Political Memoirs.

Abbott.—A HISTORY OF GREECE. By EVELYN ABBOTT, M.A., LL.D.
Part I.—From the Earliest Times to the Ionian Revolt. Crown 8vo., 10s. 6d.
Part II.—500-445 B.C. Cr. 8vo., 10s. 6d.

Acland and Ransome.—A HANDBOOK IN OUTLINE OF THE POLITICAL HISTORY OF ENGLAND TO 1890. Chronologically Arranged. By the Right Hon. A. H. DYKE ACLAND, M.P., and CYRIL RANSOME, M.A. Crown 8vo., 6s.

ANNUAL REGISTER (THE). A Review of Public Events at Home and Abroad, for the year 1892. 8vo., 18s.

Volumes of the ANNUAL REGISTER for the years 1863-1891 can still be had. 18s. each.

Armstrong.—ELIZABETH FARNESE; The Termagant of Spain. By EDWARD ARMSTRONG, M.A., Fellow of Queen's College, Oxford. 8vo., 16s.

Arnold.—Works by T. ARNOLD, D.D., formerly Head Master of Rugby School.

INTRODUCTORY LECTURES ON MODERN HISTORY. 8vo., 7s. 6d.

MISCELLANEOUS WORKS. 8vo., 7s. 6d.

Bagwell.—IRELAND UNDER THE TUDORS. By RICHARD BAGWELL, LL.D. 3 vols. Vols. I. and II. From the first Invasion of the Northmen to the year 1578. 8vo., 32s. Vol. III. 1578-1603. 8vo., 18s.

Ball.—HISTORICAL REVIEW OF THE LEGISLATIVE SYSTEMS OPERATIVE IN IRELAND, from the Invasion of Henry the Second to the Union (1172-1800). By the Rt. Hon. J. T. BALL. 8vo., 6s.

Besant.—THE HISTORY OF LONDON. By WALTER BESANT. With 74 Illustrations. Crown 8vo. School Reading-book Edition, 1s. 9d.; Prize-book Edition, 2s. 6d.

Buckle.—HISTORY OF CIVILISATION IN ENGLAND AND FRANCE, SPAIN AND SCOTLAND. By HENRY THOMAS BUCKLE. 3 vols. Crown 8vo., 24s.

Creighton.—HISTORY OF THE PAPACY DURING THE REFORMATION. By MANDELL CREIGHTON, D.D., LL.D., Bishop of Peterborough. 8vo. Vols. I. and II. 1378-1464. 32s. Vols. III. and IV. 1464-1518. 24s. Vol. V. 1517-1527. 15s.

Crump.—A SHORT INQUIRY INTO THE FORMATION OF POLITICAL OPINION, from the reign of the Great Families to the advent of Democracy. By ARTHUR CRUMP. 8vo., 7s. 6d.

De Tocqueville.—DEMOCRACY IN AMERICA. By ALEXIS DE TOCQUEVILLE. 2 vols. Crown 8vo., 16s.

Fitzpatrick.—SECRET SERVICE UNDER PITT. By W. J. FITZPATRICK, F.S.A., Author of 'Correspondence of Daniel O'Connell'. 8vo., 7s. 6d.

Freeman.—THE HISTORICAL GEOGRAPHY OF EUROPE. By EDWARD A. FREEMAN, D.C.L., LL.D. With 65 Maps. 2 vols. 8vo., 31s. 6d.

History, Politics, Polity, and Political Memoirs—*continued.*

Froude.—Works by JAMES A. FROUDE, Regius Professor of Modern History in the University of Oxford.

THE HISTORY OF ENGLAND, from the Fall of Wolsey to the Defeat of the Spanish Armada.
Popular Edition. 12 vols. Crown 8vo., 3s. 6d. each.
Silver Library Edition. 12 vols. Crown 8vo., 3s. 6d. each.

THE DIVORCE OF CATHERINE OF ARAGON: the Story as told by the Imperial Ambassadors resident at the Court of Henry VIII. Crown 8vo., 6s.

THE SPANISH STORY OF THE ARMADA, and other Essays, Historical and Descriptive. Crown 8vo., 6s.

THE ENGLISH IN IRELAND IN THE EIGHTEENTH CENTURY. 3 vols. Cr. 8vo., 18s.

SHORT STUDIES ON GREAT SUBJECTS. 4 vols. Cr. 8vo., 3s. 6d. each.

CÆSAR: a Sketch. Cr. 8vo., 3s. 6d.

Gardiner.—Works by SAMUEL RAWSON GARDINER, M.A., Hon. LL.D., Edinburgh, Fellow of Merton College, Oxford.

HISTORY OF ENGLAND, from the Accession of James I. to the Outbreak of the Civil War, 1603-1642. 10 vols. Crown 8vo., 6s. each.

A HISTORY OF THE GREAT CIVIL WAR, 1642-1649. 4 vols. Cr. 8vo., 6s. each.

THE STUDENT'S HISTORY OF ENGLAND, With 378 Illustrations. Cr. 8vo., 12s.

Also in Three Volumes.

Vol. I. B.C. 55—A.D. 1509. With 173 Illustrations. Crown 8vo. 4s.
Vol. II. 1509-1689. With 96 Illustrations. Crown 8vo. 4s.
Vol. III. 1689-1885. With 109 Illustrations. Crown 8vo. 4s.

Granville.—THE LETTERS OF HARRIET COUNTESS GRANVILLE, 1810-1845. Edited by her Son, the Hon. F. LEVESON GOWER. 2 vols. 8vo., 32s.

Greville.—A JOURNAL OF THE REIGNS OF KING GEORGE IV., KING WILLIAM IV., AND QUEEN VICTORIA. By CHARLES C. F. GREVILLE, formerly Clerk of the Council. 8 vols. Crown 8vo., 6s. each.

Hart.—PRACTICAL ESSAYS IN AMERICAN GOVERNMENT. By ALBERT BUSHNELL HART, Ph.D., &c. Cr. 8vo., 6s

Hearn.—THE GOVERNMENT OF ENGLAND: its Structure and its Development. By W. EDWARD HEARN. 8vo., 16s.

Historic Towns.—Edited by E. A. FREEMAN, D.C.L., and Rev. WILLIAM HUNT, M.A. With Maps and Plans. Crown 8vo., 3s. 6d. each.

BRISTOL. By the Rev. W. HUNT.

CARLISLE. By MANDELL CREIGHTON, D.D., Bishop of Peterborough.

CINQUE PORTS. By MONTAGU BURROWS.

COLCHESTER. By Rev. E. L. CUTTS.

EXETER. By E. A. FREEMAN.

LONDON. By Rev. W. J. LOFTIE.

OXFORD. By Rev. C. W. BOASE.

WINCHESTER. By Rev. G. W. KITCHIN, D.D.

YORK. By Rev. JAMES RAINE.

NEW YORK. By THEODORE ROOSEVELT.

BOSTON (U.S.) By HENRY CABOT LODGE.

Horley.—SEFTON: A DESCRIPTIVE AND HISTORICAL ACCOUNT. Comprising the Collected Notes and Researches of the late Rev. ENGELBERT HORLEY, M.A., Rector 1871-1883. By W. D. CARÖE, M.A. (Cantab.), Fellow of the Royal Institute of British Architects, and E. J. A. GORDON. With 17 Plates and 32 Illustrations in the Text. Royal 8vo., 31s. 6d.

Joyce.—A SHORT HISTORY OF IRELAND, from the Earliest Times to 1608. By P. W. JOYCE, LL.D. Crown 8vo., 10s. 6d.

Lang.—ST. ANDREWS. By ANDREW LANG. With 8 Plates and 24 Illustrations in the Text, by T. HODGE. 8vo., 15s. net.

Lecky.—Works by WILLIAM EDWARD HARTPOLE LECKY.

HISTORY OF ENGLAND IN THE EIGHTEENTH CENTURY.
Library Edition. 8 vols. 8vo., £7 4s.
Cabinet Edition. ENGLAND. 7 vols. Cr. 8vo., 6s. each. IRELAND. 5 vols. Crown 8vo., 6s. each.

HISTORY OF EUROPEAN MORALS FROM AUGUSTUS TO CHARLEMAGNE. 2 vols. Crown 8vo., 16s.

HISTORY OF THE RISE AND INFLUENCE OF THE SPIRIT OF RATIONALISM IN EUROPE. 2 vols. Crown 8vo., 16s.

History, Politics, Polity, and Political Memoirs—*continued*.

Macaulay.—Works by LORD MAC-AULAY.

COMPLETE WORKS.

Cabinet Ed. 16 vols. Pt. 8vo., £4 16*s*.
Library Edition. 8 vols. 8vo., £5 5*s*.

HISTORY OF ENGLAND FROM THE AC-CESSION OF JAMES THE SECOND.

Popular Edition. 2 vols. Cr. 8vo., 5*s*.
Student's Edition. 2 vols. Cr. 8vo., 12*s*.
People's Edition. 4 vols. Cr. 8vo., 16*s*.
Cabinet Edition. 8 vols. Pt. 8vo., 48*s*.
Library Edition. 5 vols. 8vo., £4

CRITICAL AND HISTORICAL ESSAYS, WITH LAYS OF ANCIENT ROME, in 1 volume.

Popular Edition. Crown 8vo., 2*s*. 6*d*.

Authorised Edition. Crown 8vo., 2*s*. 6*d*., or 3*s*. 6*d*., gilt edges.

Silver Library Edition. Crown 8vo., 3*s*. 6*d*.

CRITICAL AND HISTORICAL ESSAYS.

Student's Edition. 1 vol. Cr. 8vo., 6*s*.
People's Edition. 2 vols. Cr. 8vo., 8*s*.
Trevelyan Edition. 2 vols. Cr. 8vo., 9*s*.
Cabinet Edition. 4 vols. Post 8vo., 24*s*.
Library Edition. 3 vols. 8vo., 36*s*.

ESSAYS which may be had separately price 6*d*. each sewed, 1*s*. each cloth.

Frederick the Great.	Lord Clive.
Lord Bacon.	The Earl of Chatham (Two Essays).
Addison and Walpole.	Ranke and Gladstone.
Croker's Boswell's Johnson.	Milton and Machiavelli.
Hallam's Constitutional History.	Lord Byron, and The Comic Dramatists of the Restoration.
Warren Hastings (3*d*. swd., 6*d*. cl.).	

SPEECHES. Crown 8vo., 3*s*. 6*d*.

MISCELLANEOUS WRITINGS.

People's Ed. 1 vol. Cr. 8vo., 4*s*. 6*d*.
Library Edition. 2 vols. 8vo., 21*s*.

MISCELLANEOUS WRITINGS AND SPEECHES.

Popular Edition. Cr. 8vo., 2*s*. 6*d*.

Student's Edition. Crown 8vo., 6*s*.

Cabinet Edition. Including Indian Penal Code, Lays of Ancient Rome, and Miscellaneous Poems. 4 vols. Post 8vo., 24*s*.

Macaulay.—Works by LORD MAC-AULAY.—*continued*.

SELECTIONS FROM THE WRITINGS OF LORD MACAULAY. Edited, with Occasional Notes, by the Right Hon. Sir G. O. Trevelyan, Bart. Crown 8vo., 6*s*.

May.—THE CONSTITUTIONAL HISTORY OF ENGLAND since the Accession of George III. 1760-1870. By Sir THOMAS ERSKINE MAY, K.C.B. (Lord Farnborough). 3 vols. Crown 8vo., 18*s*.

Merivale.—Works by the Very Rev. CHARLES MERIVALE, late Dean of Ely.

HISTORY OF THE ROMANS UNDER THE EMPIRE.

Cabinet Edition. 8 vols. Cr. 8vo., 48*s*.
Silver Library Edition. 8 vols. Cr. 8vo., 3*s*. 6*d*. each.

THE FALL OF THE ROMAN REPUBLIC: a Short History of the Last Century of the Commonwealth. 12mo., 7*s*. 6*d*.

Parkes.—FIFTY YEARS IN THE MAKING OF AUSTRALIAN HISTORY. By Sir HENRY PARKES, G.C.M.G. With 2 Portraits (1854 and 1892). 2 vols. 8vo., 32*s*.

Prendergast.—IRELAND FROM THE RESTORATION TO THE REVOLUTION, 1660-1690. By JOHN P. PRENDERGAST, Author of 'The Cromwellian Settlement in Ireland'. 8vo., 5*s*.

Round.—GEOFFREY DE MANDEVILLE: a Study of the Anarchy. By J. H. ROUND, M.A. 8vo., 16*s*.

Seebohm.—THE ENGLISH VILLAGE COMMUNITY Examined in its Relations to the Manorial and Tribal Systems, &c. By FREDERIC SEEBOHM. With 13 Maps and Plates. 8vo., 16*s*.

Smith.—CARTHAGE AND THE CARTHAGINIANS. By R. BOSWORTH SMITH, M.A. With Maps, &c. Cr. 8vo., 3*s*. 6*d*.

Stephens.—PAROCHIAL SELF-GOVERNMENT IN RURAL DISTRICTS: Argument and Plan. By HENRY C. STEPHENS, M.P. 4to., 12*s*. 6*d*. Popular Edition. Cr. 8vo., 1*s*.

Stephens.—A HISTORY OF THE FRENCH REVOLUTION. By H. MORSE STEPHENS, Balliol College, Oxford. 3 vols. 8vo. Vols. I. and II. 18*s*. each.

History, Politics, Polity, and Political Memoirs—*continued.*

Stubbs.—HISTORY OF THE UNIVERSITY OF DUBLIN, from its Foundation to the End of the Eighteenth Century. By J. W. STUBBS. 8vo., 12s. 6d.

Sutherland.—THE HISTORY OF AUSTRALIA AND NEW ZEALAND, from 1606 to 1890. By ALEXANDER SUTHERLAND, M.A., and GEORGE SUTHERLAND, M.A. Crown 8vo., 2s. 6d.

Thompson.—POLITICS IN A DEMOCRACY: an Essay. By DANIEL GREENLEAF THOMPSON. Cr. 8vo., 5s.

Todd.—PARLIAMENTARY GOVERNMENT IN THE COLONIES. By ALPHEUS TODD, LL.D. 8vo., 30s. net.

Tupper. — OUR INDIAN PROTECTORATE: an Introduction to the Study of the Relations between the British Government and its Indian Feudatories. By CHARLES LEWIS TUPPER, Indian Civil Service. Royal 8vo., 16s.

Wakeman and Hassall.—ESSAYS INTRODUCTORY TO THE STUDY OF ENGLISH CONSTITUTIONAL HISTORY. By Resident Members of the University of Oxford. Edited by HENRY OFFLEY WAKEMAN, M.A., and ARTHUR HASSALL, M.A. Crown 8vo., 6s.

Walpole.—Works by SPENCER WALPOLE.

HISTORY OF ENGLAND FROM THE CONCLUSION OF THE GREAT WAR IN 1815 TO 1858. 6 vols. Crown 8vo., 6s. each.

THE LAND OF HOME RULE: being an Account of the History and Institutions of the Isle of Man. Cr. 8vo., 6s.

Wylie.—HISTORY OF ENGLAND UNDER HENRY IV. By JAMES HAMILTON WYLIE, M.A., one of H. M. Inspectors of Schools. 3 vols. Crown 8vo. Vol. I. 10s. 6d. Vol. II. 15s. Vol. III.
[*In preparation.*]

Biography, Personal Memoirs, &c.

Armstrong.—THE LIFE AND LETTERS OF EDMUND J. ARMSTRONG. Edited by G. F. ARMSTRONG. Fcp. 8vo., 7s. 6d.

Bacon.—LETTERS AND LIFE, INCLUDING ALL HIS OCCASIONAL WORKS. Edited by J. SPEDDING. 7 vols. 8vo., £4 4s.

Bagehot.—BIOGRAPHICAL STUDIES. By WALTER BAGEHOT. 8vo., 12s.

Boyd.—TWENTY-FIVE YEARS OF ST. ANDREWS, 1865-1890. By A. K. H. BOYD, D.D., Author of 'Recreations of a Country Parson,' &c. 2 vols. 8vo. Vol. I., 12s. Vol. II., 15s.

Carlyle.—THOMAS CARLYLE: a History of his Life. By J. A. FROUDE. 1795-1835. 2 vols. Crown 8vo., 7s. 1834-1881. 2 vols. Crown 8vo., 7s.

Fabert.—ABRAHAM FABERT: Governor of Sedan and Marshal of France. His Life and Times, 1599-1662. By GEORGE HOOPER, Author of 'Waterloo,' 'Wellington,' &c. With a Portrait. 8vo., 10s. 6d.

Fox.—THE EARLY HISTORY OF CHARLES JAMES FOX. By the Right Hon. Sir G. O. TREVELYAN, Bart.

Library Edition. 8vo., 18s.
Cabinet Edition. Crown 8vo., 6s.

Hamilton.—LIFE OF SIR WILLIAM HAMILTON. By R. P. GRAVES. 3 vols. 15s. each.
ADDENDUM TO THE LIFE OF SIR WM. ROWAN HAMILTON, LL.D., D.C.L., 8vo., 6d. sewed.

Hassall.—THE NARRATIVE OF A BUSY LIFE: an Autobiography. By ARTHUR HILL HASSALL, M.D. 8vo., 5s.

Havelock.—MEMOIRS OF SIR HENRY HAVELOCK, K.C.B. By JOHN CLARK MARSHMAN. Crown 8vo., 3s. 6d.

Macaulay.—THE LIFE AND LETTERS OF LORD MACAULAY. By the Right Hon. Sir G. O. TREVELYAN, Bart.
Popular Edition. 1 vol. Cr. 8vo., 2s. 6d.
Student's Edition. 1 vol. Cr. 8vo., 6s.
Cabinet Edition. 2 vols. Post 8vo., 12s.
Library Edition. 2 vols. 8vo., 36s.

Marbot.—THE MEMOIRS OF THE BARON DE MARBOT. Translated from the French by ARTHUR JOHN BUTLER, M.A. Crown 8vo., 7s. 6d.

Montrose.—DEEDS OF MONTROSE: THE MEMOIRS OF JAMES, MARQUIS OF MONTROSE, 1639-1650. By the Rev. GEORGE WISHART, D.D. (Bishop of Edinburgh, 1662-1671). Translated, with Introduction, Notes, &c., and the original Latin, by the Rev. ALEXANDER MURDOCH, F.S.A. (Scot.), and H. F. MORELAND SIMPSON, M.A. (Cantab.). 4to., 36s. net.

Biography, Personal Memoirs, &c.—*continued.*

Seebohm.—THE OXFORD REFORMERS —JOHN COLET, ERASMUS AND THOMAS MORE : a History of their Fellow-Work. By FREDERIC SEEBOHM. 8vo., 14*s.*

Shakespeare.—OUTLINES OF THE LIFE OF SHAKESPEARE. By J. O. HALLIWELL-PHILLIPPS. With numerous Illustrations and Fac-similes. 2 vols. Royal 8vo., £1 1*s.*

Shakespeare's TRUE LIFE. By JAS. WALTER. With 500 Illustrations by GERALD E. MOIRA. Imp. 8vo., 21*s.*

Sherbrooke.—LIFE AND LETTERS OF THE RIGHT HON. ROBERT LOWE, VISCOUNT SHERBROOKE, G.C.B., together with a Memoir of his Kinsman, Sir JOHN COAPE SHERBROOKE, G.C.B. By A. PATCHETT MARTIN. With 5 Portraits. 2 vols. 8vo., 36*s.*

Stephen.—ESSAYS IN ECCLESIASTICAL BIOGRAPHY. By Sir JAMES STEPHEN. Crown 8vo., 7*s.* 6*d.*

Verney.—MEMOIRS OF THE VERNEY FAMILY DURING THE CIVIL WAR. Compiled from the Letters and Illustrated by the Portraits at Claydon House, Bucks. By FRANCES PARTHENOPE VERNEY. With a Preface by S. R. GARDINER, M.A., LL.D. With 38 Portraits, Woodcuts and Fac-simile. 2 vols. Royal 8vo., 42*s.*

Wagner.—WAGNER AS I KNEW HIM. By FERDINAND PRAEGER. Crown 8vo., 7*s.* 6*d.*

Walford.—TWELVE ENGLISH AUTHORESSES. By L. B. WALFORD, Author of 'Mischief of Monica,' &c. With Portrait of Hannah More. Crown 8vo., 4*s.* 6*d.*

Wellington.—LIFE OF THE DUKE OF WELLINGTON. By the Rev. G. R. GLEIG, M.A. Crown 8vo., 3*s.* 6*d.*

Wordsworth.—Works by CHARLES WORDSWORTH, D.C.L., late Bishop of St. Andrews.

ANNALS OF MY EARLY LIFE, 1806-1846. 8vo., 15*s.*

ANNALS OF MY LIFE, 1847-1856. 8vo., 10*s.* 6*d.*

Travel and Adventure.

Arnold.—SEAS AND LANDS. By Sir EDWIN ARNOLD, K.C.I.E. With 71 Illustrations. Cr. 8vo., 7*s.* 6*d.*

AUSTRALIA AS IT IS; or, Facts and Features, Sketches and Incidents of Australia and Australian Life, with Notices of New Zealand. By A CLERGYMAN. Crown 8vo., 5*s.*

Baker.—Works by Sir SAMUEL WHITE BAKER.

EIGHT YEARS IN CEYLON. With 6 Illustrations. Crown 8vo., 3*s.* 6*d.*

THE RIFLE AND THE HOUND IN CEYLON. 6 Illustrations. Cr. 8vo., 3*s.* 6*d.*

Bent.—Works by J. THEODORE BENT, F.S.A., F.R.G.S.

THE RUINED CITIES OF MASHONALAND : being a Record of Excavation and Exploration in 1891. With Map, 13 Plates, and 104 Illustrations in the Text. Cr. 8vo., 7*s.* 6*d.*

THE SACRED CITY OF THE ETHIOPIANS: being a Record of Travel and Research in Abyssinia in 1893. With 8 Plates and 65 Illustrations in the Text. 8vo., 18*s*

Brassey.—Works by LADY BRASSEY.

A VOYAGE IN THE 'SUNBEAM'; OUR HOME ON THE OCEAN FOR ELEVEN MONTHS.

Library Edition. With 8 Maps and Charts, and 118 Illustrations. 8vo., 21*s.*

Cabinet Edition. With Map and 66 Illustrations. Crown 8vo., 7*s.* 6*d.*

Silver Library Edition. With 66 Illustrations. Crown 8vo., 3*s.* 6*d.*

Popular Edition. With 60 Illustrations. 4to., 6*d.* sewed, 1*s.* cloth.

School Edition. With 37 Illustrations. Fcp., 2*s.* cloth, or 3*s.* white parchment.

SUNSHINE AND STORM IN THE EAST.

Library Edition. With 2 Maps and 141 Illustrations. 8vo., 21*s.*

Cabinet Edition. With 2 Maps and 114 Illustrations. Crown 8vo., 7*s.* 6*d*

Popular Edition. With 103 Illustrations. 4to., 6*d.* sewed, 1*s.* cloth.

Travel and Adventure—*continued.*

Brassey.—Works by LADY BRASSEY—*continued.*

IN THE TRADES, THE TROPICS, AND THE 'ROARING FORTIES'.
Cabinet Edition. With Map and 220 Illustrations. Crown 8vo., 7s. 6d.
Popular Edition. With 183 Illustrations. 4to., 6d. sewed, 1s. cloth.

THREE VOYAGES IN THE 'SUNBEAM'. Popular Edition. With 346 Illustrations. 4to., 2s. 6d.

THE LAST VOYAGE TO INDIA AND AUSTRALIA IN THE 'SUNBEAM'. With Charts and Maps, and 40 Illustrations in Monotone (20 full-page), and nearly 200 Illustrations in the Text from Drawings by R. T. PRITCHETT. 8vo., 21s.

Curzon.—PERSIA AND THE PERSIAN QUESTION. With 9 Maps, 96 Illustrations, Appendices, and an Index. By the Hon. GEORGE N. CURZON, M.P., late Fellow of All Souls' College, Oxford. 2 vols. 8vo., 42s.

Froude.—Works by JAMES A. FROUDE.

OCEANA : or England and her Colonies. With 9 Illustrations. Crown 8vo., 2s. boards, 2s. 6d. cloth.

THE ENGLISH IN THE WEST INDIES : or the Bow of Ulysses. With 9 Illustrations. Cr. 8vo., 2s. bds., 2s. 6d. cl.

Howard.—LIFE WITH TRANS-SIBERIAN SAVAGES. By B. DOUGLAS HOWARD, M.A. Crown 8vo., 6s.

Howitt.—VISITS TO REMARKABLE PLACES, Old Halls, Battle-Fields, Scenes illustrative of Striking Passages in English History and Poetry. By WILLIAM HOWITT. With 80 Illustrations. Crown 8vo., 3s. 6d.

Knight.—Works by E. F. KNIGHT, Author of the Cruise of the 'Falcon'.

THE CRUISE OF THE 'ALERTE': the Narrative of a Search for Treasure on the Desert Island of Trinidad. With 2 Maps and 23 Illustrations. Crown 8vo., 3s. 6d.

WHERE THREE EMPIRES MEET: a Narrative of Recent Travel in Kashmir, Western Tibet, Baltistan, Ladak, Gilgit, and the adjoining Countries. With a Map and 54 Illustrations. Cr. 8vo., 7s. 6d.

Lees and Clutterbuck.—B. C. 1887: A RAMBLE IN BRITISH COLUMBIA. By J. A. LEES and W. J. CLUTTERBUCK, Authors of 'Three in Norway'. With Map and 75 Illustrations. Cr. 8vo., 3s. 6d.

Montague.—TALES OF A NOMAD ; or, Sport and Strife. By CHARLES MONTAGUE. Crown 8vo., 6s.

Nansen.—Works by Dr. FRIDTJOF NANSEN.

THE FIRST CROSSING OF GREENLAND. With numerous Illustrations and a Map. Crown 8vo., 7s. 6d.

ESKIMO LIFE. Translated by WILLIAM ARCHER. With 16 Plates and 15 Illustrations in the Text. 8vo., 16s.

Riley.—ATHOS : or the Mountain of the Monks. By ATHELSTAN RILEY, M.A. With Map and 29 Illustrations. 8vo., 21s.

Rockhill.—THE LAND OF THE LAMAS : Notes of a Journey through China, Mongolia, and Tibet. By WILLIAM WOODVILLE ROCKHILL. With 2 Maps and 61 Illustrations. 8vo., 15s.

Stephens.—MADOC: An Essay on the Discovery of America, by MADOC AP OWEN GWYNEDD, in the Twelfth Century. By THOMAS STEPHENS. Edited by LLYWARCH REYNOLDS, B.A. Oxon. 8vo., 7s. 6d.

THREE IN NORWAY. By Two of Them. With a Map and 59 Illustrations. Cr. 8vo., 2s. boards, 2s. 6d. cloth.

Von Hohnel.—DISCOVERY OF LAKES RUDOLF AND STEFANIE: Account of Count SAMUEL TELEKI'S Exploring and Hunting Expedition in Eastern Equatorial Africa in 1887 and 1888. By Lieutenant LUDWIG VON HOHNEL. With 179 Illustrations and 6 Maps. 2 vols. 8vo., 42s.

Whishaw.—OUT OF DOORS IN TSAR LAND; a Record of the Seeings and Doings of a Wanderer in Russia. By FRED. J. WHISHAW. Cr. 8vo., 7s. 6d.

Wolff.—Works by HENRY W. WOLFF.

RAMBLES IN THE BLACK FOREST. Crown 8vo., 7s. 6d.

THE WATERING PLACES OF THE VOSGES. Crown 8vo., 4s. 6d.

THE COUNTRY OF THE VOSGES. With a Map. 8vo., 12s.

Sport and Pastime.
THE BADMINTON LIBRARY.

Edited by the DUKE OF BEAUFORT, K.G., assisted by ALFRED E. T. WATSON.

ATHLETICS AND FOOTBALL. By MONTAGUE SHEARMAN. With . 51 Illlustrations. Crown 8vo., 10s. 6d.

BIG GAME SHOOTING. By C. PHILLIPPS-WOLLEY, F. C. SELOUS, ST. GEORGE LITTLEDALE, &c. With 150 Illustrations. 2 vols., 10s. 6d. each.

BOATING. By W. B. WOODGATE. With 49 Illustrations. Cr. 8vo., 10s. 6d.

COURSING AND FALCONRY. By HARDING COX and the Hon. GERALD LASCELLES. With 76 Illustrations. Crown 8vo., 10s. 6d.

CRICKET. By A. G. STEEL and the Hon. R. H. LYTTELTON. With Contributions by ANDREW LANG, R. A. H. MITCHELL, W. G. GRACE, and F. GALE. With 63 Illustrations. Cr. 8vo., 10s. 6d.

CYCLING. By VISCOUNT BURY (Earl of Albemarle), K.C.M.G., and G. LACY HILLIER. With 89 Illustrations. Crown 8vo., 10s. 6d.

DRIVING. By the DUKE OF BEAUFORT. With 65 Illustrations. Cr. 8vo., 10s. 6d.

FENCING, BOXING, AND WRESTLING. By WALTER H. POLLOCK, F. C. GROVE. C. PREVOST, E. B. MITCHELL, and WALTER ARMSTRONG. With 42 Illustrations. Crown 8vo., 10s. 6d.

FISHING. By H. CHOLMONDELEY-PENNELL. With Contributions by the MARQUIS OF EXETER, HENRY R. FRANCIS, R. B. MARSTON, &c.

Vol. I. Salmon, Trout, and Grayling. With 158 Illustrations. Crown 8vo., 10s. 6d.

Vol. II. Pike and other Coarse Fish. With 133 Illustrations. Crown 8vo., 10s. 6d.

GOLF. By HORACE G. HUTCHINSON, the Rt. Hon. A. J. BALFOUR, M.P., Sir W. G. SIMPSON, Bart., ANDREW LANG, and other Writers. With 91 Illustrations. Cr. 8vo., 10s. 6d.

HUNTING. By the DUKE OF BEAUFORT, K.G., and MOWBRAY MORRIS. With Contributions by the EARL OF SUFFOLK AND BERKSHIRE, Rev. E. W. L. DAVIES. With 53 Illustrations. Crown 8vo., 10s. 6d.

MOUNTAINEERING. By C. T. DENT, Sir F. POLLOCK, Bart., W. M. CONWAY, DOUGLAS FRESHFIELD, C. E. MATHEWS, C. PILKINGTON. With 108 Illustrations. Cr. 8vo., 10s. 6d.

RACING AND STEEPLE-CHASING. *Racing:* By the EARL OF SUFFOLK AND BERKSHIRE and W. G. CRAVEN. With a Contribution by the Hon. F. LAWLEY. *Steeple-chasing:* By ARTHUR COVENTRY and ALFRED E. T. WATSON. With 58 Illusts. Cr. 8vo., 10s. 6d.

RIDING AND POLO. By Captain ROBERT WEIR, J. MORAY BROWN, the DUKE OF BEAUFORT, K.G., the EARL of SUFFOLK AND BERKSHIRE, &c. With 59 Illustrations. Cr. 8vo., 10s. 6d.

SHOOTING. By Lord WALSINGHAM and Sir RALPH PAYNE-GALLWEY, Bart. With Contributions by LORD LOVAT, A. J. STUART-WORTLEY, &c.

Vol. I. Field and Covert. With 105 Illustrations. Crown 8vo., 10s. 6d.

Vol. II. Moor and Marsh. With 65 Illustrations. Cr. 8vo., 10s. 6d.

SKATING, CURLING, TOBOGANING, AND OTHER ICE SPORTS. By JN. M. HEATHCOTE, C. G. TEBBUTT, T. MAXWELL WITHAM, &c. With 284 Illustrations. Cr. 8vo., 10s. 6d.

SWIMMING. By ARCHIBALD SINCLAIR and WILLIAM HENRY, Hon. Secs. of the Life Saving Society. With 119 Illustrations. Cr. 8vo., 10s. 6d.

TENNIS, LAWN TENNIS, RACQUETS, AND FIVES. By J. M. and C. G. HEATHCOTE, E. O. PLEYDELL-BOUVERIE and A. C. AINGER. With Contributions by the Hon. A. LYTTELTON, W. C. MARSHALL, Miss L. DOD, H. W. W. WILBERFORCE, H. F. LAWFORD, &c. With 79 Illustrations. Crown 8vo., 10s. 6d.

YACHTING. By the EARL OF PEMBROKE, R. T. PRITCHETT, the MARQUIS OF DUFFERIN AND AVA, the EARL OF ONSLOW, LORD BRASSEY, Lieut.-Col. BUCKNILL, LEWIS HERRESHOFF, G. L. WATSON, E. F. KNIGHT, etc. With Illustrations by R. T. PRITCHETT, and from Photographs. 2 vols. 10s. 6d., each.

Sport and Pastime—*continued*.
FUR AND FEATHER SERIES.
Edited by A. E. T. WATSON.

THE PARTRIDGE. Natural History, by the Rev. H. A. MACPHERSON; Shooting, by A. J. STUART-WORTLEY; Cookery, by GEORGE SAINTSBURY. With 11 full-page Illustrations and Vignette by A. THORBURN, A. J. STUART-WORTLEY, and C. WHYMPER, and 15 Diagrams in the Text by A. J. STUART-WORTLEY. Crown 8vo., 5s.

THE GROUSE. By A. J. STUART-WORTLEY, the Rev. H. A. MACPHERSON, and GEORGE SAINTSBURY.   [*In preparation.*

THE PHEASANT. By A. J. STUART-WORTLEY, the Rev. H. A. MACPHERSON, and A. J. INNES SHAND.   [*In preparation.*

THE HARE AND THE RABBIT. By the Hon. GERALD LASCELLES, &c.   [*In preparation.*

WILDFOWL. By the Hon. JOHN SCOTT-MONTAGU, M.P., &c. Illustrated by A. J. STUART WORTLEY, A. THORBURN, and others.   [*In preparation.*

Campbell-Walker.—THE CORRECT CARD: or, How to Play at Whist; a Whist Catechism. By Major A. CAMPBELL-WALKER. Fcp. 8vo., 2s. 6d.

DEAD SHOT (THE): or, Sportsman's Complete Guide. Being a Treatise on the Use of the Gun, with Rudimentary and Finishing Lessons on the Art of Shooting Game of all kinds. By MARKSMAN. Crown 8vo., 10s. 6d.

Falkener.—GAMES, ANCIENT AND ORIENTAL, AND HOW TO PLAY THEM. By EDWARD FALKENER. With numerous Photographs, Diagrams, &c. 8vo., 21s.

Ford.—THE THEORY AND PRACTICE OF ARCHERY. BY HORACE FORD. New Edition, thoroughly Revised and Rewritten by W. BUTT, M.A. With a Preface by C. J. LONGMAN, M.A. 8vo., 14s.

Fowler.—RECOLLECTIONS OF OLD COUNTRY LIFE. By J. K. FOWLER ("Rusticus"), formerly of Aylesbury. With Portraits, &c. 8vo., 10s. 6d.

Francis.—A BOOK ON ANGLING: or, Treatise on the Art of Fishing in every Branch; including full Illustrated List of Salmon Flies. By FRANCIS FRANCIS. With Coloured Plates. Cr. 8vo., 15s.

Hawker.—THE DIARY OF COLONEL PETER HAWKER, author of "Instructions to Young Sportsmen". With an Introduction by Sir RALPH PAYNE-GALLWEY, Bart. 2 vols. 8vo., 32s.

Hopkins.—FISHING REMINISCENCES. By Major E. P. HOPKINS. With Illustrations. Crown 8vo., 6s. 6d.

Lang.—ANGLING SKETCHES. By ANDREW LANG. With 20 Illustrations. Crown 8vo., 7s. 6d.

Longman.—CHESS OPENINGS. By FRED. W. LONGMAN. Fcp. 8vo., 2s. 6d.

Maskelyne.—SHARPS AND FLATS: a Complete Revelation of the Secrets of Cheating at Games of Chance and Skill. By JOHN NEVIL MASKELYNE. With 62 Illustrations and Diagrams. Crown 8vo., 6s.

Payne-Gallwey.—Works by Sir RALPH PAYNE-GALLWEY, Bart.

LETTERS TO YOUNG SHOOTERS (First Series). On the Choice and Use of a Gun. With 41 Illustrations. Cr. 8vo., 7s. 6d.

LETTERS TO YOUNG SHOOTERS. (Second Series). On the Production, Preservation, and Killing of Game. With Directions in Shooting Wood-Pigeons and Breaking-in Retrievers. With 103 Illustrations. Crown 8vo., 12s. 6d.

Pole.—THE THEORY OF THE MODERN SCIENTIFIC GAME OF WHIST. By W. POLE, F.R.S. Fcp. 8vo., 2s. 6d.

Proctor.—Works by RICHARD A. PROCTOR.

HOW TO PLAY WHIST: WITH THE LAWS AND ETIQUETTE OF WHIST. Crown 8vo., 3s. 6d.

HOME WHIST: an Easy Guide to Correct Play. 16mo., 1s.

Ronalds.—THE FLY-FISHER'S ENTOMOLOGY. By ALFRED RONALDS. With 20 Coloured Plates. 8vo., 14s.

Wilcocks. THE SEA FISHERMAN: Comprising the Chief Methods of Hook and Line Fishing in the British and other Seas, and Remarks on Nets, Boats, and Boating. By J. C. WILCOCKS. Illustrated. Crown 8vo., 6s.

Mental, Moral, and Political Philosophy.

LOGIC, RHETORIC, PSYCHOLOGY, ETC.

Abbott.—THE ELEMENTS OF LOGIC. By T. K. ABBOTT, B.D. 12mo., 3s.

Aristotle.—Works by.

THE POLITICS: G. Bekker's Greek Text of Books I., III., IV. (VII.), with an English Translation by W. E. BOLLAND, M.A.; and short Introductory Essays by A. LANG, M.A. Crown 8vo., 7s. 6d.

THE POLITICS: Introductory Essays. By ANDREW LANG (from Bolland and Lang's 'Politics'). Cr. 8vo., 2s. 6d.

THE ETHICS: Greek Text, Illustrated with Essay and Notes. By Sir ALEXANDER GRANT, Bart. 2 vols. 8vo., 32s.

THE NICOMACHEAN ETHICS: Newly Translated into English. By ROBERT WILLIAMS. Crown 8vo., 7s. 6d.

AN INTRODUCTION TO ARISTOTLE'S ETHICS. Books I.-IV. (Book X. c. vi.-ix. in an Appendix.) With a continuous Analysis and Notes. Intended for the use of Beginners and Junior Students. By the Rev. EDWARD MOORE, D.D., Principal of St. Edmund Hall, and late Fellow and Tutor of Queen's College, Oxford. Crown 8vo., 10s. 6d.

Bacon.—Works by.

COMPLETE WORKS. Edited by R L. ELLIS, J. SPEDDING, and D. D. HEATH. 7 vols. 8vo., £3 13s. 6d.

THE ESSAYS: with Annotations. By RICHARD WHATELY, D.D. 8vo. 10s. 6d.

Bain.—Works by ALEXANDER BAIN, LL.D.

MENTAL SCIENCE. Crown 8vo., 6s. 6d.

MORAL SCIENCE. Crown 8vo., 4s. 6d.

The two works as above can be had in one volume, price 10s. 6d.

SENSES AND THE INTELLECT. 8vo., 15s.

EMOTIONS AND THE WILL. 8vo., 15s.

LOGIC, DEDUCTIVE AND INDUCTIVE. Part I., 4s. Part II., 6s. 6d.

PRACTICAL ESSAYS. Crown 8vo., 2s.

Bray.—Works by CHARLES BRAY.

THE PHILOSOPHY OF NECESSITY: or Law in Mind as in Matter. Cr. 8vo., 5s.

THE EDUCATION OF THE FEELINGS: a Moral System for Schools. Crown 8vo., 2s. 6d.

Bray.—ELEMENTS OF MORALITY, in Easy Lessons for Home and School Teaching. By Mrs. CHARLES BRAY. Cr. 8vo., 1s. 6d.

Crozier.—CIVILISATION AND PROGRESS. By JOHN BEATTIE CROZIER, M.D. With New Preface, more fully explaining the nature of the New Organon used in the solution of its problems. 8vo., 14s.

Davidson.—THE LOGIC OF DEFINITION, Explained and Applied. By WILLIAM L. DAVIDSON, M.A. Crown 8vo., 6s.

Green.—THE WORKS OF THOMAS HILL GREEN. Edited by R. L. NETTLESHIP.

Vols. I. and II. Philosophical Works. 8vo., 16s. each.

Vol. III. Miscellanies. With Index to the three Volumes, and Memoir. 8vo., 21s.

Hearn.—THE ARYAN HOUSEHOLD: its Structure and its Development. An Introduction to Comparative Jurisprudence. By W. EDWARD HEARN. 8vo., 16s.

Hodgson.—Works by SHADWORTH H. HODGSON.

TIME AND SPACE: a Metaphysical Essay. 8vo., 16s.

THE THEORY OF PRACTICE: an Ethical Inquiry. 2 vols. 8vo., 24s.

THE PHILOSOPHY OF REFLECTION. 2 vols. 8vo., 21s.

Hume.—THE PHILOSOPHICAL WORKS OF DAVID HUME. Edited by T. H. GREEN and T. H. GROSE. 4 vols. 8vo., 56s. Or separately, Essays. 2 vols. 28s. Treatise of Human Nature. 2 vols. 28s.

Mental, Moral and Political Philosophy—*continued*.

Johnstone.—A SHORT INTRODUCTION TO THE STUDY OF LOGIC. By LAURENCE JOHNSTONE. With Questions. Cr. 8vo., 2s. 6d.

Jones.—AN INTRODUCTION TO GENERAL LOGIC. By E. E. CONSTANCE JONES, Author of ' Elements of Logic as a Science of Propositions'. Cr. 8vo., 4s. 6d.

Justinian.—THE INSTITUTES OF JUSTINIAN : Latin Text, chiefly that of Huschke, with English Introduction, Translation, Notes, and Summary. By THOMAS C. SANDARS, M.A. 8vo. 18s.

Kant.—Works by IMMANUEL KANT.

CRITIQUE OF PRACTICAL REASON, AND OTHER WORKS ON THE THEORY OF ETHICS. Translated by T. K. ABBOTT, B. D. With Memoir. 8vo., 12s. 6d.

INTRODUCTION TO LOGIC, AND HIS ESSAY ON THE MISTAKEN SUBTILTY OF THE FOUR FIGURES. Translated by T. K. ABBOTT, and with Notes by S. T. COLERIDGE. 8vo., 6s.

Killick.—HANDBOOK TO MILL'S SYSTEM OF LOGIC. By Rev. A. H. KILLICK, M.A. Crown 8vo., 3s. 6d.

Ladd.—Works by GEORGE TURNBULL LADD.

ELEMENTS OF PHYSIOLOGICAL PSYCHOLOGY. 8vo., 21s.

OUTLINES OF PHYSIOLOGICAL PSYCHOLOGY. A Text-Book of Mental Science for Academies and Colleges. 8vo., 12s.

PSYCHOLOGY, DESCRIPTIVE AND EXPLANATORY : a Treatise of the Phenomena, Laws, and Development of Human Mental Life. 8vo., 21s.

Lewes.—THE HISTORY OF PHILOSOPHY, from Thales to Comte. By GEORGE HENRY LEWES. 2 vols. 8vo., 32s.

Max Müller.—Works by F. MAX MÜLLER.

THE SCIENCE OF THOUGHT. 8vo., 21s.

THREE INTRODUCTORY LECTURES ON THE SCIENCE OF THOUGHT. 8vo., 2s. 6d.

Mill.—ANALYSIS OF THE PHENOMENA OF THE HUMAN MIND. By JAMES MILL. 2 vols. 8vo., 28s.

Mill.—Works by JOHN STUART MILL.

A SYSTEM OF LOGIC. Cr. 8vo., 3s. 6d.

ON LIBERTY. Cr. 8vo., 1s. 4d.

ON REPRESENTATIVE GOVERNMENT. Crown 8vo., 2s.

UTILITARIANISM. 8vo., 5s.

EXAMINATION OF SIR WILLIAM HAMILTON'S PHILOSOPHY. 8vo., 16s.

NATURE, THE UTILITY OF RELIGION, AND THEISM. Three Essays. 8vo., 5s,

Monck.—INTRODUCTION TO LOGIC. By H. S. MONCK. Crown 8vo., 5s.

Ribot.—THE PSYCHOLOGY OF ATTENTION. By TH. RIBOT. Cr. 8vo., 3s.

Sidgwick.—DISTINCTION: and the Criticism of Belief. By ALFRED SIDGWICK. Crown 8vo., 6s.

Stock.—DEDUCTIVE LOGIC. By ST. GEORGE STOCK. Fcp. 8vo., 3s. 6d.

Sully.—Works by JAMES SULLY, Grote Professor of Mind and Logic at University College, London.

THE HUMAN MIND : a Text-book of Psychology. 2 vols. 8vo., 21s.

OUTLINES OF PSYCHOLOGY. 8vo., 9s.

THE TEACHER'S HANDBOOK OF PSYCHOLOGY. Crown 8vo., 5s.

Swinburne.—PICTURE LOGIC: an Attempt to Popularise the Science of Reasoning. By ALFRED JAMES SWINBURNE, M.A. With 23 Woodcuts. Post 8vo., 5s.

Thompson.—Works by DANIEL GREENLEAF THOMPSON.

A SYSTEM OF PSYCHOLOGY. 2 vols. 8vo., 36s.

THE RELIGIOUS SENTIMENTS OF THE HUMAN MIND. 8vo., 7s. 6d.

THE PROBLEM OF EVIL: an Introduction to the Practical Sciences. 8vo., 10s. 6d.

Mental, Moral and Political Philosophy—*continued.*

Thompson. — Works by DANIEL GREENLEAF THOMPSON—*continued.*

SOCIAL PROGRESS. 8vo., 7s. 6d.

THE PHILOSOPHY OF FICTION IN LITERATURE. Crown 8vo., 6s.

Thomson.—OUTLINES OF THE NECESSARY LAWS OF THOUGHT: a Treatise on Pure and Applied Logic. By WILLIAM THOMSON, D.D., formerly Lord Archbishop of York. Post 8vo., 6s.

Webb.—THE VEIL OF ISIS: a Series of Essays on Idealism. By T. E. WEBB. 8vo., 10s. 6d.

Whately.—Works by R. WHATELY, formerly Archbishop of Dublin.

BACON'S ESSAYS. With Annotation. By R. WHATELY. 8vo., 10s. 6d.

ELEMENTS OF LOGIC. Cr. 8vo., 4s. 6d.

ELEMENTS OF RHETORIC. Cr. 8vo., 4s. 6d.

LESSONS ON REASONING. Fcp. 8vo., 1s. 6d.

Zeller.—Works by Dr. EDWARD ZELLER, Professor in the University of Berlin.

HISTORY OF ECLECTICISM IN GREEK PHILOSOPHY. Translated by SARAH F. ALLEYNE. Cr. 8vo., 10s. 6d.

THE STOICS, EPICUREANS, AND SCEPTICS. Translated by the Rev. O. J. REICHEL, M.A. Crown 8vo., 15s.

OUTLINES OF THE HISTORY OF GREEK PHILOSOPHY. Translated by SARAH F. ALLEYNE and EVELYN ABBOTT. Crown 8vo., 10s. 6d.

PLATO AND THE OLDER ACADEMY. Translated by SARAH F. ALLEYNE and ALFRED GOODWIN, B.A. Crown 8vo., 18s.

SOCRATES AND THE SOCRATIC SCHOOLS. Translated by the Rev. O. J. REICHEL, M.A. Crown 8vo., 10s. 6d.

THE PRE-SOCRATIC SCHOOLS: a History of Greek Philosophy from the Earliest Period to the time of Socrates. Translated by SARAH F. ALLEYNE. 2 vols. Crown 8vo., 30s.

MANUALS OF CATHOLIC PHILOSOPHY.
(Stonyhurst Series.)

A MANUAL OF POLITICAL ECONOMY. By C. S. DEVAS, M.A. Cr. 8vo., 6s. 6d.

FIRST PRINCIPLES OF KNOWLEDGE. By JOHN RICKABY, S.J. Crown 8vo., 5s.

GENERAL METAPHYSICS. By JOHN RICKABY, S.J. Crown 8vo., 5s.

LOGIC. By RICHARD F. CLARKE, S.J. Crown 8vo., 5s.

MORAL PHILOSOPHY (ETHICS AND NATURAL LAW). By JOSEPH RICKABY, S.J. Crown 8vo., 5s.

NATURAL THEOLOGY. By BERNARD BOEDDER, S.J. Crown 8vo., 6s. 6d.

PSYCHOLOGY. By MICHAEL MAHER, S.J. Crown 8vo., 6s. 6d.

History and Science of Language, &c.

Davidson.—LEADING AND IMPORTANT ENGLISH WORDS: Explained and Exemplified. By WILLIAM L. DAVIDSON, M.A. Fcp. 8vo., 3s. 6d.

Farrar.—LANGUAGE AND LANGUAGES: By F. W. FARRAR, D.D., F.R.S., Cr. 8vo., 6s.

Graham.—ENGLISH SYNONYMS, Classified and Explained : with Practical Exercises. By G. F. GRAHAM. Fcp. 8vo., 6s.

History and Science of Language, &c.—*continued*.

Max Müller.—Works by F. MAX MÜLLER.

SELECTED ESSAYS ON LANGUAGE, MYTHOLOGY, AND RELIGION. 2 vols. Crown 8vo., 16*s*.

THE SCIENCE OF LANGUAGE, Founded on Lectures delivered at the Royal Institution in 1861 and 1863. 2 vols. Crown 8vo., 21*s*.

BIOGRAPHIES OF WORDS, AND THE HOME OF THE ARYAS. Crown 8vo., 7*s*. 6*d*.

THREE LECTURES ON THE SCIENCE OF LANGUAGE, AND ITS PLACE IN GENERAL EDUCATION, delivered at Oxford, 1889. Crown 8vo., 3*s*.

Roget. — THESAURUS OF ENGLISH WORDS AND PHRASES. Classified and Arranged so as to Facilitate the Expression of Ideas and assist in Literary Composition. By PETER MARK ROGET, M.D., F.R.S. Recomposed throughout, enlarged and improved, partly from the Author's Notes, and with a full Index, by the Author's Son, JOHN LEWIS ROGET. Crown 8vo.. 10*s*. 6*d*.

Whately.—ENGLISH SYNONYMS. By E. JANE WHATELY. Fcp. 8vo., 3*s*.

Political Economy and Economics.

Ashley.—ENGLISH ECONOMIC HISTORY AND THEORY. By W. J. ASHLEY, M.A. Crown 8vo., Part I., 5*s*. Part II., 10*s*. 6*d*.

Bagehot. — ECONOMIC STUDIES. By WALTER BAGEHOT. 8vo., 10*s*. 6*d*.

Crump.—AN INVESTIGATION INTO THE CAUSES OF THE GREAT FALL IN PRICES which took place coincidently with the Demonetisation of Silver by Germany. By ARTHUR CRUMP. 8vo., 6*s*.

Devas.—A MANUAL OF POLITICAL ECONOMY. By C. S. DEVAS, M.A. Crown 8vo., 6*s*. 6*d*. (*Manuals of Catholic Philosophy*.)

Dowell.—A HISTORY OF TAXATION AND TAXES IN ENGLAND, from the Earliest Times to the Year 1885. By STEPHEN DOWELL (4 vols. 8vo.) Vols. I. and II. The History of Taxation, 21*s*. Vols. III. and IV. The History of Taxes, 21*s*.

Jordan.—THE STANDARD OF VALUE. By WILLIAM LEIGHTON JORDAN. 8vo., 6*s*.

Leslie.—ESSAYS IN POLITICAL ECONOMY. By T. E. CLIFFE LESLIE. 8vo., 10*s*. 6*d*

Macleod.—Works by HENRY DUNNING MACLEOD, M.A.

THE ELEMENTS OF BANKING. Crown 8vo., 3*s*. 6*d*.

THE THEORY AND PRACTICE OF BANKING. Vol. I. 8vo., 12*s*. Vol. II. 14*s*.

THE THEORY OF CREDIT. 8vo. Vol. I. 10*s*. net. Vol. II., Part I., 4*s*. 6*d*. Vol. II. Part II., 10*s*. 6*d*.

Meath.—PROSPERITY OR PAUPERISM? Physical, Industrial, and Technical Training. By the EARL OF MEATH. 8vo., 5*s*.

Mill.—POLITICAL ECONOMY. By JOHN STUART MILL.

Library Edition. 2 vols. 8vo., 30*s*.

Popular Edition. Crown 8vo., 3*s*. 6*d*.

Shirres.—AN ANALYSIS OF THE IDEAS OF ECONOMICS. By L. P. SHIRRES, B.A., sometime Finance Under Secretary of the Government of Bengal. Crown 8vo., 6*s*.

Political Economy and Economics—*continued.*

Symes.—POLITICAL ECONOMY: a Short Text-book of Political Economy. With Problems for Solution, and Hints for Supplementary Reading. By J. E. SYMES, M.A., of University College, Nottingham. Crown 8vo., 2s. 6d.

Toynbee.—LECTURES ON THE INDUSTRIAL REVOLUTION OF THE 18th CENTURY IN ENGLAND. By ARNOLD TOYNBEE. 8vo., 10s. 6d.

Webb.—THE HISTORY OF TRADE UNIONISM. By SIDNEY and BEATRICE WEBB. 8vo., 18s.

Wilson.—Works by A. J. WILSON. Chiefly reprinted from *The Investors' Review.*

PRACTICAL HINTS TO SMALL INVESTORS. Crown 8vo., 1s.

PLAIN ADVICE ABOUT LIFE INSURANCE. Crown 8vo., 1s.

Wolff.—PEOPLE'S BANKS: a Record of Social and Economic Success. By HENRY W. WOLFF. 8vo., 7s. 6d.

Evolution, Anthropology, &c.

Clodd.—THE STORY OF CREATION: a Plain Account of Evolution. By EDWARD CLODD. With 77 Illustrations. Crown 8vo., 3s. 6d.

Huth.—THE MARRIAGE OF NEAR KIN, considered with Respect to the Law of Nations, the Result of Experience, and the Teachings of Biology. By ALFRED HENRY HUTH. Royal 8vo., 7s. 6d.

Lang.—CUSTOM AND MYTH: Studies of Early Usage and Belief. By ANDREW LANG, M.A. With 15 Illustrations. Crown 8vo., 3s. 6d.

Lubbock.—THE ORIGIN OF CIVILISATION and the Primitive Condition of Man. By Sir J. LUBBOCK, Bart., M.P. With 5 Plates and 20 Illustrations in the Text. 8vo. 18s.

Romanes.—Works by GEORGE JOHN ROMANES, M.A., LL.D., F.R.S.

DARWIN, AND AFTER DARWIN: an Exposition of the Darwinian Theory, and a Discussion on Post-Darwinian Questions. Part I. The Darwinian Theory. With Portrait of Darwin and 125 Illustrations. Crown 8vo., 10s. 6d.

AN EXAMINATION OF WEISMANNISM. Crown 8vo., 6s.

Classical Literature.

Abbott.—HELLENICA. A Collection of Essays on Greek Poetry, Philosophy, History, and Religion. Edited by EVELYN ABBOTT, M.A., LL.D. 8vo., 16s.

Æschylus.—EUMENIDES OF ÆSCHYLUS. With Metrical English Translation. By J. F. DAVIES. 8vo., 7s.

Aristophanes.—The ACHARNIANS OF ARISTOPHANES, translated into English Verse. By R. Y. TYRRELL. Crown 8vo., 1s.

Becker.—Works by Professor BECKER.

GALLUS: or, Roman Scenes in the Time of Augustus. Illustrated. Post 8vo., 7s. 6d.

CHARICLES: or, Illustrations of the Private Life of the Ancient Greeks. Illustrated. Post 8vo., 7s. 6d.

Cicero.—CICERO'S CORRESPONDENCE. By R. Y. TYRRELL. Vols. I., II., III. 8vo., each 12s.

Clerke.—FAMILIAR STUDIES IN HOMER. By AGNES M. CLERKE. Cr. 8vo., 7s. 6d.

Farnell.—GREEK LYRIC POETRY: a Complete Collection of the Surviving Passages from the Greek Song-Writing. Arranged with Prefatory Articles, Introductory Matter and Commentary. By GEORGE S. FARNELL, M.A. With 5 Plates. 8vo., 16s.

Harrison.—MYTHS OF THE ODYSSEY. IN ART AND LITERATURE. By JANE E. HARRISON. Illustrated with Outline Drawings. 8vo., 18s.

Lang.—HOMER AND THE EPIC. By ANDREW LANG. Crown 8vo., 9s. net.

Classical Literature—*continued.*

Mackail.—SELECT EPIGRAMS FROM THE GREEK ANTHOLOGY. By J. W. MACKAIL, Fellow of Balliol College, Oxford. Edited with a Revised Text, Introduction, Translation, and Notes. 8vo., 16s.

Plato.—PARMENIDES OF PLATO, Text, with Introduction, Analysis, &c. By T. MAGUIRE. 8vo., 7s. 6d.

Rich.—A DICTIONARY OF ROMAN AND GREEK ANTIQUITIES. By A. RICH, B.A. With 2000 Woodcuts. Crown 8vo., 7s. 6d.

Sophocles.—Translated into English Verse. By ROBERT WHITELAW, M.A., Assistant Master in Rugby School : late Fellow of Trinity College, Cambridge. Crown 8vo., 8s. 6d.

Theocritus.—THE IDYLLS OF THEOCRITUS. Translated into English Verse. By JAMES HENRY HALLARD, M.A. Oxon. 8vo., 6s. 6d.

Tyrrell.—TRANSLATIONS INTO GREEK AND LATIN VERSE. Edited by R. Y. TYRRELL. 8vo., 6s.

Virgil.—THE ÆNEID OF VIRGIL. Translated into English Verse by JOHN CONINGTON. Crown 8vo., 6s.

THE POEMS OF VIRGIL. Translated into English Prose by JOHN CONINGTON. Crown 8vo., 6s.

THE ÆNEID OF VIRGIL, freely translated into English Blank Verse. By W. J. THORNHILL. Crown 8vo., 7s. 6d.

THE ÆNEID OF VIRGIL. Books I. to VI. Translated into English Verse by JAMES RHOADES. Crown 8vo., 5s.

Wilkins.—THE GROWTH OF THE HOMERIC POEMS. By G. WILKINS. 8vo. 6s.

Poetry and the Drama.

Allingham.—Works by WILLIAM ALLINGHAM.

IRISH SONGS AND POEMS. With Frontispiece of the Waterfall of Asaroe. Fcp. 8vo., 6s.

LAURENCE BLOOMFIELD. With Portrait of the Author. Fcp. 8vo., 3s. 6d.

FLOWER PIECES ; DAY AND NIGHT SONGS ; BALLADS. With 2 Designs by D. G. ROSSETTI. Fcp. 8vo., 6s. ; large paper edition, 12s.

LIFE AND PHANTASY : with Frontispiece by Sir J. E. MILLAIS, Bart., and Design by ARTHUR HUGHES. Fcp. 8vo., 6s. ; large paper edition, 12s.

THOUGHT AND WORD, AND ASHBY MANOR : a Play. With Portrait of the Author (1865), and four Theatrical Scenes drawn by Mr. Allingham. Fcp. 8vo., 6s. ; large paper edition, 12s.

BLACKBERRIES. Imperial 16mo., 6s.

Sets of the above 6 vols. may be had in uniform half-parchment binding, price 30s.

Armstrong.—Works by G. F. SAVAGE-ARMSTRONG.

POEMS : Lyrical and Dramatic. Fcp. 8vo., 6s.

KING SAUL. (The Tragedy of Israel, Part I.) Fcp. 8vo. 5s.

KING DAVID. (The Tragedy of Israel, Part II.) Fcp. 8vo., 6s.

KING SOLOMON. (The Tragedy of Israel, Part III.) Fcp. 8vo., 6s.

UGONE : a Tragedy. Fcp. 8vo., 6s.

A GARLAND FROM GREECE : Poems. Fcp. 8vo., 7s. 6d.

STORIES OF WICKLOW : Poems. Fcp. 8vo., 7s. 6d.

MEPHISTOPHELES IN BROADCLOTH : a Satire. Fcp. 8vo., 4s.

ONE IN THE INFINITE : a Poem. Cr. 8vo., 7s. 6d.

Armstrong.—THE POETICAL WORKS OF EDMUND J. ARMSTRONG. Fcp. 8vo., 5s.

Poetry and the Drama—*continued*.

Arnold.—Works by Sir EDWIN ARNOLD, K.C.I.E., Author of 'The Light of Asia,' &c.

THE LIGHT OF THE WORLD: or, the Great Consummation. A Poem. Crown 8vo., 7s. 6d. net.

Presentation Edition. With 14 Illustrations by W. HOLMAN HUNT, &c., 4to., 20s. net.

POTIPHAR'S WIFE, and other Poems. Crown 8vo., 5s. net.

ADZUMA: or, the Japanese Wife. A Play. Crown 8vo., 6s. 6d. net.

Barrow.—THE SEVEN CITIES OF THE DEAD, and other Poems. By Sir JOHN CROKER BARROW, Bart. Fcp. 8vo., 5s.

Bell.—Works by Mrs. HUGH BELL.

CHAMBER COMEDIES: a Collection of Plays and Monologues for the Drawing Room. Crown 8vo., 6s.

NURSERY COMEDIES: Twelve Tiny Plays for Children. Fcp. 8vo., 1s. 6d.

Björnsen.—Works by BJÖRNSTJERNE BJÖRNSEN.

PASTOR SANG: a Play. Translated by WILLIAM WILSON. Cr. 8vo., 5s.

A GAUNTLET. a Drama. Translated into English by OSMAN EDWARDS. With Portrait of the Author. Crown 8vo., 5s.

Cochrane.—THE KESTREL'S NEST, and other Verses. By ALFRED COCHRANE. Fcp. 8vo., 3s. 6d.

Dante.—LA COMMEDIA DI DANTE. A New Text, carefully revised with the aid of the most recent Editions and Collations. Small 8vo., 6s.

Goethe.

FAUST, Part I., the German Text, with Introduction and Notes. By ALBERT M. SELSS, Ph.D., M.A. Cr. 8vo., 5s.

FAUST. Translated, with Notes. By T. E. WEBB. 8vo., 12s. 6d.

FAUST. The First Part. A New Translation, chiefly in Blank Verse; with Introduction and Notes. By JAMES ADEY BIRDS. Cr. 8vo., 6s.

FAUST. The Second Part. A New Translation in Verse. By JAMES ADEY BIRDS. Crown 8vo., 6s.

Ingelow.—Works by JEAN INGELOW.

POETICAL WORKS. 2 vols. Fcp. 8vo., 12s.

LYRICAL AND OTHER POEMS. Selected from the Writings of JEAN INGELOW. Fcp. 8vo., 2s. 6d. cloth plain, 3s. cloth gilt.

Lang.—Works by ANDREW LANG.

BAN AND ARRIÈRE BAN. A Rally of Fugitive Rhymes. Fcp. 8vo., 5s. net.

GRASS OF PARNASSUS. Fcp. 8vo., 2s. 6d. net.

BALLADS OF BOOKS. Edited by ANDREW LANG. Fcp. 8vo., 6s.

THE BLUE POETRY BOOK. Edited by ANDREW LANG. With 12 Plates and 88 Illustrations in the Text. Crown 8vo., 6s.

Special Edition, printed on Indian paper. With Notes, but without Illustrations. Crown 8vo., 7s. 6d.

Lecky.—POEMS. By W. E. H. LECKY. Fcp. 8vo., 5s.

Leyton.—Works by FRANK LEYTON.

THE SHADOWS OF THE LAKE, and other Poems. Crown 8vo., 7s. 6d. Cheap Edition. Crown 8vo., 3s. 6d.

SKELETON LEAVES: Poems. Crown 8vo., 6s.

Lytton.—Works by THE EARL OF LYTTON (OWEN MEREDITH).

KING POPPY: a Fantasia. With 1 Plate and Design on Title-Page by Sir ED. BURNE-JONES, A.R.A. Crown 8vo., 10s. 6d.

MARAH. Fcp. 8vo., 6s. 6d.

THE WANDERER. Cr. 8vo., 10s. 6d.

LUCILE. Crown 8vo., 10s. 6d.

SELECTED POEMS. Cr. 8vo., 10s. 6d.

Macaulay.—LAYS OF ANCIENT ROME, &c. By Lord MACAULAY.

Illustrated by G. SCHARF. Fcp. 4to., 10s. 6d.

——————— Bijou Edition. 18mo., 2s. 6d., gilt top.

——————— Popular Edition. Fcp. 4to., 6d. sewed, 1s. cloth.

Illustrated by J. R. WEGUELIN. Crown 8vo., 3s. 6d.

Annotated Edition. Fcp. 8vo., 1s. sewed, 1s. 6d. cloth.

Nesbit.—LAYS AND LEGENDS. by E. NESBIT (Mrs. HUBERT BLAND). First Series. Crown 8vo., 3s. 6d. Second Series, with Portrait. Crown 8vo., 5s.

Piatt.—AN ENCHANTED CASTLE, AND OTHER POEMS: Pictures, Portraits and People in Ireland. By SARAH PIATT. Crown 8vo., 3s. 6d.

Poetry and the Drama—*continued.*

Piatt.—Works by JOHN JAMES PIATT.

IDYLS AND LYRICS OF THE OHIO VALLEY. Crown 8vo., 5*s.*

LITTLE NEW WORLD IDYLS. Cr. 8vo., 5*s.*

Rhoades.—TERESA AND OTHER POEMS. By JAMES RHOADES. Crown 8vo., 3*s.* 6*d.*

Riley.—Works by JAMES WHITCOMB RILEY.

POEMS HERE AT HOME. Fcap. 8vo., 6*s.* net.

OLD FASHIONED ROSES : Poems. 12mo., 5*s.*

Roberts. — SONGS OF THE COMMON DAY, AND AVE : an Ode for the Shelley Centenary. By CHARLES G. D. ROBERTS. Crown 8vo., 3*s.* 6*d.*

Shakespeare.—BOWDLER'S FAMILY SHAKESPEARE. With 36 Woodcuts. 1 vol. 8vo., 14*s.* Or in 6 vols. Fcp. 8vo., 21*s.*

THE SHAKESPEARE BIRTHDAY BOOK. By MARY F. DUNBAR. 32mo., 1*s.* 6*d.* Drawing-Room Edition, with Photographs. Fcp. 8vo., 10*s.* 6*d.*

Stevenson.—A CHILD'S GARDEN OF VERSES. By ROBERT LOUIS STEVENSON. Small fcp. 8vo., 5*s.*

Works of Fiction, Humour, &c.

Anstey.—Works by F. ANSTEY, Author of ' Vice Versâ'.

THE BLACK POODLE, and other Stories. Crown 8vo., 2*s.* boards, 2*s.* 6*d.* cloth.

VOCES POPULI. Reprinted from ' Punch'. With Illustrations by J. BERNARD PARTRIDGE. First Series. Fcp. 4to., 5*s.* Second Series. Fcp. 4to., 6*s.*

THE TRAVELLING COMPANIONS. Reprinted from ' Punch'. With Illustrations by J. BERNARD PARTRIDGE. Post 4to., 5*s.*

THE MAN FROM BLANKLEY'S : a Story in Scenes, and other Sketches. With 24 Illustrations by J. BERNARD PARTRIDGE. Fcp. 4to., 6*s.*

ATELIER (THE) DU LYS : or, an Art Student in the Reign of Terror. Crown 8vo., 2*s.* 6*d.*

BY THE SAME AUTHOR.

MADEMOISELLE MORI : a Tale of Modern Rome. Crown 8vo., 2*s.* 6*d.*

BY THE SAME AUTHOR—*continued.*

THAT CHILD. Illustrated by GORDON BROWNE. Crown 8vo., 2*s.* 6*d.*

UNDER A CLOUD. Cr. 8vo., 2*s.* 6*d.*

THE FIDDLER OF LUGAU. With Illustrations by W. RALSTON. Crown 8vo., 2*s.* 6*d.*

A CHILD OF THE REVOLUTION. With Illustrations by C. J. STANILAND. Crown 8vo., 2*s.* 6*d.*

HESTER'S VENTURE : a Novel. Crown 8vo., 2*s.* 6*d.*

IN THE OLDEN TIME : a Tale of the Peasant War in Germany. Crown 8vo., 2*s.* 6*d.*

THE YOUNGER SISTER : a Tale. Cr. 8vo., 2*s.* 6*d.*

Baker.—BY THE WESTERN SEA. By JAMES BAKER, Author of ' John Westacott'. Crown 8vo., 3*s.* 6*d.*

Works of Fiction, Humour, &c.—*continued.*

Beaconsfield.—Works by the Earl of BEACONSFIELD.

NOVELS AND TALES. Cheap Edition. Complete in 11 vols. Cr. 8vo., 1s. 6d. each.

Vivian Grey.	Contarini Fleming, &c.
The Young Duke, &c.	Venetia. Tancred.
Alroy, Ixion, &c.	Coningsby. Sybil.
Henrietta Temple.	Lothair. Endymion.

NOVELS AND TALES. The Hughenden Edition. With 2 Portraits and 11 Vignettes. 11 vols. Cr. 8vo., 42s.

Comyn.—ATHERSTONE PRIORY: a Tale. By L. N. COMYN. Crown 8vo., 2s. 6d.

Deland.—Works by MARGARET DELAND, Author of 'John Ward'.

THE STORY OF A CHILD. Cr. 8vo., 5s.

MR. TOMMY DOVE, and other Stories. Crown 8vo., 6s.

Dougall.—Works by L. DOUGALL.

BEGGARS ALL. Crown 8vo., 3s. 6d.

WHAT NECESSITY KNOWS. Crown 8vo., 6s.

Doyle.—Works by A. CONAN DOYLE.

MICAH CLARKE: a Tale of Monmouth's Rebellion. With Frontispiece and Vignette. Cr. 8vo., 3s. 6d.

THE CAPTAIN OF THE POLESTAR, and other Tales. Cr. 8vo., 3s. 6d.

THE REFUGEES: a Tale of Two Continents. Cr. 8vo., 6s.

Farrar.—DARKNESS AND DAWN: or, Scenes in the Days of Nero. An Historic Tale. By Archdeacon FARRAR. Cr. 8vo., 7s. 6d.

Froude.—THE TWO CHIEFS OF DUNBOY: an Irish Romance of the Last Century. By J. A. FROUDE. Cr. 8vo., 3s. 6d.

Haggard.—Works by H. RIDER HAGGARD.

SHE. With 32 Illustrations by M. GREIFFENHAGEN and C. H. M. KERR. Cr. 8vo., 3s. 6d.

ALLAN QUATERMAIN. With 31 Illustrations by C. H. M. KERR. Cr. 8vo., 3s. 6d.

MAIWA'S REVENGE; or, The War of the Little Hand. Cr. 8vo., 1s. boards, 1s. 6d. cloth.

COLONEL QUARITCH, V.C. Cr. 8vo., 3s. 6d.

Haggard.—Works by H. RIDER HAGGARD—*continued.*

CLEOPATRA. With 29 Full-page Illustrations by M. GREIFFENHAGEN and R. CATON WOODVILLE. Cr. 8vo., 3s. 6d.

BEATRICE. Cr. 8vo., 3s. 6d.

ERIC BRIGHTEYES. With 17 Plates and 34 Illustrations in the Text by LANCELOT SPEED. Cr. 8vo., 3s. 6d.

NADA THE LILY. With 23 Illustrations by C. H. M. KERR. Cr. 8vo., 6s.

MONTEZUMA'S DAUGHTER. With 24 Illustrations by M. GREIFFENHAGEN. Cr. 8vo., 6s.

Haggard and Lang.—THE WORLD'S DESIRE. By H. RIDER HAGGARD and ANDREW LANG. Cr. 8vo., 6s.

Harte.—IN THE CARQUINEZ WOODS, and other Stories. By BRET HARTE. Cr. 8vo., 3s. 6d.

KEITH DERAMORE: a Novel. By the Author of 'Miss Molly'. Cr. 8vo., 6s.

Lyall.—THE AUTOBIOGRAPHY OF A SLANDER. By EDNA LYALL, Author of 'Donovan,' &c. Fcp. 8vo., 1s. sewed.

Presentation Edition. With 20 Illustrations by LANCELOT SPEED. Cr. 8vo., 5s.

Melville.—Works by G. J. WHYTE MELVILLE.

The Gladiators.	Holmby House.
The Interpreter.	Kate Coventry.
Good for Nothing.	Digby Grand.
The Queen's Maries.	General Bounce.

Cr. 8vo., 1s. 6d. each.

Oliphant.—Works by Mrs. OLIPHANT.

MADAM. Cr. 8vo., 1s. 6d.

IN TRUST. Cr. 8vo., 1s. 6d.

Parr.—CAN THIS BE LOVE? By Mrs. PARR, Author of 'Dorothy Fox'. Cr. 8vo., 6s.

Payn.—Works by JAMES PAYN.

THE LUCK OF THE DARRELLS. Cr. 8vo., 1s. 6d.

THICKER THAN WATER. Cr. 8vo., 1s. 6d.

Phillipps-Wolley.—SNAP: a Legend of the Lone Mountain. By C. PHILLIPPS-WOLLEY. With 13 Illustrations by H. G. WILLINK. Cr. 8vo., 3s. 6d.

Robertson.—THE KIDNAPPED SQUATTER, and other Australian Tales. By A. ROBERTSON. Cr. 8vo., 6s.

Works of Fiction, Humour, &c.—*continued.*

Sewell.—Works by ELIZABETH M. SEWELL.

A Glimpse of the World.	Amy Herbert.
Laneton Parsonage.	Cleve Hall.
Margaret Percival.	Gertrude.
Katharine Ashton.	Home Life.
The Earl's Daughter.	After Life.
The Experience of Life.	Ursula. Ivors.

Cr. 8vo., 1s. 6d. each cloth plain. 2s. 6d. each cloth extra, gilt edges.

Stevenson.—Works by ROBERT LOUIS STEVENSON.

STRANGE CASE OF DR. JEKYLL AND MR. HYDE. Fcp. 8vo., 1s. sewed. 1s. 6d. cloth.

THE DYNAMITER. Fcp. 8vo., 1s. sewed, 1s. 6d. cloth.

Stevenson and Osbourne.—THE WRONG BOX. By ROBERT LOUIS STEVENSON and LLOYD OSBOURNE. Cr. 8vo., 3s. 6d.

Sturgis.—AFTER TWENTY YEARS, and other Stories. By JULIAN STURGIS. Cr. 8vo., 6s.

Suttner.—LAY DOWN YOUR ARMS *Die Waffen Nieder:* The Autobiography of Martha Tilling. By BERTHA VON SUTTNER. Translated by T. HOLMES. Cr. 8vo., 1s. 6d.

Thompson.—A MORAL DILEMMA By ANNIE THOMPSON. Cr. 8vo., 6s.

Tirebuck.—Works by WILLIAM TIREBUCK.

DORRIE. Crown 8vo., 6s.

SWEETHEART GWEN. Cr. 8vo., 6s.

Trollope.—Works by ANTHONY TROLLOPE.

THE WARDEN. Cr. 8vo., 1s. 6d.

BARCHESTER TOWERS. Cr. 8vo., 1s. 6d.

TRUE, A, RELATION OF THE TRAVELS AND PERILOUS ADVENTURES OF MATHEW DUDGEON, Gentleman: Wherein is truly set down the Manner of his Taking, the Long Time of his Slavery in Algiers, and Means of his Delivery. Crown 8vo., 5s.

Walford.—Works by L. B. WALFORD.

THE MISCHIEF OF MONICA: a Novel. Cr. 8vo., 2s. 6d.

THE ONE GOOD GUEST: a Story. Cr. 8vo., 2s. 6d.

West.—HALF-HOURS WITH THE MILLIONAIRES: Showing how much harder it is to spend a million than to make it. Edited by B. B. WEST. Cr. 8vo., 6s.

Weyman.—Works by STANLEY J. WEYMAN.

THE HOUSE OF THE WOLF: a Romance. Cr. 8vo., 3s. 6d.

A GENTLEMAN OF FRANCE.. Cr. 8vo. 6s.

Popular Science (Natural History, &c.).

Butler.—OUR HOUSEHOLD INSECTS. By E. A. BUTLER. With 7 Plates and 113 Illustrations in the Text. Crown 8vo., 6s.

Furneaux.—THE OUTDOOR WORLD; or, The Young Collector's Handbook. By W. FURNEAUX, F.R.G.S. With 16 Coloured Plates, 2 Plain Plates, and 549 Illustrations in the Text. Crown 8vo., 7s. 6d.

Hartwig.—Works by Dr. GEORGE HARTWIG.

THE SEA AND ITS LIVING WONDERS. With 12 Plates and 303 Woodcuts. 8vo., 7s. net.

THE TROPICAL WORLD. With 8 Plates and 172 Woodcuts. 8vo., 7s. net.

THE POLAR WORLD. With 3 Maps, 8 Plates and 85 Woodcuts. 8vo., 7s. net.

Hartwig.—Works by Dr. GEORGE HARTWIG—*continued.*

THE SUBTERRANEAN WORLD. With 3 Maps and 80 Woodcuts. 8vo., 7s. net.

THE AERIAL WORLD. With Map, 8 Plates and 60 Woodcuts. 8vo., 7s. net.

HEROES OF THE POLAR WORLD. 19 Illustrations. Crown 8vo., 2s.

WONDERS OF THE TROPICAL FORESTS. 40 Illustrations. Crown 8vo., 2s.

WORKERS UNDER THE GROUND. 29 Illustrations. Crown 8vo., 2s.

MARVELS OVER OUR HEADS. 29 Illustrations. Crown 8vo., 2s.

SEA MONSTERS AND SEA BIRDS. 75 Illustrations. Crown 8vo., 2s. 6d.

Popular Science (Natural History, &c.).

Hartwig.—Works by Dr. GEORGE HARTWIG—*continued*.

DENIZENS OF THE DEEP. 117 Illustrations. Crown 8vo., 2s. 6d.

VOLCANOES AND EARTHQUAKES. 30 Illustrations. Crown 8vo., 2s. 6d.

WILD ANIMALS OF THE TROPICS. 66 Illustrations. Crown 8vo., 3s. 6d.

Helmholtz.—POPULAR LECTURES ON SCIENTIFIC SUBJECTS. By HERMANN VON HELMHOLTZ. With 68 Woodcuts. 2 vols. Crown 8vo., 3s. 6d. each.

Lydekker.—PHASES OF ANIMAL LIFE, PAST AND PRESENT. By R. LYDEKKER, B.A. With 82 Illustrations. Crown 8vo., 6s.

Proctor.—Works by RICHARD A. PROCTOR.

And see Messrs. Longmans & Co.'s Catalogue of Scientific Works.

LIGHT SCIENCE FOR LEISURE HOURS. Familiar Essays on Scientific Subjects. 3 vols. Crown 8vo., 5s. each.

CHANCE AND LUCK: a Discussion of the Laws of Luck, Coincidence, Wagers, Lotteries and the Fallacies of Gambling, &c. Cr. 8vo., 2s. boards, 2s. 6d. cloth.

ROUGH WAYS MADE SMOOTH. Familiar Essays on Scientific Subjects. Silver Library Edition. Crown 8vo., 3s. 6d.

PLEASANT WAYS IN SCIENCE. Cr. 8vo., 5s. Silver Library Edition. Crown 8vo., 3s. 6d.

THE GREAT PYRAMID, OBSERVATORY, TOMB AND TEMPLE. With Illustrations. Crown 8vo., 5s.

NATURE STUDIES. By R. A. PROCTOR, GRANT ALLEN, A. WILSON, T. FOSTER and E. CLODD. Crown 8vo., 5s. Silver Library Edition. Crown 8vo., 3s. 6d.

LEISURE READINGS. By R. A. PROCTOR, E. CLODD, A. WILSON, T. FOSTER, and A. C. RANYARD. Cr. 8vo., 5s.

Stanley.—A FAMILIAR HISTORY OF BIRDS. By E. STANLEY, D.D., formerly Bishop of Norwich. With Illustrations. Cr. 8vo., 3s. 6d.

Wood.—Works by the Rev. J. G. WOOD.

HOMES WITHOUT HANDS: a Description of the Habitation of Animals, classed according to the Principle of Construction. With 140 Illustrations. 8vo., 7s. net.

INSECTS AT HOME: a Popular Account of British Insects, their Structure, Habits and Transformations. With 700 Illustrations. 8vo., 7s. net.

INSECTS ABROAD: a Popular Account of Foreign Insects, their Structure, Habits and Transformations. With 600 Illustrations. 8vo., 7s. net.

BIBLE ANIMALS: a Description of every Living Creature mentioned in the Scriptures. With 112 Illustrations. 8vo., 7s. net.

PETLAND REVISITED. With 33 Illustrations. Cr. 8vo., 3s. 6d.

OUT OF DOORS; a Selection of Original Articles on Practical Natural History. With 11 Illustrations. Cr. 8vo., 3s. 6d.

STRANGE DWELLINGS: a Description of the Habitations of Animals, abridged from 'Homes without Hands'. With 60 Illustrations. Cr. 8vo., 3s. 6d.

BIRD LIFE OF THE BIBLE. 32 Illustrations. Cr. 8vo., 3s. 6d.

WONDERFUL NESTS. 30 Illustrations. Cr. 8vo, 3s. 6d.

HOMES UNDER THE GROUND. 28 Illustrations. Cr. 8vo., 3s. 6d.

WILD ANIMALS OF THE BIBLE. 29 Illustrations. Cr. 8vo., 3s. 6d.

DOMESTIC ANIMALS OF THE BIBLE. 23 Illustrations. Cr. 8vo., 3s. 6d.

THE BRANCH BUILDERS. 28 Illustrations. Cr. 8vo., 2s. 6d.

SOCIAL HABITATIONS AND PARASITIC NESTS. 18 Illustrations. Cr. 8vo., 2s.

Works of Reference.

Maunder's (Samuel) Treasuries.

BIOGRAPHICAL TREASURY. With Supplement brought down to 1889. By Rev. JAMES WOOD. Fcp. 8vo., 6s.

TREASURY OF NATURAL HISTORY : or, Popular Dictionary of Zoology. With 900 Woodcuts. Fcp. 8vo., 6s.

TREASURY OF GEOGRAPHY, Physical, Historical, Descriptive, and Political. With 7 Maps and 16 Plates. Fcp. 8vo., 6s.

THE TREASURY OF BIBLE KNOWLEDGE. By the Rev. J. AYRE, M.A. With 5 Maps, 15 plates, and 300 Woodcuts. Fcp. 8vo., 6s.

HISTORICAL TREASURY : Outlines of Universal History, Separate Histories of all Nations. Fcp. 8vo., 6s.

TREASURY OF KNOWLEDGE AND LIBRARY OF REFERENCE. Comprising an English Dictionary and Grammar, Universal Gazeteer, Classical Dictionary, Chronology, Law Dictionary, &c. Fcp. 8vo., 6s.

Maunder's (Samuel) Treasuries —*continued.*

SCIENTIFIC AND LITERARY TREASURY. Fcp. 8vo., 6s.

THE TREASURY OF BOTANY. Edited by J. LINDLEY, F.R.S., and T. MOORE, F.L.S. With 274 Woodcuts and 20 Steel Plates. 2 vols. Fcp. 8vo., 12s.

Roget.—THESAURUS OF ENGLISH WORDS AND PHRASES. Classified and Arranged so as to Facilitate the Expression of Ideas and assist in Literary Composition. By PETER MARK ROGET, M.D.. F.R.S. Recomposed throughout, enlarged and improved, partly from the Author's Notes, and with a full Index, by the Author's Son, JOHN LEWIS ROGET. Crown 8vo., 10s. 6d.

Willich.—POPULAR TABLES for giving information for ascertaining the value of Lifehold, Leasehold, and Church Property, the Public Funds, &c. By CHARLES M. WILLICH. Edited by H. BENCE JONES. Crown 8vo., 10s. 6d.

Children's Books.

Crake.—Works by Rev. A. D. CRAKE.

EDWY THE FAIR ; or, the First Chronicle of Æscendune. Crown 8vo., 2s. 6d.

ALFGAR THE DANE: or, the Second Chronicle of Æscendune. Cr. 8vo., 2s. 6d.

THE RIVAL HEIRS : being the Third and Last Chronicle of Æscendune. Cr. 8vo., 2s. 6d.

THE HOUSE OF WALDERNE. A Tale of the Cloister and the Forest in the Days of the Barons' Wars. Crown 8vo., 2s. 6d.

BRIAN FITZ-COUNT. A Story of Wallingford Castle and Dorchester Abbey. Cr. 8vo., 2s. 6d.

Ingelow.—VERY YOUNG, AND QUITE ANOTHER STORY. Two Stories. By JEAN INGELOW. Crown 8vo., 2s. 6d.

Lang.—Works edited by ANDREW LANG.

THE BLUE FAIRY BOOK. With 8 Plates and 130 Illustrations in the Text by H. J. FORD and G. P. JACOMB HOOD. Crown 8vo., 6s.

Lang.—Works edited by ANDREW LANG —*continued.*

THE RED FAIRY BOOK. With 4 Plates and 96 Illustrations in the Text by H. J. FORD and LANCELOT SPEED. Crown 8vo., 6s.

THE GREEN FAIRY BOOK. With 11 Plates and 88 Illustrations in the Text by H. J. FORD and L. BOGLE. Cr. 8vo., 6s.

THE BLUE POETRY BOOK. With 12 Plates and 88 Illustrations in the Text by H. J. FORD and LANCELOT SPEED. Crown 8vo., 6s.

THE BLUE POETRY BOOK. School Edition, without Illustrations. Fcp. 8vo., 2s. 6d.

THE TRUE STORY BOOK. With 8 Plates and 58 Illustrations in the Text, by C. H. KERR. H. J. FORD, LANCELOT SPEED, and L. BOGLE. Crown 8vo., 6s.

Children's Books—*continued.*

Meade.—Works by L. T. MEADE.
DEB AND THE DUCHESS. Illustrated. Crown 8vo., 3s. 6d.
THE BERESFORD PRIZE. Illustrated. Cr. 8vo., 5s.
DADDY'S BOY. Illustrated. Crown 8vo., 3s. 6d.

Molesworth.—Works by Mrs. MOLESWORTH.
SILVERTHORNS. Illustrated. Cr. 8vo., 5s.
THE PALACE IN THE GARDEN. Illustrated. Crown 8vo., 5s.
THE THIRD MISS ST. QUENTIN. Cr. 8vo., 2s. 6d.
NEIGHBOURS. Illustrated. Cr. 8vo., 6s.
THE STORY OF A SPRING MORNING, &c. Illustrated. Crown 8vo., 2s. 6d.

Reader.—VOICES FROM FLOWERLAND: a Birthday Book and Language of Flowers. By EMILY E. READER. Illustrated by ADA BROOKE. Royal 16mo., cloth, 2s. 6d.; vegetable vellum, 3s. 6d.

Stevenson.—Works by ROBERT LOUIS STEVENSON.
A CHILD'S GARDEN OF VERSES. Small fcp. 8vo., 5s.
A CHILD'S GARLAND OF SONGS, Gathered from 'A Child's Garden of Verses'. Set to Music by C. VILLIERS STANFORD, Mus. Doc. 4to., 2s. sewed; 3s. 6d., cloth gilt.

The Silver Library.

CROWN 8vo. 3s. 6d. EACH VOLUME.

Baker's (Sir S. W.) Eight Years in Ceylon. With 6 Illustrations. 3s. 6d.
Baker's (Sir S. W.) Rifle and Hound in Ceylon. With 6 Illustrations. 3s. 6d.
Baring-Gould's (Rev. S.) Curious Myths of the Middle Ages. 3s. 6d.
Baring-Gould's (Rev. S.) Origin and Development of Religious Belief. 2 vols. 3s. 6d. each.
Brassey's (Lady) A Voyage in the 'Sunbeam'. With 66 Illustrations. 3s. 6d.
Clodd's (E.) Story of Creation: a Plain Account of Evolution. With 77 Illustrations. 3s. 6d.
Conybeare (Rev. W. J.) and Howson's (Very Rev. J. S.) Life and Epistles of St. Paul. 46 Illustrations. 3s. 6d.
Dougall's (L.) Beggars All; a Novel. 3s. 6d.
Doyle's (A. Conan) Micah Clarke: a Tale of Monmouth's Rebellion. 3s. 6d.
Doyle's (A. Conan) The Captain of the Polestar, and other Tales. 3s. 6d.
Froude's (J. A.) Short Studies on Great Subjects. 4 vols. 3s. 6d. each.
Froude's (J. A.) Cæsar: a Sketch. 3s. 6d.
Froude's (J. A.) Thomas Carlyle: a History of his Life.
1795-1835. 2 vols. 7s.
1834-1881. 2 vols. 7s.
Froude's (J. A.) The Two Chiefs of Dunboy. 3s. 6d.
Froude's (J. A.) The History of England, from the Fall of Wolsey to the Defeat of the Spanish Armada. 12 vols. 3s. 6d. each.

Gleig's (Rev. G. R.) Life of the Duke of Wellington. With Portrait. 3s. 6d.
Haggard's (H. R.) She: A History of Adventure. 32 Illustrations. 3s. 6d.
Haggard's (H. R.) Allan Quatermain. With 20 Illustrations. 3s. 6d.
Haggard's (H. R.) Colonel Quaritch, V.C.: a Tale of Country Life. 3s. 6d.
Haggard's (H. R.) Cleopatra. With 29 Full-page Illustrations. 3s. 6d.
Haggard's (H. R.) Eric Brighteyes. With 51 Illustrations. 3s. 6d.
Haggard's (H. R.) Beatrice. 3s. 6d.
Harte's (Bret) In the Carquinez Woods, and other Stories. 3s. 6d.
Helmholtz's (Hermann von) Popular Lectures on Scientific Subjects. With 68 Woodcuts. 2 vols. 3s. 6d. each.
Howitt's (W.) Visits to Remarkable Places. 80 Illustrations. 3s. 6d.
Jefferies' (R.) The Story of My Heart: My Autobiography. With Portrait. 3s. 6d.
Jefferies' (R.) Field and Hedgerow. With Portrait. 3s. 6d.
Jefferies' (R.) Red Deer. With 17 Illustrations. 3s. 6d.
Jefferies' (R.) Wood Magic: a Fable. 3s. 6d.
Jefferies' (R.) The Toilers of the Field. With Portrait from the Bust in Salisbury Cathedral. 3s. 6d.

The Silver Library—*continued.*

Knight's (E. F.) The Cruise of the 'Alerte': the Narrative of a Search for Treasure on the Desert Island of Trinidad. With 2 Maps and 23 Illustrations. 3s. 6d.

Lang's (A.) Custom and Myth: Studies of Early Usage and Belief. 3s. 6d.

Lees (J. A.) and Clutterbuck's (W. J.) B.C. 1887, A Ramble in British Columbia. With Maps and 75 Illustrations. 3s. 6d.

Macaulay's (Lord) Essays and Lays of Ancient Rome. 3s. 6d.

Macleod (H. D.) The Elements of Banking. 3s. 6d.

Marshman's (J. C.) Memoirs of Sir Henry Havelock. 3s. 6d.

Max Müller's (F.) India, what can it teach us? 3s. 6d.

Max Müller's (F.) Introduction to the Science of Religion. 3s. 6d.

Merivale's (Dean) History of the Romans under the Empire. 8 vols. 3s. 6d. ea.

Mill's (J. S.) Political Economy. 3s. 6d.

Mill's (J. S.) System of Logic. 3s. 6d.

Milner's (Geo.) Country Pleasures. 3s. 6d.

Newman's (Cardinal) Apologia Pro Vitâ Sua. 3s. 6d.

Newman's (Cardinal) Historical Sketches. 3 vols. 3s. 6d. each.

Newman's (Cardinal) Callista: a Tale of the Third Century. 3s. 6d.

Newman's (Cardinal) Loss and Gain: a Tale. 3s. 6d.

Newman's (Cardinal) Essays, Critical and Historical. 2 vols. 7s.

Newman's (Cardinal) The Development of Christian Doctrine. 3s. 6d.

Newman's (Cardinal) The Arians of the Fourth Century. 3s. 6d.

Newman's (Cardinal) Verses on Various Occasions. 3s. 6d.

Newman's (Cardinal) The Present Position of Catholics in England. 3s. 6d.

Newman's (Cardinal) Parochial and Plain Sermons. 8 vols. 3s. 6d. each.

Newman's (Cardinal) Selection from the 'Parochial and Plain Sermons'. 3s. 6d.

Newman's (Cardinal) Sermons bearing upon Subjects of the Day. 3s. 6d.

Newman's (Cardinal) Difficulties felt by Anglicans in Catholic Teaching Considered. 2 vols. 3s. 6d. cach,

Newman's (Cardinal) The Idea of a University. 3s. 6d.

Newman's (Cardinal) Biblical and Ecclesiastical Miracles. 3s. 6d.

Newman's (Cardinal) Discussions and Arguments. 3s. 6d.

Newman's (Cardinal) Grammar of Assent. 3s. 6d.

Newman's (Cardinal) Fifteen Sermons Preached before the University of Oxford. 3s. 6d.

Newman's (Cardinal) Lectures on the Doctrine of Justification. 3s. 6d.

Newman's (Cardinal) Sermons on Various Occasions. 3s. 6d.

Newman's (Cardinal) Via Media of the Anglican Church, in Lectures, &c. 2 vols. 3s. 6d. each.

Newman's (Cardinal) Discourses to Mixed Congregations. 3s. 6d.

Phillipps-Wolley's (C.) Snap: a Legend of the Lone Mountain. With 13 Illustrations. 3s. 6d.

Proctor's (R. A.) Other Worlds than Ours. 3s. 6d.

Proctor's (R. A.) Rough Ways made Smooth. 3s. 6d.

Proctor's (R. A.) Pleasant Ways in Science. 3s. 6d.

Proctor's (R. A.) The Orbs Around Us. 3s. 6d.

Proctor's (R. A.) The Expanse of Heaven. 3s. 6d.

Proctor's (R. A.) Myths and Marvels of Astronomy. 3s. 6d.

Proctor's (R. A.) Nature Studies. 3s. 6d.

Smith's (R. Bosworth) Carthage and the Carthaginians. 3s. 6d.

Stanley's (Bishop) Familiar History of Birds. 160 Illustrations. 3s. 6d.

Stevenson (Robert Louis) and Osbourne's (Lloyd) The Wrong Box. 3s. 6d.

Weyman's (Stanley J.) The House of the Wolf: a Romance. 3s. 6d.

Wood's (Rev. J. G.) Petland Revisited. With 33 Illustrations. 3s. 6d.

Wood's (Rev. J. G.) Strange Dwellings. With 60 Illustrations. 3s. 6d.

Wood's (Rev. J. G.) Out of Doors. 11 Illustrations. 3s. 6d.

Cookery, Domestic Management, &c.

Acton.—MODERN COOKERY. By ELIZA ACTON. With 150 Woodcuts. Fcp. 8vo., 4s. 6d.

Bull.—Works by THOMAS BULL, M.D.

HINTS TO MOTHERS ON THE MANAGE-MENT OF THEIR HEALTH DURING THE PERIOD OF PREGNANCY. Fcp. 8vo., 1s. 6d.

THE MATERNAL MANAGEMENT OF CHILDREN IN HEALTH AND DISEASE. Fcp. 8vo., 1s. 6d.

Cookery, Domestic Management, &c.—*continued.*

De Salis.—Works by Mrs. DE SALIS.

CAKES AND CONFECTIONS À LA MODE. Fcp. 8vo., 1s. 6d.

DOGS: a Manual for Amateurs. Fcp. 8vo., 1s. 6d.

DRESSED GAME AND POULTRY À LA MODE. Fcp. 8vo., 1s. 6d.

DRESSED VEGETABLES À LA MODE. Fcp. 8vo., 1s. 6d.

DRINKS À LA MODE. Fcp. 8vo., 1s. 6d.

ENTRÉES À LA MODE. Fcp. 8vo., 1s. 6d.

OYSTERS À LA MODE. Fcp. 8vo., 1s. 6d.

PUDDINGS AND PASTRY À LA MODE. Fcp. 8vo., 1s. 6d.

SAVOURIES À LA MODE. Fcp. 8vo., 1s. 6d.

SOUPS AND DRESSED FISH À LA MODE. Fcp. 8vo., 1s. 6d.

SWEETS AND SUPPER DISHES À LA MODE. Fcp. 8vo., 1s. 6d.

TEMPTING DISHES FOR SMALL INCOMES. Fcp. 8vo., 1s. 6d.

De Salis.—Works by Mrs. DE SALIS—*continued.*

FLORAL DECORATIONS. Suggestions and Descriptions. Fcp. 8vo., 1s. 6d.

NEW-LAID EGGS: Hints for Amateur Poultry Rearers. Fcp. 8vo., 1s. 6d.

WRINKLES AND NOTIONS FOR EVERY HOUSEHOLD. Cr. 8vo., 1s. 6d.

Harrison.—COOKERY FOR BUSY LIVES AND SMALL INCOMES. By MARY HARRISON. Cr. 8vo., 1s.

Lear.—MAIGRE COOKERY. By H. L. SIDNEY LEAR. 16mo., 2s.

Poole.—COOKERY FOR THE DIABETIC. By W. H. and Mrs. POOLE. With Preface by Dr. PAVY. Fcp. 8vo., 2s. 6d.

Walker.—A HANDBOOK FOR MOTHERS: being Simple Hints to Women on the Management of their Health during Pregnancy and Confinement, together with Plain Directions as to the Care of Infants. By JANE H. WALKER, L.R.C.P. and L.M. L.R.C.S. and M.D. (Brux.). With 13 Illustrations. Cr. 8vo., 2s. 6d.

Miscellaneous and Critical Works.

Allingham.—VARIETIES IN PROSE. By WILLIAM ALLINGHAM. 3 vols. Cr. 8vo, 18s. (Vols. 1 and 2, Rambles, by PATRICIUS WALKER. Vol. 3, Irish Sketches, etc.)

Armstrong.—ESSAYS AND SKETCHES. By EDMUND J. ARMSTRONG. Fcp. 8vo., 5s.

Bagehot.—LITERARY STUDIES. By WALTER BAGEHOT. 2 vols. 8vo., 28s.

Baines.—SHAKESPEARE STUDIES, AND OTHER ESSAYS. By THOMAS SPENCER BAINES, LL.D. With a biographical Preface by Prof. LEWIS CAMPBELL. Crown 8vo., 7s. 6d.

Baring-Gould.—CURIOUS MYTHS OF THE MIDDLE AGES. By Rev. S. BARING-GOULD. Crown 8vo., 3s. 6d.

Battye.—PICTURES IN PROSE OF NATURE, WILD SPORT, AND HUMBLE LIFE. By AUBYN TREVOR BATTYE, B.A. Crown 8vo., 6s.

Boyd ('A. K. H. B.').—Works by A. K. H. BOYD, D.D.

AUTUMN HOLIDAYS OF A COUNTRY PARSON. Crown 8vo., 3s. 6d.

COMMONPLACE PHILOSOPHER. Crown 8vo., 3s 6d.

CRITICAL ESSAYS OF A COUNTRY PARSON. Crown 8vo., 3s. 6d.

EAST COAST DAYS AND MEMORIES. Crown 8vo., 3s. 6d.

Boyd ('A. K. H. B.').—Works by A. K. H. BOYD, D.D.—*continued.*

LANDSCAPES, CHURCHES AND MORALITIES. Crown 8vo., 3s. 6d.

LEISURE HOURS IN TOWN. Crown 8vo., 3s. 6d.

LESSONS OF MIDDLE AGE. Cr. 8vo., 3s. 6d.

OUR LITTLE LIFE. Two Series. Cr. 8vo., 3s. 6d. each.

OUR HOMELY COMEDY: AND TRAGEDY. Crown 8vo., 3s. 6d.

RECREATIONS OF A COUNTRY PARSON. Three Series. Cr. 8vo., 3s. 6d. each. First Series. Popular Ed. 8vo.,6d. swd.

Butler.—Works by SAMUEL BUTLER.

EREWHON. Cr. 8vo., 5s.

THE FAIR HAVEN. A Work in Defence of the Miraculous Element in our Lord's Ministry. Cr. 8vo., 7s. 6d.

LIFE AND HABIT. An Essay after a Completer View of Evolution. Cr. 8vo., 7s. 6d

EVOLUTION, OLD AND NEW. Cr. 8vo., 10s. 6d.

ALPS AND SANCTUARIES OF PIEDMONT AND CANTON TICINO. Pt.4to., 10s.6d.

LUCK, OR CUNNING, AS THE MAIN MEANS OF ORGANIC MODIFICATION? Cr. 8vo., 7s. 6d.

EX VOTO. An Account of the Sacro Monte or New Jerusalem at Varallo-Sesioa. Crown 8vo., 10s. 6d.

Miscellaneous and Critical Works—*continued.*

Francis.—JUNIUS REVEALED By his surviving Grandson, H. R. FRANCIS. 8vo., 6s.

Halliwell-Phillipps.—A CALENDAR OF THE HALLIWELL - PHILLIPPS COLLECTION OF SHAKESPEAREAN RARITIES. Enlarged by ERNEST E. BAKER, F.S.A. 8vo., 10s. 6d.

Hodgson. — OUTCAST ESSAYS AND VERSE TRANSLATIONS. By W. SHAD-WORTH HODGSON. Crown 8vo., 8s. 6d.

Hullah.—Works by JOHN HULLAH.

COURSE OF LECTURES ON THE HISTORY OF MODERN MUSIC. 8vo., 8s. 6d.

COURSE OF LECTURES ON THE TRANSITION PERIOD OF MUSICAL HISTORY. 8vo., 10s. 6d.

Jefferies.—Works by RICHARD JEFFERIES.

FIELD AND HEDGEROW : last Essays. With Portrait. Crown 8vo., 3s. 6d.
THE STORY OF MY HEART : my Autobiography. Crown 8vo., 3s. 6d.
RED DEER. With 17 Illustrations. Crown 8vo., 3s. 6d.
THE TOILERS OF THE FIELD. Crown 8vo., 3s. 6d.
WOOD MAGIC: a Fable. Crown 8vo., 3s. 6d.

Johnson.—THE PATENTEE'S MANUAL: a Treatise on the Law and Practice of Letters Patent. By J. & J. H. JOHNSON, Patent Agents, &c. 8vo., 10s. 6d.

Lang.—Works by ANDREW LANG.
LETTERS TO DEAD AUTHORS. Fcp. 8vo., 2s. 6d. net.
BOOKS AND BOOKMEN. With 19 Illustrations. Fcp. 8vo., 2s. 6d. net.
OLD FRIENDS. Fcp. 8vo., 2s. 6d. net.
LETTERS ON LITERATURE. Fcp. 8vo., 2s. 6d. net.

Macfarren.—LECTURES ON HARMONY. By Sir GEO. A. MACFARREN. 8vo., 12s.

Max Müller.—Works by F. MAX MÜLLER.
HIBBERT LECTURES ON THE ORIGIN AND GROWTH OF RELIGION, as illustrated by the Religions of India. Crown 8vo., 7s. 6d.
INTRODUCTION TO THE SCIENCE OF RELIGION : Four Lectures delivered at the Royal Institution. Cr. 8vo., 3s. 6d.
[continued.
NATURAL RELIGION. The Gifford Lectures, 1890. Cr. 8vo., 10s. 6d.

Max Müller.—Works by F. MAX MÜLLER.—*continued.*
PHYSICAL RELIGION. The Gifford Lectures, 1890. Cr. 8vo., 10s. 6d.
ANTHROPOLOGICAL RELIGION. The Gifford Lectures, 1891. Cr. 8vo., 10s. 6d.
THEOSOPHY OR PSYCHOLOGICAL RELIGION. The Gifford Lectures, 1892. Cr. 8vo., 10s. 6d.
INDIA : WHAT CAN IT TEACH US ? Cr. 8vo., 3s. 6d.

Mendelssohn.—THE LETTERS OF FELIX MENDELSSOHN. Translated by Lady WALLACE. 2 vols. Cr. 8vo., 10s.

Milner.—COUNTRY PLEASURES: the Chronicle of a Year chiefly in a Garden. By GEORGE MILNER. Cr. 8vo., 3s. 6d.

Proctor.—Works by RICHARD A. PROCTOR.
STRENGTH AND HAPPINESS. With 9 Illustrations. Crown 8vo., 5s.
STRENGTH: How to get Strong and keep Strong, with Chapters on Rowing and Swimming, Fat, Age, and the Waist. With 9 Illus. Cr. 8vo, 2s.

Richardson.—NATIONAL HEALTH. A Review of the Works of Sir Edwin Chadwick, K.C.B. By Sir B. W. RICHARDSON, M.D. Cr., 4s. 6d.

Roget. — A HISTORY OF THE 'OLD WATER-COLOUR SOCIETY' (now the Royal Society of Painters in Water-Colours). By JOHN LEWIS ROGET. 2 vols. Royal 8vo., 42s.

Rossetti.—A SHADOW OF DANTE : being an Essay towards studying Himself, his World, and his Pilgrimage. By MARIA FRANCESCA ROSSETTI. With Illustrations and design on cover by DANTE GABRIEL ROSSETTI. Cr. 8vo., 10s. 6d.

Southey. — CORRESPONDENCE WITH CAROLINE BOWLES. By ROBERT SOUTHEY. Edited by E. DOWDEN. 8vo., 14s.

Wallaschek.—PRIMITIVE MUSIC: an Inquiry into the Origin and Development of Music, Songs, Instruments, Dances, and Pantomimes of Savage Races. By RICHARD WALLASCHEK. With Musical Examples. 8vo., 12s. 6d.

West.—WILLS, AND HOW NOT TO MAKE THEM. With a Selection of Leading Cases. By B. B. WEST, Author of ' Half-Hours with the Millionaires '. Fcp. 8vo., 2s. 6d.

www.ingramcontent.com/pod-product-compliance
Lightning Source LLC
Chambersburg PA
CBHW031139120726
47905CB00006B/1743